ORBUS

NEAL ASHER

ORBUS

The Third Spatterjay Novel

NIGHT SHADE BOOKS
New York

For the big 50s.
You know who you are!!

Acknowledgements

Cheers to the *new guard* at Tor Macmillan who seem to have snatched up the baton and taken off as if their feet are on fire, these including Julie Crisp, Chloe Healy, and many others besides. Also to Peter Lavery who, despite retiring, cannot quite give up his scary pencil and continues editing. My best wishes to others working diligently at Macmillan selling foreign rights or copy-editing, including Liz Johnson and Eli Dryden; in fact to all there who help bring this book to the shelves. Further thanks must go out to all those running numerous websites across the Internet who, for bugger-all payment, take the time to review my books with such precision and care, and, of course, to all those who buy them – without you I'd need to get a proper job! And, as ever, thanks Caroline for the steady supply of coffee, for accepting that my time ranting on the Internet is research . . . oh, and for being my wife!

1

It's well known that the spatterjay virus optimizes its host for their mutual survival, sometimes causing weird transformations in the said host when this survival is threatened. However, there is still much debate about the extent to which it can alter the structures of the human brain. With some Hoopers, as the residents of Spatterjay are called, long-term viral infection can result in the brain becoming hard-wired so that those affected become incapable of learning anything new or reacting usefully to any situations arising outside of their normal day-to-day lives. Yet it has also been shown that in some other Hoopers the virus is perpetually tampering with the brain, actually connecting to cerebral structure, and that information is exchanged between mind and virus. Some of this information, it would seem, cannot arise simply from that mind's own experiences, and scientists speculate that, as well as storing an eclectic collection absorbed from the genomes of the creatures it has been hosted by, the virus is capable of storing mental information too. Those who enjoy this close connection between mind and virus also seem to possess greater mental capacity, remembering a great deal of what they have read and experienced. This should not be surprising of course, since one of the greatest instruments for optimizing the survival of a Human is that organ lying between his ears.

– From HOW IT IS by Gordon

A varied collection of interesting crates, boxes, storage cylinders and oddly shaped objects wrapped in crash-foam is strapped securely in the quadrate cargo scaffold of the enormous zero-gravity hold space of the *Gurnard*. Numerous aisles run through this scaffold to provide access for the autohandlers, which are machines like giant grey earwigs presently crouching in recesses in the distant walls, their job completed some days ago. Amidst the latest cargo to be loaded rests a big plasmel crate, and now, emitting a high whine, a silvery blade stabs through the surface from inside it and cuts round, splitting the crate in two. Then, spreading metal tentacles, the object within the crate pushes the two halves of it apart.

The war drone Sniper blinks open his crystal orange eyes and peers about himself in the darkness, which isn't actually darkness to him since his sensorium spans so much wider than the limited Human spectrum.

'Do you think they'll find out?' his small companion enquires, as it drifts from the depths of the crate alongside him.

'I don't reckon so,' says Sniper. 'By the time they realize we're not still hiding in a sea cave, we'll be well away.'

While trapped in a static position as the Warden of Spatterjay for ten years, Sniper watched that same world changing, and guessed it would soon no longer be such an exciting place for him. There he obtained this new drone shell for himself – a gleaming nautilus three metres in diameter, constructed of highly advanced ceramal and diamond-fibre composite, which in turn was plated with nanochain chromium, and contained enough lethal weaponry to obliterate a city, or two – and considered heading elsewhere. However, shortly after loading his mind, essentially himself, into this shell, events unfolding upon that world – with the Prador Vrell trying to escape, and the Prador Vrost arriving in a massive space dreadnought to stop him – once again drew him in and allowed him to exercise his special talent for mayhem. But that's all over and the whole world now seems set to become more civilized; perhaps too civilized for a drone who specializes in blowing things up.

'It's not fair,' says his companion.

Sniper peers at Thirteen, an erstwhile submind of the previous Spatterjay Warden, which now occupies a drone body in the form of an iron seahorse with topaz eyes. The little drone wraps his tail round one of the cargo-frame struts as he studies their surroundings.

'No such thing as fair,' Sniper snorts.

Despite his heroic efforts in fighting for the Polity, Sniper is considered a bit of a loose cannon, or rather several loose cannons rolled into one. In fact, many of the Polity's controlling AIs consider him plain dangerous or, him having obtained that very high-spec drone body, even positively lethal. At the end of the conflict involving Vrell and Vrost, Sniper rescued a Prador war drone containing a downloaded copy of Vrell's mind. The AIs hadn't liked that either and, though Sniper made some alterations causing the Prador drone to switch loyalties to the Polity, they nevertheless confiscated it for 'further study'. Next came the order for Sniper himself to report for 'assessment', at which point this seven-hundred-year-old veteran of the Prador/Human war, and numerous subsequent conflicts, decided it really was time to be elsewhere.

'But you're a free drone,' Thirteen complains, 'just like me.'

Sniper ponders the old and much-abused concept of 'freedom'. Yes, he is indeed as free as any other citizen in the Polity, and is also given a great deal of freedom of action when it comes to dealing with its enemies. However, he is now very powerful and dangerous and if, just for one moment, the controlling AIs feel his mind is too unstable, or that in some other way he might become a threat, they will be down on him like a falling space station. He doesn't really understand what it is about his recent behaviour that has impelled them to order him in for assessment, but he has no intention of waiting around to find out.

'Let's take a look around in here.' Sniper pushes himself out from between the two halves of the crate to enter the nearest aisle. Propelling himself forward, and steadying his course with deft touches of his tentacles against the surrounding framework, he begins scanning. Thirteen pushes off after him, lowering his tail down onto the bigger drone's shell and sticking there.

The cargo immediately around them was loaded along with their own crate and consists of numerous items acquired on Spatterjay: some big crates of whelk shells; one small crate of wartime artefacts including slave collars, a couple of spider thralls, a complete Human skeleton with something metallic in its skull from which metal threads run down the spine – a full thrall unit, in fact – and a couple of very old pulse-rifles. Sniper recognizes all these illegal exports instantly, because at one time he himself turned a tidy profit by finding and selling such artefacts. Also here rest three cylinders with enviro-control consoles affixed to the exterior. Scanning inside, Sniper observes slow writhing movement and recognizes that each one contains a tangled mass of Spatterjay leeches.

'I wonder who wants *them*,' wonders Thirteen.

'Always a market for immortality,' Sniper replies.

'Yeah, but who wants *that* kind?'

Though the bite of a Spatterjay leech infects its victim with the primary virus of that world, the longevity it imparts is a mixed blessing. Reinfection at constant intervals is necessary and, if the one infected is injured or starved, the virus can take over completely and turn him into something no longer really Human. This might once have been considered a small price to pay for what amounts to virtual immortality, but with present Polity technologies making it possible for anyone to extend his lifespan indefinitely, it is one most are no longer prepared to pay. More likely those buying a bite from these leeches are attracted more by the idea of turning into something like an Old Captain: a nearly unkillable superhuman capable of bending iron bars with his eyelids.

Next along from these containers is one enormous item secured in another longer and wider cylinder. Scanning inside this, Sniper identifies a creature like a whale with mandibles, its body temperature reduced to just a little above zero, while being held in stasis by chemical and electrical means. Someone, somewhere, must actually want a living ocean heirodont? Maybe that same someone is putting together an aquarium based on the sea-life of Spatterjay, and this and the leeches are intended for that. Such an aquarium would clearly have huge entertainment value, but its owner would have to be damned careful when cleaning the glass.

Beyond the Spatterjay cargo are packed other odd and disparate cargoes. One area contains tons of wood that Sniper tentatively identifies as English oak, boxes full of jars containing either black or green olives in brine, living oysters held in stasis, a hydrogen-powered trial bike, a mass of limestone blocks, some gel-sealed barrels of whisky, living prawn eggs also held in stasis, and much more besides. He surmises that some of these cargoes have been stored here for a very long time while awaiting an opportune moment to be sold – a moment that has never come so far and, in some cases, probably never will.

'Oops,' says Thirteen abruptly.

Sniper notes movement from the autohandlers and now one of them peels itself out of its wall recess, and impelled by gas jets, begins drifting up the aisle towards them. The big war drone trains a high-powered laser on it, but otherwise does not react, since he has been expecting something like this. The handler does indeed look like an earwig, albeit one ten feet long, its rear pincers jointed and overly large in proportion to its body, its legs similarly longer and ending in two-fingered grabs, and its head looking more like that of a huge fly. As it draws near, it squirts its gas jets to bring itself to a halt, then reaches out with one of those two-fingered grabs to grasp a nearby stanchion of the cargo framework.

'I only recollect one time in the past when stowaways were found aboard,' it declares. 'The Captain at that time wanted to eject them out of an airlock and, though I thoroughly agreed with his feelings on the matter, I could not allow it. The same Captain went off for mental adjustment shortly after that, his penchant for black mem-loads having caught up with him.'

'We're not stowaways,' Sniper announces. 'We're cargo – check your manifest.'

'Oh yes,' says the *Gurnard*'s AI. 'Crate SPJ15 containing wartime data in secure storage and also a seahorse sculpture. Very amusing.'

'Well,' says Sniper, 'my mind is that same data, and my body the secure storage, and Thirteen here is a fine piece of artwork.'

'Why, thank you, Sniper,' says Thirteen.

Gurnard ignores this exchange. 'Whilst you remained in your crate, I could overlook your presence aboard, but you have now made the transition from cargo to stowaways, or even passengers. If you return to your crate and seal it up, I will forget I ever saw you. If you remain outside of your crate, there will be a further charge to pay.'

'How much?' Sniper and Thirteen had been ensconced in that crate for many days and, though he could easily scan far beyond it, he had reached his boredom threshold.

'Since you do not require food, or air to breathe, the charge will be no more than a third more than the cargo payment,' the ship AI decides, 'though your presence aboard would have to be registered at any Polity port we should arrive at.'

'I see,' says Sniper, wondering what the 'however' is going to

6

be. Gurnard has to be fully aware that Sniper and Thirteen are fugitives from Earth Central Security.

'However,' says Gurnard, predictably, 'should you sign on as members of the crew, I need provide no further details than that two free drones are aboard.'

Sniper is sure there is no rule about listing passengers, because their presence would be registered the moment they left the ship at any Polity destination, so why does the AI of this ship want to sign them up?

'And, to answer the question you are doubtless asking yourself,' Gurnard continues, 'after a brief visit to Aerial Space Station, your presence aboard might be very helpful, for we then head off for some less salubrious destinations in a particularly notorious sector of space.'

'That being?'

When the AI tells them where the *Gurnard* will be going, Sniper joyfully spins on the spot like a coin.

'Sign us up,' he says.

Before becoming a sea captain himself, Orbus spent a century of wandering and crewing on the sailing ships of others, followed by a decades-long period of suicidal wildness, before he finally built his own sailing ship. He vaguely recollects that, at about that same time, he experienced optimism and joy when, knowing he was practically immortal, he decided to properly relish his existence. He is not sure when things then started to fall out of shape, though he knew the cause lay further back in his past, in his long and brutal journey to the world of Spatterjay, from which even now he remembers the first taste of raw Human flesh.

Centuries of violence ensued, during which – aboard two separate ships, for the first was burned down to the keel while in port – he gathered about him a crew amenable to his personal tastes. A sadist ship captain in charge of a crew of masochists – really, who could object to that? But often it went too far, and some innocents were hurt because they joined the crew without really knowing what kind of ship they were joining.

One of Orbus's longest-serving crewmen stands beside him now, not this time aboard a wooden sailing ship upon that savage ocean, but aboard the old space-hauler the *Gurnard*, travelling deep in vacuum. Currently they occupy the bridge, which, with its faux-Victorian decoration and high-tech controls cleverly concealed in polished brass, cast iron and wood, might well have been designed by Jules Verne himself.

'I don't like your name,' says Orbus abruptly, a bitter worm coming back to nibble at his mind.

His crewman, who has answered to the name Drooble for longer than most people have lived, squints up at him while trying to think of something provocative to say in response. He finally gives up and asks, 'What's wrong with it?'

Orbus represses a surge of irritation because he isn't even sure why he spoke. Being less than candid, he replies, 'It sounds like a blend between dribble and droopy, or trouble and . . . it's a silly name.' Then his feeling of irritation is back, redoubled, because of the utter pointlessness of this exchange.

Drooble's expression screws up with the effort of setting his thoughts along unfamiliar courses, so all he manages is, 'Well, what about the name Orbus?'

'Nothing wrong with that name,' says Orbus, trying to quell the familiar and horribly attractive anger growing inside him. 'What's your first name?'

The crewman again squints in deep and painful thought, then tentatively replies, 'Iannus . . . I think.'

'Then that is the name I will use to address you from now on.'

There, conversation over, no need to get annoyed. Orbus takes several long steadying breaths and tries to shunt it all aside.

The vessel they occupy, along with its reserved and spooky artificial intelligence, is four miles long and precisely the shape that its name implies: it is a spaceship fashioned in the shape of a bottom-dwelling fish, steely-grey in colour, like some chunk of rococo decoration inadvertently snapped off a cast-iron gate. The two men, these two tough, durable and incredibly long-lived Hoopers, gaze out upon blackness through the chainglass window forming one fish eye. Orbus stands a full head and shoulders above his companion, possesses arms as thick as most people's legs, a rhino-thick body, a grey queue of hair trailing down his back and a sad expression behind a flattened nose. He wears clothing fashioned of heavy canvas and heirodont leather, since any less durable fabrics he would inadvertently tear like wet tissue paper, and coiled at his belt hangs a flexal bullwhip to remind him of the time when he was not such a nice person.

By comparison with his captain, Iannus Drooble is small – yet he is bigger than the Human average. He wears a white cloth shirt and baggy canvas trousers, hobnail boots and a headband. He was infected with the Spatterjay virus some centuries after Orbus, and therefore was not one of the original prisoners of Jay Hoop, but it will not be so long before he, too, will need to start seeking out more durable attire.

Orbus continues to gaze pensively upon the blackness, until a sudden light glares up from below, whereupon he peers down to watch an entire world rise into view, with their destination, the Ariel space station, silhouetted before it like a massive iron cathedral displaced into vacuum.

Back on Spatterjay his mutually sordid relationship with his crew came to an end when a renegade Prador called Vrell, who had been hiding under the sea for ten years, sank the captain's ship and kidnapped the lot of them to turn into slaves. They were thralled – implanted with Prador enslaving technology – and then forced to work upon the wrecked spaceship that once belonged to Vrell's father. But something else happened too for, deprived of certain essential nutrients, Orbus and his crew came close to being transformed by the Spatterjay virus infecting them into irretrievably *unhuman* creatures. Later rescued and fed the required diet, they returned to Humanity. In Orbus's case, it was a return to an earlier self, one not quite so bitter and sadistic. However, now he wonders about the permanence of that change; and if habits acquired over centuries are so easy to banish.

'So who is it we're here to see?' Drooble asks.

'One of the co-owners of this ship, a certain Charles Cymbeline.'

'So y'gonna stay with it?'

'It's a second chance for us, Iannus,' replies Orbus succinctly.

After being rescued back on Spatterjay, he knew he had to get away. He had lost his sailing ship, even his love of inflicting pain, and the majority of his crew had undergone a transformation similar to his own – in their case losing their love of the pain he inflicted, which was the only thing that made them feel alive. Staying in that familiar environment, he knew he could easily fall back into his old pointless existence, so when Captain Ron offered him the position of Captain aboard this spaceship it seemed sensible enough to accept, but now he is having second thoughts. During this first crossing from one star system to another, there seemed altogether too much time for reflection . . . too much time for nightmare memories to resurface.

'You have permission to dock, Captain,' states a sepulchral voice. 'Do you wish to take this vessel in yourself?'

'You do it, Gurnard,' Orbus replies. 'It seems pointless me relieving you of a task that you can perform well enough alone.'

He has wondered what was even the point of an AI-controlled ship like this having a Human, or nominally Human, Captain. He himself isn't needed to pilot it, and many of his tasks just seem like make-work. However, during some long conversations with Gurnard, he has begun to discover there is more to it than that. The AI controls handler and maintenance robots, and one or two survey drones, and though they can deal with much inside the ship, there is also much they cannot manage. Some cargo items require special handling, even certain maintenance, sometimes feeding. Whenever the *Gurnard* reaches port, Orbus's job will be to leave the ship and deal with the officialdom at those destinations that aren't themselves AI-controlled. Also there is the task of obtaining new cargoes, or securing payment from reluctant recipients of existing cargo. All those Human interractions to consider . . . However, these do not seem like jobs for a Captain, and with some technological upgrades, Gurnard could probably handle them. He rather thinks that, this being a privately owned vessel, someone like himself is the cheaper option. He also knows that AIs often deliberately include Human crews simply for company, to keep them grounded, to keep them from disconnecting totally from the material world. And then he wonders if he and Drooble are really the best choice for that role.

The *Gurnard* shudders slightly and, back towards his right, Orbus glimpses a glare of white light as a fusion drive ignites, then knives of blue flame from steering thrusters. The space station swings around until it lies directly at the ship's nose, thus visible in neither of the adjacent big eye windows, though now centred on the viewing screen positioned on the wall opposite the Captain's large reinforced chair. Orbus wanders over and plumps himself down in it, whilst Drooble takes the seat positioned inside a horseshoe console just to the left of him. From here, in the unlikely event that the ship AI should cease to function, they can control the ship, though the option of dropping it into U-space would be lost to them.

As they draw closer to the space station, it grows and grows until once again visible in both eye windows. Checking some readings on a touch-screen that flips up from the ship's slab currently resting on the arm of his chair, Orbus is amazed to see they are still a hundred miles away from the space dock.

'Big old place,' comments Drooble.

Orbus is impressed because, as he understands it, Ariel Station is, in Polity terms, considered a rather provincial and unimportant place. For many centuries he was not really paying much attention to events or progress away from his homeworld, or really anywhere beyond his old sailing ship, the *Vignette*. Obviously quite a lot has changed since, and maybe he now has the chance to make some remarkable discoveries. Perhaps being the Captain aboard this ship might really be a good thing for him, after all? Perhaps.

After some minutes, the forward fusion drive ignites, underscoring all their views with its white glare and lighting up the station ahead, then, as that cuts out, they come in over a massive platform and slide underneath what looks like a series of Gothic arches fashioned of iron. Beyond this the ship eases into a great quadrate framework, steering thrusters firing rapidly to position it. About them are docked other ships, though mostly of a more immediately functional design than the *Gurnard*. Snaking between them, from big fuel tanks, umbilici twine like vines, and docking tubes run to station access points hanging amidst this tangle, like great metal flower bulbs on thick stalks. With a crash and a shudder the ship halts, and echoing through its interior can be heard the sound of the station's docking hardware engaging.

Orbus finds himself urged to his feet by an unaccustomed excitement, and for a very brief moment feels truly *alive* without there being any pain involved, either that of others or his own. He picks up the ship's slab from the chair arm, its texture like slate against his calloused fingers, then turns to Drooble. 'Remember, these people ain't Hoopers, so be careful with them. They're delicate.'

Drooble grins weirdly and nods. Orbus studies him for a moment, not convinced that this crewman has lost his love of pain, and feeling certain he is neither safe nor stable, then heads out the back of the bridge located in the *Gurnard*'s head, Drooble trailing along behind him.

'A representative of Charles Cymbeline will be waiting for you by the drop-shafts at the far end of First Port Concourse,' intones Gurnard. 'You will require no paperwork or other verifications of identity, since all the required information has already been forwarded from Spatterjay.'

That gives Orbus pause for thought as he wonders just what information about him has been sent. It isn't as if either his history or his reputation is particularly good.

The spine corridor actually curves down into the main body of the ship, but because the floor is grav-plated that curve cannot be perceived. A twenty-minute walk brings them to a point behind the *Gurnard*'s head, from which they take a side corridor leading to one of the airlock stations in the ship's docking ring. Drooble starts whistling tunelessly through his teeth; a sound that in previous centuries always annoyed Orbus, but which he now forces himself to ignore. Through the airlock they enter a ribbed docking tube, then after that pass through another lock into a brightly lit cylindrical room, where a reception committee awaits.

'Your name is Jericho Lamal Orbus,' states the Golem.

Captain Orbus gazes at this machine fashioned in the shape of a Human, and surmises it is a late-series model, then he eyes the eight port-security officers standing behind it. They wear what look like bulky envirosuits but which he guesses, by the odd bulges here and there and by the cyber-assisted gauntlets, must incorporate exoskeletal armour. They also carry slammer rifles and wear pepperpot stunguns holstered at their hips. They certainly aren't taking any chances with him, but then again, why should they? His reputation has preceded him.

'Haven't heard my full name in a long time,' he says, chest tightening.

'Bit of an odd name, if you ask me,' comments Drooble, at his side.

Orbus glares at him, resisting the impulse to slam the back of one hand across the man's face, and Drooble grins back at him. The Golem studies both of them but, not having heard their previous exchange about names, is left guessing. Orbus returns his attention to the machine-man in front of him.

The Golem, who appears just as big and heavily muscled as Orbus himself, shrugs briefly. 'We obtained your full name from records that pre-date the destruction of Imbretus Station, but obviously what concerns us most here is the information forwarded to us about your life after that event.'

Orbus does not remember much from the time before the Prador seized Imbretus Station and herded himself and so many other Human captives aboard their ship. He knows that, because they subsequently hit the station's reactors with particle beams, the destruction was so complete that no one in the Polity even realized that captives had been taken. Of course, during the height of the war the AIs could not spare the resources for a rescue, but that did not leaven the bitterness he still feels. The brutality and horror of the ensuing journey is never completely clear in his memory, but it gives him nightmares even now, seven centuries later. He knows that he did terrible things in order to be one of the few survivors to reach Spatterjay alive, where he and those remaining were handed over to the pirate called Jay Hoop. And, once on the planet he now calls home, he clearly remembers being made to walk through tanks of leeches to ensure he was infected by the Spatterjay virus and, later, other unsavoury games.

'Would that be directly afterwards?' he asks, peering down at his right hand, which has begun shaking. 'I don't think there was much recorded about that time.'

Humans thus infected by the alien virus became incredibly tough and practically immortal, but Jay Hoop wasn't giving this to them as a gift; he was simply ensuring they were durable enough to withstand coring and thralling, a process whereby most of their cerebrum was chopped out and replaced by Prador thrall technology. All the Human captives were destined to become mindless slaves of the Prador. Orbus himself managed to avoid that process, but still hates to recollect, even vaguely, the things he did in order to survive until ECS police action on Spatterjay freed him and many like him after the war was over.

'Our greatest concern is your more recent record – namely information recorded since Spatterjay has been under the remit of an AI warden.'

'Spatterjay is not a Polity world,' Orbus growls, 'so anything that happened there is the province of those who rule it.' Old Captains, like himself, and the living sails that occupy the spars of their ships.

The Golem nods polite agreement. 'I am not here to arrest you, or to hold you to account for anything you did on your homeworld. I am merely here to deliver a warning.'

Orbus folds his arms to still their shaking, the ship slab still clutched in one hand.

The Golem continues, 'Whilst you are here aboard Ariel you will be watched very closely, and if you attack anyone, if you resort to violence of any kind, we fully understand that we cannot afford to limit our response. You are one of the original Old Captains, and we are well aware of your capabilities.'

Orbus closes his eyes and dips his head in thought for a moment. Steady, even breaths. *Steady.* 'I get you, but that seems a bit unfair. What if someone attacks me?'

The Golem ventures an amused grin as Orbus looks up again. 'Old Captain Orbus, I don't think we have anyone aboard who would be that suicidal.'

'Okay,' says Orbus. 'Message understood.'

The Golem turns and nods to his fellow security officers, and they begin to filter away towards the drop-shaft at the rear of the room.

'What's your name, sonny?' Orbus asks the Golem.

'Triax,' the Golem replies.

'Well, Triax,' says Orbus through clenched teeth, 'you might find this hard to believe, but I'm a reformed character now. You won't get any trouble from me.'

The sincerity of that statement is somewhat undermined by crewman Drooble's snigger.

The Prador Vrell is now hardly recognizable as one of its own kind. The transforming effect of the Spatterjay virus has converted this new adult from an enormous crablike creature with a body shaped like a vertically flattened pear into something much more sleek and dangerous-looking, almost evil. His colouring, once a combination of purple and yellow, is now entirely black. His carapace has grown disc-shaped, with the concave surface underneath nearly following the convex line of his back. His visual turret – at what was once the apex of the pear shape – and his mouthparts have detached from his main body and now extend on a long muscular neck, while his numerous limbs are longer and sharper. However, none of this is visible at the moment for, now aboard the ship the Prador King sent to hunt him down, precisely because he knew Vrell was likely to make such a transformation, he is concealed inside thick and heavy armour.

When Vrell tore out the previous occupant of this metal outer shell, he discovered it possessed a body shape vaguely similar to his own. It seemed that the Prador, the 'King's Guard' aboard Captain Vrost's massive dreadnought, had also been transformed by the Spatterjay virus, but wore armour whose exterior appearance more closely matched the normal shape of their kind. They were all part of the Prador King's extended family, while Vrell's crime was simply one of genetics. He isn't part of that family and, with the viral transformation also producing a massive increase in his intelligence, the King considers him too dangerous to live.

The King is right.

As Vrell clatters through the wide corridors of the huge vessel, he pauses to eye a collapsed King's Guard who is clad in armour like himself. It possesses the exterior shape of armour worn by a sizeable first-child, but Vrell knows that what lies inside is a second-child heavily mutated like himself. It seems that only because, throughout his own transformation, he was severely starved can he manage to fit himself into the same-size armour, for he is a mutated adult.

The fallen Prador waves a claw weakly as oily smoke trickles from its armour's vents. Vrell has seen others like this still showing signs of life, but they are in the process of dying and many more are already dead. The replicating nanite he fashioned to destroy the nervous systems of those with a particular genetic code – *their* genetic code, not his – has been very very effective, but Vrell does not intend to allow himself any complacency. Though most of the King's Guard switched from their armour's air supply as soon as they arrived aboard, and thus started breathing in the nanite, there is no guarantee all of them did so, and certainly there will be those still working in damaged areas open to vacuum who did not. Also there is the matter of how fast the nanite spread. If any fast-thinking individual had acted quickly enough, many areas of the ship might easily have been sealed off. And then there is the Captain himself. It seems likely that, shortly after the ship dropped into U-space, Vrost would have ascertained something was seriously wrong and sealed off the Captain's Sanctum.

At the end of the corridor, a drop-shaft leads down into the ship's bowels where the Sanctum is located. The shaft is currently not functional, but whether that is due to the recent damage Vrell inflicted on the ship by crashing his own craft into it at Spatterjay, or to some security measure, he is uncertain. He hesitates. Enthusiastic after his success with the virus, it was his intention to head straight for the Sanctum – but maybe that is not such a good idea. If Vrost has not succumbed, he will now be totally on his guard and doubtless in control of some lethal security measures.

Entering the shaft, the ship's schematics already memorized from his armour's CPU feed, Vrell rapidly clambers upwards. The pull from various grav sections of the ship is disorientating, but not enough to slow him down, for he knows he could be in danger here. Massive gravity immediately engages within the shaft, an irised gravity field slamming down upon him like a falling boulder, but he throws himself up against it and in a moment drags himself away from its pull and into another corridor.

'So, you survived,' a familiar voice observes.

'Are you a *child*, Vrost?' Vrell enquires, meanwhile considering other schematics of this ship, the likely death toll aboard and the presently recorded damage, and then beginning to formulate his plans. Ever since boarding, he has been running his armour's CPU at maximum capacity and rapidly absorbing information in audio, visual and pheromonal form. He now, if his guess about Vrost is correct, probably knows more about this ship than its Captain, though not the secret security protocols of course.

'So *you* are not a child,' Vrost remarks, his tone deliberately devoid of emotion.

So, thinks Vrell. *I now understand the situation fully.* King Oberon was the first adult Prador to have been transformed by the Spatterjay virus. The Prador dying around Vrell are the King's second-children and third-children, also transformed but still fully controlled by Oberon. Also, considering the sheer number of the 'King's Guard' spread throughout the Third Kingdom, Oberon must also have found a way to continue breeding such useful off-spring.

'You are a first-child,' Vrell decides.

Though all of the King's children have been similarly transformed, Vrell realizes that the change in them is not exactly the same as in him, being an adult. Vrost has made errors he himself would not make – because Vrost is simply not as intelligent. Only the King, Oberon, is therefore Vrell's equal. However, it would be stupid to underestimate Vrost, so what would Vrell do now if he was currently in the Captain's situation?

Working with his present knowledge of the ship, Vrell begins making a statistical analysis. It seems likely that with the damage the vessel sustained, at least a hundred of the Guard are currently in secure armour, while making repairs in the evacuated sections. Judging by the speed of the nanite dispersal, and Vrost's likely reaction time, a further two hundred would probably have managed to close up their armour in time to save themselves. Vrost, being a first-child, should have little regard for his personal safety, and so will have sent all the remaining Guard in pursuit of Vrell. Then there is another problem: the war drones aboard this ship, being run by the frozen brains of adolescent Prador, will all have survived as well. The situation, he feels, is about to get a little fraught.

Vrell does an inventory of his present resources: he possesses this armour which, though tough, will not survive a sustained attack; one rail-gun, presently fixed in its clamps below his armoured carapace, and half a load of inert missiles; three grenades; a quarter-power supply and some com lasers.

He realizes he needs time, lots of time, but unfortunately he does not have it. No matter what their defences, the Prador here cannot remain free from the nanite for long, because Prador, being creatures who can survive abrupt changes in air pressure, and even survive vacuum for an appreciable length of time, tend to be somewhat lax about atmosphere security. Even the Sanctum, doubtless originally made secure against biological attack, will not be able to keep the nanite out for long. It will eventually worm its way in through old seals, and between the gaps in mechanically worn components, or maybe even through holes chewed into the insulating layers by ship-lice. Vrost probably knows all this, and realizes that he too possesses limited time. And when that time runs out, Vrost will most likely run the destruct sequence on this ship.

Vrell finally reaches the location he has been searching for and, of course, the armoured doors are sealed. However, he knows the weaknesses here – but first some privacy. Initiating his com laser he loads to it one of the viral-attack programs residing in the library of his armour's CPU, swiftly making alterations to it as he does so. Locating one of the ship eyes in the rough walls here, he fires the laser at it. Vrost takes this as an attack, and counter-attacks through the same com connection. All feeds to Vrell's CPU blank out, as expected, but the further result is that all the ship eyes in this area are now out of action for as long as it takes Vrost to run diagnostics on them to ensure nothing nasty lurks in their computer architecture. Now reaching down, Vrell slides one claw into the slots in a floor grating, and heaves. With a snapping of bolts, it comes up and he tosses it to one side. Next he unclips his rail-gun and inserts it downwards into the cavity below, which is squirming with ship-lice, and then fires it towards the underside of the door, fanning across its entire lower section. The ensuing racket is incredible as shattered metal, glowing white-hot, explodes up out of the floor cavity. The half-load gone, he tosses in the three grenades over towards one side of the door, then moves swiftly back.

Fire erupts from below and the blast throws up numerous floor gratings along the corridor. The door, like all Prador doors, is constructed to divide diagonally, with the two halves revolving back into the walls on either side. Thoroughly understanding the mechanism and its weaknesses, Vrell knows that the bottom rail, which takes the weight of the left-hand door, will be the one most weakened. Returning to it, he feels a slight twinge of satisfaction to be proved correct: for the door has dropped right down into the floor below it, leaving a gap he might just be able to squeeze through.

After a couple of attempts to push through, Vrell has to admit that the gap is not wide enough. To get in, he needs to remove his armour. Removing his armour would usually be a simple matter of sending an instruction to its CPU, but that is now shut down. That means manual routine. He tilts his extendable head down inside the dome of the armour's turret, and inserts his mandibles into the required control pits. Fast eject ensues.

The upper carapace rises up on silvered rods, and then hinges back, while compressed air blows his limbs, lubricated with a special gel, out from the armour's limbs. He lands with a crash just beyond the abandoned armour, then turns to gaze at it contemplatively. It still stands as if occupied, which might be handy. He clatters over and heaves it round to face down the corridor where he might expect an attack to come from. Again detaching the rail-gun, he slots it over one claw, then reaches inside the armour to operate the control to close it, and the carapace lid hinges back and closes down with a thump. Now it looks as if an armed Prador stands waiting in the corridor.

Vrell turns back to the door.

Something cracks within his shell as he squeezes through the gap, and he feels certain that, now he is free of the restricting armour, the physical changes within him will continue apace. He turns his head – something he could not manage in his earlier form – and observes a star-shaped crack in his carapace, opened out and now rapidly filling with new carapace. Another spurt of growth in process. When does this end? *Does* it end? Now he feels free to inspect his surroundings – and emits a sigh of satisfaction.

The armoury is filled to brimming with numerous lethal toys. Twenty new suits of Prador armour stand tilted like close-growing toadstools, harnesses with sensory masks crouch like the desiccated corpses of giant spiders ranged on high shelves, multi-barrel rail-guns are racked ready, ammunition aplenty, explosives stacked in octagonal crates – including CTDs – and some portable particle cannons glitter temptingly. Vrell immediately grabs up a breach section for a missile-launcher and drags it over to the door, hauls up a floor plate and shoves the breach section down inside, finding purchase for it underneath the dropped door, and heaves it back up into place, turning and jamming the breach section to hold it there. Next he finds a welder and quickly welds the two doors together, finishing the job just as the clattering racket of rail-gun fire sounds from out in the corridor.

Still holding the welder, Vrell scuttles about the room rapidly locating, from his memory of the ship's schematics, all the ship eyes located in the rough walls, and systematically burns them out. Next he pulls out a maglev toolbox from storage, and tows it across behind him towards the suits of armour. The CPUs are easily accessible, with the suits open, and it is only a matter of minutes to disconnect them from the ship's systems and select a new frequency for them. All CPUs like this, he knows, contain attack programs that can control the armour without the intercession of the individual wearing it. If the occupant is severely injured, perhaps parboiled by a microwave beam, he could, within limited parameters, make his armour continue fighting for him. Working through one CPU, Vrell finds these programs and, with a speed any normal Prador would find incomprehensible, begins making certain alterations.

Outside, the sound of rail-guns is replaced by the sawing shriek of a particle cannon. A detonation shudders the door, and it drops a little but holds. Vrell quickly dons a light weapons harness, makes a rapid selection from all the lethal toys available, then goes to find a large box of hull-buster limpet mines. These he places all around the walls of the armoury, seeking out the weakest points that give access to other corridors and chambers of the ship. Placing the CPU link mask of the harness across his lower eyes and mouthparts, he uses his mandibles to tap away at the internal control pits and to link his CPU to the same frequency as the twenty suits of armour, and then instructs them to arm themselves with a large variety of weapons. Twenty empty armour suits move forward with robotic precision, taking up rail-guns, grenades, missile-launchers and portable particle cannons, then move back into a nice neat line.

But the next task is not so easy.

These suits all contain fusion tactical explosives so that the occupant can destroy himself if captured, or so that Vrost can detonate it should the occupant be reluctant to do so. This is all about keeping secret the viral transformation of those occupants. However, for obvious reasons, the tacticals remain offline while these suits – in fact while all the suits of the King's Guard – are aboard ship. It now takes Vrell some minutes of frustrating reprogramming to override that and get the bombs ready to detonate again. Then he is ready. Taking up the detonator for the limpet mines, he begins pulling up floor gratings, even as the sawing note of the particle cannon modifies, and the doors into this room glow red-hot.

The first two of the King's Guard to enter the armoury immediately open fire on the suits of armour, which are moving to take cover. The empty suits fire back with their nasty selection of weaponry. One of the Guard is slammed back out into the corridor, all the legs on one side of his body sheared off. The other dives for cover behind a rack of massive replacement coils for a coil-gun. More of the Guard charge in, and soon the air is filled with a sleet of fast-moving chunks of hot metal, gouts of fire, and a thickening haze of smoke cut through with the sabre slashes of beam weapons. Stored chemical munitions begin to detonate, and damaged power supplies start to discharge, spreading miniature lightnings down the racks and across the floor gratings. Then the hull-busters begin to go off.

The first takes out a section of wall twenty feet across, tearing through to an area crammed with loading conveyors supplying the ship's big guns. The back-blast topples racks and tosses fifteen-ton armoured Prador about like autumn leaves. Four of the suits Vrell controls now make their exit through there. Further blasts open gaps into a main corridor, into a putrid nursery full of dead third-children, and into an adjacent drop-shaft, and into other rooms and other corridors. All but two of the remote-controlled suits exit and flee, fighting a retreat against the pursuing King's Guard.

Soon the armoury is empty of fighters, though the frequent detonations and discharges continue.

After some minutes have passed, Vrell protrudes one palp eye up through a gap in the floor gratings he is concealed beneath, then quickly snatches it back down as into the room floats a Prador war drone, a big sphere of metal with rail-guns mounted on either side, and other weapons and communication pits studding its surface. He crouches even lower, his legs spread out and his flat, disc-shaped carapace nearly filling up the gap below the gratings. Time to move, so carefully he drags himself off to one side, where the adjoining third-child nursery was partially torn out, extends his head through the narrow gap and raises it slightly, one palp eye directed back towards the war drone. After a moment the drone turns slowly and drifts towards where the Guard set off in hot pursuit of those empty suits of armour, now heading for the hull guns.

Using one of his manipulatory hands, Vrell draws a laser, scans the room ahead and targets ship eyes, firing rapid and accurate shots that sear the things out of their sockets. Certainly many of them were dead, at least temporarily, having been knocked out by the EM generated during the battle, but he is just making sure. Now he heaves himself through the gap and, half-scuttling down the wall, drops to the floor. He tugs on a cable, and the maglev toolbox follows him out to crash on the floor then rise again on its maglev field. He tows it across to the further wall and there hunches down for a moment.

All this activity has made him rather hungry, and here lies an ample supply of meat. He flips his harness mask aside, reaches out with one long and slightly translucent claw to snag up one of the dead third-children. It is already showing signs of viral mutation, but its carapace is still soft, which makes things easier. He feeds its small claws into his mandibles first, crunching them down like a Human eating a stick of celery, works his way around all the legs and small underslung manipulatory limbs, then champs into the main body like a burger. It takes three of the dead to satisfy his appetite and he wonders where all this meat is going, since his carapace has grown so attenuated. Then abruptly his stomach roils and he squats to emit a great flood of watery excrement, which partially answers his question. He flips his mask back into place.

Accessing the frequency of the armoured suits, he soon discovers that five of them have now been destroyed, but that the battle area continues to spread throughout the ship. Soon, at least two or three of those suits will reach particular areas he has selected. Vrell now focuses his attention on the wall before him, reaches out and flips up the lid of the toolbox, and takes out a stud extractor. He knows that directly behind the big rough-metal wall section before him lies a ten-feet-thick layer of foamed porcelain. This is part of the shock-absorbing internal structure of the ship, and that foam-filled cavity extends deep down inside, to where the Captain's Sanctum lies.

2

As the technology for transporting people and objects through space evolved, it went through many transformations, and the carrier shell is now a relic of a previous military form. When U-space drives were first developed, they were too big for the kind of ships made to manoeuvre in atmosphere or in crowded solar environments. Two methods were adopted to solve this: the mother ship and the carrier shell. The mother ship, a large vessel containing the drive itself, would transport a whole host of smaller ships. The problem with this of course, in a battle, was that if the mother ship was hit, then all the smaller ships would immediately be stranded. Carrier shells were therefore developed to counter this. They comprised a U-space drive, usually toroidal, into which one of the smaller ships could insert itself. With these devices, smaller ships could be deployed at many locations, and the carrier shells, being relatively small, were easily concealed. And should shells and ships be destroyed during a battle, it was statistically likely that most of the remaining ships could get away, even if not in the same carrier shells they arrived in.

– From THE WEAPONS DIRECTORY

'There's a drone watching us,' says Drooble.

Orbus glances up and locates something that looks like a polished chrome catfish floating some twenty feet above their heads, just below the glass ceiling above which there seems to exist some sort of garden, for the area is packed with plant life.

'Not a problem,' he says, lowering his gaze to the concourse lying directly ahead. He finds it odd to see so many people gathered in one place, none of whom he recognizes. For centuries, whenever he attended any gathering on Spatterjay, which was rarely, there was always someone trying to warily avoid him or else issuing some politely trite greeting – or, in the case of another Old Captain, swearing at him. Though here one or two of the surrounding crowd are surreptitiously studying him and Drooble, probably because they recognize the mottled blue scarring on their skins – a sure sign of what they are and where they come from – most of those present just ignore him,

'Come on.' Orbus leads the way into the crowds, peering about at his surroundings. At ground level, on either side of the concourse, lie entrances to shops, bars, restaurants, and other establishments whose purpose he cannot even guess. Here and there, transparent tubular drop-shafts waft people to upper levels or bring them floating down. What look like private homes, or maybe hotels, rise above the shops and below the ceiling, and tiered all the way along, up there, are chainglass bubble windows and balconies.

The concourse itself is divided in two by long pools studded with fountains whose spray is twisted into curious shapes by some artistic use of field technology. Little bridges span these pools where, below rainbow weeds, dart shoals of small blue flatfish, while below these can be seen brightly-coloured crustaceans bumbling along the bottom.

'Well, excuse me!'

Orbus immediately halts, having just inadvertently walked into another man and caused him to drop a bag that spills various pieces of computer hardware and optic cables across the floor. Orbus has tried to be careful, but these people just keep getting in his way. It is very irritating indeed. He steps over the strewn hardware and starts to move on.

'Oh, never fucking mind, will you,' grumbles the individual, stooping to pick up the scattered mess and scoop it back into his bag.

The Captain halts again, a shiver of indignation running down his spine, his hands clenching and unclenching and a sudden rage coiling in his belly. No one ever steps in his path back home – because no one there is that stupid. But, of course, they do not know him here. This little man with his twinned augs, cropped red hair and loud shirt does not know that Orbus is capable of pinching off his head just using a thumb and forefinger. He glances aside and notes Drooble watching him curiously, then he glances up and notes that the drone has descended some ten feet, and meanwhile opened a wide black port in its belly. With utterly rigid self-control, Orbus turns back and squats down.

'My apologies, that is rude of me,' he says, reaching out to help the man scoop his bits and pieces back into the bag.

The fellow slaps his hand away irritably. 'Oh go away.' Then he pauses to stare at the hand he is dismissing, then after a moment raises his gaze to take in Orbus fully. Perhaps it was he, whilst using his augs, who had been the one unaware of his surroundings. Perhaps the fault is his and it was he who had blundered into Orbus. But now he is focused, intently, on the huge figure now squatting before him.

'That's . . . that there . . .' He points a finger at the mass of ring-shaped blue scars mottling the back of Orbus's hand.

'It's caused by the plug-cutting bite of the Spatterjay leech,' explains Drooble, standing behind Orbus with a vulture-like patience.

The Old Captain realizes in that instant that Iannus Drooble is just waiting for him to fail; for him to return once again to the comfort of mindless violence; to become again what he was.

'Once again, my apologies.' Orbus stands and turns, moving away, glimpsing the brief flash of disappointment in Drooble's expression.

'He just doesn't know how close he came to a Davy box,' Drooble remarks.

'He is nowhere near one at all,' says Orbus, but with very much more apparent certainty than he feels.

At the end of the concourse lie the drop-shafts Orbus had been directed to. He sees a woman watching him from beside them and guesses, as she now approaches, that she is Charles Cymbeline's representative. He studies her and observes that like most females here, she is devoid of the familiar blue scarring and increased muscle bulk characteristic of Hooper women. Her hair is an unnatural green-black, whether through dye or some genetic tweak, he cannot guess. She is pretty and uniformly professional-looking in white businesswear skirt, white jacket, red blouse and spring heels, wears a discreet white aug behind one of her mildly elf-sculpt ears, silver earrings in the shape of fishes, and an inset sensory ruby adorns her forehead. Compared with some of the others he has already seen about here, she is positively prosaic.

'Captain Orbus,' she says, holding out one delicate hand.

Orbus stares at the hand for a long moment, then carefully takes and shakes it, all too aware that with the slightest miscalculation he might turn it to pulp. As he releases her hand, he feels his estimation of this woman rise. Certainly she must be aware of the danger.

'And you are?' he enquires.

'Jan,' she replies. 'Jan Crosby. I'm here to take you to Charles.' She gestures with one hand to the drop-shafts, and is about to set out towards them when she notices Orbus's wary expression. She abruptly changes course and heads towards some side stairs.

'I guess she could have matched your grip,' says Drooble, as they mount the stairs behind the woman.

'What?' Orbus glances at his crewman.

'Golem.' Drooble nods up towards the woman preceding them, who glances round with a smile.

Orbus feels slightly lost. He just did not recognize this fact for himself, yet it is a general trait with Hoopers that they can tell the difference between real and ersatz humans. It seems his voyage of discovery into his new life has well and truly begun. Charles Cymbeline is another odd stopping-off point on that same journey, but Orbus has at least seen his kind before on the massive Spatterjay ship named the *Sable Keech*.

Charles Cymbeline, co-owner of the *Gurnard*, occupies an office overlooking the gardens above the First Port Concourse. Glancing through the wide-span bubble window, Orbus can see a fringe of jungle growth on either side of the glass roof covering the concourse itself, and numerous gardens suspended over that, all interlinked by equally suspended walkways.

'It's a premium view,' says Cymbeline. He waves in dismissal towards the Golem woman, who departs with a smile, before he takes a puff on an unfiltered cigarette.

Cymbeline is seated behind a wide marble-topped desk cluttered with com equipment, stacks of reusable paper and one or two models of spaceships – one of them the *Gurnard* itself. After gazing out at the gardens for a further moment, Orbus takes the visitor's chair placed before the desk, which is obviously intended for him, for it is unusually big and made out of ceramal. Drooble drops into the more prosaic chair beside it.

'Why do you smoke?' Drooble asks.

Cymbeline stares at him for a moment with glass eyes, then snorts some smoke out of his nostrils, a further little wisp of it departing via his ear. 'Iannus Drooble, no less – recruited to the population of Spatterjay three centuries ago, following a career that spanned the disciplines of fusion-drive tech, runcible tech, U-space geometry and also a slight digression into spear-fishing for Klader sea dragons, before, at that particular time of your life, you decided you'd like to try your luck on an even more dangerous ocean.'

Orbus glances at Drooble. The Captain is sure that at some time in the past he has heard all this, but it is a surprise to hear it fully recited again.

Though looking somewhat nonplussed, Drooble persists. 'But *why* do you smoke?'

'Did you know, Iannus, that your wife is still alive?'

This firmly shut the crewman up.

'I, too, would like to know why you smoke,' says Orbus.

'I smoke because I enjoy it, and it's a difficult habit to break.' He thereupon takes another drag, and this time a little wisp of smoke rises up out of the tightly buttoned jacket of his rather expensive-looking suit.

'I would have thought death might have broken the habit,' Orbus notes.

Charles Cymbeline is blond, thin, wears an expensive suit that probably requires special cleaning, and is very very dead. He is a reification – a corpse with preservative chemicals running through its veins. His skin is like old leather, that is worn through in places, for his knuckle bones are showing through, along with the metal of some of the cybermechanisms that keep him mobile. Like the reifications who boarded the *Sable Keech* on her disastrous maiden voyage, his mind has been stored to a crystal contained inside the mulch that was once his brain.

'I chose to not let it do so,' he explains. Then, leaning forward, he continues, 'Jericho Lamal Orbus . . .' Cymbeline pauses to glance at Drooble, when the smaller man sniggers. 'You once flew shuttles and insystem ships, and I believe studied force-field dynamics as a hobby, but that was seven hundred years ago. One would think I might worry about you taking charge of the *Gurnard*, but I learned a lot from Captain Ron about you Old Captains. The ones that survive are those whose brains are not too petrified by the viral fibres, and who, despite lack of any effort, have just kept on acquiring new knowledge throughout their lengthy lifespans.'

Orbus shrugs, not quite sure what this man is getting at, and very much disliking his own subordinate role here.

Cymbeline continues, 'Since the Polity police action on Spatterjay just after the war ended, you've all had limitless access to information and I know that, throughout those long sea voyages, you've had opportunity to read and study a great deal. Some of that information might not have stuck, but we're talking about entire centuries of reading, learning, potentially becoming wise.'

Orbus shrugs again: yes, it wasn't all just keel haulings and floggings during those lengthy voyages, and he has indeed read a bit, learnt a few things, though not so much in latter years.

'Tell me, Captain, for I'm curious to know: what procedure do you prefer to follow when removing a Singlosic thermister junction from a Deplan steering thruster.'

Orbus explains the entire procedure, not entirely sure why the reif wants to know. It is usually the kind of thing you get a qualified engineer to sort out. Cymbeline smiles – not a pleasant sight, since the movement of the cybermotors in his face expose a grey slit along his jawbone – and he studies the end of his cigarette. 'Now let's get down to business. You are now the Captain of the *Gurnard*, you are a Hooper like Captain Ron before you, and you also have a certain reputation.'

Orbus holds up a hand. He wants to retain control of his own responses, and now feels this is going too fast for him. 'I'm not sure I want to continue as Captain of that ship.' Doubts haunt Orbus, and he doesn't like the way this reif said 'certain reputation'. Orbus needs to slow this down a bit.

'That would indeed be a shame,' says Cymbeline, 'because you are perfectly suited to what I have in mind.'

Orbus raises a questioning finger. 'Which will be hauling cargo, of course.'

'Oh yes.' The reif nods, causing puffs of smoke to issue from a hole in one side of his neck. 'In the Graveyard.'

Orbus shivers, hears something creak, then glances down at his hand gripping the chair arm. He carefully relaxes his hold, noting some hairline cracks have appeared in the tough metal. Imbretus Space Station had been there, located in that place the reif has so casually mentioned. And it is very close, close to them – those fucking vicious crab things.

The Prador/Human war did not end in real victory for either side. The Polity was just beginning to push the aliens back, and to reclaim lost worlds, when the then King of the so-called 'Prador Second Kingdom' was usurped – rather messily it was rumoured, being skimmed out across the homeworld sea with diatomic acid eating away at him from the inside. Throughout this usurpation many Prador ships withdrew, and as the 'Prador Third Kingdom' then arose, it became evident that the new King understood he could not win. He therefore withdrew the rest of his forces to where the original border had lain, and there established a series of defensive space stations. The Polity proceeded to establish similar stations, but not without leaving a large buffer zone between them and the Prador. Later agreements officially designated this an area where neither Prador nor Human warships should venture. This area was subsequently called No Man's Land, or the Wasteland, but the final name settled on was the Graveyard, simply because that's what it was. Billions had died there, living worlds had been killed, massive wrecks still drifted through the dark. It is like an interstellar version of the dead and cratered ruination found between planetary battlefronts, and only rats live there.

'The Graveyard,' echoed Drooble, the very mention of it seeming to perk him up.

'What interests do you have there?' Orbus asks tightly.

'They are numerous and varied,' says Cymbeline. 'As you yourself must be aware, considering where you come from, there is currently a great interest in wartime artefacts. Within the Graveyard, numerous teams of . . . prospectors are collecting items of interest to sell in the Polity. Presently I have agents at various locations there, buying up such desirable items so as to put together one large cargo to ship back into the Polity. But, as you must also be aware, the Graveyard is a dangerous place, and I would prefer that the Captain who takes the *Gurnard* there is capable of dealing with the difficulties he is, unfortunately, certain to encounter.'

Orbus just grunts at that. On the one hand he wants to escape his sadistic past, but on the other . . . the prospect of action and some *difficulties* offers a horrible attraction. Perhaps, nevertheless, he should avoid such things for a while? Perhaps he should just *get out*?

He leans forward. 'Well, perhaps we should now discuss my pay, and some sort of profit-sharing scheme?'

Cymbeline's grotesque grin reappears.

Even with all the wall panel's rivets removed, it still hangs stubbornly in place, so Vrell takes up from the toolbox that essential piece of Prador metals technology, a huge lump hammer, and begins crashing it against the panel to help loosen the metal from

35

the underlying foamed porcelain. After a moment he spots two further rivets he has not yet removed. They must be a later addition, for they are nowhere on the schematics he has carefully memorized. He places the extractor over each in turn, winds them out, then takes up another tool, a crowbar, jams it behind the panel and levers. The panel comes out with a crack, totters in place for a moment, then slams down on the grav floor, spattering ichorous flesh from the third-child corpse it crushes underneath it.

Vrell emits a bubbling sigh and now reaches into the toolbox for a device like a large handgun devised to fit a Human hand. This trails a superconducting cable into the toolbox itself, where it plugs into the box's power supply. Holding this device in one of his underhands, Vrell directs it at the wall of green foamed porcelain before him, and presses the trigger. The vibro-debonder makes not a sound, but the porcelain retreats before it like expanded plastic before a blowtorch, as the precise frequency now emitted turns it to dust. Vrell pulls his mask back on, making use of his harness air supply while he works, for soon he is surrounded by a white haze. Within minutes he cuts open a space into which he can easily fit, first dropping the toolbox inside, then climbing in himself. Reaching back out with one claw, he hauls the wall panel back up into place, bonds it there with a squirt of epoxy from the toolbox's ample supply, then begins to slice downwards through the foam.

As he works his way downwards Vrell checks, via his CPU, the current situation with his fighting suits of armour. Obviously the King's Guard must understand that most of the suits will be empty but, because of the variance to the standard fighting programs, they will believe that Vrell occupies one of them and is exerting some control over the rest. Thus far they have destroyed nine of them, with only minor injuries to their own side. This is perfectly to be expected, but now three separate suits have nearly reached three crucial areas of the ship, and Vrell realizes he needs to move faster to get his timings right.

At about every twenty-foot interval in his progress downwards Vrell cuts a cavity to one side and scoops all the accumulated powder into it. This isn't entirely necessary since the stuff does not greatly restrict movement, and he is anyway using his harness air supply. After a while he does not bother scooping away the powder, and fifty feet down is soon submerged in the stuff, but continuing to work. Then he discovers a good reason for shifting the powder, since it blunts the effectiveness of the vibro-debonder. Again he opens a large cavity to one side and, using all his under-hands, scoops the mass of accumulated powder into it.

But still he is not progressing fast enough. His armoured suits are now fighting at two of the locations required, and others will reach the third location within minutes, and yet he has at least fifty feet to go. It is time to take a risk.

This internal shock wall contains no security measures. It is basically a blindspot – it having been considered as much a waste of resources to place security measures here as it would be to place them inside a structural beam. However, because of its function, it does contain sensors that relate to the integrity and structural strength of the ship as a whole. Vrell now unclips from his harness a weapon consisting of a heavy polished tube, the rear section equipped with heat-dispersing fins and claw grip, an s-con cable trailing from it to the harness power supply. This particle cannon can easily cut down through the foamed porcelain, but he did not use it at first because of those sensors. If the beam cuts close enough to them to defeat the insulating properties of the foam, they will instantly detect the heat, so he needs to be extremely accurate with his shooting.

Vrell now begins assessing precisely where he is within the wall. Because he is no longer connected into the ship's computer system, he cannot use it to locate his exact position, so he instead begins triangulating from the shifting positions of the other CPUs in his own little network of mobile armour, whilst also relying on his memory of the ship's schematics. This should be an impossible task for anything less than a Polity AI, or else one of the surgically removed and enhanced first-child minds the Prador use to control their own spaceships, but Vrell is confident in his own abilities. He aims the cannon downwards, checking the angle of its barrel on his mask display and also its distance from the centre-point of his own CPU, aiming directly between sensors he can see only in his own mind, and triggers it.

The beam flashes ragged purple for half a second, then turns a hot green as it heats up the floating porcelain dust, then punches downwards through the hard foam. Hot gas and dust blast up at him as, from the initial point of aim, he slowly spirals the beam outwards, carefully counting away the seconds. The cavity he occupies rapidly rises in temperature and he folds in his under-hands as they begin to sear. The sharp tips of his legs soon begin to hurt too. He knows he will sustain some physical damage, but retains much faith in the recently discovered regenerative proper-ties of his virally transformed body. Then finally he shuts off the beam.

A glowing cave spears down into murk till lost to sight. With his spare claw Vrell takes up the toolbox, then releasing his hold on the wall, he drops. Just a little under fifty feet, he hits bottom, sharp feet stabbing into red-hot foamed porcelain. Before the pain grows too intense, he swings round the vibro-debonder in one of his manipulatory hands and begins turning the remaining porcel-ain into dust. A hole punches through, furnace-hot gas and dust blowing down into it under pressure. Soon he exposes a cavity below, between two walls braced apart by piston shock absorbers. Movement sensors within these measure the changes of stress and strain inside the ship. And beyond one braced wall lies very heavy security. Now it is time to do something about that.

The last target location within the ship is finally covered by the mobile suits of armour, and his whole plan now teeters on the edge of disaster. Because at one of the other locations only one suit survives and, currently under fire from eight members of the King's Guard, it will not survive for much longer. However, in a way this is a little piece of luck in view of what Vrell next intends, for maybe Vrost will think that his rival himself occupies that last suit and has decided to take out as many of the enemy as possible before being struck down. Vrell sends the detonation signal to the fusion tactical of that one suit, which is fortunately the first one that needs to be destroyed.

The armour detonates, excavating a massive burning hole within the ship and not even the smallest fragment of itself escaping obliteration. A seemingly unintended consequence of this explosion is huge damage to the casing of a nearby combined fusion and fission reactor, which now begins spewing radiation into the surrounding area. Automatic safety protocols shut down certain power feeds there, and divert others. Vrell now sends similar detonation signals to the other remaining suits, but those exploding in two particular locations are the most important. One detonation sends an inductive surge of power along a nearby s-con conduit and burns out part of the ship's distributed computer network, while the other actually shears through some main power conduits. The final result of this is a cut to all power in a particular section of the ship – the portion directly below Vrell.

He sweeps the beam of the particle cannon across, severing numerous shock absorbers, then drops down into the space below him. The rivet extractor already in one hand, he applies it rapidly to the sheet of hull metal facing him, the loosened rivets clattering away into the darkness below. Shortly, the sheet of metal falls after them, jamming with a crash between shock absorbers below. Vrell throws himself into the space beyond and, with a satisfied sigh, eyes the mass of hardware, optics and s-con cables packed in the spaces all about him. This place was last entered many centuries ago, when the ship was first built, and then closed up. Here are all the main feeds and computer connections to what lies directly below him: the Captain's Sanctum.

Ensconced in his chair on the ship's bridge, Orbus gazes at a distant cloud-swathed world. Like so many once-inhabited worlds in the Graveyard, a glittering ring of debris now encircles it, though in this case the ring is neat and precise, having been shepherded by a sulphurous moon. The planet is called Paris and long ago was a thriving Polity world with a Human population surpassing a billion. Great satellite space stations orbited here, and huge high-tech industries occupied the equatorial deserts down below. This place was rich in every resource – surrounding space also swarming with asteroids heavy in rare metals. It took the Prador less than a day to turn those satellites into that ring of debris, before going on to depopulate the planet itself and turn it into a hell which only now, after seven hundred years, is cool enough for a few bases to be established down on the surface.

'Got it sorted yet?' he enquires.

'Jeesh, Captain, you should see this thing,' Drooble replies from the little-used shuttlebay of the *Gurnard*. 'It's probably older than you are!'

'The shuttle,' Gurnard informs them both coldly, 'is perfectly serviceable, and will probably continue to be perfectly serviceable long after you have both found your own graveyards.'

Orbus clenches his hands into fists. He really does not like the way Gurnard sometimes phrases things, for the ship AI seems to alternate between plain spooky and threatening. It is also frustrating that it remains so disembodied and beyond his grasp . . . not that he wants to do anything harmful to it. Certainly not, for he is a reformed character.

'Don't see why we gotta use the bugger at all,' Drooble complains.

'It's the law here,' says Orbus. 'Or maybe more of a tradition now.'

The *Gurnard* changes course, and Orbus eyes their destination as it slides into better view on the forward screen. The 'Free Republic of Montmartre' is a massive space station built up over a long period of time from salvage collected within the Graveyard. However, there is no denying that some of that salvage is well utilized. Orbus recognizes the brassy glint of Prador exotic metal used in exterior construction, numerous gun turrets and the throats of big rail-guns. The rule that no ships larger than a certain size can approach the station dates back to the time when this place was just a conglomeration of bubble units, and therefore easily damaged or destroyed. Back then even ship shuttles had to be transported in by a station grabship, though this rule has been dropped over the last few centuries. Now Orbus glances down as a subscreen flicks into life in the bottom corner of the main screen.

'I have transmitted docking coordinates and an entry course to your AI.' A bored-looking ophidapt, with slightly protruding fangs, peers at Orbus. 'If you deviate from that course, you could be subject to a fine not less than one thousand New Carth shillings.'

Orbus nods acceptance. 'There'll be no problem.'

The subscreen flickers off, and he stands up, grabbing a small heirodont-hide carry-all, and heads for the shuttle bay. Having thoroughly checked out the history of this place, he knows that five centuries ago any deviation from approach rules would have resulted in the offender getting smeared by one of those big rail-guns out there. Things have moved on, however, and civilization is even infiltrating places like this. Then again, it seems that civilization here has penetrated only as deep as this station's skin, for inside this place is one of those *difficulties* Cymbeline mentioned.

The shuttle bay is a plain cylinder with a suiting room to the rear and space doors at the other end, opening through the hull. Crammed into it is one craft that must be the *Gurnard*'s original shuttle, for it appears to be a product of the same designer. It looks like a short lamprey, but one with a miniature pattern on its hull of the same curved scales as adorn the *Gurnard* itself. In its side, a long door follows the curve of its hull and divides horizontally so that its bottom half, with inset steps, can fold down to create a stair. At the moment it stands open, and light of a more yellowish tint than the surrounding bay lights illuminates the interior, whence can be heard the sounds of Drooble moving about, and occasionally swearing.

Orbus clumps up the steps and ducks inside to peer around. Much as he expected, the interior of the shuttle is also faux-Victorian. The main controls, set below two slanting screens, are all brass and wooden levers and wheels rising out of a glass console below which turn numerous interlocking brass cogs and gears like those of a Babbage difference engine. The two chairs positioned before this are of wood, but with leather upholstery secured by big round-headed brass tacks. Studying his crewman's sour expression, Orbus feels something quite strange boil up inside him, something it takes him a moment to identify as amusement. But then that dies away as he understands the reason for his initial inability to identify this feeling: it is because he has not really been amused by anything for centuries. So when, in fact, was the last time he laughed? Yes, he'd done that of course, usually while flogging the skin off someone's back or keel-hauling them or breaking their bones with a wooden club, but that can hardly be described as arising from anything as healthy as the simple amusement he has just experienced.

'Memories of your high-tech qualifications coming back to haunt you, Iannus?' he asks, resting a hand momentarily on Drooble's shoulder.

Drooble gazes at him for a moment, his expression suddenly confused, then shivers as if icy water has just run down his spine. 'Why dress it up *old* like this?'

'Why not?' the Captain replies, as he plumps himself down in the chair before the small column-mounted helm, and tries to figure out how he is going to fly this thing. After a moment he realizes it won't be particularly difficult since white enamel labels, imprinted with a flowing Cyrillic script, clearly identify every control arrayed before him.

'Take a seat, Iannus,' he orders. 'Let's go for a little ride.' Reaching over he pulls back an ivory-handled lever, and actually feels some feedback through the handle itself as the shuttle's door groans shut. The lever just next to it is for controlling the space doors, and once he pulls that back, a ship's bell begins ringing. He wonders, just for a moment, if all this stuff was designed precisely with Old Captains in mind, then dismisses the idea. This might all be ersatz ancient, but it is definitely *old* and part of the original overall design of the *Gurnard* – a ship certainly built well before Cymbeline decided to start hiring Orbus or his kind.

Taking hold of the helm, he is momentarily at a loss, until he spots that the helm column itself can move up and down as well as backwards and forwards, and that a series of foot pedals runs along the floor against the lower half of the console.

'This should be interesting,' he says as Drooble finally drops into the seat beside him.

Ahead, the space doors slide open, revealing their join to consist of interlocking crenellations. When they reach nearly all the way apart, a red light on the console flicks out to be replaced by amber, then green. He eases the helm forward on its column, and with a low rumble the shuttle slides out into space. Now, easing back on the helm again, he brings the shuttle to a halt relative to the *Gurnard*, then spends some time manoeuvring it around the larger ship to thoroughly familiarize himself with the controls, aware that any thousand-shilling fine would probably be deducted from the profit-sharing bonus he has agreed with Cymbeline.

'So,' says Drooble, 'this Smith character is being a little difficult?'

'He rents the warehouse in which is stored the entire carapace of a Prador adult that Cymbeline's agent retrieved from the wreckage of a dreadnought destroyed somewhere out this way,' Orbus explains. 'The price was agreed beforehand, but now there's an additional handling charge being demanded which has trebled the initial cost. Apparently such a delicate and expensive item might be badly damaged if it is not moved by an expert team.'

'Protection racket,' observes Drooble.

Orbus glances at him and notes he is smiling, then returns his attention to Montmartre. Yes, it might be simply about shoving up the price, but the situation has other slightly more worrying aspects. It seems Cymbeline's agent and his crew, and his survey ship, dropped out of contact shortly after delivering the carapace here.

They now approach the docking coordinates, and Orbus sees that the facilities here consist of a series of three old carrier shells: large structures in the shape of hexagonal-threaded nuts, once running the big engines for shifting over large distances the smaller vessels that slotted into their central holes. In one of these shells a shuttle is currently docked, but the next one along is empty and it is to this one Orbus is directed. He reduces speed as the station structure looms all about them, the shuttle sliding into shadow glinting with navigation lights. A few deft alterations with steering thrusters set the shuttle drifting into the central hollow of the carrier shell, then Orbus brings it to a full stop, aligning not the side doors but a rear airlock.

'OK, we pay the agreed cost and collect the carapace,' Orbus states. 'I'm sure this can all be resolved without any unpleasantness.'

With a double thump against the hull, gecko-pad docking clamps engage. Orbus reaches over and and clicks down a brass-toggle electric switch and, below the main forward screens, concertinaed wooden shutters open to expose a series of smaller viewing screens. These last are slightly bulbous, almost like ancient cathode-ray televisions. Here he observes a view of the clamps – just two hydraulic cylinders terminating in wide circular pads presently stuck to the hull on either side of the airlock. Between these, the steel tube of a docking tunnel – terminating in a univeral lock that can adjust to encompass just about any size of airlock – is being extruded from the carrier shell. He watches the lock slowly expand and then affix itself to the hull, using the same technology as the gecko clamps. A particular red light turns to amber then green, and inside the glass console a wheel revolves into view an enamel plaque informing them that the tunnel is properly engaged and therefore ready to use.

'Let's go.' Orbus stands, picks up his bag and heads to the rear, Drooble quickly on his heels. Both of them cram into the shuttle's airlock, then through the tunnel towards the station lock.

The interior of the carrier shell is cramped, zero-gravity and very old. Although visitors can propel themselves through here while hardly touching the interior, the metal walls are in places worn down to an underlying layer of insulation, and in many other places patches have been welded in place. Oddly, there is also a vine growing across these walls, its gnarled trunk as thick as a man's leg in places and spined with twiggy growth putting out green and red buds. The two pause in here, holding on to vine wood polished by the touch of many hands, whilst a hatch opens to extrude a saucer-shaped security drone. This buzzes to itself for a moment, blue lights flickering around its rim, then shoots out of sight again, the same hatch slamming shut. Orbus focuses his attention on the station door, but it remains resolutely closed.

'I believe you are already aware of the rules governing entry to the Free Republic of Montmartre?' enquires the snooty voice of the ophidapt station official.

'No weapons likely to damage the station structure and no dangerous biologicals,' replies Orbus, turning a suspicious eye on Drooble.

Drooble shakes his head. 'I ain't got nothin', Cap'n.'

'What's the problem?' Orbus asks, wondering just when, in situations like this, the urge to start smashing things up will cease to torment him.

'The scanning drone has detected a large quantity of an as yet unidentified alien viral form,' the ophidapt informs them. 'Until it is identified and proven safe, I cannot allow you into the station.'

Through clenched teech Orbus asks, 'Have you got some sort of fault in your bio files?'

'What do you mean?'

'We're Hoopers.'

After a short pause the drone once again pops out and scans them, this time for a lengthier period.

In a flat voice the ophidapt announces, 'You may enter, but please be aware that the station owners classify any physical augmentation as a weapon. You will face severe penalties if you damage station structure, and you will also be ejected should you attack registered station personnel.'

A lock clonks in the station door and Orbus pushes himself over, pulls it open, and enters the grav-plated vestibule beyond. Here a payment console awaits, and he makes a money transfer from his ship's slab to get them through the next door into the station proper. He has no intention of attacking registered personnel. The owners of the station, the Layden-Smiths, and the 'free citizens' who keep it maintained, collect a nice tithe from their tenants but do not concern themselves with how those tenants run their businesses. The rule about weapons and damage to the station structure is an old one, for it dates from times when the firing of any weapon might have caused an atmosphere breach. As he understands it, the rule now only concerns damage to the main heavy superstructure, airlocks, floors and ceilings, and all the service networks, but most of everything else within here is the property of those same tenants. Orbus decides he will just have to choose carefully if it becomes necessary for him to shove someone's head through a door or a wall.

The female lies slumped against the blank white wall, and shiplice begin to edge closer, detecting death well before the onset of decay. The Human woman, Sadurian, holds up one hand, and the two Prador third-children, clad in close-fitting chrome armour, halt immediately, placing their equipment on the polished metal floor and themselves settling down onto their stomachs. Behind them the droge – a big upright cylinder with compartments all about its outer surface, containing further equipment – subsides with a hiss of compressed air. Sadurian herself squats on her haunches, the motors in her exoskeleton balancing her perfectly, and tries to recapture some of her original feelings of awe and privilege.

When the Brodis made his approach on Cheyne III, offering Sadurian a job and any salary she cared to name, she was somewhat doubtful. She had been approached like this before and, since the expertise and extensive knowledge she had acquired over a century of research had made her independently wealthy, she knew that only ECS or one of the stellar corporations could possibly afford her. And, even then, more than money was required, for she only wanted work that *interested* her – and back then very little but her own heavily esoteric pursuits did that. Blank-faced, she suggested a truly huge sum.

'First payment will be by electronic transfer, thereafter in Prador diamond slate and etched sapphires,' Brodis replied, taking out a palm console. 'If you could send me your account details, I will immediately transfer one month's salary, which you may keep even should you reject the commission I am about to offer you.'

Somewhat more curious by then, Sadurian took up her own palm console from one of her laboratory counters, keyed it to the signal from the other console, and sent her bank account details. Brodis carried out the transfer at once, and Sadurian blinked at the phone-number figure that appeared on her screen.

'Are you ECS?' she enquired.

'No.'

'Which corporation?'

'My master is not based within the Polity.'

'Your master?'

'My master and possibly your employer is neither Human nor artificial intelligence.'

That doesn't leave much else. 'A high-ranking Prador.'

'The highest.'

The journey into the Prador Third Kingdom took many months, skirting the Graveyard as it did and involving many transfers between ships. As Sadurian penetrated deeper into that shadowy realm where the two races traded, she found Humans increasingly strange as they adapted themselves to those they did business with. There were people with additional cybernetic limbs, so that as well as their own natural hands they might sport claws, and there were those whose vicious pursuits were entirely in keeping with Prador tastes, but remained capital crimes within the Polity. The first Prador she met she realized must be as different from the Prador norm as these Humans were from the Human standard, so she decided not to base any assessments of their kind upon it.

Penetrating deeper into the Kingdom, she found vicious individualists whose base instincts were utterly focused on the destruction, usually in the most messy and painful way imaginable, of their competitors. To begin with she could not understand how creatures like this ever managed to run a stellar kingdom. But when she first encountered the King's Guard, she realized that here was a different kind of Prador who, along with their King, were the glue that held it all together. And when she finally came before her employer, King Oberon, she found something utterly different again, something in a constant state of change, even then, which was a hundred years ago.

Sadurian continues gazing at the dead female. Polity AIs, while making genetic assays of Prador males, just about got the physiology of the females right and were correct in their assumptions about their social position, though way off in their estimates of Prador female intelligence and what form it took. But she is the first free Polity citizen to actually *see* one of their kind, for her involvement with them is all part of the job she was offered. She soon learnt that Oberon and his original children, mutated by the Spatterjay virus, were locked into a kind of stasis. The virus prevented Prador children from growing up – more effectively even than the hormonal controls Prador generally use – and it also rendered the King infertile. Gradually, through the slow attrition of accident and murder, the number of Oberon's children was dropping, and if their number dropped below a certain level, Oberon would not be able to hang on to the reins of power. Sadurian's job, as arguably the most able xenogeneticist the Polity had ever seen, was to change this state of affairs. And she did.

The female is twenty feet wide and resembles, if anything, the horseshoe crab of planet Earth. Unlike the male her shell is more helmet-shaped, with a wide skirt underneath which her legs and underhands can be folded out of sight. Saurian ridges extend from the facial end of the carapace to the ovipositor tail. The visage itself consists of two large forward-facing eyes between which rise two clublike eye-stalks, each sporting one short-range pupil and one other fibrous sensor whose spectrum does not venture out of the infrared. Her mandibles are long and heavy and almost serve as limbs themselves, in that they once could rapidly extend to snatch up prey. Her claws, though short and broad, possess a clamping pressure that could crack ceramal. This particular female's claws are both crushed, and her mandibles have been shattered, though her lethal ovipositor remains undamaged. She is lying on her side, tilted up against the wall, her underside split and viscera bulging out. Such are the consequences of a mating with the King.

'Okay, let's see what we've got here,' says Sadurian, easing herself to her feet.

The two armoured third-children hoist up their equipment and advance on the corpse, the droge rising again to dog their footsteps. First they use long electric probes to ensure that she is actually dead, then they open compartments in the droge to take out further tools required for the task. With hydraulic cutters they snip away her underarms to expose more of her underside, then they wield carapace saws, vibroblades and their own motorassisted claws to pull all this covering away, and with careful cutting expose her internal egg sacs.

This operation has become all but routine over the last eighty years, and though there is much other work to do involving viral mutation and the raising of tank-grown Prador young, Sadurian now finds plenty of time to speculate about the Prador Third Kingdom.

Oberon's usurpation of the Second King's rule brought the Prador/Human war to an end, and certainly Oberon and his children *are* the glue that holds this insane species together within the new kingdom, but what about *before*? Oberon received his viral infection from the planet Spatterjay, a place unknown to the Second King until the war with the Humans actually began, which meant that previous monarch seemed likely to have been a normal Prador. So what was the particular glue that held the Second Kingdom together, and the First Kingdom before it? What enabled such vicious and destructive creatures to build both a civilization and a technology to take them to the stars?

The whole thing remained a mystery to her until her fiftieth year within the Prador Kingdom. Then she learnt how simple historical circumstances had resulted in the First King, but then the Second King rose to power because of the machinations of a legendary being called The Golgoloth, which is a name still used to terrify Prador children.

3

Those who wonder why naturally exoskeletal creatures would want to clad themselves in yet further layers of armour obviously do not understand the psychology of adolescent Prador. Humans want to own their own homes, which they will furnish and decorate to their own taste; on more primitive worlds they will even put locks on the doors and windows, install home defences and alarms. But adolescent Prador do not have homes as such. For them the territory they can call their own lies within their own shells, and can only be extended by adding extra layers. Aware of their tenuous hold on life, they forever strive to build up their mobile defences and therefore gladly rather than reluctantly accept the armour provided for them by their controlling parent, and so believe themselves just that little bit safer. Each armoured Prador is its own fortress; yet each has a back door open to that same controlling parent – a door that is invariably used.

– MODERN WARFARE lecture notes from E.B.S. Heinlein

Sniper clings tight to the great scaly flank of the *Gurnard*, with Thirteen affixed by his tail to his shell. At first Sniper could not understand why the ship's AI did not inform the vessel's captain of their presence but, after scanning that shuttle as it headed over to Montmartre, he now understands.

'I don't suppose he'd be overjoyed to see me,' says the big drone.

'That is my own assessment of the situation,' replies Gurnard.

Back on Spatterjay, Sniper once saw Captain Orbus from a distance as he himself, still in his old drone shell, was trading illegal artefacts on the Island of Chel. Knowing the Captain's reputation, he did not bother approaching him to check if there was anything he might buy or sell. During his ten years as Warden of Spatterjay, Sniper had gained access to Polity files on Orbus and found them very interesting reading. The man was a sadist and though little evidence was available, seemed more than likely to be a murderer too. Later, rehoused in his present form, Sniper was ordered to search an area of the ocean for a particular Golem android the Polity AIs were worried about, and Captain Orbus's ship, the *Vignette*, lay within that same search area. The Captain, not being the most stable of characters, rejected Sniper's request to be allowed to search his ship, in fact objecting most strongly with a pulse rifle and flexal bullwhip. Sniper, always robust in his response to that kind of objection, left the Captain tied by the ankles to a cross-spar with his own bullwhip. Of course, later he rescued Orbus and some of his crew from Vrell's spaceship as it surfaced from the ocean depths, but Sniper doubts that the Captain is the kind to take that favour into account, even if he had been in any fit condition to know what was going on.

'But he's all recovered now?' Sniper enquires.

'Apparently,' says Gurnard. 'According an assessment of him, made by the other Old Captains, the traumatic events he suffered on Spatterjay have allowed him to recover his sanity. Perhaps that is a debatable point, for it seems likely his mental illness was abating anyway, and those events just expedited the process.'

'So he might be okay with me?'

'He may no longer be fighting the nightmares of his past, and he may no longer be submerged in that sick world he created for himself on the *Vignette* . . .'

'But?'

'He might indeed be regarded as sane, but that does not guarantee he has suddenly turned non-violent and sweet-natured.'

The AI pauses as if considering something else. 'I think it best he does not know about you for the present. However, I think it will be a good idea for you to be ready to back him up – as it seems likely that the situation here is more dangerous than one might suppose. I want you to locate the Prador carapace we are here to collect, and probe that station thoroughly – assess the true situation there. I cannot get clear readings because there's too much exotic metal armour in the way.'

'An Old Captain who needs back-up?' exclaimes Thirteen disbelievingly, and is instantly shushed by Sniper over their private channel.

With a shove of his tentacles, Sniper now propels himself away from the *Gurnard*'s hull. Twenty yards out, he engages his chameleonware, whereupon he and Thirteen disappear from sight. Under the effect of that shield, he fires off simple chemical propellant thrusters and speeds towards the station.

'Dodgy,' says Thirteen, coming back on that private channel to Sniper.

'Bloody right,' Sniper replies. 'That Gurnard is up to something, and it ain't just about collecting some shit for a museum.'

'No Polity warships allowed here,' Thirteen observes. 'Nor any Prador warships either.'

'Exactly,' says Sniper.

Of course, he has been manipulated. Any AI of sufficient ability could have predicted how Sniper would react to being called in for 'assessment', and that he would rapidly be using his contacts in the illegal artefacts trade to find a way offworld. That same AI would probably be aware that the *Gurnard* was the only ship currently in orbit about Spatterjay which was taking on such cargo. Sniper is now precisely where some Polity AI wants him and, that being so, some sort of shit is about to hit the fan, because no AI will employ Sniper if a talent for diplomacy or advanced macramé is required. He focuses his attention on the station lying ahead and studies it intently.

Montmartre, though essentially a conglomerate of junk built up over centuries, has certainly been refined in recent years, bound together more securely, rebuilt in sections, combined into more of a single unit. Its main body is essentially spherical – now even more so since large segments of Prador exotic metal armour have been affixed around the outside – but with spindleward towers and one long extrusion at the equator containing carrier shells converted into docking facilities. Sniper avoids the carrier shells, because most of the station sensors cluster about them, and heads instead directly towards one of those sections of exotic metal attached to the main body. A couple of squirts of his thrusters soon bring him to a near-standstill in relation to the station, and he stretches out one tentacle to grasp the edge of what was once a laser com port in the Prador ship this expanse of brassy metal was salvaged from. He pulls himself in, drags himself across the surface like some huge space snail, and peers over the rim of the armour.

Support frameworks curve from the armour's edge right round to the next segment of armour nearly half a mile away. Sniper surmises that the intention here is to eventually cover the entire station with this stuff, as and when it becomes available. Directly below this rim lies the curve of an old bubble unit, then other curves, as well as interconnecting tunnels, the occasional converted spaceship, or even a section of some other space station: in fact a great complex of airtight habitats folded into this one ball and secured with bubble-metal beams. There are also signs of further construction in progress – the intervening spaces being gradually enclosed.

'Ooh, looky looky,' says Thirteen.

'What?'

The little drone detaches from Sniper's shell, impelled by

compressed air jets, and settles down to the edge of the armour. His seahorse tail then divides, one half of it grasping a nearby bolt head, the other tapping against a casting flash along the edge of the armour section. 'That shouldn't be there.'

Sniper ups his magnification and studies the line running along the armour edge. It is ragged and sharp, but if this huge chunk of metal was retrieved from some wreck, that ridge should have been neatly ground away because, when being installed on a ship, these sections must butt up against each other with micrometric precision.

'Could have been a dreadnought under construction,' Sniper suggests.

'I suppose,' Thirteen replies grudgingly.

Sniper now pulls himself across the armour's edge, and worms down into the station structure just as far in as he can fit himself. Once past the layer of exotic metal, he finds it easier to scan deep into what lies ahead, and there finds things much as expected. Even the scan shielding covering many areas, so that they appear very hazy under scrutiny, is entirely in keeping with the kind of people who live or trade here. Doubtless the Prador carapace currently resides in one of those shielded areas, and it will be difficult for the drones to see what happens to the Captain should he enter one of them.

'Looks like a lot of dirty secrets in there,' remarks Thirteen, presently linked into and riding on Sniper's more powerful scanners.

'Looks like *you*'ll have to go inside,' Sniper rejoins.

'Yeah,' says the little drone, 'I thought so.'

Scanning in his immediate vicinity Sniper locates the positions of all the nearby station sensors and personnel. Below the bubble unit lies a very large enclosed area divided into accommodation for tenants, and an internal street lined with shops and other commercial establishments, behind which stand warehouses, but not the storage facility they seek, for this warehousing seems entirely packed with crates of spaceship components. Numerous blind spots are available, and Sniper chooses an apparently little-used tunnel connecting the warehousing to a large shop rising five floors tall.

'Over there,' he says, indicating in memory space that location to Thirteen. 'You shouldn't have too much trouble since there are free drones aboard.'

'Right,' says Thirteen doubtfully.

Sniper reaches out and sets the spatulate end of one of his two larger tentacles against the bubble-metal beam presently blocking his progress. The edge of the spatula begins vibrating at high speed, microscopic chainglass teeth running round it on a series of threadlike belts. Throwing out a stream of powder, it slices easily through the beam just there, and then at a point lower down. Sniper moves the cut-out section to one side and drifts on through, before replacing it behind him and fixing it in position with a squirt of vacuum-hardening epoxy. Cutting through two more beams similarly, and bending off to one side a duct containing fibre optics, he finally arrives above the connecting tunnel.

'Okay, inside,' he orders the little drone.

Thirteen sighs, but knows precisely what is required. Sniper withdraws his head and tentacles inside his big nautiloid shell, in order to make a space for his companion, and Thirteen positions himself within the mouth of the shell. Now Sniper presses that same mouth down against the roof of the tunnel, initiating a gecko seal about the shell's rim and pumping air into the cavity Thirteen now huddles inside. This is to bring the pressure in there up to the same as that found within the tunnel, because station sensors are especially sensitive to any changes in air pressure, since any such variance aboard a space station is always a serious matter. Thirteen meanwhile coils himself up tight whilst Sniper uses that spatulate tentacle to cut through the tunnel wall and lower a disc of it down inside. Thirteen uncoils and floats down inside the tunnel.

'Find Orbus and stick with him,' Sniper advises. 'I'll stay in contact and keep watch, but I'm also going to have a nose-around myself.'

'If I get too close to him, he might recognize me.'

'Not a problem so long as you stay out of reach of that bullwhip of his.' Sniper pulls the disc back up into place, and starts applying an epoxy that sets quickly in atmosphere. Floating on AG, Thirteen drifts off down the tunnel below, muttering to himself.

Within the cramped space, Vrell touches a control on the side of the toolbox, whereupon it settles to the floor and unfolds to display its varied contents. Now studying his surroundings more intently, the Prador begins to identify the purpose of the superconducting cables, the ducts containing fibre optics, the computer components and other hardware here. He reaches out and takes up a small diamond saw, chooses one particular duct and, with extreme care, cuts through its casing, removing a yard-long section to expose the mass of fibre-optic cables inside. Many of these are colour-coded, and from his memory of the ship's schematics he picks out those he does not need and eases them to one side. Fifteen cables remain. Next he takes up a ring-shaped external optic interface and plugs its own optic feed into his harness CPU, before snapping open the ring and closing it about the first cable. Prador computer language – blocky hieroglyphs – begins running diagonally across his mask's screen, and after studying these for a moment he realizes they aren't encoded, so this optic is not the one he requires. Taking a moment more to study the glyphs, he sees that this feed is simply data running into the Sanctum from the ship's engines.

He selects another cable and checks again, this time to report on the status of five of the ship's fusion reactors. The eighth cable is the one he is after.

The computer code now running across his mask is supposed to be unbreakable, but he long ago learnt that there is no such thing as an unbreakable code. Vrell does not even bother copying it to his CPU memory, just memorizes it himself and applies his intellect to it. He runs code-breaking programs in his mind, discarding elements of them and altering them as he goes along. Eidetically clear in his mind is the Prador language, which includes text, sound and pheromones, and he runs perpetual comparison between the code and his language's structure. This takes him an hour, and he wonders if he has cracked it as fast as Polity AIs would manage the same chore. Thereafter, Vrell does not even apply a translation program through his CPU, but simply reads the code directly. First he samples back to the moment he began memorizing and replays the communications in his mind.

'. . . likely he is in that armour,' Vrost has just finished saying.

'We can't go in there yet – it's too hot even with armour,' comes the reply, along with a pheromonal signature identifying the Prador concerned. Vrell sees how the Spatterjay viral mutation has distorted the signature from the norm. This is something he would never have spotted from the outside if he were a normal Prador receiving communications from one of the Guard. Obviously they translate their signatures for any com outside their own family, so as to keep their real nature hidden.

Next comes a data packet Vrell translates as readings from air samplers. Vrost must have studied this for a moment before saying, 'Trace organics, but they could come from the Guard incinerated in there. I want you to try and find anything remaining of that suit and take direct samples.'

'There won't be anything left.'

Vrell is surprised at this comeback. Obviously the King's Guard – these mutated second-children – are allowed more of a free rein than normal Prador, since conversations between second- and first-children of the latter kind usually consist simply of orders and direct obedience.

'If you are concerned about losing more of your unit,' says Vrost, 'do not be. We are all dead anyway – because, with that nanite aboard, this ship will not be allowed back into the Kingdom and, since we know it slowly penetrates glathel seals, the extent of our lives is limited to three hours.'

Interesting. Vrell knows the nanite can penetrate some porous substances – but glathel seals? He does a high-speed analysis incorporating his knowledge of the hard rubbery substance his kind employ to make airtight seals, and comes to a rapid conclusion: the nanite cannot penetrate a static seal, but will work its way down through the laminated layers of that same substance while it is in movement, precisely as it is now being moved in the joints of the armoured suits worn by the Guard.

'Why then is it necessary for us to find out if he is inside that suit?' enquires the King's Guard. 'In two hours this ship, and we along with it, will cease to exist.'

Ah, thinks Vrell, *Vrost himself hopes to find some way of surviving.* For the seals about the Sanctum just might all be intact, he surmises, and are certainly static.

'Because our father so instructs,' replies Vrost. 'Do your duty.'

Their father: King Oberon himself.

This particular communication closes down and for the ensuing hour only routine information packages are exchanged. From these Vrell puts together a mental image of the search now in progress: the Guard being sent one after another into the area devastated by the fusion-reactor explosion, then sickening in the perpetual sleet of radiation and withdrawing to find somewhere to curl up and die. Then, in present time, comes a communication Vrell recognizes as channelled through an exterior route.

'That I can still obtain a response from your U-space communicator means you have disobeyed me,' says someone. Vrell studies the complex pheromonal signature and, though recognizing some of the organic compounds as having a Prador as their source, know these are but a small proportion of the whole.

'Father,' replies Vrost, 'I wish to ascertain that Vrell has either died aboard this ship or still remains aboard it when I detonate.'

So, that signature is King Oberon's. Vrell studies it more intently, identifying those same distortions he saw in the signature of that member of the King's Guard, but seeing even further distortions and a huge complexity that goes way beyond any mutation he has so far observed or himself experienced. However, does this mean anything more than that the King is making sure his signature is difficult to copy? Vrell feels it does. He does not know how old Vrost or any of the Guard here are, but certainly the King is over seven hundred years old. Who could know what he has become in that length of time?

'If you had detonated, as instructed,' replies Oberon, 'Vrell would certainly have been inside. Obviously, throughout the long period of your watch over Spatterjay, you have gained a degree of independence from me and are able to disobey. This is now more than evident since the remote detonation code I sent to your ship from here has not worked.'

'Father, Vrell cannot escape.'

'Have you at least disabled all the U-space escape pods? Please tell me that you were able to follow that simple order?'

'I have.'

'Oh good.'

Vrell allows himself a Prador smile, which consists of twisting his mandibles to a particular angle normally used to gut a certain kind of crustacean considered a delicacy on homeworld. He is ambitious for a lot more than simple survival, and did not even consider taking that escape route; he will seize control of this ship or die.

'Presently we are searching for traces of his remains, since he—'

The King interrupts. 'I have studied the data. You will find no traces, for Vrell is almost certainly still alive, and probably even now somewhere near you.'

In the midst of this conversation comes a spurt of a very complex code. Vrell studies it intently but finds himself struggling to make any sense of it. He works at it harder, applying more and more of his mental capacity. Slowly he begins to make some headway and realizes that, oddly, this intricate code only contains a very simple message.

'So, Vrell, doubtless you have intercepted this.'

Vrell suddenly feels very insecure and rises up higher on his legs, unclipping his particle cannon.

Oberon continues, 'Despite my constant cautions to Vrost, he has become both arrogant and independent. He does not realize what you are and that, now you are aboard his ship, he cannot hope to survive. Though he disabled my option to destroy his ship remotely, he will certainly attempt to destroy both himself and his ship the moment your nanite penetrates his seals. But that's not enough, is it?'

Thinking very fast, Vrell yanks the optic interface away. But he is not quick enough, for the virus the King now sends propagates through his CPU and blooms on the screen of his mask. His mind, having been closely applied to the previous code so as to uncover the message, is therefore receptive to the thing that now enters through his eyes and penetrates his brain. Vrell tries to control a sudden impulse to turn the particle cannon upon himself, then tries to disrupt the self-assembling worm in his head that starts his limbs jerking while it causes other organic reactions actually inside his body.

Managing to swing the cannon across he fires upon two particular superconducting cables, severing them so that their massive discharge of power arcs towards the floor. Knocking his mask aside, he directs his lower turret eyes at the hideously intense arc-light of the discharge, and shrieks as the front of his head smokes and his optic nerves burn out. Now, seeing only with his palp eyes, he closes a claw around the optics before him, tears them free, then smashes that same claw into the casing of one of the components of the Sanctum's distributed computer network. That should now delay any destruct signal Vrost might send.

The worm in Vrell's head, disrupted by the intense flash of light and the pain, starts to fall apart, and he shuts down selected parts of his mind to ensure this, though the rest of his mind notches up a number of gears and starts operating so fast it feels like it is beginning to burn. All the schematics he has memorized come to the forefront of his consciousness: all he understands about Prador technology, the materials of the ship around him, in fact just about everything he knows resurfaces for conscious perception, and he processes it to find a solution.

Swivelling round, Vrell reaches up and tears off the casing of another of those computer components, then tries to bring his limbs sufficiently under control so that he can reach inside with a small abrading tool clutched in one of his manipulatory hands. Finally, with delicate precision, he cuts across two miniature gold wires and presses them together, before turning again to grab up one of the superconducting cables by its insulating layer and then slam it into the side of a hydraulic fluid reservoir. Now he fires the particle cannon beyond the same container; aiming precise shots at twenty-three different locations on the wall, before hurling himself at it. The panel, its twenty-three rivets incinerated, collapses under his charge, and he falls through and down towards the floor twenty feet below. Even as he falls, he opens fire on the King's Guard standing at the end of the corridor, concentrating on the magazine of a missile-launcher strapped on its back. The subsequent detonation slams the Guard into the side wall, but Vrell's aim does not waver even as he lands, and further detonations send the armoured Prador tumbling further down the corridor, where it comes to rest, probably still alive but with its suit's systems knocked out and the nanite doubtless already penetrating various damaged seals.

Vrell spins towards the big heavy doors of the Captain's Sanctum and watches as, despite Vrost's efforts to make sure they stay firmly closed, the doors begin to vibrate. Simple hydraulics: the power surging into the reservoir is heating it up and expanding the fluid, forcing it the wrong way against valves, then something finally gives and high-pressure fluid slams into the door cylinders, and the doors crash open. But, even as Vrell hurls himself forwards, some part of the worm still inside his head collapses into a different shape. It loses its impetus and becomes simply a message.

'Next time, then, Vrell,' says the King of the Prador Third Kingdom. 'But now I'll allow you to deliver my displeasure to Vrost.'

It takes away some of the pleasure of victory for Vrell to know that his real opponent is possibly even more lethal than himself.

Gazing up through the hollow core of Harper's Cylinder, towards internal elevator tubes and a stair winding up around the internal wall, Orbus surmises that this cylinder was once the spin section of a very old ship – one built before grav-technology advanced sufficiently to become usable. Now, as part of this space station, it is like a tower block with grav operating from the lower end and with all sorts of commercial establishments lining the interior. Smith's front office – with access to the storage area he owns, which is positioned just outside the Cylinder – lies somewhere near the top. However, Orbus has some business to conduct first at a place halfway up.

'There's a drone watching us,' says Drooble.

Experiencing a moment of déjà vu, Orbus glances at his companion, then follows his gaze up and over to one side. There is indeed a drone up there, one made in the shape of a seahorse and presently clinging to the stair rail by its tail, but whether it is actually watching them is debatable. Now studying the thing, Orbus feels it is somehow familiar, but then everything possesses a degree of familiarity once you've been knocking about for over seven hundred years. More likely this is something Smith himself sent to watch them and, hopefully, that is all the two behind them are here for too.

'Iannus,' he says, 'I think we should worry more about *them*.' Orbus stabs a thumb over his shoulder at the two rather large individuals who have been trailing them since shortly after they boarded this station.

There is something he very much does not like about the way they move: a sort of wooden gait but with no unnecessary movement of any other parts of their bodies. He suspects they might be early-series Golem or some other make of android, but something niggles at his memory, some rather black areas of his memory.

Drooble glances over his shoulder at their two shadows. 'Do you reckon we should go and have a word with them?'

Orbus heads for one of the elevator shafts. He doesn't like drop-shafts but this should be okay because at least he'll have something solid under his feet. 'What will be achieved by having a word with them?' He hits the call button and the doors ahead slide open. Stepping inside with Drooble close behind him, he quickly selects the floor he requires. The two big men pick up their pace, and Orbus studies them more closely through the still open doors. Both of them wear long heavy coats, baggy trousers and large boots. They also wear gloves, and pork-pie hats pulled low on their foreheads, and though gazing directly at both Orbus and Drooble, their meaty features express a kind of dead indifference. Orbus feels something crawl up his spine and for a moment that errant memory nearly surfaces. Then the elevator doors close, and he and Drooble are whisked upwards through Harper's Cylinder.

Arriving at the floor they want, Orbus soon locates their first destination by the Anglic script scrawled above the double chain-glass doors, and even as he heads over, the doors slide open at his approach.

'Captain,' says the individual inside as, with a sigh of exoskeletal motors, she stands up from a very old-fashioned computer console. 'You will understand, I hope, if I don't shake your hand?'

Her skin is a yellowish orange, her long hair a silvery white, while her eyes possess a metallic glitter. Even the bulk of her exoskeleton cannot disguise how thin she is, for she is an Outlinker: a Human adapted to living in zero gravity, usually aboard one of the outlink stations that border the Polity. People like her can survive for an appreciable time in vacuum, being able to store a great deal of oxygen inside them and seal their bodies against zero pressure. However, her bones and muscles possess very little strength, so her fear of an Old Captain's handshake is utterly comprehensible.

'Not a problem, Reander,' says Orbus with rote politeness, before reaching into his carry-all to pull out the ship's slab.

She points to a small round table beside her console, then turns her attention towards Drooble, who is peering down into a glass-topped display box.

'If you see anything you're interested in, I'm sure I can give you a special price,' she informs him.

The place is packed with hardware stowed on shelves that retreat into cobwebby darkness, while the mezzanine floor above, with steel stairs leading up to it, is stacked to the ceiling with boxes. There seems likely to be something here to excite interest in just about anyone.

While Reander is using an optic cable to connect the ship's slab to her console, Orbus eyes a large reinforced-chainglass machete. He doesn't require such an item to chop through the thick dingle of Spatterjay, but something deep down is telling him it might come in very useful, and soon.

'Iannus,' he warns. 'Keep an eye out.' He nods towards the door, and Drooble heads over that way, ostensibly to study a display case full of laser lighters just beside it.

Reander watches this exchange just for a moment, then returns her attention to the screen. 'Dear oh dear, that ship is full of junk,' she observes. 'However, I think we can do business on at least some of the cargo.'

Orbus steps up beside her, trying not to notice how she flinches away from him, and peers at the ship's manifest currently displayed on her screen. Upon first boarding the *Gurnard*, he had taken a stroll through the grav-plated areas of the hold and been astounded at the sheer quantity of goods stored there, also by their variety and, in many cases, their sheer age. Some of the stuff is even in the process of making the transition from junk to antique. And yet the grav-plated areas of the hold contain only half the total available storage space.

'These.' Reander highlights some of the cargoes on the list: fifty tons of Bishop's World onyx and three crates of toy pulse-guns. This space station couldn't possibly have a use for such a quantity of onyx, but doubtless she has a customer to sell it on to who will then transport it elsewhere. Though curious about its possible destination, the Captain does not let this concern him too much. He picks up the ship's slab and, so Reander cannot see, checks the minimum price these two cargoes must be sold for, adds 20 per cent, and allows the price to display on her screen. She sighs and they begin the ancient Human pastime of haggling, but the Captain's heart isn't in it and he soon lets her buy the goods for only 5 per cent above minimum.

'So what can you tell me about Smith Storage?' he asks, as she now sits down to carefully work her way through the rest of the manifest.

She glances up. 'Still got problems with that carapace?'

She herself was the intermediary aboard Montmartre who found a place for that item to be stored.

'Still got problems,' Orbus confirms.

'That's odd.' She frowns. 'Anyway, that question is one being asked a lot around here lately.' Now she does look up. 'They've been in business for only a year, but they've bought up a lot of station space and have been bringing in a lot of goods, yet they don't seem to do much business. They did, apparently, sell the new exotic armour you can see out there to the station owners, and they've done a bit of smaller trading, like with your particular item, but it still doesn't seem enough to cover their expenses.'

'What's the general station consensus on them?'

'They're arms traders who've been sold a special licence to operate from here, or they're a big Polity concern preparing to move into the Graveyard, or they're a Separatist cover company, or else they're the owners, the Layden-Smiths themselves, gradually reac-quiring full control of the station.' Reander now begins highlighting various food cargoes held in stasis.

'Your own opinion?'

'The last,' she says. 'Business has picked up in the Graveyard over the last twenty years and I reckon the owners want a bigger share of the profits. They've been operating for a long time so they'll have the contacts, and I also don't think it's coincidental that the new concern is called Smith Storage.' She shrugs. 'It seems a sensible move – though I still don't get why they're being so awkward about one Prador carapace.'

After a pause she adds, 'It seems they undercut all the other storage companies to get the business.'

'Cap'n,' interrupts Drooble.

'They here?'

'Just the drone.'

'Keep watching.'

'You're being followed.' Reander abruptly stands up. 'I've got just a small business here and, for readily apparent physical reasons, I cannot afford to get involved in anything nasty. The station grabship will head over to the *Gurnard* for the items we've agreed upon. You'll now inform your ship AI?'

Orbus taps a finger briefly against the ship's slab, before unplugging it and dropping it back in his bag. 'Already done – there's a direct link.' Abruptly he realizes it wouldn't be fair on her if those two heavies broke in here and caused a problem, for minor violence that might bloody any normal person's nose could crush her skull. 'One last question?'

'Go ahead,' she says.

'Cymbeline's agent delivered the carapace to you for storage. Do you know what happened to him afterwards?'

She shrugs. 'He left – that's all I know.'

Turning towards the door, Orbus pauses by the chainglass machete. 'How much for this?'

Reander walks over, meanwhile pulling a plastic sheath and

shoulder strap for the blade from the shelf behind. Tossing them to him she says, 'Take it with my compliments – I was always nervous about having that thing in here anyway.'

Orbus picks up the big blade and weighs it in his hand. Reander cringes back, so he slides it into its sheath, nods to her briefly and departs.

The little survey ship is not even concealed behind any shielding, merely docked at one of the Layden-Smiths' private docks. It is a simple bullet-shaped craft with a small hold and exterior twinned U-engine nacelles, of the kind used all across the Polity, so Sniper would not have even bothered scanning it had he not noticed the damage. The vessel has been hit with a high-intensity laser burst from the dock's defences, the beam punching through the hull in a very particular area to the rear of the crew compartment. Here, the old war drone knows, was almost certainly where the ship's AI, if it had one, would be positioned. Scanning inside the vessel, he sees that it had indeed possessed an AI, but that entity is now merely a slag of shattered and molten crystal. Scanning further, he finds that the rest of the crew has done no better.

'The survey vessel belongs to Charles Cymbeline's agent in this area,' Gurnard confirms, after Sniper tight-beams an update back out of the station.

'Well,' says Thirteen, also listening in, 'that solves one riddle.'

'And he's still aboard,' Sniper replies.

The corpse in question is well on the way to skeletonhood, but Sniper possesses more than enough knowledge of human anatomy and forensics to know what has been done to him, especially when taking into account certain other items scattered on the floor about his feet. Someone glued him to a wall and tortured him. They used an autodoc on him, so they could deliver the maximum amount of pain and still keep him alive. They used psychotropics, pain inducers and a good old-fashioned bit of bone breaking and electrocution, and even relieved him of all his fingernails. The final finesse was the use of a specially-adapted augmentation to ream out his mind. Obviously, whoever did this wanted to learn every-thing the agent knew about something, and there is no doubt they obtained that information. As for the rest of the crew, they received similar treatment. Only one was not interrogated, for quite likely it was essential to take him out of action as quickly as possible. And how.

'Um,' remarks Sniper to both Gurnard and Thirteen, 'seems there's something around here capable of tearing apart a Golem android.'

'I think I can guess who did that,' says Thirteen.

'Enlighten me.'

Thirteen sends him an image of two large and bulky individu-als climbing into a lift. 'I thought there was something funny about them and, judging by the looks he was giving them, Orbus does too.'

'And what exactly is funny about them?' enquires Gurnard.

Thirteen changes the image to an X-ray view. Where in normal humans only the bones would now be visible, along with any metal items carried about their persons, these two are only reduced to translucence. However, it is possible to see the hardware sitting inside their skulls and the threads of metal spearing down their spines. Sniper at once recognizes what these two are, and knows that two of them certainly could manage to tear apart a Golem android.

'Warn the Captain about them,' Gurnard instructs.

'Without getting into debates about who I am and why I'm here?' Thirteen asks.

'I think things have moved beyond that,' says Gurnard, 'but try to be subtle.'

'Subtle, right,' says Thirteen. 'Yeah, I remember subtle.'

Outside Reander's establishment, Drooble stabs a finger towards where the seahorse drone is still hovering above the entrance to the elevator shaft. Orbus nods as he continues over, then, before stepping into the elevator, peers up at the drone and asks, 'What do you want?'

'Many many things,' replies Thirteen. 'But right now I want to know why so much of this station is shielded, and why two very old men, who once made a brief and traumatic visit to Spatterjay, are keeping tabs on you.'

'Two very old men?' Drooble queries, but in Orbus the memory finally surfaces and he now knows precisely who the two heavies are – or, rather, what they were. It is as if someone has just slapped him, slapped him harder than anyone has been able to manage for centuries. Hearing an odd creaking sound, he realizes it is the noise of his own muscles tightening up like knots of steel cable.

'Anything else you want to know?' Orbus asks the drone.

'I'd like to know why a Prador carapace is so important. I'd like to know why Smith Storage, which is, as Reander Asiera guessed, a concern started up by the owners of this station, is bringing in a lot of cargo but transporting none out, and why the owners themselves – the five descendants of the original Layden-Smith family – haven't been seen for over a year.'

'And why do you want to know these things?'

'Because I work for Gurnard and I'm here to back you up.'

Orbus stares at the drone, not sure whether to be amused or angry, then steps into the elevator after Drooble and selects the floor on which Smith Storage lies. Stepping out from the elevator upon arrival, he is greeted at once by the sight of the two heavies waiting on either side of a quite possibly genuine wooden door. Switching his heirodont-hide bag to his left hand, he thereby frees up his right hand and keeps it up ready by his left shoulder, within easy reach of the machete now strapped across his back. He knows that these two will not notice something so obvious as this, though perhaps whoever is looking through their eyes will.

'Is Mr Smith in?' he enquires as they reach the door.

'Fuck,' says Drooble abruptly.

Orbus glances at him, realizing he's just caught on. Neither of the two heavies responds, though the door immediately begins to creak open. Orbus realizes that, just after talking to the drone, he should have turned round and headed straight back to the *Gurnard* for some explanations, or maybe mooched off to buy passage on some other ship out of here. However, the presence of these two at the door stirs up in him a deep reservoir of anger, and a horrible joy at the certainty that here at last he will be able to express that anger.

'I just go through?' he asks, pointing ahead and, without waiting for a response, steps through.

A reception office waits beyond the door and, judging by the splash of old blood behind the desk, which itself now lies in two halves on the floor, the receptionist will not be greeting them. Beyond this lies a set of double doors.

'I guess the storage area is this way?' Orbus strides ahead.

Drooble glances back at the two heavies, the main door closing behind them as they lurch in to follow. Orbus slams a boot into the centre of the two doors ahead. One smashes back against the wall adjacent and the other goes crashing end over end down the corridor extending beyond. Here they have not bothered to remove the corpses, and two lie on the carpet, stains spread out about them. They've obviously been here for some time, being now rotted down to bone and parchment skin. Both of them seem to have their heads on backwards.

'Probably the Layden-Smiths, or their staff,' Orbus observes, striding ahead. 'I'm guessing our two chums originally came in this way.'

'Hey, Cap'n,' says Drooble, 'glad to have you back.'

A further set of double doors leads to a bubble-metal stair running down along the wall to terminate in a small storage room stacked with plasmel boxes. At the rear of this room stands a large heavy door, probably taken from a ship's bulkhead. After glancing back to see their two companions now picking up their pace, Orbus jumps.

'Come on, Iannus!' he yells.

Orbus hits the floor with a crash, denting it, and Drooble lands somewhat more lightly beside him. Behind them, the two pursuers start to negotiate the stairs, probably as they always have done, this method of descent being recorded as a program in what might be called their minds. Orbus doesn't bother with the handle of the bulkhead door, for he can see it is locked down in its recess and therefore it should only be possible to open it from inside. This area, then, is supposed to be the killing ground. He knows this door is most certainly station property, but surmises that the Layden-Smiths are beyond objecting to the damage he will now cause. Dropping his small bag, he smashes a fist into the metal beside the door, twice, to leave a dent, lodges both hands in this to grab the door and heaves. His Old-Captain strength, grown incrementally over seven hundred years, his body wound so tight with viral fibres that his muscles are as dense as old oak and his bones like toughened steel, is not to be long resisted. Ceramal locking mechanisms snap clean off, and the door swings round to crash against the wall.

Within lies a large darkened warehouse, shelves reaching up to

the high ceiling, large cargo containers towards the rear, monolithic stacks of boxes all around, in fact an area little different in
appearance to the *Gurnard*'s hold. From behind come two loud
crashes, as their pursuers finally receive instructions not to waste
time negotiating the stairs. Drooble, so long in service of his
Captain he can nearly read his mind, ducks to one side, drawing a
ceramo-carbide hunting knife from his boot.

'Mr Smith!' Orbus calls out.

The two come in behind, and without even looking round
Orbus draws his machete and spins, the blade describing a perfect
flat arc all about him. The tug of contact is hard, of course, for the
blade is slicing through flesh and bone just like his own. Along
with a rigid chunk of Prador hardware. Now Orbus unhooks his
bullwhip with his free hand and lashes it sideways, the snake of
flexal coiling around the legs of the second heavy. He pulls, and
the man goes down on his back, the big pulse-gun he just drew
sent skittering from his hand. His companion, now headless, still
stands upright, one hand vibrating at the edge of his severed but
utterly dry neck. He hasn't realized he is dead. He hasn't realized
he actually died seven hundred years ago.

Drooble, ready to snatch any opportunity, skitters over and
picks up the pulse-gun, then steps over and begins firing it down
into the head of the fallen man. He empties the weapon, firing
until nothing remains of the head but a smoking fibrous mass and
the glowing metal of a thrall unit.

'Fucking blanks,' he spits.

Indeed they are. These two are what Orbus would have
become on Spatterjay centuries ago had he not managed to avoid
being cored and thralled, if the war had not ended and rescue
finally come. Slowly, like a building demolished by specially placed
charges, the headless human blank collapses first onto his knees,
then tilts over forwards, before slumping down onto his side.

'Mr Smith!' Orbus calls again viciously, turning away to survey the entire storage area.

In a wide aisle between shelves, beside masses of jury-rigged consoles, lies a great brassy-coloured object that Orbus recognizes as basically the same shape as a Prador carapace. For a moment he thinks that this must be what, ostensibly, they came here for. However, it heaves itself up onto its numerous legs and spins, reaches out with one claw to tear down some shelving and cast it aside, then extends its other claw, in which it holds a massive rail-gun.

Orbus begins to shake, but cannot tell whether this is from fear or excitement.

'I don't think you're Mr Smith,' he manages.

4

The no man's land between the Prador Kingdom and the Polity, which quickly acquired the name 'The Graveyard', did not remain as barren and lifeless as its name implies, but quickly filled with lowlife. Certain members of both the Prador and Human races found it convenient to locate their businesses where, by treaty, warships cannot be sent and where the security services of both sides have limited ability to intervene. Separatists base themselves there, as do criminal syndicates, the makers of black memloads and smugglers of illegal technologies. It is argued that these traders in Human suffering could easily be cleared out without the use of warships. It is also noted that such an environment is a useful one in which to conduct black operations, and that both sides therefore want the Graveyard to continue just as it is.

– From HOW IT IS by Gordon

'Now what are two Human blanks doing here?' wonders Sniper.

'It's not so unusual as you might think,' Gurnard replies. 'Though many were returned to the Polity in recent years, it is certain that many more still remain within the Third Kingdom, and certainly they tend to turn up out here in the Graveyard – usually having been sold to some criminal organization.'

'So that's what we're dealing with here, is it?' Sniper asks sarcastically, 'a "criminal organization"?' Scanning into the dock he now observes something he has noted elsewhere round and about Montmartre: the Layden-Smiths possess their own internal tubeway network and, fortunately, the bubble carriages they use are larger than Sniper himself. Not being one to let such an opportunity slip by, he begins to subvert security systems around the dock so that he can open a door into it – the cargo bay immediately beyond connects into that same tubeway network. He is extruding something like an electronic lock-pick into the door control when he realizes that Gurnard is not going to be forthcoming with a reply.

'So let me work my ignorant way through this,' Sniper continues. 'The *Gurnard*, a ship owned by the private individual Charles Cymbeline, is sent into the Graveyard to gather up wartime artefacts collected in this area by his agents. There is a problem with the first of these artefacts that it comes to pick up, and Spatterjay Human blanks are involved. Coincidentally I, a Polity war drone, happen to be aboard the *Gurnard* and, coincidentally, the Captain of the *Gurnard* is an Old Captain – someone who narrowly avoided being turned into a blank himself and who has every reason to hate the Prador.'

'It is a large universe,' Gurnard observes, 'and the mind, be it AI or Human, with its tendency to search for patterns, will often find coincidences.'

'Bollocks.' With the cargo door now open, Sniper slides into the small vacuum bay. The tubeway network beyond, which is also used for transporting the cargoes delivered here, is a vacuum network, and so Sniper enters it easily.

'I am not quite sure what you're driving at here, Sniper.'

'I smell a rat.'

'A tendency not unknown to Polity AIs.'

'Are you going to elaborate on that?'

Now actually inside the Layden-Smiths' realm, Sniper is well within all the shielding, and more freely able to scan the areas about himself. Almost at once he begins to notice Prador metals and technology. This can be explained by the fact that most of this station is built from salvage, but what cannot be explained is why so much of it is not the superannuated technology of the war.

'Let us say that there is something about King Oberon and his hugely extended family that he wants to keep a complete secret even from the rest of his own kind.'

'Yeah, I'm with you on that.' Sniper knows precisely what that secret is, and if he knows, it is certain that Earth Central Security knows too.

'Let us say that the Graveyard is a very sensitive area, where ECS forces and the official forces of King Oberon must not come into contact with each other, for that might lead to the start of another all-out-devastating interstellar war.'

'Right, let's say that.'

'However, let us also say that King Oberon is being a bit too pushy and for some years now has been infiltrating his forces into the Graveyard, it being a moot point whether this is in preparation for war or to more firmly secure his defences. ECS will not want open confrontation in this matter, but would rather take limited actions to scotch that infiltration.'

'I'm sort of with you so far . . .'

'Having now discovered the major infiltration of a certain space station in the Graveyard, ECS would need to do something about it, but would also want to conceal precisely what they are doing about it. Say they know an agent of Oberon is gradually taking control of the said space station, and they therefore send to that station an item that will reveal, in Polity hands, the secret nature of Oberon's family. The agent aboard will have to seize said item, and ensure that any knowledge of it cannot be passed on. Those coming to collect the item must also be dealt with and, as we know, when it comes to Prador, "deal with" almost always means kill. However, *coincidentally*, the privately owned ship sent to collect the item happens to have, in its complement, an Old Captain who, as you say, has every reason to hate the Prador, and also a renegade veteran war drone from the Prador/Human war, currently occupying a state-of-the-art drone shell.'

'One could guess that some plausibly deniable mayhem might ensue,' remarks Sniper. 'Was it also part of the plan that those aboard the survey ship should die?'

'That was most unfortunate,' Gurnard opines. 'They were merely supposed to deliver the item I mentioned and—'

'You mean,' Sniper interrupts. 'The carapace of a Prador, most likely that of a second- or first-child, heavily mutated by the Spatterjay virus?'

'Yes, exactly – it was assumed that you knew more than you are letting on.'

'Oh, I'm full of stuff I'm not letting on.'

Gurnard ignores that jibe and continues with, 'They were merely supposed to deliver the carapace and then swiftly depart. However, it would appear that Oberon's infiltration here is more extensive than was first thought, and his agents or agent on the spot moved faster than expected.'

'Hang on a minute.' Sniper draws to an abrupt halt. 'When you say agent or agents, you're not talking about Humans allied with the Prador are you?'

Before Gurnard can reply, Thirteen's urgent summons comes through, 'Sniper! Get over here now!' And along with it come some very interesting scan images.

Sniper accelerates, no longer concerned about keeping himself concealed from the various security systems around him. The tubeway isn't really designed to have a fusion engine fired up in it, but Sniper is not hugely concerned about that. He occasionally crashes into the walls, causing more damage to them than to himself. And as he hurtles through the station he starts running a system check of his weapons which, of course, could not have been any more functional.

The huge Prador looming immediately ahead of Vrell is clad in heavy armour, looks as big as an adult but, unlike most adults, possesses all of its limbs. Sometimes adults do choose to wear armour like this, the limb casings empty but run by small control units grafted into the adult's empty limb sockets, but Vrost is not such a creature and certainly still possesses all his limbs. Vrell does not give Vrost a chance to do any more than register his presence before he opens fire, the particle beam directed solely at one of Vrost's legs.

Vrost shrieks and skitters sideways, trying to protect the one targeted limb, as he himself swings up a rail-gun. Vrell leaps straight up, unencumbered by armour, as a stream of solid projectiles shoots underneath him to smash into hot shrapnel in the corridor behind. He catches one leg against the top of the door, spins round and skitters up the uneven wall, yet, even while doing this, still firing the particle cannon, the beam not wavering from its target for a second. The armour on Vrost's leg turns white-hot and then gives up, something inside exploding and splitting it open.

Still moving rapidly along above the door, rail-gun missiles cutting a groove through the wall just behind him, Vrell redirects his aim at Vrost's visual turret, but only for a second because missiles then slam into his own back end, taking off one of his legs and punching through some carapace there. He pushes out from the wall and drops, deliberately not turning to land on all limbs, but hitting edge-on with carapace edge directed towards Vrost to present the smallest target. He throws himself into a roll, heading towards Vrost like a huge plate revolving on its edge, rail-gun missiles ricocheting or cutting grooves down the back of his shell.

Even while rolling, he redirects his aim for one short burst that slices into the power feed for Vrost's weapon. This blows, the s-con cable arcing to the floor, as Vrell tips over and comes down on all limbs. Vrost now moves back, the spin of the rail-gun's multiple barrels gradually waning. He makes an odd bubbling sound and staggers whilst Vrell aims again at his visual turret, but Vrell does not fire, for he knows this battle is already over.

Vrost had obviously felt secure enough in here to leave his armour vents open. Now they emit an oily brown vapour. Vrell did not need to break the seals on that armour by hitting the leg, because shortly after those doors began to open, Vrost began to die, the nanite invisibly filtering into the Sanctum and doing its work.

Vrost abruptly collapses, his legs folded underneath him, claws still held up threateningly, but even they begin to subside as if too heavy a weight to bear. Now Vrell whirls round and studies the wall around and above the doors. Here the armouring is not so thick as on the exterior, and therefore all the systems less well protected. He makes some close adjustments to the focus and power setting of his particle cannon, and aims at a particular point above and to the left of the doors. The narrow beam punches through the wall, cutting a hole just an inch across. For a moment Vrell thinks he has hit the wrong point, but then boiling hydraulic fluid jets from the hole, and the two doors begin to grind shut. It will be hard to get them open later on, but more important right now is keeping the surviving King's Guard outside. Vrell returns his attention to his victim.

Vrost is still managing the occasional weak movement, but no more than that.

'Are you dead yet?' Vrell enquires, turning to inspect the damage to his own back end. One leg is missing, and though he can see the site of the puncture through his carapace, it has filled with a white tissue that is already skinning over. The pain too is diminishing, now becoming more like that he had felt as a child while shedding carapace prior to a growth spurt. He wonders how long it will take for his leg to grow back. Certainly, sight is already returning to lower eyes he blinded only minutes ago.

'Not going to die,' Vrost manages, and Vrell turns back in time to see him heaving himself up a little, then collapsing again.

'You are right, of course.' Vrell clips away his particle cannon, then goes over to study the C-shaped wall of pit controls and hexagonal screens via which Vrost controlled his ship, and its crew. Vrost should also possess control units shell-welded to his own carapace and linked into his nervous system – these for greater finesse in control of his drones, certain ship systems and any Human blanks, if he happens to have them aboard.

'Yes, you won't die,' Vrell continues, 'in the usual sense.' Vrost has ceased either to be able to hear or to reply, for there is no response. However Vrell, having been so long without anyone to really talk to, carries on with his explanation.

'The nanite destroys your nerve tissue, first entering through the nerves directly under your carapace, and then eating its way in. The biggest lump of nerve tissue, your major ganglion, or brain, it will take longer to destroy.'

The pit controls are genome-keyed to Vrost, encoded and presently shut down because of the damage Vrell himself did above. If he can get out of here to reconnect things up there, whilst avoiding being fried by the remaining members of the Guard who will now be gathering about this Sanctum, the destruct order that Vrost himself almost certainly input would carry on through. That same order would have only been sent via optics, since no Prador would trust such a major function to any kind of electromagnetic means. The control units on Vrost, then – they are the only way.

'Now, with a normal Prador this would result in death and

decay, but like me you're full of the Spatterjay virus, so the virus will begin to transform you into something else based on its eclectic collection of bits of genome derived from the Spatterjay ecology. It will mindlessly try to survive, though how that will work itself out inside your armour I just don't know yet. Maybe you'll just turn into a big Spatterjay leech inside there, before lack of nutrients puts you into biological stasis. I'll be interested to find out.'

Vrell now goes back over to Vrost and begins minutely inspecting his armour. When a Prador seals itself up in such armour, there are only a few ways to get it open again: either the Prador inside opens it, a superior Prador possesses the codes to open it, or it has to be blown open or sliced apart. Vrost's superior is Oberon himself, so the exterior-code option is probably no option at all. Vrost certainly won't willingly open the armour, and probably can't open it by now. Vrell squats down before his victim and considers how best to approach the problem.

Within Vrost's visual turret lies the simple manual option for opening the armour, therefore all Vrost needs to do to get himself out is insert his mandibles simultaneously into two control pits. Vrell stands to carefully survey the Sanctum, wishing he'd taken the time to bring the toolbox down with him, but knowing that even seconds counted and such delay could have killed him. Doubtless Vrost's own tools reside in the various sealed cavities scattered about here, but all of them are only accessible either through punching the correct code into their pit-control locks or by sending a signal from one of the control units presently bonded to Vrost's own body. So all Vrell has available is the small abrading tool he still clutches in one of his underhands, as well as the particle cannon, a laser and a selection of grenades. With weary annoyance that no simpler and more elegant approach occurs to him, he moves over to Vrost and climbs up onto his shell.

The particle cannon, currently at its lowest and most narrow-beam setting, splashes off the dome of Vrost's visual turret, and in its range of spread sets the far wall of the Sanctum smoking. After a minute its constant bombardment upon the same spot begins to ablate the exotic metal away, turning the beam splash from fuzzy turquoise to a hot red. When Vrell estimates that only a minimal layer of the armour remains, he shuts the beam off.

Now the abrading tool, which uses up its entire supply of shaped diamond dust to slice out a two-inch circle of exotic metal no thicker than a leaf. Underneath this lie alternate layers of foamed porcelain, s-con grid and inner seal that Vrell simply digs out with the sharp tip of one extended claw, to finally open into a cavity just above Vrost's head. This confirms that Vrost is of a similar shape to Vrell, for any normal Prador's immovable head would merely butt up against the seal. However, Vrost's colouring is very different, in fact distinctly odd.

The next task is interminably frustrating. Vrell snips off a length of fibre-optic cable leading to his harness CPU, feeds the bare end of it into the cavity he has created and uses it as an internal camera; but only after a great deal of poking round does he get some idea of what lies inside there. He locates both the pit controls and Vrost's weirdly distorted mandibles, and sees he will need to move Vrost's head quite a bit to line up the two. This he accomplishes by using the laser to burn holes in the top of Vrost's skull, into which he inserts the tips of his claws to manip-ulate it round. Finally, with things properly lined up, he strips down s-con wires, burns further holes through Vrost's head, then inserts the wires down to the appropriate muscle groups. Though the Prador underneath him is all but dead, and his nerves eaten away, his muscles still respond to simple electricity. The whole business takes hours. The first jerk of those mandibles, as Vrell feeds in power from his harness, completely shifts Vrost's head out of position. Only when he finally combines abrading tool, laser and the snout of his particle cannon to jam the head in place, do Vrost's mandibles stab themselves into the required control pits.

Vrell leaps back as the upper carapace of the armour rises on silver poles, then hinges back. With a crash and explosion of gas, Vrost is hurled up and forwards from his armour, and lands on the floor of the sanctum with a heavy loose-limbed thump. Vrell moves over to study his erstwhile opponent, and wonders if this is what he himself is destined to become.

There is no way of telling if Vrost is a first-child; in fact no real way of telling, on first inspection, that he is a Prador at all. Certainly he possesses the correct number of limbs, claws and underslung manipulatory hands, but Vrost is a rosy pink in colour, though dotted with brown burns caused by the nanite, their position mapping out the major nerve groups. His carapace is elongated slightly, and possesses a scalloped dorsal crest running from behind his long folded neck to his short spiky tail. His head, like Vrell's, is no longer a turret, and even the turret eyes have separated out on their own stalks.

Now entertaining a suspicion, Vrell steps delicately over and prods Vrost's carapace. As he suspects, it is soft. Has Vrost spent so long within armour that somehow the Spatterjay mutation has dispensed with his own hard outer layer? Vrell, normally so cold in his assessment of just about anything, now feels a species of deep disgust. Vrost is soft and floppy like those animals with internal skeletons. Like Humans, in fact. Then comes a horrifying attendant thought. The Spatterjay virus gathers up parts of the genome of its various hosts. Could it be that Vrost *is* partially Human? And could it therefore be that Vrell himself might have acquired some part within him of those contemptible creatures?

This is not a notion Vrell wants to pursue, so he quickly applies himself to the next task in claw and, containing his disgust, heaves Vrost up and over to expose the series of six hexagonal Prador control units bonded to his rubbery skin. With the limited tools to hand, and much ingenuity, he begins to remove them. The task is one he did before, aboard his father's ship, when he fixed a control unit to his own carapace and rooted it into his own nervous system, then later fixed two more. Six units should not be too much for him to deal with, since he has also learnt much about partitioning such units.

Having thus removed Vrost's six control units from their rooting modules, Vrell now sets about taking them apart. Each time he encounters a problem that requires a tool, he squats and considers the same problem for a short while, and each time comes up with a solution amidst the limited hardware available. By the time he has the six units sufficiently disassembled for his purpose, his particle cannon and much of his harness, Vrost's rail-gun and some parts of his armour also lie disassembled and scattered across the floor. Vrell mates the major components of the six units to form three units, subsequently removing his own three units from his own body, but leaving their rooting modules in place. He plugs the three new jury-rigged units into the modules, and sends the internal signal to initiate them. Immediately, a tsunami of data floods his mind and he shrieks and flips over on his back, completely losing control of his body.

Orbus knows that cored and thralled Human blanks were sold to any Graveyard scum that could afford them, and assumed that Smith Storage was being run by scum of that kind, which might well have included the Layden-Smiths. Upon hearing from the little drone that the owners of this station have been out of contact for a while, and upon seeing the wrecked office and then the corpses that lay beyond, he assumed that some Human criminal must have moved in and taken over. But that the two Human blanks were actually controlled by a Prador did not occur to him, and he now realizes it was a rather lethal error to make. He feels a fist clenching up in his guts, as old horrific memories clamour for his attention. The very shape of the thing standing before him burns deeply into his consciousness.

'Run!' he shouts at Drooble, but the order is superfluous, for the crewman is already hurling himself behind a big stack of storage boxes.

The Prador hesitates for a moment, then swings its rail-gun away from Orbus and opens fire. The pile of boxes explodes into shreds of plasmel, foam packing and numerous toy soldiers scattered far and wide. With rage surging up through the well of memory, Orbus raises his machete and, with long experience of handling such blades, throws it just as hard as he can. The point of the blade slams into the Prador's armoured turret with a resounding clang but, as the Prador swings back towards him, it then simply drops out.

'Bugger,' says Orbus, his mouth suddenly arid, mesmerized as the monster begins to aim its rail-gun again.

Now lasers flash through air turned dusty by the exploded boxes, their beams issuing from the seahorse drone as it hurtles into the warehouse.

'Get to cover, you fool!' the little drone shouts.

Orbus jerks into motion, a cold sweat suddenly suffusing him, and the tightness in his stomach turning to nausea. He heads off running the opposite way to Drooble as rail-gun fire tracks across the ceiling, raining down shattered metal in a trail behind the speeding iron seahorse. The little drone has momentarily blinded the Prador with what Orbus guesses is merely a powerful burst from a com laser, and that is enough for the drone now to become the enemy's prime target. Ducking into an aisle between shelves, he continues running, intent on losing himself inside this place, at least for a while. Really, he explains to himself, up against a normal Prador of that size he would have faced some pretty serious problems, but to encounter one in exotic metal armour and armed with a rail-gun? He needs to get himself out of here just as fast as he can, and hopefully take Drooble with him if the man is still in one piece. Then something looms at the end of the aisle, and Orbus skids to a sudden halt.

'Twice bugger,' he says, and checking to either side of him sees nowhere to dive for cover amidst the crowded shelving.

He has seen something like this not so long ago back on Spatterjay: a floating sphere of exotic metal ten feet across, its surface poxed with the pits for housing weapons and com equipment. In fact it was something like this that first snatched Orbus and his crew from the *Vignette*, before sinking that hapless ship. For not only is there a damned Prador here, but one of their war drones too.

Then a particle beam repeatedly stabs down from the ceiling, cutting numerous holes and searing across the spherical war drone. A massive detonation ensues, its painfully bright fire spreading across a hardfield wall the drone itself has generated. *Should have used the missile first*, thinks Orbus, as a blast wave picks him up off his feet and flings him backwards.

As he hits the floor, flat on his back, the Captain watches the drone hurl itself sideways, smashing over a whole row of shelving. Up above it the ceiling now looks like a colander, as beam strikes and missiles slam down through it. The drone is obviously being pushed, for something explodes inside it, almost certainly a hardfield generator, and it spews fire from one of its com-pits. It drops a little, its top glowing white-hot under the impact of further beam strikes, then within a moment it has another hardfield up. Below the drone, unnoticed by anyone but Orbus, something punches up through the floor and, making an odd whickering sound as little steering jets alter its course, it loops round and shoots straight into the drone's burnt out com-pit.

Sneaky, thinks Orbus, as a second blast-wave picks him up and hurls him back to deposit him in a pile of twisted shelving. He sees the war drone crashing sideways, fire spewing from all the pits in its surface. It bounces and thunders into another row of shelves, bringing them down, while further explosions inside it shoot jets of flame across the warehouse.

Pushing a plasmel crate out of his way, Orbus looks straight across, now the shelving is down, towards the armoured Prador. It has shed the tips of one claw and is firing upwards from this with a previously concealed particle cannon, the turquoise beam lancing up through a snow of fire-retardant foam. Smoke and that same foam form a maelstrom, as an atmosphere breach at one end of the warehouse sucks them straight out into vacuum. Then the floor underneath the Prador erupts, and numerous silver tentacles spear up to wrap around the armoured monster. The Prador shoots upwards, a huge nautiloid drone now clinging to it, and painfully bright fire burns from where they lie in contact. Orbus recognizes this newly arrived war drone immediately, for it once tied him by the ankles to the spar of his own ship.

As drone and armoured Prador crash up through the damaged ceiling and disappear from sight, Orbus feels something like disappointment, but at what he cannot readily analyse. Still tightly wound, he snatches up some twisted shelving metal and crunches it up in one fist, something halfway between a groan and a snarl of frustration issuing from deep within his chest.

'It might be a good idea to get out of here, Captain!'

Orbus glances to one side to see the seahorse drone hovering there. It points with its tail towards the maelstrom, now sucking entire plasmel cases into its core. Returning his attention to the drone, he just stares at it, slowly opening his hand to drop the ball of scrunched-up metal.

'Captain,' the drone repeats, backing well out of range.

Orbus abruptly heaves himself from the battered shelving, glances at the rips in his clothing, then at a big chunk of metal embedded in his right biceps. He tugs this out and flings it away, its flat trajectory slamming it with the force of a bullet into one wall, where it shatters. A very small amount of blood wells for a moment as the deep wound snaps closed like a prudish mouth. Orbus reaches up and wipes his eyes, which he can only assume are watering because of the smoke in here, then he goes to find Drooble.

'Little bit fraught in here!' the crewman bellows over the roar of the wind, as Orbus uncovers him. Drooble is grinning, despite the large ragged hole punched right through his righthand side just above his hip and, not having been infected with the Spatterjay virus so long as his Captain, he is bleeding. However, flat ribbons of tissue worm about in his wound as they slowly pull it closed.

One-handed, Orbus grabs him by the belt and picks him up, then runs for the door. The pull from the atmosphere breach is now intense and he leans forward into the gale, chunks of the wreckage all around constantly bouncing off him. Once through the big door, he only has to pull it away from the wall against which he earlier flung it, and the suction slams it shut. For a moment there comes a whistling of escaping air, but this is a bulkhead door and the air pressure on this side soon closes it down on its seals.

'This is better than being on the *Vignette*!' Drooble exclaims excitedly.

Orbus glances down at him, noting that his eyes are slightly crossed and his expression definitely not quite right. He surmises that the damage in his crewman's side must be more extensive than it appears, for Drooble is already being tampered with by the virus inside him – would that Orbus himself had the same excuse. He slings the man over his shoulder.

'You should get back to the *Gurnard*,' suggests the seahorse drone, now drifting up the stairway ahead.

Orbus peers up at it. 'Should I?' he growls. 'Should I really go back to the *Gurnard* and see if I can get myself dropped into another shitstorm like this?'

'I'm sure that wasn't the intention,' says Thirteen, not even bothering to eliminate the doubt from his voice.

'Whatever,' Orbus spits, striding on up the stair. He wants answers, he tells himself, and if necessary he will tear the *Gurnard* apart to find them. Yet, on some level, his own reasoning feels false. I want to know how to stop, something whispers. I want to know how to control it, and I want to know why I started to cry back there . . .

Outside Smith Storage, klaxons are blaring and a little way along from the door a crowd is now gathering about some kind of wall access. Orbus only realizes what they are up to when he notices those on the periphery pulling on survival suits – simple impervious and reinforced paperwear with a transparent visor and a limited oxygen supply, and the possible difference between life and death in a situation like this. He heads straight for the lift.

'Hey, Cap'n,' says Drooble, 'I think you can put me down now.'

Orbus hoists the man off his shoulder and stands him on his own two feet.

'See, I'm—' Drooble's legs give way and he just slumps to the floor. 'That's odd,' he adds.

Orbus nods to himself. The hideous impact of a rail-gun

missile, as well as cutting a chunk out of Drooble's side, has severed his spine. It will take the man a while longer yet before he is up and about, and he will need to be well fed with non-Spatterjay food items just to stop him becoming markedly stranger than he is already. Orbus again picks him up one-handed and slings him over his shoulder, then enters the lift. Thirteen zips in beside the pair, then heads up to the roof of the compartment, perhaps trying to keep out of the Old Captain's reach. Orbus hits the touch-pad for the bottom floor, inadvertently driving it through the lift's wall, and they descend rapidly . . .

But obviously they have not been moving fast enough. 'Step out of the lift and kneel down on the floor!' a voice instructs, as the door opens.

Orbus recognizes the ophidapt official, now standing behind four men clad in visored helmets and combat armour, and all armed with pulse rifles – every barrel pointing at Orbus. Doubtless the moment the atmosphere breach occurred, station security personnel started watching the images on their screens from the cams located within the area.

Stepping out of the lift, his legs quivering with the urge to hurl himself forward and just scatter these fools, Orbus enquires viciously, 'Did you know you've got a Prador aboard?' Though he wonders if the Prador *is* still aboard, because it seems likely the war drone that attacked it dragged it to where their fight would be less likely to cause inadvertent casualties.

The ophidapt just stares at him for a moment, then again orders him to, 'Kneel on the floor!'

'I need to speak to any one of the Layden-Smiths,' says Orbus, fighting to introduce some calm into his voice. 'But let me guess, they've been out of direct communication with you for a while?'

'Station property has been severely damaged,' says the ophidapt, seemingly unable to process what Orbus has said. 'You are in the area, and obviously have been involved in some way, so I must take you into custody.'

'I've no time for this,' Orbus growls, groping down for his bull-whip, but it is still up above somewhere.

'When I fire,' says Thirteen, 'run for it.'

Red com-laser light flashes on four visors, and across the eyes of the ophidapt. Orbus ducks to one side and takes to his heels, pulse-gun fire hammering into the lift behind him. He deliberately circumvents the reception committee, so as to put them out of his own reach.

'Ow!' says Drooble, and glancing down the Captain sees his crewman's foot is smoking, so obviously one of the shots was on target even after the drone blinded the marksmen.

Still hurtling along, Orbus soon reaches the long tunnel leading to the docking area. Behind him he hears shouting, but no one starts firing because only a thin skin of metal separates this area from vacuum. Reaching the other end, he takes a couple of turnings to reach the door into the carrier-shell atrium. He kicks it in and strides through, then enters the zero-gravity shell itself. The security drone, obviously alerted, shoots out of its alcove, but Orbus is already sailing across towards it, with one hand reaching out. The drone must be semi-AI and intelligent enough to know its chances of survival, for it snaps back inside its alcove, the hatch slamming shut. Thirty seconds after that, Orbus boards the shuttle and is soon strapping Drooble into a chair.

'Of course' – Thirteen settles down to wind his tail around one of the console levers – 'there's the problem with all this station's armament.'

Orbus seats himself, then reaches forwards to click a brass switch positioned before a very archaic-looking horn-shaped mouthpiece. 'You there, Gurnard?'

'I am always here,' the distant ship AI replies.

'Right,' says the Captain, 'you dropped me into this mess and now I want you to get me out of it.'

'You should be safe enough,' the AI replies. 'Sniper informs me that the Prador had seized control of the station weapons but, presently being otherwise occupied, will not be able to deploy them. However, I am now moving in to assist in the unlikely event of any problems.'

The moment the universal dock disengages, Orbus wrenches up the helm and, on steering jets, accelerates the shuttle out of the carrier shell, just far enough not to cause too much damage to the station when he engages the fusion drive. Torch firing up, the shuttle then hurtles out of the station structure, only a few surfaces singed by the fusion flame. Next he flings the shuttle into a hard turn. Numerous red lights ignite on the console and Orbus does not need long to interpret the archaic-looking displays of information on those little screens before him. The missile from one of the big rail-guns just misses them, which means someone has managed to get the weapon up and working, but is firing on manual.

'I see,' says Orbus, knowing he might not be so lucky next time.

The Golgoloth shifts in uneasy slumber, all the tubes and wires mating with its ancient Prador body rattling and squirming wetly in the armoured lair surrounding it. The two internal ganglion grafts it uses for internal monitoring, which never sleep, note that the new muscle grafts to its five-chambered heart have bonded nicely, and sends a signal via cybernetic implant along one of the fibre-optic cables sprouting from scarred and heavily shell-patched carapace. This signal simultaneously shuts down the mechanical pump that is circulating the creature's green blood and sends electric impulses to probes buried inside heart muscle. The much patched and repaired heart takes up the slack at once, smoothly taking over the task the mechanical pump has performed for the last decade.

Slowly, since the creature is in no hurry to be anywhere, automated systems within its lair begin bringing the Golgoloth's other external ganglia online, bringing it to consciousness. By incremental degrees it begins to observe its surroundings through both its turret and palp eyes, then makes a visual inspection of all the equipment that keeps it alive and has kept it alive for an appalling time. The only notable damage is to a pipe leading to a blood scrubber, which it must have crushed with its latest single claw graft while in uneasy slumber. But because of the tenfold redundancy in the equipment surrounding it, this isn't a problem. Next the Golgoloth focuses its attention on the numerous readouts from the array of hexagonal screens standing before it like a chunk of honeycomb, and begins to check upon the running of its abode beyond this armoured lair.

The creature's children all grow nicely and some of them will soon be ready for harvesting. They are a direct product of the Golgoloth for, being a hermaphrodite, it possesses both Prador sexes and, with a little technical assistance, can mate with itself.

Specifically it studies the largest of its seven hermaphroditic first-children, secured in a slowly expanding growth framework, nutrient feeds and monitoring optics mated into sockets surgically implanted in its body. The child's remaining claw is now big enough for removal and grafting. Like the Golgoloth itself when it was younger, this first-child's entire body has grown asymmetrically; one entire side growing twice as fast as the other and therefore one claw reaching the point when it could be harvested before the other one. The Golgoloth now sports the largest of those two claws as a replacement for a previous graft that came under attack from its ridiculously rugged immune system, just like its legs, which are presently under attack and turning an odd custard yellow and will soon need replacing. This first-child cannot provide those limbs, since its own legs were removed to provide the Golgoloth with internal muscle about the socket of its new claw, but the other children are coming along nicely.

The Golgoloth now pushes itself up onto its yellow legs, whilst engaging the antigravity unit on its underside to take the bulk of its weight. As it moves towards the door of its lair, subsidiary feeds automatically separate from its body to snake back to their sources through the foot depth of water upon the floor, whilst its two main life-support units detach from their floor sockets and switch over to internal power. As it advances to the doors, these two units – fat upright floating cylinders with numerous protrusions and inset pit-consoles – drift along behind, keeping their numerous optics and pipes slack enough not to pull free, but not so slack they might become entangled about the creature's legs.

The doors open and the Golgoloth moves out into the wide corridor, eyeing the mutated ship-lice crawling along the walls to keep pace with it, ever ready for the occasional graft that might drop off. They are a necessary pest here, because they keep the place clear of the build-up of organic detritus. At the end of the corridor the hermaphrodite Prador begins to descend one of the numerous ramps in its abode, and now, with its heart having undergone sufficient testing, begins bringing online more of its external ganglia. In a moment it attains full temporal consciousness, which puts it at the intelligence level of a wakeful and bright but normal Prador. And the Golgoloth begins to remember and consider its immense lifespan.

In the early planet-bound days of the Prador, their aggression kept them in an Iron Age lasting many thousands of years. During that time, technical knowledge was gathered and jealously guarded by various individuals and factions. However, since alliances tended to change very quickly, with betrayal and murder of one's allies an utterly accepted political tool, this technical knowledge gradually spread. Towards the end of this age of iron, one particular Prador rose to power and achieved planetary dominance first by dint of being extremely aggressive and cunning, and second through the creation of a liquid explosive that led to the invention of the gun. This was a legendary time of rigid control over the factions and rapid technological advance, and by the time the First King became the victim of one of his own jealously guarded weapons, Prador were building flying machines and computers, and had even advanced their biotechnology to the point where they could keep their children in perpetual childhood and install thralls in many of their homeworld creatures. Prador even managed to get into space, and the first bases were established on the two homeworld moons at the end of the First King's reign.

After the death of the First King, a thousand years of warfare ensued. Knowledge was never lost, only jealously guarded, and after a large alliance of factions managed to run a scientific project for long enough to split the first atom, the entire race faced extinction with the onset of the nuclear age. Startlingly, however, some sanity prevailed, and the Prador managed to agree amongst themselves rules of engagement that would not result in their world ending up as a radioactive wasteland. And it was during this time that the Golgoloth hatched from an egg implanted in one of the seashore birth molluscs.

Reaching a wide armoured portal leading into the nurseries, the Golgoloth sends a coded signal and slowly the portal divides diagonally, its two heavy halves rolling back into the walls. Entering the long chamber, it studies the large first-child lying directly ahead. The child's turret eyes are locked perpetually on an array of screens before it. But its palp eyes turn towards the creature that is both its father and mother, and it struggles ineffectually in the framework keeping it permanently imprisoned. Then it jerks suddenly. Obviously it did not give the required response to something appearing on one of its screens, and therefore received its punishment shock. The Golgoloth learnt long ago that just as exercising its children's muscles results in the best limb grafts, keeping their minds active results in the best ganglia either for internal grafting or for connecting into its distributed mind.

It meanwhile moves on. Later it will activate its surgical robots and take that claw perpetually flexing under electrical stimulus.

The Golgoloth supposes itself a product of mutation because, despite controls of nuclear weapons being introduced before it hatched, they were used previously and still used later on occasion. Usually, one such as itself is not even allowed to survive into third-childhood, for adult male Prador are ruthless in their selection of those children they allow to live. But the Golgoloth's father was an oddity himself, with very low fertility – perhaps the mutation actually began with him – and because of a strange interest in the grotesque he allowed the Golgoloth to live and kept it as a curiosity. Only later did he realize that this odd asymmetric and crippled child possessed a formidable intelligence. He realized it too late, only shortly before the self-renewing diatomic acid the Golgoloth invented had eaten right through his shell.

After murdering its father, the Golgoloth moved to take over their home's security system and use it to exterminate all its first- and second-children kin. Thereafter it used chemical and thrall control over the remaining third-children, and itself stayed hidden and undiscovered for many years. During this time it studied and experimented and, by delivering a few severe lessons, discouraged its neighbours from trying to seize its land or other property. It also studied history, particularly its favourite period: the time of the First King. The Golgoloth felt that the Prador way was ridiculously wasteful, for with them strictly controlled under some powerful autocrat, all the stupid internecine conflicts could be terminated. The Golgoloth considered itself for that position, but knew a king *must* be visible and that, upon seeing the Golgoloth, all the other Prador would turn upon it. Studying its neighbours, however, it saw few candidates suitable for the position, and so set about experimenting upon itself.

The first self-fertilized eggs it produced, and itself injected into a birth mollusc, simply died, and after some months of study the Golgoloth came to the conclusion that though sperm and egg were sound, the fertilized eggs were not receiving the required nutrients in its body. Next it tried removing such fertilized eggs from its own body and inserting them into one of Father's wives, but they would not let the Golgoloth anywhere near them, so it became necessary to completely delimb one of them for the process. The eggs grown inside this female, and then manually injected into a birth mollusc, did actually hatch out, but they produced many grotesques even more distorted than the Golgoloth itself. They also produced three Prador who, though having some internal mutations, appeared to be sound, so the Golgoloth allowed those to live.

Now reaching the next first-child, the Golgoloth peers closely at legs permanently stretching and flexing within the framework. Really, even the ones on the child's fast-growing side aren't yet ready for removal and grafting, and the Golgoloth knows that, unless it raids its emergency supply, it will be losing some of its own sickly legs before replacements are ready here. No matter, the hermaphrodite long ago created blocks and filters for its nerves; the process is no more painful than shedding old carapace, and it can increase antigravity support for its body. Next time it will ensure more children are available for spare parts, for it has come a long way in this process from its first attempts.

One of those children it allowed to survive from its first brood died before reaching third-childhood – a fault in its digestive system – and a second died from a minor injury because its blood possessed no clotting agent. The third survived to grow and learn quickly under the Golgoloth's guidance. He was intelligent, this Prador, and quite normally aggressive and competitive. The Golgoloth trained him to direct this aggression much more constructively than his fellows, and through gradual stages relinquished responsibility, turning from master to teacher and adviser. The Prador grew to adulthood with the Golgoloth ever there in the background; like a weirdly distorted shadow. Then, with only a light guiding claw, this adult began to make astute moves, ruthless takeovers, very specific assassinations. He mated frequently and produced a rapidly growing batch of children, though their number did not match that of those that were meantime necessarily and secretly destroyed. The Golgoloth trained these children, then went on to use the same techniques on the children of those Prador who became allies.

Two decades of conflict and expansion followed, then a final large conflict that for a brief time went nuclear. At the end of this the homeworld was ruled by a new King, and they called his reign the Second Kingdom, in deference to the legendary First Kingdom. The Golgoloth was both mother and father of this King – kingmaker in every sense.

5

They metabolize oxygen in a similar manner to Human beings, though the blood they use to transport it is based on copper rather than iron. However, never has a creature been more suited to space without having undergone some sort of modification. Certainly anoxia will kill them, but not as quickly as it will kill a Human. They can withstand the extreme cold of space, since it finally drives them into a natural cryosleep rather than killing them. Pressure changes are not a problem to them either and, supplied with oxygen, they can survive in vacuum. It has been noted incidentally that, because of this, the atmosphere integrity of Prador ships would never pass Human inspection. They possess numerous limbs for moving about in zero gravity, numerous 'underhands' with which to manipulate their complex environment, and numerous eyes with which to observe it. The shame is that they bring to that same environment the minds of psychotic lobsters.
– From HOW IT IS by Gordon

The war drone is easy, for Sniper has much experience in dealing with them. They aren't particularly bright and tend to over-focus on the current attack, so the *distract while putting a missile up the tail-pipe* routine works in eight out of ten encounters. There is also, he feels, a deep underlying psychological problem with Prador war drones: for, being run by the surgically excised and then flash-frozen cerebral matter of first- and second-children, and being utterly subject to the will of the Prador controlling them, it is impossible for them to pursue their evolutionary imperative to finally become adults and themselves reproduce; they can take no pleasure in the basic things in a Prador's life, like eating and bullying their juniors, and they will never be anything but war drones until the day some enemy missile shafts them from behind. In essence, he suspects war drones possess no hope and that deep down they want merely to die. However, this armoured Prador most certainly does *not* want to die.

The moment he wraps his tentacles about the beast, Sniper immobilizes its most dangerous limbs, namely the ones wielding its rail-gun and particle cannon, then pulls himself in close and begins extruding a thermic lance. This method of penetrating exotic-metal armour was used in close-quarters combat between drones during the war, and Sniper engages close like this because he wants the Prador to think he is trying to avoid combat that resulted in large burning holes throughout Montmartre and lots of bloated Human corpses floating about in vacuum, which is precisely the case, though Sniper is also being sneaky again.

As the Prador struggles to bring its particle cannon to bear, Sniper hurls the two of them on antigravity upwards through the ceiling. He strains against the claw, the motors in the Prador's armour seeming to evenly match the strength of his tentacles. Smashing through the ceiling, they enter a cavity where smoke and debris sketch lines towards where Sniper cut his way in from the tubeway, causing the atmosphere breach, and the gale of escaping air now draws them towards the tubeway, just as Sniper wants. As they enter it, he apparently manages to stick a small mine to the Prador's armour. The blast flings them both along the tubeway in one direction, but the mine is too small to do anything more than score the Prador's covering. Sniper, however, had not intended it to do any more. Now, with a flickering of a com laser, the Prador tries to open communication.

Sniper prepares himself for any computer viruses or worms, and allows com.

'The moment you penetrate my armour, you're dead too,' the Prador informs him.

'Really.' Sniper is thoroughly aware that armoured Prador like the one he is grappling contain tactical fusion bombs to completely obliterate them. On Spatterjay he witnessed Vrost's armoured guard either destroying themselves or being destroyed remotely by Vrost, whenever there was danger that an opponent might defeat them, and thence possibly discover what their armour contained.

'If you persist I will be forced to fire my particle cannon,' says the Prador coldly. 'I will not hit you, but Human casualties will result.'

It is trying to plumb Sniper's apparent weakness and he shuts off the thermic lance, though still holding it in place. 'So, what do we do now?'

'You must release me.'

Not a chance. Letting this bastard go free would be like releasing one's hold on a rattlesnake and expecting it not to bite. At that very moment they ricochet off the side of one of the tubeway transports parked along this section of the route. It is enough to dislodge the stalemate and the Prador now brings its particle cannon partially to bear on Sniper's shell. For the first few seconds the beam simply bounces off, then it begins to penetrate the layer of nano-chain chromium, and burn. Sniper reignites his thermic lance.

'We can come to some arrangement,' says the Prador.

Just words, Sniper knows. The only accord they can possibly reach from this point onwards is that in which only one of them remains alive. Prador do not deal, especially those of them like this one, which is not an adult and certainly under orders it cannot disobey.

They hurtle out of the tubeway into a small dock, smash against the hull of a small private transport, then fall out and away from Montmartre. Now, having kept the Prador distracted long enough to get it out of the station, to where its self-destruct won't kill a few thousand inhabitants, Sniper decides it is time to stop playing around. Scanning all about himself, he sees the *Gurnard*'s shuttle dodging shots from a rail-gun fired regularly but inaccurately from the station – one of the big ones shooting off missiles weighing in at four hundred pounds each. The *Gurnard* itself is now accelerating in towards the station, firing a powerful maser that is turning at least a few of those lethal missiles into lines of burning gas. Briefly igniting his fusion drive, he sends himself and the Prador hurtling towards the firing line of the big gun, meanwhile factoring in Orbus's manoeuvres and the tracking of the throat of the rail-gun, whereby he makes some quite esoteric ballistics calculations – something he is very very good at.

'Okay, let's come to an arrangement,' says Sniper.

He extends his tentacles, now applying their true full strength, stretches out from the Prador and turns his fusion drive right round towards his opponent's visual turret, ignites it at a precisely judged moment, and finally releases his hold. The two hurtle apart, and the Prador, thoroughly blinded, tumbles back towards the space station, shrieking, while firing both its particle cannon and rail-gun randomly about it.

'I'll arrange for you to meet Mr Big-Fuck Rail-Gun,' jibes Sniper.

The missile, travelling at one quarter the speed of light, slams into the Prador and turns the creature, and itself, into a hot cone of plasma reaching rapidly out into space. The fusion bomb inside the thing's armour does not even get a chance to explode, but it still makes a big enough firework display.

Sniper now abruply swings himself round. The rail-gun is still firing and still a danger and, even if it were to result in the death of the operators of the great weapon, that would not have influenced his subsequent actions. However, he knows the loading and firing mechanisms of the gun are automatic, and that it is actually being aimed from some remote control-room. Between spates of firing, the missile he launches enters the throat of the big gun and detonates, spewing molten metal out into vacuum. It does not fire again.

Sniper accelerates past this geyser of molten metal, abruptly changes direction and shoots back inside the station structure. Whatever else they were here for, the ostensible primary task has not yet been accomplished. Soon finding the dock, he once again enters the tubeway system and works his way back to Smith Storage. He rather doubts that what he seeks still exists, for surely the King's Guard he just killed must already have destroyed the evidence? The warehouse is now in complete vacuum, and grav is out. Ruination lies within, much of the contents of the warehouse floating about in big clumps of debris. Sniper carefully begins to scan all this, and very quickly finds a large package sprayed over with crash foam. Perhaps, for its own obscure reasons, the Guard did not follow orders? Sniper grabs up the package and rapidly heads back out of the station, for even at that moment station staff are fitting an airlock to the other side of the bulkhead door.

It feels to Vrell like his brain is boiling and, through the haze of pain and confusion caused by the data overload, he now understands his mistake. He foolishly assumed that, though not a normal Prador adult, Vrost was handling data at the rate of one, for he held the position of an adult. Vrell has badly underestimated Vrost, because the Captain of this ship was processing data at about twice the usual rate – at the rate Vrell himself found himself able to handle back on Spatterjay. But after doubling up Vrost's control units to insert them into three rooting modules, Vrell is now receiving four times the data density of a normal adult.

It hurts.

Lying on his back with his legs waving in the air, for a little while he is just too confused to know what to do. Then, through the haze, he manages to regain some self-control and extend an underhand to grab one of the doubled-up control units and pull it free. Even with this relief of the pressure, the density of data flowing into his mind is almost too much but, determined not to sacrifice another unit, he concentrates first on just flipping himself back onto his legs, then on encompassing the data.

Slowly, through the units, he begins to assimilate just what now lies under his control. Turning, still a little unsteady, he sends a particular coded signal, and in response all the alcove storage units along one wall pop open. They are packed with equipment for Prador, since even the captains of vessels like a large selection of tools close at claw.

Through these units he can also get visual and audio feed from about a hundred and fifty of the King's Guard, and knows a further fifty-four feeds are absent because he is currently receiving requests for Vrost himself to respond from two hundred and four sources. The war-drone cache aboard also lies within his compass, though all but three of the drones are somnolent and can only be activated through the pit controls of the console. Access to many other ship systems, like diagnostics and damage control, is his too. However, through these units he cannot detonate the fusion tacticals in the armoured suits of the King's Guard – those being offline, since the Guard are inside the ship – and he cannot control the ship's weapons, life-support or anything else of use *against* the Guard. Obviously Oberon learnt the lesson of the war: that transmitted com can be intercepted, decoded by AI, then turned against his kind.

Gazing through the sensors of various suits of armour, and through the ship eyes, Vrell sees that the group of Prador originally ordered to recover some part of Vrell himself from the highly radio-active area of the ship – in fact one of the many highly radioactive areas of the ship, he now finds – have just ceased work. Normal Prador, unless ordered to do otherwise, will continue with their task until it eventually kills them all. These ones know something is up and are waiting to find out what.

'—optic com to local broadcast is out,' the leader of their unit is announcing. 'No response via ship broadcast. We did not get him here.'

The reply from a Prador only a short distance from the Sanctum is, 'Currently investigating.' That particular Guard is not visible, so doubtless it is now in the part of the ship Vrell previously occupied up above the Sanctum.

'Optic feeds cut,' the Prador confirms. 'He heated the hydraulic fluid to force the door cylinder.'

'He is inside the Sanctum?' the other enquires.

'One Guard disabled outside the Sanctum currently dying – nanite penetration of his suit – currently seeking confirmation.'

Besides that one group comprising nearly thirty of the Guard, it seems the rest of the Guard occupy the area all around the Sanctum, so really Vrell does not want to send any self-destruct orders, because such a concentration of blasts will kill him too.

What to do?

Though Vrost was communicating with those outside via the optics Vrell severed above, the Captain also possessed the option to talk to them through the control units – the 'ship broadcast' mentioned. This is an option probably only used when communications do not need to remain utterly secure. However, with Vrell still not knowing the full convoluted extent of Vrost's security measures, which almost certainly extend to how communications are couched, the Guard will soon realize he is not Vrost. Noting that the disabled Guard in the corridor outside has been dragged off into a side corridor to be interrogated by two of his fellows, Vrell listens in.

'Dropped from . . . wall panel,' the dying Prador manages.

'Is it Vrell?'

'Do not know shape . . . Vrell.'

'What did you see?'

'Mutated . . . black.'

'It *is* Vrell,' the two interrogators confirm to each other at the same time.

Further questions receive no answer as the Guard member finally expires.

Damn, Vrell needs more than just these control units, he needs the pit console, and that is disconnected above him. He squats down to mull the problem over.

Of course, once the nanite penetrates the glathel seals of all those suits out there, which, according to Vrost, will now take less than two hours, the remaining Guard will cease to be a problem. However, the dying Guard having confirmed that Vrell is in here with their Captain, the rest at once begin shifting some of the heavy equipment previously being used to repair the ship. Vrell recognizes most of the machines they bring towards the Sanctum, and knows that the big short-beam cutter, which is based on the same technology as the particle cannon, and the massive hydraulic clawjack, will be enough. If he does not find a way to stop them, they will be in here within their remaining time. That they will die shortly after finishing him off is no consolation.

The drones . . .

The three war drones, apparently detailed to search the ship for him, still follow a search grid, so are not in the communication loop with the King's Guard. War drones are usually quite dumb, and stubborn to a terminal degree, so Vrell decides to try something.

First sending Vrost's pheromonal signature, he orders them, 'Secure . . . com,' whilst deliberately breaking up the signal. 'King's Gua . . . mutiny . . . attacking Sanctum . . . protect.'

Even if the drones fall for this ruse, it won't be enough to stop the King's Guard, but maybe it will delay them for just a little longer. Vrell focuses his attention on the alcove storage and quickly scuttles over. After a brief search he finds precisely what he wants: a spray gun for putting protective coatings on different surfaces, and containers filled with a selection of such coatings, in different colours.

Ebror watches carefully as his fellows bring the required equipment down the drop-shaft leading to the corridors located on the same level as Vrost's Sanctum.

'Take the cutter down first,' he instructs.

Ever since Vrost fell out of communication, authority has devolved on Ebror as, at three centuries old, he is the most senior second-child remaining alive after the appalling carnage Vrell wrought here. Like all of the King's Guard, Ebror possesses a greater degree of self-determination than normal Prador children. This is because, though all the Guard are utterly incapable of disobeying their father, and are in fact pheromonally and psychologically locked into obedience, there being so many of their kind it is very infrequent that any one amongst them will receive a direct order from King Oberon. Ebror's orders come from the next one up in the hierarchy from himself, which in this case is Vrost, and he can always question, within limits, the source of those orders. It is also the case that the Guard are more intelligent than normal Prador, and not faced with the prospect of being killed by their father once they begin to mature. Ebror has been a second-child for three centuries and knows that, because of the virus matted through his body like river weed, he will never become a first-child.

'When you get those doors open,' he instructs, 'we go straight in.'

Of course, it is now a certainty that he will not remain a second-child for much longer. Checking an internal display he studies the counter that numbers the remaining minutes of his life. Briefly, he wonders why he is bothering, and feels a momentary surge of irritation at Vrost for not at once enabling the Guard to detonate their own fusion self-destructs. He knows why, though: Vrost hopes to stay alive, somehow, and does not want the Guard, should they somehow find out about it, obeying the order to destroy the ship which Oberon has almost certainly sent. Right now, a destruct order sent to every suit aboard would do the job nicely.

'Ebror,' reports one of those now moving the big cutter out of the drop-shaft, 'one of the war drones just turned up.'

Ebror feels another surge of irritation. He does not like dealing with any Prador who is not a member of his own family, and members of Oberon's family are never turned into drones or ship minds. The drones in the cache here are part of this ship's original complement and older even than him, in fact they date from the war. They are run by the flash-frozen brains of the children of some Prador adult who took the wrong side when Oberon usurped the previous King. That adult, the previous Captain here, was taken alive and sealed up with crash-foam in some wall aboard. It has always been a matter of debate amongst the Guard which wall that might be.

Ebror descends the drop-shaft and exits behind the moving mass of machinery. Engaging antigravity in his armour, he ascends to the ceiling and passes over above it all and, descending on the other side, spots the war drone hovering at the end of the corridor, both its side-mounted rail-guns directed towards the team that is moving the machinery.

'Why are you here?' Ebror asks. 'You were ordered to grid-search for the intruder.' None of the Guard had bothered to tell the three drones to stop searching, really, they were a bit superfluous anyway and only of use in any action occurring outside the ship.

The drone simply says, 'Protect Sanctum.'

'Who ordered you to protect the Sanctum?' asks Ebror, already guessing.

'Captain Vrost.'

'Listen, drone,' Ebror hisses. 'The order you received comes from the intruder, who even now is inside the Sanctum with our Captain.'

'Protect Sanctum,' the drone insists stubbornly.

Damn, if the Guard continue trying to bring the equipment through here, the drone will attack them. Ebror has no doubt that he and his fellows can destroy it, but meanwhile, the equipment might get damaged. He swings round to the team moving the machinery. 'Take it down there for now.' He points with one claw into a side corridor then, shutting off the outside address, opens a private channel to one of those ranking directly below him in the Guard hierarchy. 'Agreen, what's the situation now?'

'One drone at each end of the main sanctum corridor, and one sitting right before the doors,' the Prador replies. 'They're not listening.'

Ebror again feels one of those familiar surges of annoyance. The drones are simply stubborn robots following orders, but he cannot help but feel resentment at the knowledge that for them time is not an issue here. Being of a different genetic heritage to the Guard, they will not die even if the nanite does penetrate through to their microscopic frozen brains.

'Very well,' he says, 'bring down the big portables. We'll deal with this problem once the equipment is out of the way.' He does not add the need for alacrity, since they are all aware of the limit to their lifespans.

Ebror rises into the air again and retreats behind the cutter and the enormous clawjack, then ascends through the drop-shaft. Already some of the Guard are moving towards the shaft entrance above, towing behind them equipment of a rather different nature. With some satisfaction he eyes the missile-cluster launchers, thermal mortars and particle cannons, all of them perfect weapons for combating drones confined by corridors.

'Don't wait for further orders,' he instructs those carrying these weapons. 'Just destroy them as quick as you can.' Stopping beside a group of eight of the Guard who are burdened with weapons, he says, 'Bring those and come with me.' Then, as he heads off with the same eight in tow, he explains his plans to Agreen.

'Understood,' his junior replies.

The intruder, Vrell, Ebror realizes, is obviously a seriously clever and dangerous individual who has used his only recently acquired knowledge of the ship layout to perfect advantage. Ebror intends to do much the same.

'This way.' He waves a claw towards a side tunnel, which in turn leads to a corridor running back parallel to the previous corridor. In his armour CPU he pulls up ship schematics and begins to analyse precisely where he wants to be. As he finally leads the eight into an empty storage room which, by the lingering smell, was obviously once full of food, the rumbling and crashing of weapons fire issues from below.

'Why are we here?' asks one of the eight.

'We are here because drones are stupid,' Ebror explains. 'You two' – he points a claw at the two carrying missile-cluster launchers

– 'stand here, and here.' He directs them to either side of an empty patch of floor, then reaches over and takes a pack of thermal mortar bombs from another Guard and, twisting off their safety caps, places them one by one evenly spaced in a circle on that floor. 'When they start to drop through, launch your missiles straight down.'

Ebror now sends an internal signal through his armour, whereupon the tips of his right claw drop away. Pointing the twinned throats of his particle cannon at the mines he planted, he sets it for wide dispersal – enough to turn them white-hot but not enough to blow them out of position – and then fires. Within a second all but a few of the thermal mines ignite with a sun-bright glare, turning into balls of heat intense enough to cut through just about anything. They begin sinking into the floor, which begins to sag. Even before Ebror can give the order, the two Guard step over this inferno and fire their cluster missiles downwards. Seven missiles from each launcher punch down through the softened metal and detonate below. The massive concussion throws the floor up, hurls all the armoured Prador waiting there up against the ceiling in an eruption of debris, then they crash down through the weakened floor into the corridor below, and Ebror has the satisfaction of seeing the drone positioned outside the Captain's Sanctum rolling aside, now just a shell of armour hollowed out by fire.

'Agreen!' he calls. 'Situation?'

'The one at the drop-shaft access is down,' Agreen replies.

'That way!' Ebror shouts to his comrades, firing his particle cannon towards where the surviving drone is retreating towards them, its hardfields up before it, under fire from the other end of the corridor. Immediately a hail of thermal mortars and clusters of missiles hurtle towards it. The drone has no time to defend itself from behind, and the non-stop blasts fling it forward, its hardfields failing, straight into the attackers before it. The back-blast picks Ebror and his companions up off the floor and flings them back too, but that's what their armour is for and they soon recover. Some of those the drone crashed into are not so fortunate, and Ebror sees that a few of them have fallen.

'Get that equipment down here now!' he bellows, all too aware of how quickly his time is running out. Less than an hour remains of the two hours which, he estimates, is how long it will take to break into the sanctum – unless this Vrell has even more surprises for them.

Those still mobile quickly drag aside their comrades who are either stunned or dead, then roll back the big drone shell and push it down into the drop-shaft. Soon they draw the particle-beam cutter into view. Running on big heavy wheels rather than maglev, it looks like a sawn-off version of the weapon used in warfare, with its cooling fins, massive power supply and numerous armoured s-con cables leading to a straight and simple barrel. As soon as they position it before the double doors and lock its wheels, Ebror clambers up behind it, inserting his claws into the guide-pits. He swings the barrel off to one side of the doors, meanwhile checking ship schematics via his CPU, then targets the shaft of one of the big hydraulic cylinders within the wall.

The beam appears with a thump: a rod of blue light lancing between barrel and armoured wall. At first it splashes – hazy violet fire spreading down to the floor and up to the ceiling – then, when the thick metal there hits the right temperature, a mass of molten globules explode from a steadily deepening hole. Soon he is through the thick armour, and the hydraulic shaft is visible. This, being composed of a simple steel alloy, evaporates under the intense blast, and a crash and explosion of sparks issue from the hole as the cylinder drops inside the wall. Three more hydraulic shafts follow, then Ebror cuts two large holes in the middle of the doors, on either side of the diagonal line where they meet, into which the jaws of the clawjack can now be inserted. He clambers back down to the floor.

'Move it!' he bellows, when it seems several of the Guard here are getting a bit tardy, but then he sees one of his fellows staggering to one side and collapsing, and realises the nanite is beginning to kill them.

Those still able to function unlock the short-beam's wheels and help Ebror move it aside.

'Agreen, the clawjack!' Ebror instructs.

'I am sorry,' says the junior, his legs giving way underneath him.

'Get the dead ones out of the way and fetch that clawjack in here,' Ebror orders those who are still able. Most obey him instantly, but he notices others just turning round and heading off to find somewhere quiet to do their dying. Ebror himself even considers doing the same, but does not relish the prospect of contemplating his end in silence.

Soon they draw the clawjack, which is simply a giant hydraulic claw, into position and insert its tips into the holes Ebror has cut. Its driving motor begins humming and its hydraulic cylinders drive the claw apart. Freed of their own hydraulics in the walls, the two heavy doors begin to part.

'Prepare yourselves,' Ebror instructs needlessly.

He looks around to see about fifty of the Guard now cramming the corridor, but even some of these are starting to sag and collapse.

'You two.' He gestures two of them towards the doors, and they move into position unlimbering heavy rail-guns.

The moment the gap draws wide enough, the beam of a particle cannon stabs out from inside, hitting one of the two directly. Both retreat, one with his armour smoking. The beam lances out again, hitting the clawjack, while one of them pokes his weapon through the gap and fires at some target Ebror cannot see. The firing ceases abruptly. Can that be it? Has Vrell been hit? When the doors draw far enough apart for an armoured Prador to enter whilst tilted on its edge, the first Guard goes in, rapidly followed by the second. Ebror scuttles up behind them, wondering why his legs are beginning to hurt; then, checking his time display, he understands. The two ahead of him open fire again, but only briefly, then Ebror is in behind them.

Vrell is dead.

Ebror walks unsteadily over to the black monster that crouches immobile against one wall, to inspect the great wet cavities gouged in its body by rail-gun fire. Since, like all the children of Oberon, he has been instructed directly by his parent to never remove his armour unless in absolute privacy, Ebror has only ever seen his own mutation. How his fellows look inside their armour is a mystery to him, and he therefore wonders if any of them look like this. Vrell is horrible, for there seems something soft about him.

Ebror now turns to Vrost. 'Captain?' he asks tentatively.

He expects no response and receives none. Either Vrell managed to somehow penetrate Vrost's armour, or the nanite did his work for him. Ebror's legs give way. Now his entire body starts to burn and he bites down on a scream. Aware of how the nanite works, he knows the pain will be intense for a while, but even now it is drawing in a numbness behind it as it destroys his nerves. Already he cannot feel his legs.

Other members of the Guard enter the Sanctum, some to prod at the black mutated Prador corpse, one or two collapsing, others wandering off to find somewhere else to die. After a little while the only movement is from flames issuing from a hole in one wall as hydraulic fluid burns. Smoke sits in a flat fog against the ceiling. Then some sensor comes back online, or some system repairs itself, and cold gas extinguishes the flames. Ebror has now receded to a small point of awareness. Most of his body feels like dead meat and his eyes ache and start to grow dim. Hearing a hiss and crump, and seeing an armoured suit opening, he feels only vague curiosity until it impacts on him that the open suit is Vrost's. The Prador now standing before the suit is hard and black and lethal-looking. Vrost?

'I wonder if you can hear me?' the figure says.

Ebror can't respond; does not want to respond.

The black mutated Prador continues, 'I was right to assume that none of you even knows what Vrost looks like. All you did know was that a black mutated Prador came in here, so it was a small enough task to give Vrost's corpse a black coating, arm him with a particle cannon, and then fire it remotely.'

Ebror continues fading . . . and ceases to care.

With internal flesh parted, three pairs of egg sacs lie exposed in a gullet-like cavity. As Sadurian steps forward, the two chrome-armoured third-children move respectfully to one side. She stoops to the sacs and presses her fingers against them, checking the tension of their surfaces to ensure they are fully charged with Oberon's sperm, for sometimes a mating can be unsuccessful, with the female ending up dead and disembowelled before the King concludes his business. These sacs are certainly full, so next Sadurian pulls an ultrasound micro-scanner from her belt and places it against one of them, pulling up an image on the screen of eggs shaped like Human blood corpuscles floating amidst a mass of strange objects like fleshy tuning forks.

Some of the two-pronged sperms spear their targets and are gradually drawn inside – as is usual in a normal Prador mating – but others spear eggs and merely suck the substance out of them. These sperms are actually eating the eggs they attach to. Running a program through the scanner, Sadurian calculates the proportion of each kind of sperm, then pauses to observe a new phenomenon: sperms attaching themselves in reverse to eggs and using them as a base to attack other eggs and sperms. She isn't greatly surprised, because there is always some new phenomenon like this at each mating, what with the King's sperm being just as vicious and adaptive as the creature that produces it.

'Okay,' she says, 'we've got about twenty per cent hostiles.' She turns to just one of the two Prador. 'Delf, get it collected and down to the laboratory as quickly as you can. Use autobot separation for the first hour, then nanobots thereafter. But do it in batches of just half a litre – we don't want a transferable mutation this time.' They'd lost the product of an entire mating last time when using little nano-robots to hunt down and kill the hostile spermatazoa. The Spatterjay virus had caused a rapid mutation in one sperm enabling it to chemically kill nanobots and then, within minutes, this mutation had spread virally to all the other spermatazoa, including those that weren't hostile. It was a disaster and Oberon had not been greatly pleased since: though he enjoys mating, it is not something he can indulge in very often, what with females physically suitable for him having to be grown and then surgically altered especially for the purpose.

The armoured third-child Delf now punctures each sac in turn with the spout of a vacuum collector – the spout resembling a female's ovipositor and the collector a small magnetic pump connected to twin chainglass collection bottles. With a sucking gurgling sound each sac deflates and the bottles fill with a pale orange fluid. When Delf is finished, he detaches the two bottles and carefully places them in a padded box, before inserting the pump and spout of the collector into a sterilizing sheath. Then he quickly retreats with his prize and heads off through the aseptic corridors. No other Prador will stand in his way and if any should foolishly assume he is a normal third-child who can be treated with violence, that foolish Prador will soon end up eating the hot end of a particle cannon installed in Delf's armour.

'Yaggs,' Sadurian addresses her second Prador assistant, then points towards the dead female. 'Eggs sacs, oviduct and ovipositor and required muscle groups. We'll use these this time rather than the machines – make it all as natural as possible.' Of course Prador cannot pick up on the Human sense of irony, though they have plenty of a sense of their own.

Yaggs quickly turns to the droge, removing gleaming surgical tools from its numerous compartments, and begins cutting out the required items. They need to be utterly scoured of hostile sperm before they can be used; after which the egg sacs can be refilled with fertilized eggs for the initial growth stages, then inserted into a birth mollusc. It is all a very complicated process, but the King's juice is a lethal thing. Even in the early days, when females could still survive the actual matings with him, his sperm would eventually spread throughout their bodies and consume them like some flesh-eating virus. In fact the stuff has been used as a method of execution for those who displease the King sufficiently, though it only consumes those uninfected by the Spatterjay virus. The King's own children it doesn't kill, though after a long period of suffering what remains of them has to be destroyed.

Making a last cut around the back end of the female, Yaggs withdraws a great muscular sac and, as he does so, the attached spike of the ovipositor is pulled out of a hole in the rear of the female's armour. This oviduct and ovipositor, with the muscles that drive the fertilized eggs from the former through the latter, the third-child now places in a refrigerated compartment within the droge. Next he moves on to cutting around the flaccid eggs sacs, then suddenly pauses before going down flat on his stomach. As a huge shadow draws across this diorama, Sadurian feels a shiver run up her spine. There comes a heavy crump to one side and she glances over to see a complex armoured foot indenting the floor, serrations running in triple ridges up the leg above it, to the first heavy joint.

'We'll be done here soon,' says Sadurian, without looking up.

The foot rises and withdraws from view. The King is obviously in no mood for conversation, for he does not reply, but just moves away. Later, Sadurian knows, he will return to the dead female, and when the King is finally done, and the ship-lice after him, there will be nought to clear away but a few remnants of hard carapace.

6

In the past, gold, platinum and precious stones were the substances whose ratio of value to volume was the greatest, but as it became possible first to manufacture precious stones and then to mine asteroids and other worlds – some worlds where gold is as common as iron is on Earth – their value fell. The items of the greatest value then became complex electronic chips, AI crystal – in other words, small objects requiring intensive manufacturing. But the techniques employed in making these continually improve, and now the greatest value-to-volume ratio is attached to rarity: Prador diamond slate (thus far mined on only one world), unique organic molecules, or Human and alien antiquities for which there is a thriving black market . . .

– From QUINCE GUIDE compiled by Humans

'So this is what all the fuss is about?' says Orbus, peering at a large package resting on the floor of this particular grav area of the *Gurnard*'s hold. For a moment he half-expects Drooble to comment on the sarcasm in his boss's tone, but the crewman is presently in the ship's small medbay, strapped to a slab and with an autodoc force-feeding the required nutrients into his reluctant mouth.

Orbus is calmer now, managing at last to accept the futility of bellowing threats at an AI whose location within the ship he has not been allowed to know, though he has left numerous fist-shaped dents in the *Gurnard*'s walls. Perhaps he still possesses some hard, stubbornly sane core deep inside him that can still make itself heard.

'Ostensibly, this is what all the fuss is about,' replies Gurnard.

'Nice word that . . . "ostensibly",' says Sniper from where he currently rests on the other side of the package from Orbus. The drone spears out one big spatulate-ended tentacle, which emits a high whine as it runs across the object lying between them. Dust rises into the air from the contact point, then the drone reaches in with several thinner tentacles to pull the package apart. Within a minute he is piling chunks of crash foam to one side, and then he strips away an inner layer of plasmel to reveal the contents.

The carapace, which extends three metres long, is oval, dished like a crab's and slightly segmented across the back. It isn't as deep as the Prador carapaces Orbus has seen, and possesses no visual turret, though there is a large natural-looking hole lying just ahead of the turret's usual position on the shell. Even so, looking at this thing, he feels it trying to insert itself in that burnt and nightmarish place within his memories.

'That ain't Prador,' he says doubtfully, not even sure whether he wants it to be.

'He doesn't know, does he?' says Sniper.

Orbus glares across at the drone. Yes, he wasn't in his right mind when he occupied the position of Captain of the *Vignette* on Spatterjay, but he still hasn't forgotten the humiliation of being hung from the spar of his own ship by his ankles by this very drone. Admittedly this same drone then rescued him and a few of his crewmen from Vrell's ship as it rose from Spatterjay's ocean, but that just seems to add insult to injury.

'As Captain of this ship,' he says succinctly, 'haven't I got some say about who's allowed aboard and who can become part of the crew?'

'You do have some say, Captain,' Gurnard replies. 'But the ultimate decision rests with Charles Cymbeline.'

'Right . . . what is it I don't know, then?' Orbus asks resentfully.

Perhaps because of Orbus's obvious anger at both Sniper and the controlling AI of this ship, Thirteen drifts down from where he was hovering above, to anchor his tail against the top of the exposed carapace.

'What you *do* know, Captain,' the little seahorse drone explains, 'is what happens to Humans infected with the Spatter-jay virus.'

'Oh really, do I?'

'Since the objective of all life is to eat and breed,' says Thirteen sniffily, 'it is not particularly unusual for life-forms alien to each other to take some sustenance from each other. The effect on Humans of alien viruses and bacteria, or their equivalent in the chain of life, ranges from the insignificant to the catastrophic. And the effect of the Spatterjay virus on Humans, though remarkable, is not unheard of within a planetary ecology. On Earth, too, are found parasites that increase the survivability of their hosts so as to increase their own chances of survival and thus breeding prospects.'

'Is this going anywhere?'

'Certainly.' Thirteen tilts his equine head for a moment. 'The Spatterjay virus collects parts of the genome of its hosts. It toughens up its hosts in a remarkable way, making them virtually immortal and very hard to kill. This is simply about evolution, for a durable and tough host can remain a carrier of the virus for longer—'

'Ain't you forgetting about the leeches?' Orbus interrupts. *Yeah, I'm calm,* he tells himself, *I can talk about all this reasonably.*

'No, I am not forgetting. A mutualism exists between the leeches of your homeworld and the virus – they spread the virus by their bite, and the virus turns its host into a perpetually reusable food resource for the leeches. Such complicated arrangements are often found in very old ecologies.'

Orbus shudders, remembering the thousands upon thousands of such bites he has received, right from the start when the Prador ship brought him to Spatterjay. When added up over the length of his very long life, the sheer quantity of plugs of flesh he lost to those creatures would fill this very hold.

'As I was saying,' the little drone continues. 'The virus collects up the genomes of its many different hosts and is unusual in that it can actually employ said collection of genetic material to mutate its host, rapidly, into something more able to survive, should circumstances change. As I said before, such a basis for survival is remarkable in a contained planetary ecology, but still remains within evolutionary parameters. However, that this same virus can use the Spatterjay genome to mutate Human DNA is more than remarkable. In fact it quite simply cannot be something that naturally evolved.'

Orbus has never heard of this before. The virus has been part of him for so long and its effects so familiar to him and his fellows, that he long ago ceased to question it. Now, described like this, he realizes just how odd it is.

'Polity AIs have been studying the virus and its effects for some time and have come to the conclusion that it is an artefact, though there is still much debate amongst them as to whether it is a mutated artefact, a random mix of some nanotechnology with a living virus or whatever, but certainly it is fundamentally an artefact. When it was first discovered that it could do to Humans what it already did to the creatures of its own world, some doubt remained about its antecedents. However,' Thirteen taps his tail against the carapace, 'now we know that it can do the same to another race that *is* alien to it, there is no doubt.'

Orbus stares at the carapace and with a shudder remembers the Prador Vrell lurking in his own father's spaceship under Spatterjay's ocean. Vrell looked like no other Prador that Orbus had ever seen, but he had not thought deeply about the reasons for this, in fact preferred to push such memories down deep with those *other* memories. Anyway, at that time he'd had enough problems, like fighting off his own crewmen who were themselves being transformed by the virus inside them whilst they starved, having revived from being harpooned and then drowned, or like trying to fight the control of the spider thrall Vrell had surgically installed in the back of his neck. So this, then, is why Vrell looked the way he did.

'Are *all* Prador infected?' he asks. Prador, he feels, are bad enough in their natural form, but Prador toughened up like an Old Captain? This is the stuff of the worst possible nightmares, and Orbus has quite enough of those to contend with as it is.

'Nope,' says Sniper abruptly, 'just King Oberon and his extended family – and our friend Vrell.' The big drone taps a tentacle against the carapace. 'This thing here is the shell of one of Oberon's Guard – one of his second-children – and this is a secret Oberon will do just about anything to keep.'

Orbus now steps forwards and walks around the shell, perpetually reminding himself this thing is dead and cannot harm him. But now it seems to loom here, inspiring the same feelings of illogical fear in him as some others feel upon seeing a Human skull.

'Damned big for a second-child,' he says. 'So that's why Vrost, one of the King's Guard, wanted to kill Vrell. And that's why the Prador here had tried to wipe out anyone with knowledge of this shell.' He pauses for a moment. 'But there's more to this than us simply coming here to collect this?'

'You wanna tell him?' Sniper asks.

'No,' Gurnard replies.

The big drone refocuses its orange eyes on Orbus. 'This shell was Polity property specially routed through Montmartre so the

Prador that infiltrated that space station would grab it. The private company that apparently owns it, sends a ship that just happens to be crewed by an Old Captain and a war drone who both really don't like Prador. Got the picture?'

'Earth Central Security?' Orbus asks.

'It's all about deniability,' says Sniper. 'ECS action in a sensitive area – better than sending a warship into the Graveyard and having the Prador respond with one of their own. ECS employed Cymbeline for this.'

'I was instructed by Charles Cymbeline,' says Gurnard, 'to tell you both, once you found out, that you may return to your homeworld or go wherever you want from here. He will pay you both a year's standard wage.'

'So ECS paid him well,' says Orbus. 'How many more of these Prador have infiltrated the Graveyard?'

'Two more that we know of, and there may be others,' replies the ship AI.

'So where's the next one?' Orbus asks, not able to identify what causes that sick feeling in his stomach. Is it excitement or fear, or something like both tangled together in the twisted wiring of his brain?

'Inside a small moon right near the edge of the Prador Kingdom.'

'So how do we get to that one?' Sniper enquires.

'Does it matter?' Orbus asks.

Thirteen just sighs and drifts back up into the air.

Before leaving the Sanctum, Vrell checks and rechecks the situation out in the ship through his control units. It takes a further hour before the last of the Guard collapse and expire, and then the ship is completely his. However, it is still travelling through U-space towards the Prador Third Kingdom, and in its present condition it will survive just about as long as it takes another warship to reach it once it surfaces back into realspace. He needs to take full control as fast as possible.

From Vrost's storage alcoves, Vrell quickly finds the necessary tools and begins taking apart the C-shaped pit console. Every pit-control is genome-coded to Vrost, which is a fact that Vrell puzzles over until going to inspect the Captain's armour and finding that the armour on each claw, and on his underhands, can open and fold back so the pits can sample the organic material required from him. He first takes apart each pit control and removes the tiny computer chips encoded with a permanent sample of Vrost's genome, then wipes clean all remaining programming and memory storage within each control. Next he finds a collection of blank chips, placing them in a reader to encode them with his own genome, before inserting them into each control. The entire task takes a full two days.

That a store of extra blank chips lies available here in the Sanctum is unusual, and further study reveals to him that there is a degree of leeway in the encoded genome. Both the store of chips and the lack of precision in each chip point to a simple fact: Prador infected with the Spatterjay virus are in a perpetual state of mutation. The chips installed can handle this transition for a period but, as the mutation continues, will periodically need to be replaced. While he works, Vrell occasionally snips off a piece of Vrost and gobbles it down. But, reminded by the way these chips work, he knows that this diet, Vrost's body being laden with the virus, is not the best one. Humans infected with this virus need to regularly ingest certain virus-free nutrients to prevent yet further mutation, and he has no doubt that the same applies to him too.

Finally Vrell reassembles the pit console, which now lies under his control but still remains disconnected from the rest of the ship. He takes up one of the ubiquitous Prador toolboxes and heads out of the Sanctum, leaps up onto the rough wall of the corridor and climbs further up to where he first entered it. It takes him a further two days' work to reconnect all the optics and repair the other damage he has caused up there. Now to get to that pit console and ensure the destruct order has been deleted, and to then search out all the programming traps Vrost has doubtless left spread throughout the computer architecture of this ship.

Returning to the Sanctum after a lengthy period of work, Vrell reaches out with one claw to again snip away a chunk of Vrost's body, which is now lacking many of its limbs because Vrell has already eaten them. The body shudders and shifts away from his probing claw. Vrell pauses to study it. Though nerveless and mindless, the chunk of flesh before him is still filled with the virus, still alive and now probably undergoing rapid mutation. Its main purpose, once it achieves some sort of transformation, will be to seek food, and the nearest source of that in here is Vrell himself. Vrell backs away from it then goes over to pick up his discarded particle cannon and reattach it to his harness power supply. Setting the beam to wide focus, he fires upon Vrost's remains. The effect is quite astounding.

As soon as the corpse begins to burn and char, all its remaining limbs fall away and numerous deep holes open in its surface. Like a hundred tongues, numerous pink leech ends issue from these, their horrible thread-cutting mouths extending like trumpets. Leech ends also extrude underneath and, like starfish legs, try to move Vrost's remains away from the source of intense heat. Vrell keeps the beam focused on this thing, surprised at how long a lump of semi-living matter can survive a beam able to evaporate steel. Finally it slumps back against one wall, now just a burning oily mass. Vrell keeps the beam on it until absolutely nothing remains, and the adjacent wall and floor begin to burn. Then he finally switches it off.

This, he realizes, is the kind of transformation already occurring in the hundreds upon hundreds of suits of armour aboard. Fortunately it seems an insentient change – base-level survival – and, whatever any Guard turns into, it will not be able to escape its enclosing armour. However, he recalls there were unarmoured Prador aboard, who died when first he released the nanite here: very young Prador yet to receive their armour, and others out of armour for whatever reasons. These, too, will have undergone transformations, and may even now be roaming the ship in search of sustenance. Before getting involved with sorting out the pit-console, Vrell decides he had better take some precautions.

He clips the particle cannon back onto his harness and, one at a time, heaves the members of the Guard who expired within the Sanctum out into the corridor. Next he detaches the clawjack, drags it to insert it, on the inside, into the same holes cut through the door, starts up the jack and draws the doors closed. Now that he feels safe enough to continue, he turns to the console.

First Vrell inserts his claws and begins running primary routines up on the hexagonal screens, then he inserts his manipulatory hands into other pits and begins to explore the underlying code to each routine. In every case he finds subroutines which, if the code is being strictly applied to its task, should not be needed. A brief study of one of these subroutines reveals that if he tries to shut down the engines without inserting a certain eight-digit number, they will simply continue functioning. It is all surprisingly easy to deal with, and he understands that all these precautions were taken in case some influence outside the Sanctum itself tried to usurp control. Vrost never expected any enemy to penetrate this far or, rather, Vrost did not care if they did, for he knew that at that point it would no longer matter to him. After checking and checking again, Vrell finally sends the instruction that does in fact shut down the U-space drive. The ship mind, a disembodied and flash-frozen brain of a Prador first-child capable of no more than handling U-space maths, intercepts this instruction and applies it. With a shuddering twist, the ship at last returns to realspace.

Vrell bubbles contentedly to himself, then begins to inspect astrogation data. The ship has surfaced into interstellar space within the Polity, some twenty light-years from the nearest inhabited star system. Within a matter of days some Polity watch station is bound to detect his presence out here, if it has not already been detected, for though light from his ship will take twenty years to reach those Polity sensors positioned to record the radiations of realspace, certain other sensors, as sensitive as the legs of spiders resting on the strands of a web, will very quickly detect the U-space disturbance this ship just caused. He estimates it will take a minimum of ten days for the Polity to get ships here to investigate, unless he is extremely unlucky and Polity ships are already positioned nearby. He must quit this position within eight days, if he does not wish to leave a wake through underspace that any pursuing ship can follow.

Now returning his attention to the rest of the vessel, he begins to run diagnostics and make an extensive inspection of the massive damage he himself inflicted upon it. The outer hull is breached in numerous places; even the exotic armour was unable to sustain the massive impact of his own ship travelling at near relativistic speed. However, Vrell sees that, by altering the internal structure of the ship, and by using spare armour in its stores, the main hull can now be reintegrated as a whole. And, using the same approach to much of the other damage, order can be restored elsewhere: weapons and computer systems put back online, life-support returned to areas now devoid of air, steering thrusters reinstated and sensors replaced or rebuilt. However, a rather large problem remains because, though he can see how all this could be achieved, there is no crew available to do it.

Rattling his legs against the floor, Vrell begins to examine an idea that germinated in his mind the moment he entered this vessel's armoury. Certainly the ship possesses automatic repair robots that even now are mindlessly trying to fix the damage. Other automatics are putting out the remaining fires and steadily cleaning up radioactive areas; also some of the war drones are provided with manipulators rather than just weapons and thus can be put to work, but all of these measures are nowhere near enough. Vrell needs a *workforce*, and he knows precisely where one is available.

By consigning many files to compacted storage, he begins to open up programming and memory space, into which he first dumps copies of those programs he used to control those suits of armour taken from the armoury. Gradually he begins to develop these programs, taking them beyond anything Prador generally use, since they become increasingly self-governing and complex, and thus approach that capability hated by most Prador, of artificial intelligence. When he is finally ready, he transmits ten test copies to ten close locations, and through ship eyes observes the result.

Ten of the dead King's Guard abruptly lurch to their feet, while their suits run self-diagnostics. They test every joint of their legs, every joint of their underslung arms and manipulatory hands, snip their claws at the air, if air surrounds them, check their turret vision, audio and other sensory apparatus, then stand ready for orders. Vrell loads to them a schematic revealing one small section of ruination aboard, gives them instructions on how this schematic must be changed, then directs them to the necessary stores of equipment and materials, before proceeding to watch them intently on every level, to ensure they function as predicted.

Vrell ponders how ghoulish this all is. In a way it is rather like some Prador version of those animated corpses the Humans call reifications, though admittedly, reifications are run by the crystal-stored minds of the Human corpse's previous occupant rather than the simplistic sub-AI occupants of these suits of armour. He even feels some strange doubts about setting into motion suits still containing the semi-living remains of their previous occupants, for those remains, no matter how insentient or lacking in nerves, will be receiving a perpetual feed-back of motion and data from the suit sensors, and he does not know what effect that might have. But right now he simply has no other options, so he sidelines those doubts as he puts a further fifty suits to work. Within hours, every suit is in motion and the entire ship fills with the racket of reconstruction. Vrell, however, has little time for satisfaction, for within minutes of the last suit picking up a wire-welder and heading out onto the hull to repair cracks, the ship's sensors begin warning of a U-space disturbance less than a quarter light-year from Vrell's present position.

Immediately analysing the disturbance, Vrell becomes aware of what will be surfacing into the real, a microsecond before it does so. The shape of the thing is inherent in the disturbance it is causing, though the light that would confirm that shape would take a quarter of a year to reach the conventional sensors of this ship. It is a cylinder a mile long, with nacelles a quarter of a mile long jutting from either side on wide stanchions, and with a big rear fusion-drive array and a long needle of a nose. No Prador ship possesses such a shape; this is some Polity dreadnought.

Further disturbances follow, one of them only a few millon miles away from him. How did they get here so fast? But, even as he poses himself the question, Vrell knows the answer. Vrost threatened the Polity and conducted an assault on Spatterjay which, though not actually a Polity world, does come partially under Polity aegis. Doubtless the Polity AIs made their own threats, and also made their own preparations. Though they were unable to get warships to Spatterjay in time, they must have sent warships on an intercept course to tally with Vrost's predicted departure route.

It seems unlikely to Vrell that Vrost's attack did not cause casualties on Spatterjay, so these ships must be here for some payback. Vrell now has a serious problem for, though repairs can continue whilst his ship travels through U-space, there is still much that cannot be done to the exterior hull within that continuum. Surfacing into the real again, he will still be vulnerable – will in fact almost certainly be obliterated by ships now close enough to be able to trail him wherever he might go. There seems only one dangerous solution left, that being to take this ship where, by treaty, neither Prador nor Polity warships are allowed to venture. It is also a place where he might find further much-needed supplies, for certainly his own kind will be there watching for an attack, just as Humans watch there for the same reason.

Inputting coordinates to the disembodied mind of his vessel, Vrell gives the order for his ship to immediately drop into U-space, despite the fact that, with repairs ongoing, he will lose some of those suits still busy out on the surface of the hull.

As the dreadnought drops out of the real, he remembers the Human name for his new destination: the Graveyard.

The Prador border stations have been in position long enough for light reflected from them to reach the present position of the *Gurnard*. In fact, powerful telescope arrays in the Polity can detect them, and even deeper within the Polity other arrays can look over seven centuries into the past, to the time when these stations were being constructed. At forty-eight light-years away, resolution here is good enough for Gurnard to provide a clear image of the nearest station, and Orbus now studies that image.

'Utility overcame aesthetics,' he observes with a grimace,

knowing exactly what will be scuttling about inside those massive constructions.

'That started back during the war,' remarks Sniper, 'with the ships.'

Orbus turns to gaze at the drone. At first he hoped to avoid Sniper up here on the bridge because, though the drone can traverse most of the ship's corridors, it previously couldn't fit through the bulkhead door leading into here. However, Sniper has made short work of that problem by cutting out both frame and door, bringing up materials from the ship's hold, and then rebuilding it all so that now the original door sits within an even larger one.

'Really,' says the Captain.

'Most of 'em, deliberately constructed in the shape of their makers, were built before the war, or up to about halfway through it,' Sniper explains. 'When the Second King twigged we weren't gonna roll over and die, he must have decided that sticking to the crab shape was a waste of metal. A lot of the later ones were still that traditional shape, but only because a lot of their shipyards didn't get a chance to retool. Elsewhere they didn't stick to it as strictly, and their stations were built without their egos governing the blueprints.'

'Thank you for the history lesson,' says Orbus flatly.

'Not a problem,' Sniper replies. 'But there's something else to chew on.'

'That being?'

'Oberon ordered these stations built, and he may not love the Prador form as much as the rest of his kind . . . or, rather, the kind he once used to belong to.'

Orbus returns his attention to the station.

It bears some resemblance to a titanic brass vase just hanging in vacuum, but many extrusions and incrustations adorn its

surface, and certainly what blossom from its mouth are not flow-
ers. This collection of long straight cylinders, scaffolds and square-
section pipes is in fact an array of near-c rail-guns, particle cannons
and wide-spectrum lasers. Perpetually powered by the tidal forces
exerted by the brown dwarf it closely orbits, this defence station
can throw out missiles and energy with a destructive potential
more often associated with solar flares than with anything built by
a sentient race. Such a station would of course be useless should
any attacker choose to bypass it through the U-continuum.

Grudgingly, since Thirteen is currently down in the Medbay
with Drooble, and since he knows he should get himself on a civil
basis with Sniper, Orbus asks, 'So how does it stop ships travelling
through U-space?'

Sniper points a tentacle towards the screen. 'The same grav-
generators running off that brown dwarf are used to power a big-
fuck series of USERs.'

'USERs?'

'Underspace interference emitters,' the drone explains. 'We do
it by rattling a singularity in and out of a runcible gate. Here they
go for the bang method. The moment they detect a U-signature
within twenty virtual light-years, they invert a U-drive inside a
high-powered grav-sphere. The disruption wave through U-space
knocks any attacker back into the real. Bit silly, and all for show
really, like the Maginot Line.'

Orbus nods, because he has read enough history to understand
that reference. Why would the Polity, should it want to attack,
send its ships into the Prador Kingdom this way? The Graveyard
only extends between where Polity and Kingdom converge, and
the main concentration of defence stations is here only. Just as the
Nazis circumvented the Maginot Line, so could the Polity go
around all this. But of course the reverse applies too and the Polity
defence stations on the other side of the Graveyard can equally be

bypassed. The whole point is display: each side reminding the other of just what kind of weapons could be deployed, and how many billions might die should they once again go to war.

Orbus knows that the stations on both sides regularly conduct drills and test firings. It seems all very much like the sabre-rattling of the twentieth century, at the very beginning of the nuclear age: the atomic tests that were not really to see if the bombs worked but simply a message: *'We've got this, so watch it.'*

'But this isn't why we're here, is it, Gurnard?' Orbus asks.

The image on the screen fades and is then shunted aside by another. Into view slides a small dark moon orbiting far out from a frozen planet not much bigger than Earth. With the distances involved here, the sun they both turn about looks only a little larger than the other near stars. The moon itself possesses no particularly distinguishing features; like so many trillions scattered throughout space it is just a ball of rock turned dusty and grizzled by appalling reaches of time.

'There are indications of a landing on the surface, which is somewhat remiss of the occupant here,' the ship AI lectures. 'Deeper scan reveals underground caverns of unusual orderliness.'

'Do you reckon they'll fall for all this?' Orbus asks.

They had made it generally known aboard Montmartre, as those resident there cleared up the mess and fought each other for ultimate control, that the *Gurnard* was heading out this way to search for wartime artefacts before moving on to the next Human population centre in the Graveyard. They'd meticulously scanned one entire world, numerous asteroids and moonlets, and even discovered a small cache of munitions which, just to keep up the façade, it had been necessary for them to take aboard. Coincidentally, Prador-hating drone and Old Captain would now stumble on a secret Prador station . . .

'It's not a case of whether they'll fall for this,' says Gurnard.

'The Prador will know, after this next encounter, that ECS is stomping on its infiltrators in the Graveyard. However, because ECS has sent no military ship, no treaties have been broken so they cannot respond militarily.'

'But they can respond covertly,' says Sniper. 'Beside their other agents here there's descendants of Prador refugees in the Graveyard . . . so you can bet someone'll be on our arses soon enough.'

Orbus turns and gazes at the drone. 'Refugees in the Grave-yard?'

'Yeah, there's a few renegade adults – descendants of families who escaped when King Oberon started clearing house,' Sniper replies. 'Some of 'em still want to get back into favour and return to the Kingdom, and others will reckon it a good idea to get into favour even if they intend staying here. Remember, all Prador believe the war unfinished business.'

'So what's the difference between them and the likes of this one?' Orbus gestures at the screen.

'Very speciesist of you, Captain,' quips Sniper. 'Just because every Prador every Polity citizen has met is a murderous conniving shit doesn't mean they all are.'

Gurnard explains, 'Prador like the one at Montmartre and the one below have all installed themselves secretly, and are all directly supplied with weapons and materials from the Kingdom. They have been covertly establishing a foothold here, a dangerous foot-hold that puts them closer to the Polity than our rulers can tolerate. However, the other Prador established here have shown no inclin-ation to do more than keep their heads down and survive.'

Whilst they speak the moon draws closer on the screen, expanding to nearly fill it. Checking the instruments available to him, through the controls in the arms of his Captain's chair, Orbus sees that the *Gurnard* now sits geostationary above it. He stands, turns and walks back, circumventing Sniper and stepping out into the corridor leading down into the ship. The big drone turns with deceptive silence and drifts along behind him like a huge steel spectre.

'I'll want to be armed this time,' remarks Orbus.

'There is a small armoury inward of the docking ring in "A" segment,' Gurnard replies, its voice now issuing from the walls. 'Iannus and Thirteen will meet you there.'

Orbus has spent much time wandering about this ship and he knows precisely where A segment lies within the docking ring, but cannot recollect seeing an armoury there. It also occurs to him that this description '*small* armoury' might well mean that there is also a big one aboard.

'I'll meet you down on the moon,' says Sniper, abruptly taking a side route to another area of the docking ring and to an airlock he uses to exit the ship. He, of course, has no real need of the contents of an armoury.

Soon, after taking a few twists and turns of corridor and descending a spiral stair installed in what was once a drop-shaft, Orbus steps out to where Thirteen and Drooble wait in a feature-less corridor. Inspecting the crewman, Orbus wonders if Drooble will be safe handling weapons. Though there is now no visible sign of the massive wound in his side, he still looks a little . . . odd. But then Orbus cannot recollect a time when Drooble did not look a helmsman short of the full crew.

'So where's this armoury?' the Captain asks.

'Thirteen says it's here.' Drooble grins and bangs a fist against the blank wall, and, almost as if in response to this, the wall divides vertically and begins to part. Soon lights come on within the room lying beyond, and Drooble steps inside.

'Looks like everything is ready for you, Cap'n.' Drooble waves his little finger towards a massive, heavily reinforced spacesuit supported in a framework.

Inspecting this item, Orbus notes designs with a nautical theme etched into its surface. This is all entirely in keeping with the rest of the *Gurnard*, but the sheer size of the suit indicates it was made for an Old Captain – probably for Captain Ron when he held the post Orbus now occupies.

'Ceramal and diamond-fibre composite plated with nanochain chromium,' pipes up Thirteen, while hovering right above the suit. 'Just what Sniper's covered with.'

As Drooble meanwhile goes over to a rack of proton carbines and makes a selection, Orbus reaches out and presses a control on the front of the suit. With eerie silence the thick chainglass visor withdraws up into the helmet, which in turn hinges back, while the chest plate and groin armour open like double doors, as do the hams of the legs. The rest of the armour of the arms and legs expands on shiny rods. It is all ready for him to step inside and, now it is open, Orbus sees that the suit's layers are nearly three inches thick in places. He hesitates only for a moment, then turns his back to it, reaches up and grips two bars of the support frame positioned around it for this purpose, heaves himself up and first inserts his legs. Next, as if putting on a coat, he inserts his arms, and the spacesuit methodically draws closed around him.

Orbus steps away from the framework, the suit feeling as light on him as his own clothing. He realizes it possesses motorized joints and wonders why, since he is hardly a weakling. The visor remains open and, raising his arm, he inspects the pretty much standard control panel set into it. On a small screen he can call up information about his air supply, suit diagnostics, the external conditions, and all this and much other information can be transferred to a visor display. Carefully pressing the buttons adapted to his now huge but still oddly sensitive fingers, he checks a few things and finds that the suit's assister motors are of a design called Lamion.

'Lamion?' he enquires.

'Standard assister motors don't even match the strength of an Old Captain,' the drone Thirteen informs him, as it drifts down before him. 'Lamion motors use nano-scale molecular interactions between microscopic layers of ceramic – they can multiply your strength by up to four times.'

'So whoever designed this suit had encounters with armoured Prador in mind,' the Captain observes. 'I wonder how long ago this was all planned. I wonder if Captain Ron was the one originally intended for this job.'

Drooble has now loaded himself with a proton carbine, a solid-state hand laser and a bandolier of grenades. There is no suit for him here since the standard suits provided aboard will do him fine. Studying the other contents of the armoury, Orbus looks for suitable weaponry to complement his present outfit, and there it is, resting down beside the support framework. He stoops and picks up the huge shiny carbine with a multiplicity of barrels. A heavy power cable trails from it, the plug at its end perfectly designed to fit into the socket positioned just over the captain's hip. He plugs it in and his visor slams instantly closed. Cross-hairs appear on it, shifting as he moves the gun itself. A side-menu lists a selection of firing modes: laser, particle cannon and a selection of projectiles ranging from inert to high explosive.

'Rail, inert,' he says, and the cluster of barrels turns. He rests his sensitive forefinger against the trigger and points the weapon at Drooble, who abruptly backs away, but not without an expression of horrible anticipation.

'Disarm, now,' Orbus adds, then unplugs the power cable and rests the weapon across his shoulder. 'Let's go.'

Drooble follows his Captain back out into the corridor, his expression now one of disappointment. Orbus wonders if the man is disappointed at not being shot, or by his own wish that he had been, but it is difficult enough for him to sort out his own emotions without getting into those of his deranged crewman. Why, for example, is he himself sweating, and why does he now feel a sickness in his guts almost like hunger?

The trip down to the surface is marked only by Drooble's constant litany of complaints as he struggles into a spacesuit with the appearance of a diving suit from Jules Verne's novel *Twenty Thousand Leagues under the Sea*. Orbus brings the shuttle down on the floor of a valley between mountains of grey stone cut through with striations of white like hoar frost. Because of the sheer size of the suit Orbus wears, they necessarily depart the shuttle one at a time through the airlock.

'Something odd here,' comes Sniper's voice over the suit radio.

They bounce easily up a nearby slope to enter what is ostensibly a natural cave mouth, where in Orbus's visor light amplification kicks in. Hissing between his teeth he peers down at the recognizable footprints of sharp Prador feet in the ochre dust. As Gurnard noted: it is remiss of the occupant here to leave signs of a recent landing on the surface, and just as remiss to leave signs like this if its mission is supposedly covert. Advancing into the gloom, he swings his multigun across to align the visor cross-hairs over Sniper, as the drone revolves to face them.

'Looks like he's already had some visitors.' Sniper gestures with one tentacle to the back of the cave where a ceramic airlock door, its exterior disguised with a layer of rough stone, lies in two halves on the floor. Beyond this the inner door is gone, as is the intervening airlock chamber itself.

As they cautiously make their way in, Orbus immediately notes severed trunking clips, now empty, along one wall and the many similarly empty cavities intended to hold some sort of equipment. The s-con cables and fibre-optics have been torn out of here, other hardware also removed. The rock also bears molten scars, blast craters, laser burns, and the distinctive jagged grooves cut by rail-gun fire.

'Abandoned?' wonders Thirteen, poised over one blast crater.

'Someone hit this place *hard*,' says Sniper. 'Dunno if anyone here would have been capable of doing any abandoning.'

'Bugger,' says Drooble, gazing with disappointment at his proton carbine.

Orbus also feels a leaden disappointment, though countered by an odd sense of relief. Will he ever know what he really wants? Will any of his emotions ever be unambiguous?

A thorough exploration of all the caves reveals the same story throughout: most of the equipment that must have occupied these spaces is now gone. Orbus begins to notice how this place was stripped selectively. Ceramics and plastics were left behind, but just about every scrap of metal taken. He notes bolt-holes in floors where reactors were once mounted, what seems likely to have been a storage cave, and empty bolt-holes in regular patterns across the floor where even the racking was looted. Other holes and fixings indicate where armouring was previously fixed around certain deep chambers. Apart from the few aforementioned scraps, only one other thing remains: this place's erstwhile resident.

'No useful metal in him,' Drooble quips.

'Or still on him,' Sniper adds.

Obviously this one was not a member of the King's Guard, since the burnt remains lying curled against the wall show none of the mutations displayed by the carapace retrieved from Montmartre, or by the Prador Vrell, and anyway, as Orbus now understands it, any attack upon one of the King's Guard would result in the attacker being incinerated when the Guard, if losing the fight, detonates its armour's fusion tactical. Perhaps the fact of the resident here not being such a formidable opponent is why this place was chosen as a target. He walks over to the creature's remains, his multigun never wavering from it, and peers down carefully. This is the best sort of Prador to encounter: a dead one.

'What the hell is going on here?' he asks. 'If this is the result of a Polity operation, we wouldn't have been sent here. So who did this?'

None of his companions can supply an answer.

'Gurnard?' he enquires.

The ship AI's reply is immediate. 'Time for you to leave that place, just as quickly as you can.'

'Why?'

'A Prador kamikaze just exited U-space and is on its way here, now.'

7

Prador are not constrained by any morality concerning treatment of their children. Their youngest, their third-children, they keep in confined conditions and encourage to fight with each other. Many of these children are literally torn apart, and those severely wounded soon become the victims of their fellows. In second-childhood the competition continues, but now the children are also selected for intelligence and technical ability, while those not making the grade become lunch for the others. This process continues in first-childhood, though those that fail the challenge are very often not just killed. Much has already been invested in such a child, so its brain and part of its nervous system are cut out to serve as the controlling intelligence in either a drone or a spaceship. It was therefore not unexpected that during the war such children were used as U-space kamikazes – massive flying antimatter bombs used to destroy Polity capital ships, space stations, or sometimes entire worlds.
– WEAPONS DIRECTORY NOTES, E.B.S Heinlein

Records aboard Vrost's vessel supplied the location of the Graveyard outpost, but the haul is disappointing. Its lone occupant being a single Prador first-child is a sufficient explanation for the outpost's evident poverty: it is merely a watchpost to relay early warning to the border-defence stations, occupied by a first-child supplied by some Prador family other than King Oberon's own. It seems that if Vrell wants to track down bigger hauls of resources and materials of Prador manufacture within the Graveyard, he needs to find the location of the King's Guard. This, then, poses the further problem of how he takes those resources away from them without them wrecking the whole lot when they fusion-suicide. Perhaps it would be better instead to hit a few of the Human settlements here?

In the fluctuating glare of an unstable green sun, Vrell's spaceship hangs like a pomegranate crushed and split in many places and swarming with mites. Repairs continue apace and, by lying in close orbit to the erratic output of lethal radiation, this offers perfect cover as the ship slowly changes shape, its work-force of sub-AI armour steadily drawing closed the gaps in its hull. The present weapons complement is now 40 per cent func-tional and, though the internal structure still lies some way from optimum, Vrell is pleased.

After defrosting and then rapidly consuming steaks of flesh hewn from a homeworld decapod food animal, he carefully inspects himself. Ever since ceasing to consume anything containing the Spatterjay virus, he has noted the changes in himself slowing. His form, which was completely disc-shaped when he boarded this ship, has lengthened slightly and the sharp spike of a tail has appeared, something a little like the ovipositor of female Prador – indeed a worrying development. Donning armour he recently adjusted to fit his now elongated form, Vrell decides it is time to tour his new domain, not because there is any of it he cannot easily view from the Sanctum, but because he feels the need for exercise and because *things* he can hunt scuttle and slither in some of the more shadowy sections of the vessel.

He'd first spotted them while scanning internal repairs to the hull armour overlying one area of the ship that contained, amongst other things, a third-child nursery. Doubtless that is where they came from: the Spatterjay virus having worked its grotesque magic upon the nerveless living dead in the nursery itself. Further scanning confirms this conjecture when Vrell sees that the nursery is utterly empty of corpses.

Arming himself with both a rail-gun and a particle cannon, he sends a control-unit signal to the now repaired Sanctum doors and steps out into the corridor. Even as he enters the drop-shaft at one end, he notes that two of his armoured servants have removed sections of wall to get to the damaged structural members lying beyond, where they are currently welding into place some triangular strengtheners at the beam joints. Briefly accessing their programming, he sees this is growing increasingly complex as it adapts to new circumstances. They are strengthening the superstructure because certain repairs to the hull armour have repositioned load points within the ship. This is something Vrell has already considered with the intention of studying later. He does not know whether to be glad or worried that his slaves have got to the problem before him.

Vrell studies their programming a while longer and notices something else: how odd corruptions in that same programming are generating inadvertent limb movements. Perhaps this is all part of their increasing complexity, for that must give greater room for error, but he doesn't like it. Later he will have to study this development more closely and, if necessary, shut them all down and reprogram them. It isn't something he wants to do, seeing how fast their work is now progressing.

Throughout the ship, new metal and new welds gleam, some of the specialized alloys already beginning to take on a dull patina as their outer layers oxidize into a hard coating. Wherever Vrell goes there is activity: maglev trains shifting materials to where required; floating pallets of ordnance being taken to those rail-guns once again operational; numerous pallets of scrap metal and various materials on their way to internal factories for reprocessing; his slaves removing burnt-out optics, computer hardware, re-insulating s-con cables, rebuilding structure. It is all very very gratifying, but Vrell remains utterly aware that no matter how spaceworthy this ship is made, it is still only one ship.

Abruptly halting at a shaft leading down to the third-child nursery, Vrell momentarily draws his thoughts away from the day-to-day mundanities of repairing his vessel and considers what else he wants. On Spatterjay it was all about survival, for he knew that there could be no escape for him whilst Vrost's ship orbited that same world. Vrost would never have allowed Vrell's ship to leave the planet, and would have scoured the surface until finding and killing him. But what now? In either the Third Kingdom or the Polity he has no doubt that he would be hunted down, because King Oberon will want any dangerous adversary dead, and the Polity AIs would not want a Prador destroyer freely roaming their realm. Within the Graveyard neither side will want to deploy warships for the task, but covert forces will still be arrayed against him. But why bother remaining in any of these three zones when there is a whole universe out there he can lose himself in?

Like all Prador he is instinctively aggressive, and has never questioned his urge to strike back hard at any attacker. Now, questioning this natural response, he feels that the answer involves more than just a survival reaction. In either Polity or Kingdom he cannot hope to remain free, but nor does he want to just run away. *Why should he?* The bottom line, Vrell surmises, is that he feels himself the subject of a huge injustice. It is simply *unfair*. And Oberon is now his prime target simply because the King tried to have him killed. Vrell realizes that his present notions of fair and unfair are not natural to the Prador, and he wonders therefore how such Human concepts have lodged themselves in his mind.

Still mulling all this over, he steps into the irised gravity field of the drop-shaft and descends. Then, after negotiating a few corridors and passing on through into a portion of the ship whose ruination does not effect the vessel's overall running, it is a welcome distraction for him to find monsters there that lie outside his own mind.

A knot of wreckage occupies an area extending half a mile across. Occasional gravplates still function, but often lying athwart each other to create strange effects of perspective. Some lights still work, a few of them casting odd portions of the spectrum as elements in them have burnt out or been dislocated into some infrequently used setting. Superconducting cables, their insulation damaged, occasionally short themselves against twisted I-beams, gases leak to create off-colour fogs twisted into strange shapes by damaged gravplates.

Even for Vrell this is a spooky place, and when the first of the new residents suddenly appears, it seems perfectly in keeping with its surroundings.

The thing looks only vaguely like a Prador third-child. Its numerous legs have grown extensively, in the process acquiring a few more joints, and have now shifted to its four quarters. Studying the thing as it eases itself through the wreckage towards him, Vrell realizes that this new leg positioning is well suited to this partially zero-gravity environment. Its body is now globular, and a huge trumpet-like leech mouth sprouts from its near end, while like Vrost it possesses stalked eyes, though they sprout in a ring about the base of that ever-questing mouth.

Vrell continues watching it, fascination overriding his initial reflex to blast the thing as soon as it appeared. Maybe he should just let it continue on its way, but this is no resident of a planetary jungle going about its day-to-day life; it is a creation of the mutating effects of the virus, searching for food in a place where little food exists. In whatever passes for its mind – some leech-based organ recently grown inside it – any movement means food and, once through the tangle of metal, it throws itself at the moving thing that first attracted it.

Vrell raises his free claw and snaps it closed about the creature's globular body. It struggles with surprising strength, the sharp tips of its legs scraping frantically against his armoured turret, then the trumpet mouth thunks down against his claw, its complex internal mouthpart of saw-edged discs and bony blades grating against the armour. He pushes it further away from him to inspect it better. To be able to move like this it must have at least grown a rudimentary nervous system, and since Vrell's nanite is still everywhere throughout this ship, that nervous system must be based on something other than the genome of the third-child it once was.

Further movement out in the tangle of wreckage attracts his attention, and he realizes that other creatures of a similar nature are moving in. He could easily toss this one away from him and hit it with the particle cannon, before turning both of his weapons on the others now approaching, but his curiosity has been stirred. Still clutching his trophy, he abruptly backs out of the area into the better-lit corridors, and retreats to the nearest door. As he goes through, the racket of pursuit reaches him, and turning back he watches through the closing gap in the door the approaching horde of monstrosities. None of them can reach him before the door closes.

Next, Vrell formulates and dispatches new orders through his control units to his armoured slaves, instructing them to destroy any of the mutated Prador they encounter, barring themselves of course, except those in this particular area, which is to be totally sealed off but for this one entrance. Strange random bits of code accompany the acknowledgement received from them. *Later, he will deal with that later.* He turns and takes his struggling captive towards one of the medical research units aboard the vessel, all weapons forgotten and his focus now upon research.

Having survived the winnowing-out process of third-childhood, Nool makes it to second-childhood as a strong and vicious creature – but no more so than all his contemporaries, since they have undergone the same process. Competition is strong in the ranks of second-childhood, where both their responsibilities and their likelihood of dying increase. Nool soon learns that, though it is an honour to be allowed to serve Father, and such servitude increases the possibility of one being raised to first-childhood, Father's Sanctum is a very dangerous place to be. Always jealous of his own position and wary of contenders for it, Father's first-child Golt is ever prepared to crack a youngster's shell should it step out of line, or even show too much perspicacity. Then there is Father himself, who will deliberately set those directly below him against each other, or often, when the urge takes him, will without hesitation dismember and eat a second-child.

For many years Nool manages to avoid Sanctum duty but, merely his avoiding it for so long and carrying out his assigned tasks with a quiet efficiency inevitably brings him to Father's notice. With two other second-children, he is given the duties of bringing megafauna steaks for Father to eat, and then cleaning his mandibles afterwards, and this is the first time he even comes within a hundred feet of his ancient parent.

Father is utterly limbless, his massive carapace supported above the gravplates of the Sanctum by grav-units attached to his underside. Control units dot his carapace below his huge heavy mandibles, some of them commanding the five Human blanks arrayed against the back wall of the Sanctum. When he is not wearing his prostheses – metal claws, legs and underarms that slot neatly into cybernetic sockets positioned where his former limbs had been – these Humans sometimes act as his hands. Nool is quick to learn that when Father does don his limbs, this is usually because he wants to make a meal of something that will certainly have other ideas on the matter. Nool sees his first two co-workers go that way, shrieking and bubbling as Father tears them apart and feeds them into mandibles that Nool is instructed to clean afterwards. Thereafter he sees another twelve second-children perish similarly. Why they were chosen and he is not, he can never fathom, but is simply grateful to survive.

The change in him begins to occur shortly after a biological weapon opens in the hold of the ship and wipes out nearly a quarter of the children aboard. Golt tears apart those second-children responsible for in-hold security, and apparently works hard to find the source of this weapon, and to ensure one never gets aboard again. Nool realizes that the first-child is actually terrified for, though conveniently Golt blames those working the hold area, the buck ultimately stops with him. Whilst all this uproar goes on, Nool, when it comes to feeding time, is redirected to a different larder. Shortly after he begins eating the rich meats which, he soon realizes, are not laden with suppressant hormones, his body begins to grow and change. Golt's reaction, upon seeing these changes, tells Nool all he needs to know: he is turning into a first-child.

Golt becomes immediately violent, attacking him in a corridor in order to tear off one limb and crack his shell, but this mistreatment only seems to accelerate the change, and shortly afterwards Nool is sent on a mission down to the surface of a Prador world, well out of Golt's reach. When he finally returns, he has attained full first-childhood and, summoned to the Sanctum, finds Father, in full prosthetic array, holding Golt down on the floor and meticulously tearing off all his limbs while the victim shrieks and begs for mercy. Father likes to do this sort of thing himself, though it is two of his Human blanks that operate the surgical machine that eventually opens Golt's shell and cuts out his major ganglion and a large proportion of his nervous system. This organic material is subsequently flash-frozen and placed in storage for later installation in a drone shell. As a result, Nool is now Father's first-child.

His ascendancy in that position does not last long.

It seems Golt himself, knowing the hormones and other chemical cocktails that kept him locked in perpetual childhood were no longer working so well, deliberately created the first weaknesses in ship security. Managing to beat Father's chemical control of him, he wanted his parent dead so that he himself could make the transition to adulthood. Next realizing that some second-children, for Nool was not the only one, were being raised to first-childhood, he became desperate and further weakened security to allow in one of the perpetual attacks devised by Prador competitors. After Golt's fall, another weakness shows itself straight away with a shell-eating nanite in Father's food supply, one that eats away part of his mandible before he can resort to an anti-nanite.

The summons to the Sanctum comes shortly afterwards and, still utterly and rigidly under his father's control, Nool can do nothing but obey it. Father waits, prosthetics already in place, and orders him to the centre of the floor. Nool fights the command but his limbs obey – limbs that are soon being torn out of their sockets and tossed about the Sanctum. This agony lasts for hours, only decreasing and finally shutting down as the most essential parts of Nool are cut away and flash-frozen.

A long time must have passed while Nool sat there in storage. Awake now and gazing out through the numerous sensors in his new shell, he does not recognize the portion of the universe he is seeing. The great defence station he launched from had existed in his own time but is now much changed, and data accessible to him makes him aware that three hundred years have passed. Utterly obedient to command, he flings himself away from the station, making the required U-space calculations to get himself to a particular location. He has weapons lying under his control, but only to be used against any interloper who tries to prevent him getting there – but none do.

As he arrives above the moon, he is able to now study himself through his own sensors. He is now a torpedo of metal with two U-engine nacelles to his rear on either side of a one-burn fusion drive. At once he knows that his existence in this form will be brief, for he recognizes what he has become. Still unable to do anything but obey, he sets a course to the surface of the moon, engaging the fusion drive, which burns dirty and hard, racking up an acceleration that no creature of flesh could survive unaided. The surface comes up at him fast, and just a microsecond before impact, he carries out his final purpose: detonating the massive contra-terrene device that is his core.

There is no pain, merely a brief unbelievable brightness.

Then nothing.

A great black macula appears on the screen, entirely covering the moon, then slowly fades to show its orb glowing bright and laval, and expanding like bread dough. Great fountains of fire explode from its surface, tearing holes in it and licking out into space. The moon continues to expand and come apart, sheets of molten rock the size of small countries peeling out into vacuum.

'Now that seems a bit drastic,' says Drooble.

'Doesn't it just?' Orbus replies, as he swings the shuttle round and heads in towards the *Gurnard*.

'Got any explanation for that?' he asks generally, as he brings the shuttle into the docking bay. Sliding past the bay doors, he observes the silvery shape of Sniper darting in to one side, heading for his own entry point to the ship.

With Gurnard showing no inclination to reply, Thirteen steps in. 'You could speculate that the Prador King does not want us to obtain any information from there.'

'But the place had already been hit,' says Orbus. 'There was nothing there that would be of any use to anyone.'

Thirteen is silent for a while, mulling this over, then from his position with his tail tethering him to the console to one side of Orbus, simply shrugs.

Soon the shuttle lies again in its bay, the docking clamps locking it down. Orbus waits impatiently for the bay to fill with air, then, when that is done, steps out and hurries through to an adjacent suiting area. Here he orders his suit to open for him. It seems to release its hold on his body reluctantly and, since there is no supporting framework here for it, folds itself down to the floor to sit like some strange metallic sculpture. Drooble also unsuits, more slowly than his Captain, and follows him as he stomps impatiently towards the bridge.

'So what the hell is going on?' he asks, as he slumps down in his Captain's chair and Drooble takes his place at the horseshoe console.

'As yet I have no explanation,' replies Gurnard, 'though certainly something very big is occurring.'

The screen image of the moon now shows it as just a spreading cloud of detritus and hot gas.

'Yeah, that's big,' agrees Drooble, then muffles a giggle.

Orbus glances at him suspiciously, then says, 'Maybe this isn't about information. Maybe the Prador simply don't want anyone to have proof of their spies inside the Graveyard?'

'Screw that.' Sniper now looms in the bridge behind them.

Orbus glances over his shoulder. 'Which means?'

'I think Sniper means,' explains Gurnard, 'that both sides have spies and supposedly secret outposts in the Graveyard, and both sides know it. They are always fighting for advantage here – it is what was once called a cold war.'

'But discovery of such a base might mean some sort of treaty violation,' Orbus suggests.

'Not, I would suggest,' Gurnard replies, 'as big a treaty violation as the sending of a Prador suicide bomb into the Graveyard to destroy such a base.'

'I see.'

'I am glad you do,' the ship AI replies, 'but I certainly don't.' Then after a pause adds, 'I am receiving communications.'

Orbus continues gazing at the spreading cloud of debris. He, Sniper and this ship have been seconded into a secret war here in this borderland: a stupid game of spies and a struggle for some advantage that might never be used. They had been used to remove an advantage gained by the Prador; then been sent to remove another one, only to find someone else got there first. Surely the Prador must know what had happened to their agent down inside that erstwhile moon, so why, upon detecting a Human ship here, did they take the dangerous and unprecedented step of sending a bomb to destroy the remains of both agent and base? No matter what angle he looks at this, he can find no plausible answer.

Abruptly the screen image flickers out, to be replaced by something very different.

'What is this?' the Captain asks.

'Even as the Graveyard was first being established, ECS was sending its robotic spies into the Third Kingdom, just as the Prador were sending theirs into the Polity,' Gurnard lectures. 'On both sides many were intercepted, but so many were sent that certainly some must have been missed. A seed, no larger than a wheat grain, was fired into the Prador Kingdom seven hundred years ago and, upon encountering a piece of spaceborn rock, it stuck and germinated, digesting rock and turning itself into a multispectrum scanner and tight-beam U-space broadcast array. Until now it has had nothing much to report.'

But it certainly seems this little electronic spy has now hit the jackpot.

In vacuum, the ten dreadnoughts wink into being, faint sparkles of spontaneously generated photons marking their entry point back into realspace. Bearing some resemblance to their makers, they are recognizable as Prador dreadnoughts; however these are sleeker than usual, stretched out so they resemble teardrops – silver teardrops. Their formation is a ring, presently viewed just off from the side. Then something else appears with a massive splash of photons in vacuum, at the precise centre of this ring.

'Bloody hell!' Orbus exclaims.

He knows just how big Prador dreadnoughts can be, often extending as much as five miles across, and those dreadnoughts out there look like the largest kind. But this thing utterly dwarfs them. Its shape is that of an upright cylinder, at least fifty miles from end to end, topped with a disc, off-centre and jutting forward, while down on its lower end, affixed on either side, are two massive nacelles in the shape of cored olives. Also positioned randomly along its length are numerous other protrusions: weapons systems, communications arrays, and even ships docked to its surface like aphids clinging to a stem.

'It seems King Oberon himself has arrived at the border,' Gurnard observes. 'But it also seems he is not the only one showing an interest.'

The scene abruptly switches to another area of space. Here, hanging in vacuum, are Polity dreadnoughts of designs as various as the ages in which they were produced. Most are spherical, though often with chunks excised from them and numerous pro- trusions about their surfaces; others are huge raptorish vessels aerodynamically shaped for battle in atmosphere or spatial gas cloud; and one is a weird-looking thing like a huge metalized liver, but its numerous tubes deploying drives and weapons instead.

'The other side of the Graveyard, I presume,' says Orbus.

'You presume correctly,' Gurnard replies. 'And now Charles Cymbeline himself would like to talk to you all.'

'Realtime U-com?' Orbus enquires.

'Yes, it is,' replies the seated corpse who now appears on the screen.

'I don't recollect anything in my job description about chasing and offing Prador spies,' says Orbus, not because he truly objects but because he feels he ought to say something.

'But since you did not take your year's pay and leave, I presume you accept that your job, for which you will be even further well paid, has changed?'

Drooble emits a snigger and Orbus turns to glare at him for a moment, before returning his attention to the screen.

Cymbeline continues, 'It seems that we have a bit of a situation at the border.'

'Huh, no shit,' says Sniper.

Cymbeline grimaces, and it isn't a pleasant sight, what with various holes opening up in his face. 'The situation is this: King Oberon, supposedly unaware that the secret is already known by Polity AIs, is determined to keep from us, and from the other Prador in his kingdom, the fact that he and his family have been heavily mutated by the Spatterjay virus. To this end he sent a certain Vrost to Spatterjay specifically to obliterate the Prador Vrell who, whilst not a member of the King's family, has also been mutated. For, knowing that Prador can be changed by the virus, it would not take long for anyone with half a brain to figure out why the King is never seen and why his family – his so-called King's Guard – always wear armour.'

'This is old news for us,' says Orbus. 'We were there, remember.'

'But Vrost failed,' says Sniper abruptly, 'didn't he?'

Orbus turns to peer at the big drone, but there is no recognizable expression to read in that molluscan face and those implacable orange eyes.

'How did you know that?' Cymbeline enquires.

'Vrell is a very very clever Prador,' says Sniper. 'When he crashed his spaceship into Vrost's, destroying his own ship in the process, he wasn't actually aboard. I saw him, returning to Vrost's ship along with the King's Guard. He'd managed to snaffle a suit of their armour.'

Cymbeline nods. 'ECS would have had no idea what happened after that, if not for one stroke of luck. ECS dreadnoughts were already en route to intercept Vrost's ship and knock it out of U-space. They weren't actually going to destroy it, because fortunately Vrost caused no loss of life on Spatterjay, but some display of power was required to make it clear to King Oberon that such ships will not be allowed to enter Polity territory with impunity. However, Vrost's ship surfaced into the real along that route before a USER could be deployed against it. The Polity dreadnoughts moved to intercept, whereupon it dropped back into U-space and fled, not, as one would have expected, along a direct route past the Graveyard and to the Prador Kingdom, but on a convoluted course into the Graveyard itself.'

'And that means?' Orbus prompts.

'Polity AIs were unsure of what this meant until some debris was retrieved, shed by Vrost's ship as it departed for the Graveyard. Included amidst that debris was one of the King's Guard, who appeared to be completely inactive. Using telefactored robots, because of the possibility of the fusion tactical within the armour being detonated, a forensic AI opened it and made a startling discovery.'

'Oh, do enlighten us,' says Sniper with affected boredom.

'The mutated Prador within was effectively dead, its nervous system eaten away by a very sophisticated and specific nano-weapon – one specific in fact to King Oberon's genome. It seems certain that this weapon was created by Vrell, and taken aboard Vrost's ship. It also seems certain that all aboard but Vrell are now dead and that he is in control of that ship. He fled to the Graveyard because, other than heading away from both Polity and Kingdom, that is the only place where neither Polity nor Kingdom ships can pursue without causing a very dangerous political incident.'

'So it was Vrell that killed our friend down on the moon here?' asks Orbus, adding with a grimace, 'Or what was once a moon.'

'It seems likely,' Cymbeline replies. 'The suicide drone was not sent to cover up evidence of a spy outpost, but to destroy any possibility of us finding evidence concerning Vrell's nature, which could easily have been left there at the scene.'

'Now ships from both the Polity and the Kingdom are waiting either side of the border,' Orbus observes.

'The situation, so I am told, is this,' Cymbeline explains. 'If ECS decides that Vrell's entry into the Graveyard is a treaty violation, and follows him, it seems likely that the King will enter too, which could be . . . very dangerous. ECS is holding off, but if Oberon enters the Graveyard first, in pursuit of Vrell, then Polity ships must perforce be ready to counter that incursion.'

'Bit of a stand-off,' observes Orbus.

'Supposedly, but it is speculated that, despite appearances, Oberon is actually aware Polity AIs know his nature, and he does intend to enter the Graveyard to *apparently* go after Vrell, hoping

ECS will see such an expedition as merely due to his need to keep his family's secret, and so will not move sufficient forces to counter it, or order other forces into place to back them up.'

'Right,' says Orbus, scratching his head.

Cymbeline continues, 'It may be, however, that he intends to seize Graveyard territory. It is also a possibility that all this has been manufactured as a diversion to cover the initial moves of an all-out attack.'

Sniper snorts with derision.

Cymbeline peers beyond Orbus at the drone. 'Yes, it seems unlikely, and the reasoning convoluted. However, if the correct moves are not made to counter this possibility, and ECS is proved wrong, that could be a mistake costing billions of lives.'

'Serious stuff then,' interjects Drooble, in a not particularly serious tone.

'This is all very interesting,' says Orbus firmly, 'but what's it got to do with us?'

'The *Gurnard* is under contract to ECS, and it is the largest apparently non-military vessel ECS has in the area.' Cymbeline is as expressionless as a corpse as he continues: 'ECS knows that, after attacking there, Vrell moved into a certain large sector of the Graveyard, but does not yet have him precisely located within that sector. You are to enter it and begin searching, because before any action is taken, we need to know where Vrell is, what he is doing, and what he intends.'

'You mean talk to him?' asks Orbus, a deep anger rising in his chest.

'Yes, I mean talk to him.' Cymbeline now gives a jerky shrug. 'And perhaps, if you see an opportunity, then do something about him.'

Sniper's laughter is hollow.

★

The Golgoloth moves on past the last of its first-children, then turns into the aisle taking it past its numerous second-children. For a moment it stops to study some that it has been trying to force into growing symmetrically, by using chemical controls and deliberate starvation of nutrients to certain portions of their bodies. In only one case out of the five has this experiment been a success, but the resultant creature is kept jerking permanently under punishment shocks as it makes no response to its screens. Checking data streams feeding straight into one of its external ganglia, the Golgoloth sees the creature is brain-dead.

Best to cut the losses now. A simple signal increases the punishment shocks to all five children, four of which scream and bubble within their frameworks, smoke rising from their carapaces. After a minute or so all movement ceases, whereupon all the feeds detach from their bodies and all the clamps open. Five Prador corpses drop to the floor below the frameworks, and ship-lice move in on this new bounty. The Golgoloth moves on, considering all it has done to keep itself alive.

Whilst the king he had made consolidated his power, the Golgoloth took some time to confront something that was becoming a bit of a problem for itself: mortality. It had already lived four times the artificially extended span of a normal Prador, but now it was becoming apparent that if it did not do something soon, it might not live to five times that span. The loss of limbs, which heretofore had only been a problem for other normal Prador of extreme old age, had begun to affect even the Golgoloth. It first lost some of its underlimbs and then a leg, but what finally impelled it to action was the loss of a claw.

Many Prador used thrall-controlled beasts, and their own kin, to serve them, and many ancient Prador were without any limbs at all, but the Golgoloth understood that, along with the loss of limbs, old Prador begin to lose contact with reality and end up being assassinated either by competitors – and all Prador are natural competitors – or by their own inadequately controlled first-children. This route was not appetizing for the Golgoloth, so something had to be done.

At the time, Prador already had a long history of experimentation with transplant technology, and why not, since there were plenty of their own kin available to supply the spare parts. But their immune systems being so powerful, rejection was always a severe problem, and the Golgoloth realized that in being able to produce kin of a very close genetic match to itself, it might be able to allay this problem somewhat. But this time, from the brood it produced it selected, rather than normal Prador, those who more closely matched itself.

When its first hermaphrodite child grew to the point where its parts might be harvested, the child acted, obviously aware of what lay in store for it. The creature nearly penetrated through to the Golgoloth's lair with one of the new beam weapons of that time, and therefore had to be incinerated by the security system. The Golgoloth thus realized that those most closely matching itself genetically were just as intelligent and dangerous as itself. Its next brood it confined in secure cells until they grew large enough, whereupon it could make its first harvest.

The most essential replacement at that point involved a large proportion of an organ that is a combination of both liver and kidneys. To be able to make this transplantation, the Golgoloth spent many years perfecting surgical robots controlled by the increasingly sophisticated computers of the Prador. The job was then done, but the Golgoloth required massive doses of anti-rejection drugs thereafter.

History advanced apace. The Prador race as a whole, though prepared to use sophisticated computers, was never prepared to develop them into artificial intelligences. Instead they used transplant and thrall technology to enslave the organic minds of their own kin. Thus engines for throwing spaceships through underspace were designed by a conglomerate of first-child minds which was immediately exterminated thereafter, for it was felt to be too powerful a thinker. Other similar conglomerates were made and then destroyed and technology advanced rapidly and, still within the era of the Second King, the Prador went to the stars. Upon encountering Humans, their natural xenophobia pushed the Prador to even greater technological advances, and very soon they were ready.

By this time the Golgoloth had perfected its very own personal transplant routine and, after a group of its children attempted to escape their cells, it first tried severing their major nerve trunks and directing all other physical control externally by optic feeds, but that resulted in the degeneration of nerve tissue. Thereafter it took the precaution of confining them in frameworks little different from these now standing before it. This turned out to be the safest and most productive method of confinement, though now the Golgoloth takes the precaution of surgically installing optic feeds in its offspring, so it can more closely observe the growth process, make required refinements, and conduct experiments. Perfecting such techniques during the first encounters with Humankind had also been a necessity, because the Golgoloth realized it would soon need to be able to survive independent of the rest of the Kingdom.

The Second King ignored the Golgoloth's advice against attacking these horrible soft but obviously quite advanced creatures called Humans. Whilst continuing in an advisory capacity, the hermaphrodite rapidly prepared itself for the predicted fall of the Second Kingdom, for its King was now ancient, stubborn and prone to error. It expected this fall to be brought about by the Humans, so it came as a surprise when a Prador mutated by the Spatterjay virus returned to homeworld to usurp the Second

King. In the vessel it had diverted funds from nearly one-tenth of the Prador economy to construct, the Golgoloth managed to escape the ensuing – and lengthy – bloody aftermath.

Exiting the long chamber containing its utterly confined and steadily growing children, the Golgoloth heads for the main communication centre of its vessel. The equipment in that place is easily enough accessed from its armoured lair, but the hermaphrodite is wary of so confining itself, for that leads to a hermetic and defensive state of mind, and it needs to stay sharp if it is to survive in this ever-changing universe.

Upon assuming power, the Third King halted the attack on the Polity and withdrew Prador forces, and the Humans, showing more restraint than any of the Golgoloth's own kind would have shown, only followed them as far as the original border between their two realms. Had they been Prador, the war would have continued further, probably resulting in yet more denuded planets and further billions dead, and ultimately both the Polity and the Prador Kingdom falling apart. The Golgoloth felt some admiration for these soft creatures until it realized that had it been entirely down to them, the war *would* have continued, but it was their artificial intelligences that made the cold assessment that a war of extermination was not worth the cost.

Oberon, then as now, was incredibly intelligent and dangerous, and had he understood the true nature of the previous King's rise to power, he would not have let the Golgoloth escape. However, shortly after establishing himself on homeworld he found this out, and dispatched numerous returning warships to search for the escapee. The Golgoloth then fled from hideaway to hideaway in the Third Kingdom, coming close to capture on many occasions. Finally it chose a destination where warships could not follow, and established itself in the borderland, the Graveyard.

Entering its spherical communications centre, the Golgoloth

climbs onto a circular dais positioned at the very centre, which is then propelled upwards by a wide pillar. From here it can observe the hundreds of surrounding screens, and sometimes, using those same screens, create VR effects about itself that entirely banish the surrounding room and produce the illusion of placing the hermaphrodite just about anywhere its sensors are positioned. Through an external ganglion it initiates a whole bank of hexagonal screens directly before it. For a moment they show only an enormous wide open area, all aseptically white. Then something even more monstrous than the Golgoloth itself steps into view.

'So you are not dead,' says this thing.

'And you, as always, are very much alive, King Oberon,' the Golgoloth replies.

Consciousness slides within grasp, and then away again, in the mind that knows itself as the Prador Ebror – yet, in brief moments of lucidity, knows that it cannot be Ebror. Does not the nanite Vrell released destroy all nerve tissue, including the major ganglion? How can Ebror now exist without a brain to hold him?

The armour within which these thoughts occur first contained Ebror's heavily mutated Prador body, whose shell had softened over the years, and often, in those years immediately before his death, attached itself to the inside of his armour. But now rapid change is occurring. The original Prador nervous system is gone, but the Spatterjay virus immediately seeks to replace it by copying from the relevant strands of some glister genome it contains.

Growth is rapid but the viral organism in which this network of nerves and neurons grows rapidly burns up nutrients, and is soon starving. Aware, on some base level, that it is constantly in motion, the organism grows leech mouths with which to feed, but they suck ineffectually against the armour's interior. It tries a human skull, jaws and teeth, lines it with flesh, but this also beats itself to no purpose against hard metal confining it. It attaches glister nerves to Prador eyes and other senses, sees that it truly is moving in an environment where other things move, other things that must surely be food, but it just cannot reach them. In its efforts to do so, it reattaches to Prador muscles that also fight against the armour, but to no effect. It grows hard little claws, tubular siphons, belts of teeth and, surprisingly, even manages to obtain some nutrient as it chews up the softer lining inside the armour, but this is a limited resource.

Once all this insulation is gone, along with anything else that can possibly be digested, the viral creature goes through its entire collection of Spatterjay genomes as it tries every possible insentient strategy it can find to feed – and gets nowhere. Genetic strands are tried, energy burnt, and the strands themselves digested as the virus hungrily breaks up the phosphates, sugars and other compounds that bind them together. Working its way down through the layers of collected genomes, it eventually runs out of familiar options to try and reaches those segments of alien code that lie at its heart.

The moment the virus touches the first segment, rapid change ensues. The alien genome keys in to certain ancient chemical sockets within the virus, and takes command of it, impelling it to immediately link to every other fragment of alien code it contains. Now completely in control, the alien genome begins shutting down all futile attempts to escape from the enclosing armour. It shuts down every superfluous use of energy and applies all remaining resources to grow a new neural structure: a brain. It then begins loading into this the mind of the Prador Ebror, which – even though Ebror's brain has been destroyed – is imprinted on the virus itself. It shortly follows this with an upload of quantum-stored information from itself, though only a little, for there is not yet enough room for it all. The segments also begin to throw off the structures of life, *its life:* its equivalents to proteins, amino acids, enzymes and RNA, and gradually unravels throughout the process. All of these structures are infinitely more complex, yet more ordered, than everything used beforehand, and they quickly begin to digest and displace their predecessors.

As the new brain grows, the larger portions of it take over control of the viral mycelium and use it to explore its environment, building a virtual model of that environment within the mind, applying other loaded data, then coming up with entirely new strategies. The mycelium uses acids to etch away metal from the interior of the armour, forms this into nano-wires at its core, creates an electrical network and wires it into organo-electric interfaces in the brain. Free ends of the mycelium then connect into little joins and junctions in the armour, and begin inserting the nano-wires. It makes connections at random, some direct and some inductive, but, utterly not at random, it interprets the data gathered and tentatively begins to input some of its own.

Sub-AI programs created by Vrell begin to change, corrupt, and reorder themselves, and the armour they control begins to shift and shudder in disturbing ways.

And something that has been dead for four million years starts to open its eyes.

8

It has been well documented that those who survive catastrophic events, in which they see many of their fellows die, will suffer survivor guilt. This guilt is stronger still when they have done things in order to survive for which they have every reason to feel guilty. But the concentration-camp victim forced to stack decaying bodies or feed them into the furnace is not the one I am referring to here. No, it is the one who survives at someone else's direct and immediate expense. When Jay Hoop and the rest of the Eight established their massive concentration camps on Spatterjay, they delighted in forcing such a situation upon their captives, and the horrible games they played are legend. They regularly conducted 'hunts' through the island dingles, using one captive as a 'hound' and another as a 'rabbit'. If a hound did not bring down a rabbit during such a hunt, the hound himself went for coring; and if he did, then it was the rabbit who was taken away to have his brain and spinal cord cut out. Other groups of captives were forced to vote on who in their group would go for coring next; and similar groups were sometimes stuck in a room with just one open door, and the first five to fight their way out got to survive that day. Sometimes victims were made to perform sex-acts with animals, and men were instructed to rape and often torture women, other men or children for the entertainment of the Eight. If they did not follow instruction they were cored. In this way no depravity was neglected. Jay Hoop especially enjoyed forcing some of the captives to skin others alive, which goes some way to explaining his later incarnation as The Skinner. Many of those who thus survived the rule of the Eight on Spatterjay were later hunted down and killed by more innocent survivors. Many eventually killed themselves, though some still exist, it is said. Certainly they understand the concept of survivor guilt.

– From QUINCE GUIDE *compiled by Humans*

The stink of Human excrement is almost a taste in the air, and the groaning, the crying and sometimes the screaming whenever someone wakes up to find a ship-louse chewing into him provides a perpetual racket. In the crowded hold, Orbus nudges the blanket-wrapped bundle at his feet, then reaches over to drag it closer. With shaking hands he opens the short penknife the Prador have not bothered to relieve him of, leans down and pulls at the stained blanket and, after a moment, a child's arm flops out. It is still warm, so he checks for a pulse but finds none, then he reveals the head, and one glance is all he needs to confirm this little girl is dead. Her head is misshapen, crushed by an inadvertent blow from one of the second-child guards that comes in to snatch up the latest complement of corpses.

Checking about furtively Orbus sees that those nearby are too lost in their own misery to even notice what he is doing. Many are asleep, which is one of the best reliefs to the perpetual gnawing hunger, others just stare blank-eyed into shadows. The lack of light will help him here too, since he is some distance from the phosphorescent growths on the wall. He cuts into the muscle just below her elbow, sawing down to bone, then cuts down along the bone itself to just before her wrist, then out again, and extracts a chunk of flesh the size of a banana. Pulling the heat-sheet he has stolen from another corpse over his head, he leans forwards and tries to bite off a piece of the child's flesh. It is raw, salty, and causes his mouth to well with saliva, but in the end he can't get his teeth through it, so has to cut through it with his penknife held in front of his mouth. A great deal of chewing later, with bits of sinew lodging between his teeth, he finally swallows the great claggy lump and comes close to vomiting. But he cannot allow that, and soon the nausea passes.

The remaining flesh he cuts carefully into small pieces, feeding them one after another into his mouth, then he leans forward again and quickly cuts further chunks from the corpse, concealing them in his jacket. Upon spotting one of the other prisoners nearby beginning to take notice off him, Orbus covers the girl's remains, stands up and moves steadily away. He takes a drink from the wall spigot – at least water is no problem here – before returning to seat himself with his back against the wall – a place he has made his own, and manages to retain because he remains physically strong while others weaken. He left just in time. A sudden hysterical screaming issues from the girl's mother as she discovers what has happened to her daughter's corpse. Later, the small self-elected group of vigilantes present beats to death a man who happens to be lying nearby, but even they are weakening and it takes them some time. Later still, the second-children come and empty a small bag of decaying human food on the floor, then with unerring precision collect both the girl and the innocent victim of the vigilantes. The mother makes no protest this time, which Orbus thinks unfair. She shrieked blue murder upon discovering some occupant of the hold had cut away parts of her little girl for food, yet keeps silent when these monsters take the dead girl away for precisely the same reason.

'We are all going to die,' says the youth seated against the wall next to Orbus.

'I'm going to live,' Orbus murmurs quietly.

The Old Captain snaps out of uneasy slumber, then carefully removes his fist from the hole he's just smashed into the wall beside him. The lights in his cabin are on, activated by this sudden movement.

It wasn't just a nightmare; if only that were the case. The

memory has never before been so utterly clear and horribly detailed. He heaves himself up on his bed and rests his back against the wall, gazing into those memories, that clear one and others not so clear. The vigilantes caught four others who were surviving by using the same horribly practical method as himself. They killed two of them outright, but only managed to kill one of the other two while she was asleep. The remaining cannibal spoke out and won others to his side, even some of the vigilantes themselves. The choice was to either eat Human flesh or die. Orbus pretended reluctance, eating what was given to him, but supplementing it from the cache in his own jacket.

Orbus wonders why such an utterly clear memory has surfaced now, and finds a confusing answer just as a sudden surge of anger sends heat flushing down his back.

Vrell.

Before the mutated Prador seized both Orbus and his crew, everything had been so blessedly hazy. By subjecting him to old horror, Vrell shook him back to consciousness, yet . . . Yet, though he feels a deep instinctive rage against the Prador, he also feels a gratitude. The animal organic part of himself wants to retreat into rage, mindless violence and sadism, but everything superior to that – all that might be described as his higher self – is glad of this return to painful sanity. Yet, again, though he might be grateful that Vrell's actions coaxed him to his present condition, the Prador had not intended to do him a favour. It had subjected him to hideous pain, drowning and thralldom, and even Orbus's higher self feels that is a debt to be repaid. Then, again, is his higher self being influenced by . . .

Orbus angrily throws back the cover, swings his legs over the side of the bed and stands. He walks over to gaze at a wall mirror and inspects the massive bulk of his naked body, blue rings of scar tissue cicatricing its surface so it looks almost scaled. Centuries of leech bites, centuries spent in a place deep inside his skull where memories could not find him, and now standing here with a body that is more viral fibres than Human flesh.

Am I still Human?

He turns away and opens a cupboard, takes out his neatly stacked clothing and dons it, then swiftly exits his cabin and heads for the bridge, even now realizing that it wasn't any surfacing of old memory that woke him, but the *Gurnard* surfacing into the realspace of their destination.

Vrell ignores the hissing and clattering racket behind him, instead studying intently the nanoscope images displayed on the hexagonal screens before him. It seems that the mutated third-child, now struggling perpetually against the clamps securing it to a surgical saddle, is a complete viral organism. Previously, its mutated genome had remained distinct from the viral fibres occupying its body, but now there is no distinction between them. The separate cells of its body are blurred together, and the engines of cell division and growth sit in a nub at the end of each viral fibre penetrating every cell. Using nanoscopic tools Vrell excises one of these nubs, opens out great lumpy strands of genetic tissue and begins mapping it. Five hours later he realizes that the processing space he has provided for this task is nowhere near enough, and so provides more.

Checking the ship's records of genome samples, Vrell at length realizes that this creature's nervous system regrew by using a combined blueprint of both the Spatterjay glister and hammer-whelk. He then sets programs to automatically check everything being mapped against records whilst the process itself continues. After ten hours, less than 3 per cent of the entire genome has been mapped, but even in that small portion Vrell finds that within its collection the virus holds strands of the genomes of the ocean heirodont, the lung-bird, the frog-whelk and of course the Spatter-jay leech itself, though only fragmented strands. Vrell tips back with a sigh and considers what he is doing and how this might help him achieve his own ends, and realizes such research will probably be of no help at all. He understands then just how radically he himself has changed, for no real Prador would allow scientific curiosity to divert it from the serious business of vengeance.

Mildly distracted, he is considering the mass of genetic tissue now being revealed when an errant thought occurs to him. Since any planetary ecology has at its root, in the far past, the same life-form, there should thus be a sizeable duplication of code across various species. Even Prador possess much of the same code as simple seaweeds back on their homeworld. Vrell has so far found neither duplication nor junk genetic material, yet without these this sample is far too big and complicated. The entire ecology of Spatterjay could easily fit into about a quarter of it and, even if Human DNA and some of the other species they took to that world with them were to be included, that still leaves a lot of genetic material unaccounted for.

Vrell shakes himself. Stupid . . . and paranoid. Almost certainly the genetic bulk he is seeing is due to junk genome and pointless replication he has yet to discover. Life only conforms to the logic of environment, not the kind of mathematical logic of those who build artificial life-forms. There is always a huge amount of waste, redundancy, parasitic genetic tissue . . . Still Vrell feels an unease he cannot shake, for everything he is now seeing, besides lacking such waste, seems far too logically ordered, far too much like the construct of some builder rather than the product of normal evolution.

The program comparing the genetic material with everything on record steadily continues to build up a list, and only now does

Vrell note how it is perpetually rescanning certain molecular constructs already mapped. Checking, he sees that it has there found complex strands it cannot identify. These must be from life-forms on Spatterjay yet to be discovered, and their genomes mapped. It is only upon closer inspection, upon discovering that the unidentified segments are a form of trihelical genetic material whose bases don't even come close to that of the Spatterjay samples, that Vrell realizes he has in fact found something utterly alien. Perhaps, far in the past, there were other visitors to that world . . . It must have been far in the past, because the collection of genetic material seems to be layered in a historical pattern, and these are down deep – the deepest of all.

Vrell shivers, his unease growing. He now abruptly focuses his study upon the viral strands holding all this together, and allowing only parts of it to replicate. Gradually he builds up a picture of it in his mind, keying together molecular components and attempting to understand the underlying logic of its structure. Realization slams into him all at once. Now focused on the virus rather than its eclectic collection of genetic material he understands perfectly what he is seeing. A large proportion of this virus is no natural product of evolution, though evolution has made its weight felt and the thing has been changed by it. The virus was tampered with, added to, the additions being something made by an intelligent mind. Though these extras resemble what is described as life, they are in fact an incredibly complex collection of organic-base nanomachines working in perfect concert. And they must have been added long before either Humans or Prador crawled out of their ancestral mud.

A worrying thought now occurs to him. Could there be some connection between this and the odd code, and behaviour he has been noticing in the King's Guard? No, surely not. Though what exists inside their armour might bear some resemblance to this creature, it has no source of nutrient and so will eventually become somnolent, and hibernate.

He backs away from the screens and turns to inspect the creature clamped into the surgical saddle, and notes that its shell, such as it is, has turned rubbery underneath the clamps, and the creature is already gaining a greater compass of movement. Suddenly reaching out, Vrell disconnects the clamps and, as the creature tries lunging for him, closes his claw about its body and carries it across to a large cryostore, opens the circular portal, then thrusts it inside and slams the door shut. Peering through a small window in the door, he observes the thing crashing about inside, knocking sample bottles out of their racks as, using a pit control, Vrell winds the internal temperature down to minus a hundred and fifty degrees Celsius. As the cryostore's systems struggle to bring its interior temperature down to that level, the creature's antics grow steadily more sluggish and here and there it begins to develop cracks in its body. But even when the pit control emits its even tone indicating that target temperature has been achieved, the thing is still moving.

Continuing to watch, Vrell notes that its carapace has turned a bright yellow, and that some tar-like substance has begun oozing out of the cracks to seal them. Still it moves, very slowly extending a transparent siphon into a puddle of spill from one of the sample bottles. Perhaps it was some organic sample, Vrell speculates, before even thinking to turn on the small screen beside the cryostore and study its manifest.

The store contains genetic samples of Terran life-forms, but this does not arouse any suspicions in Vrell. This thing has quite obviously detected a source of nourishment. He knocks the temperature setting down even lower, as the thing now squirts some black fluid down through its siphon – still liquid even at this temperature – into the sample, which dissolves, whereupon the creature slowly sucks it all back up again. Now, in utter slow motion, the creature raises one armoured tentacle and brings it down on another bottle. But its movements are becoming so slow, they are almost indetectable. Vrell moves away from the cryo-store, putting together in his mind a series of experiments he now intends to conduct. However, just then he receives a notification through one of his control units: a ship has arrived in this same sector of the Graveyard.

'What is it that you are seeking?' the Golgoloth asks, peering at the monster displayed on the screens before him.

'I seek to become,' replies Oberon, King of the Prador. 'But I have a problem,' he adds.

'You have a problem,' the Golgoloth repeats, simultaneously analysing that first statement, which is one Oberon often comes out with. Certainly, over the centuries in which the Golgoloth has communicated with the King, his form has changed radically. But precisely what does Oberon seek to become?

'Do you for ever want to remain a refugee, Golgoloth?' Oberon counters. 'Would you not prefer to come home?'

'Of course, but the ruler of the kingdom I fled has always shown far too much interest in me, and . . .' the Golgoloth pauses momentarily, '. . . it is never healthy to be the subject of any ruling Prador's interest.'

'That statement is true,' replies Oberon, 'if the ruling Prador is of the normal Prador stock, but I, like yourself, can hardly be described as such.'

'Even so, I still think it unlikely that your interest in me concerns my good health, long life and happiness.'

'But this time I mean you no harm.'

The Golgoloth pauses. Over the centuries they have conducted this discussion in many different forms, and every now and then

Oberon has offered amnesty if the Golgoloth will return to the Kingdom to work for the King himself. However, on every previous occasion the Golgoloth saw through that offer and discovered, through his own robotic spies within the Kingdom, that there was something specific the King was after that required the Golgoloth's input. On early occasions that input included tracking down the Second King's treasury, and also finding a secret military base where biological weapons were being developed. On a more recent occasion it was to find the Golgoloth's own abandoned memstores that were packed with a mass of useful data about Prador genetics, and some more besides about the viral form of Spatterjay which, when Golgoloth resided within the Kingdom, had only been known about for a few decades. But now things have changed.

The Golgoloth gazes at the creature displayed on his screen. Once the King was a pure Prador, but is nothing like that now. The hermaphrodite knows Oberon possesses a formidable intelligence that, in the beginning, was the equal of the Golgoloth's own. But that intelligence has grown over the centuries, perhaps now surpassing the Golgoloth's, even though the Golgoloth has perpetually added to its own brain-power with internal and external ganglion grafts. This is perhaps why Oberon's offers of amnesty have gradually tailed off, since Oberon, growing in mindpower, wants less and less from the Golgoloth. In fact, their infrequent communications have, over the last century, mostly been complex conversations of the kind Oberon cannot conduct with any of his fellows inside the Kingdom. The Golgoloth is a like mind, someone to bounce ideas off and with whom to debate increasingly obscure branches of science and philosophy, but otherwise has become an irrelevance.

'What do you want?' the Golgoloth asks.

'You understand, of course,' says Oberon, 'that I no longer

require anything from you related to your previous hidden influence within the Second Kingdom. You understand that if you were to return here now, you would be of value to me only as a mind that can grasp at least a little of my own compass of thought.'

'Arrogantly Pradorish.'

'The truth, nevertheless.'

'So you're asking me to come back just to be your buddy, are you?'

'In time, perhaps, but really I am offering you something you'll want to come back for – something you have always wanted to come back for.'

The Golgoloth shifts uncomfortably. 'I am not sure there is anything in the Kingdom I want that much.'

'Of course there is, Golgoloth,' says the King. 'Do you think I don't understand you at all? You have remained alive for longer than just about any creature within either the Kingdom or the Polity, except – and this is the entire point – those creatures which were native to Spatterjay long before either Humans or Prador arrived there, for on that planet reside living sails and deep-ocean whelks who exceed you in age by an order of magnitude.'

'This is no news to me,' the Golgoloth interjects.

'You, Golgoloth, have an appetite for life that exceeds that of our fellow Prador, and also possess the intelligence and skills to maintain that life. You butcher your children to provide you with an endless supply of transplants, and I have no doubt that you have obtained a sample of the Spatterjay virus. So why haven't you used it?'

'I proceed with caution.'

'You proceed with fear and too rigid a grasp on your existence. You will never allow that virus into your body until you fully understand it and what it will do to you, what it will do to you over the ensuing centuries of your life, because, my friend, I well understand that you intend to live until the suns go out and, if at all possible, even beyond that time.'

The Golgoloth dips its head in appreciation. 'An accurate assessment.'

'And,' the King now adds, 'there is only one place where you can study the long-term effects of the Spatterjay virus on Prador – and only certain Prador you particularly want to study. And those are myself and my family.'

'I see. So what is this problem I can help you with, for which you are prepared to allow me access to youself and your children?'

'The problem is called Vrell,' Oberon replies. 'He is an adult Prador hiding in the Graveyard, an adult Prador recently infected with the Spatterjay virus, and as such a rather younger version of myself. He is dangerous, and I need him to cease to exist, and quickly.'

In light of this latest revelation, the Golgoloth immediately begins to assess in depth everything Oberon has already told him. Does the King genuinely fear he will be usurped by this younger version of himself? Surely not, for seven centuries lie between them, and Oberon has to be vastly superior in development to the younger version. Oberon obviously does not want to send forces straight into the Graveyard because, no matter how advanced the King himself now is, he is still an organic being and would be dropping himself into a whole world of hurt if he went up against the Polity and its artificial intelligences. So why this, now? Why, really, should the King be sufficiently concerned about this Vrell to be prepared to call on the Golgoloth's assistance?

The Golgoloth onlines the ganglion, long unused and there-fore sluggish to respond, in which he has stored all his knowledge about the Spatterjay virus. It has not used this ganglion for some time because, just as the King said, he wants to study the virus's long-term effects – a line of research truncated here in the Grave-yard. Once again it finds itself reminded that the virus is an arti-ficial life-form that as well as holding within its matrix a collection of Spatterjay genomes, also holds there something utterly alien. Could the King's present fear be something to do with that? Could it be that this young Prador might find something there that the King has missed, or take some course the King himself has neglected?

Or is it that Oberon has no real fear of this youngster? That this is merely a way of bringing the Golgoloth out of hiding?

'I am waiting for your response,' says the King.

The Golgoloth shakes itself out of its reverie. When dealing with a being as complex as the King, there are just too many possibilities, too many probable convolutions to his plans, his plots. However, if it is true that this Vrell is in the Graveyard, as described, the Golgoloth wants to study him.

'I will find this Vrell,' it replies.

'Is that your only response?'

'For the moment.'

With frightening speed for something so large, King Oberon moves out of view and the Golgoloth closes down the link.

Of course, a simpler explanation covers all this. Vrell, just like the Golgoloth itself, is a potential competitor, and getting compet-itors to try and tear each other apart is an old manoeuvre in the Prador Kingdom. Just politics really.

Stepping into the bridge of the *Gurnard*, Orbus gazes out at the glimmering stars and suddenly feels very alone. The ship seems unnaturally quiet with neither the drones nor Drooble present here. But it is impossible to be truly alone on a ship like this.

'Have you detected the target?' he enquires.

After a noticeable delay, Gurnard replies, 'I have.'

'That was quick.'

'Vrell has placed his ship in close orbit around an unstable green sun, which is enough to conceal it from long-range detection but not enough to conceal it from me here.'

'How far away is it?'

'One and a half light-years.'

'So why aren't we closer?'

'Our arrival in this sector of the Graveyard in one jump is something Vrell might consider a coincidence. But if we now jump to his present location, he will know for sure we are here searching for him.'

'And?'

'I was waiting for some input from my Captain and crew. And I also have further news to impart.'

Orbus walks round his Captain's chair and seats himself there. 'Where are they?'

'Sniper, who has been spending rather a lot of time scanning the contents of my holds, is even now on his way. Thirteen, who has been supervising Iannus Drooble's latest visit to the Medbay for intravenous nutrients, is bringing Iannus here.'

Orbus impatiently rattles his fingers on one chair arm, and after a moment becomes aware of a shadow looming up into the bridge. Glancing round he observes Sniper enter and then slide round to one side of him, settling down on the floor with a heavy crunch.

'Orbus,' the big drone acknowledges him.

'What's so interesting in the hold, then?' Orbus enquires.

'Some weird items down there.' Sniper waves a spatulate tentacle towards the rear doors of the bridge. 'There's an entire ocean heirodont in stasis and another cylinder full of leeches.' The big drone pauses for a moment. 'Oddly, there's even a cargo of sprine, and some multiguns specially formatted to deliver it as a weapon. . . . Any idea what that's all about, Gurnard?'

Again the delay before Gurnard replies. 'It was placed aboard by the same agent who approached Cymbeline about the original mission out here. He thought it might be useful to have some of the substance aboard, since it seems likely we will be encountering the King's Guard, who are all virally mutated.'

Orbus feels himself go cold at the mention of sprine. It is an Old Captain's get-out clause. The stuff is produced in the bile ducts of giant ocean-going leeches on Spatterjay when they make the transition from plug-feeders to eating whole prey. It quickly kills the virus within that prey, enabling the leech to then digest it. Sprine extracted from those bile ducts, and then refined, kills virally infected humans even faster. Old Captains, being virtually unkillable by most normal means, always like to keep some to hand in case life should became too unbearable for them. They also keep it just in case they fall into Spatterjay's ocean, so they can choose a quick death rather than the nightmare of an endless agonized existence under the waves. But Orbus is puzzled.

'Seems a daft idea when all the Guard always wear armour,' he says. 'I can't think of many portable delivery systems that can punch through that.'

'The multiguns will certainly not punch through Prador armour,' Gurnard concurs. 'I believe the agent just wanted to make another option available, no matter how remote the chances of it ever being used successfully. It is not as if it is taking up useful space . . .'

It seems a dubious explanation.

Thirteen floats in next, with Drooble in tow, clutching to his tail so that the drone looks like some sort of toy balloon.

'Cap'n,' Drooble murmurs, his expression slightly bewildered.

'You all right now, Iannus?'

'Never better,' says Drooble, releasing Thirteen's tail and going to take his usual seat at the horseshoe console.

Orbus studies him for a moment. Despite the ongoing medical care, he seems worse than he appeared directly after his first visit to Medbay. That sometimes happens, of course – a delayed reaction to the effects of the virus gaining ground in a patient's body. Drooble requires watching, which is why, Orbus suspects, Thirteen is never far off. Orbus turns away.

'Now, let's get something straight,' he says. 'Our instructions are to find out what Vrell is up to, and possibly do something about him? I'm buggered if I know how we can achieve either.'

'Ah, but we gotta use our own initiative,' says Sniper sarcastically.

Orbus shakes his head, 'For all we know, Vrell might have turned into a Prador version of the Skinner, so I doubt he'll be reasonable.'

'We don't really know that,' says Drooble, his voice somehow yearning in tone.

Orbus glances at him, wondering just what is going on in his mind, then continues, 'I'm betting that the moment we move in close, he'll attack and try spreading the *Gurnard* all over vacuum, and then he'll find somewhere else to hide.'

'Which is why,' interjects Gurnard, 'you need something to offer – something that might be of real value to him.'

'Like what?' asks Sniper.

'Like an amnesty for crimes he committed within the Polity, and also the freedom to live there without interference,' Gurnard replies.

'You what?' says Orbus in surprise.

'You heard,' the ship AI replies.

'One of my crew died inside his ship,' growls the Captain.

'There is sufficient doubt about how that man died. We cannot prove it was not an accident, just as Vrell claimed at the time.'

'Yeah, but is that very likely?'

'Who can say?' Gurnard wonders. 'Who can say how certain members of the crew aboard your sailing ship, the *Vignette*, met their end over the years?'

'So ECS is offering Vrell an amnesty,' says Sniper, now that Orbus falls silent.

'King Oberon wants Vrell dead because, through him, Polity AIs might learn about virally infected Prador and come to understand Oberon's nature,' says Gurnard.

'Wait a minute,' says Sniper. 'What about this being a possible seizure of Graveyard territory or the first moves in an attack on the Polity?'

'Though that idea was mooted,' Gurnard observes, 'it has now been dismissed. If Oberon wants to seize Graveyard territory he would do better to just seize it without warning, and the same rule applies to any attack on the Polity. Therefore leading Polity AIs have now gone back to first causes: Oberon wants Vrell dead, and the fact that he has positioned himself, and a portion of his forces, at the border inclines those AIs to now believe there is some time factor involved here. Oberon wants Vrell out of circulation fast, and is perhaps not prepared to wait until he decides to venture outside the Graveyard.'

'Time factor?' asks Orbus, looking up again.

'Vrell has shown himself to be very dangerous indeed but we still cannot see how a virally infected Prador could pose a real danger to Oberon. Unless, of course, some other factor is involved. Earth Central believes there is something else about Vrell, something else about this whole situation, that is not entirely clear yet.'

The ship lurches abruptly, the screens greying out, then Orbus feels his brain trying to turn inside-out as the vessel drops into underspace.

'How long will it take us to get there?' Orbus asks.

'With the current U-space geometry, just twenty minutes.'

Orbus nods, stands up, and abruptly departs the bridge. Doubtless, once they arrive, Gurnard will try communicating with Vrell, and just maybe things will proceed without too many problems thereafter. However, Orbus does not really expect things to go so easily, and so heads directly to the docking ring to find his armoured spacesuit. Upon his arrival in the suiting room, he gazes at the thing still folded into a strange sculpture on the floor and seemingly waiting for him. He steps into the boots and the suit starts to fold itself up around his body, quickly enclosing him, whereupon he steps over and picks up the multigun that keys into the suit. Pausing for a moment, he studies the weapon, then thoughtfully puts it down again whilst opening com through the suit itself.

'Where are those multiguns that can deliver sprine?' he asks Gurnard.

The ship AI's reply is prompt this time. 'I've just sent a guidance package to your suit, so follow it down into the hold.'

Orbus's visor abruptly closes up, whereupon an arrow starts to blink down in the bottom corner. He follows it to the exit from the suiting room, then down a corridor leading towards the zero-gravity hold area. He pauses for a moment at the doorway into that large dark space, peers at quadrate frameworks packed with mysteriously wrapped cargoes, and begins checking his suit controls for the gecko function of the boots, or the impeller jets. There is no need, however, for out of the shadows comes one of those disconcerting earwig handler-robots. Clasped in its pincers is a package, a long, brushed-aluminium case, and he presents it. As

Orbus takes it, the handler opens its pincers wide with a loud snap, then turns and jets itself back into its benighted home.

In the corridor outside the hold, Orbus opens the aluminium case to reveal a multigun inside, secured in shaped foam, with all its auxiliary devices, spare ammunition and necessary power packs. He begins hanging the spares on his belt, then pauses to inspect a tubular magazine: Sprine MXC – explosive needle bullets containing sprine. Checking over the multigun he also finds an option for firing a beam of magnetically accelerated sprine dust, but the rest of the weapon's functions are much the same as those of the one he left behind in the suiting room. He takes it up and heads back towards the bridge.

'I see you are taking precautions,' Sniper observes as he re-enters.

Ignoring the comment, Orbus heads for his chair but, peering at it, realizes that wearing this spacesuit he won't fit. Instead he lays the multigun down on it, and turns to gaze at the greyness currently displayed on the screens. After a few minutes it flickers, and again Orbus experiences that horrible twisting sensation as the *Gurnard* surfaces into the real. A beat, and then the stars to one side are blanked out by a massive explosion.

'Evasive manoeuvres,' announces Gurnard flatly.

'Are you speaking to Vrell?' Orbus enquires.

No reply.

'He's a bit busy now,' Sniper observes, as the ship lurches and the still visible starfields spiral. Something silvery flickers past one of the eye windows, and a boom echoes deep within the ship. Orbus feels grav fluxing underneath him.

'A suit might be a good idea at that,' says Drooble, standing up only to be flung sprawling as the ship lurches again.

'Vrell is not talking,' explains Gurnard, voice still monotone.

Orbus, still perfectly in balance, his suit motors and now the gecko function of his boots keeping him upright, turns to Sniper. 'How good is your chameleonware?'

'The best,' Sniper replies.

'Good enough to cover me as well?'

'I guess.'

Orbus turns to Drooble, as the man drags himself back to his seat. 'You have the bridge, Iannus.' Back to Sniper, 'You and I are going to find an airlock.'

Sniper turns and, with all speed, shoots out of the rear of the bridge. Orbus snatches up his weapon then runs after the drone, his suit again compensating for balance and powering him along so that, even with grav fluctuations, he runs smoothly.

'I cannot stay here for much longer,' announces Gurnard.

'When we've gone, pull back, but try to keep track of him,' Orbus replies, swerving to keep up with Sniper as the drone heads for an unfamiliar part of the docking ring. 'I'm presuming you have some sort of negotiating package from Earth Central concerning this amnesty?' Soon they pass through a cargo tunnel into an empty shuttle bay, the door automatically clanging shut behind. As soon as pumps begin to suck out the air, Orbus's suit visor slams shut.

'I do,' Gurnard replies through his suit com.

'Transmit a copy to Sniper, and to the memspace of my suit.'

'Done.'

A little icon lights up down at the bottom of Orbus's visor, blinks for a moment and goes out.

'You sure about this?' Sniper asks.

'As sure as I can be about anything,' the Old Captain replies.

Sniper's tentacles enwrap his body and draw him close, as grav shuts down and the interlocking crenellations of the doors begin to pull apart. Then they are outside, falling through night, the *Gurnard* veering away just as the beam from a particle cannon scours past it. Momentarily they hover in the light glare of *Gurnard*'s fusion motors, then comes massive acceleration, which Orbus feels even in such a protective suit, as Sniper pulls them clear. The *Gurnard* folds out of existence, and Orbus finds himself hurtling down towards a Prador dreadnought that looks like it has been sent out too early from its construction yard.

'This is going to be rough,' Sniper informs him. 'I can't use my engine until we're in real close, so we'll hit hard. Your suit should be able to handle it, and you might be able to as well.'

A massive scaffold spears up past them, and a great wall of brassy metal hurtles up like the top of an elevator. Fusion flame, blinding, and Orbus feels himself being compressed into one side of his suit. Momentary corrections from steering thrusters next, then, rather than hit the wall of exotic metal, they slam into scaffolds and tension cables, Sniper's shell taking the brunt of the impact. They crunch down in a maze of twisted metal, to finally land in a ninety-degree conjunction between something like a sheet of riveted steel and a wall composed of diamond-shaped chunks of foamed porcelain. Sniper's tentacles star out all about them, holding them in place as the Prador dreadnought makes another one or two vicious manoeuvres, then zero-gravity gradually returns. Orbus just lies there thinking that only a tap will be necessary to remove him from this outer garment now. His whole body feels as if it has been smashed to jelly.

9

Even the Prador have their myths and legends, but they are very different from those that Humans propagate. They do not have gods, demons and fairies, nor has any past Prador been deified. Until the war ended and some cultural contact became allowed, it was assumed they had no conception of the supernatural. Now we know there are things Prador can fear even more than their own fathers. The Golgoloth is such a creature: an eternal monster who holds Prador young for ever captive, and in some vampirish manner slowly feeds on them to extend its own life. This is an odd myth and one wonders why young Prador so fear this creature, for it could cause them no more sorrow than their fathers already do. The adult male of any family fulfils amply the role of some spiteful god, with his power to kill on a whim or even to sentence his children to eternal hell.

– From HOW IT IS by Gordon

Ensconced once more in the Captain's Sanctum, Vrell studies in minute detail the data recorded about the intruder ship, and comes to some immediate conclusions. Though to all intents the unknown craft seems like a cargo hauler with a rather odd and inefficient design of hull, it is clearly something more than that, for it possesses particle cannons and rail-guns which, just by measuring their bulk and positioning within the hull, Vrell surmises are of up-to-date Polity design. Almost certainly the ship is a covert Polity vessel and therefore its crew and AI work for Earth Central Security. But why did it come here?

Though armed, the vessel could not hope to match Vrell's

dreadnought, and it did not even try, instead running and U-jumping away just as quickly as it could, once having delivered its packages. Vrell, now somewhat more paranoid since his problems over the message he earlier received from Oberon, immediately consigned the one information package to secure processing space. Now taking every precaution available, he slowly and carefully opens it, studying its basic structure before going anywhere near its content. The thing seems fine – simply a message recorded in Prador com code – so finally Vrell listens to it, his mental finger poised on the off button.

'I am the artificial intelligence aboard the ship you are presently firing upon and, of course, knowing your history I understand your paranoia. I bring you a message direct from Earth Central itself. The ruling intelligence offers you amnesty and sanctuary within the Polity, but obviously with some provisos. You must there obey Polity laws and you must give up your vessel, since we cannot have a fully armed Prador dreadnought travelling at will within Polity space. You must allow Polity AIs to study you for a period of no more than one Solstan year, during which time all your needs will be provided for and you are assured those investigations will not subject you to any discomfort. After that time you will become a free citizen of the Polity, provided with funds equal to the value of the vessel you hand over.'

Vrell listens to the message four or five times, then lays it out as Prador text for further study. Sending instructions to the mind controlling the dreadnought, he turns the vessel round rather than fleeing to some other location, as had been his intention. This offer requires further investigation for, though he still aims to exact some sort of vengeance for King Oberon's shabby treatment of him, it might still be a good idea to leave some other options open. The offer, he realizes, is not a bad one, but what about guarantees? And of course, more importantly, what about the other two packages? What about the war drone and armoured Human who have just boarded his ship? What are *their* intentions?

Vrell turns to his screens, observing interior scenes throughout the dreadnought whilst simultaneously processing data through his shell-welded control units. The drone's chameleonware is very good and Vrell would not have known the two were aboard were it not for their violent impact with part of the ship undergoing repair, and thus constantly monitored, and their subsequent penetration of another area of the ship he is also constantly monitoring: that section where the mutated third-children reside. The drone and the Human are currently moving through tangled superstructure, and seem to be showing no inclination to hide themselves. They are conversing, too, so Vrell decides to listen in.

'Do you think he's spotted us yet?' asks the armoured Human.

'Almost certainly,' replies the drone, now moving into an area where the ship eyes can finally get a clear view of it.

Vrell feels a sudden disquiet, for he recognizes this drone as the one called Sniper. It is the one that once, in a previous drone shell, knocked his father's ship out of Spatterjay's sky and which later, in its present form, managed to penetrate that same ship and rescue some of the Human prisoners Vrell had seized. But this is also the drone that detected him returning to Vrost's ship and yet gave no warning to Vrost. Vrell is ambivalent in his feelings about this Sniper, but certainly this is a dangerous drone that must be taken very seriously.

The drone continues, 'If he didn't detect us smashing into his ship, then almost certainly one of the ship eyes will have picked us up by now.' Sniper points precisely at the eye Vrell is watching them from. 'Like that one.'

'So what do you reckon his reaction will be?'

'He'll either try to talk or try to kill us,' Sniper replies. 'My money's on the latter option, so I'm guessing he'll send some of the crew after us.'

'But the ship's crew is dead.'

'Yup, but despite that they seem quite active.'

'What?'

'I'm guessing some sort of control program operating their armour. We've got dead Prador wandering about this ship in mobile coffins.'

'Oh, that's nice.'

'There's also some nasty-looking things in this section of the ship, which are now starting to close in on us. I'm not entirely sure what they are.'

At hearing this, the Human checks the controls on his complicated-looking assault rifle, then holds it up in readiness, swinging it perpetually to cover any possible approach. Vrell checks through other eyes in the same area and sees that mutated third-children are indeed closing in, then returns his attention to the two intruders. Studying the Human intently, Vrell realizes that, though the man wears a bulky powered spacesuit, that does not fully account for his size. However, there is no facility for any kind of deep scan at the Human's current location, so he cannot be sure. Yet, from what he understands of Human behaviour, Vrell realizes this man seems very ill at ease, despite being physically big, armed and armoured, and accompanied by a lethal war drone.

He studies the face he can see through the visor, but it is just a Human face, and they all look the same to Vrell. He considers opening communication with the two, but abruptly scotches that idea. By just watching and listening he might learn more. Perhaps, at some point, they will think he does not know they are aboard, and so say something more revealing. Certainly, once the mutants attack, Vrell will learn more about the armament they carry, which he cannot do simply by scan until they reach a part of the ship where intensive internal scanning is available.

The first mutant third-child ascends from below, its multiply jointed legs easing out of a circular duct so as to then heave its soft body out, till it pops like a cork coming out of a bottle. Vrell notes that though its body and legs resemble those of the one he captured, the rest of it is at wild variance. Its head is a long spike with eyes running all down the sides, it has sprouted leech mouths underneath it where its legs join its body, and it possesses a whip-like, two-pronged tail.

'What a horrible fucker,' says the man, immediately directing his weapon towards the monstrosity. 'But there's something a bit familiar about certain parts of it.'

'The number of legs is the same as a Prador's,' Sniper observes, 'and those things underneath it look suspiciously like leech mouths.'

The creature orientates itself, then hurtles towards them, leaping at the very last moment towards the Human. One of Sniper's tentacles sweeps out and bats it to one side, where it hits hard against a canted wall. The thing quickly unpeels itself, and merely attacks again. Again Sniper smacks it against the wall, and again it starts to unpeel itself.

'This could get rather repetitive,' says the drone.

'Well, it's obviously hostile,' the man observes.

'Orbus, your speed of comprehension is blinding.'

Orbus.

It takes Vrell a moment to dredge up the memory and to realize why that name is so familiar. In that same moment, Orbus fires his weapon, its beam setting cutting the attacking creature in half.

Orbus was the captain of that sailing ship Vrell attacked on Spatterjay, capturing him and his crew to use as slave labour to repair Father's spaceship. He is an Old Captain, of course, so that accounts for his size.

'Look at the bugger now,' says Orbus.

The two severed halves are still moving, folding in on themselves to produce two creatures but with a lesser complement of legs. And now other mutated third-children begin to appear and hurl themselves towards the newcomers. Sniper lashes out with all of his tentacles that are not gripping the twisted wreckage around them, sending the creatures crashing into the surrounding darkness. As the first of them begin to return, he opens up with a powerful laser, but even that takes a couple of seconds to render each of their assailants inert.

'Let me try something,' says Orbus, quickly making an adjustment to his weapon.

The next mutant to attack – a repellent creature whose legs are making the transition into tentacles, and whose body has become squidlike and sports two trumpet mouths surrounded by a ring of eyes – he shoots just once with some sort of explosive bullet. Detonating inside the creature, the bullet tears a gaping hole, but still that should not be enough to stop it. However, the creature clings to wreckage, utterly still for a moment, then it begins to shiver. Black fluid oozes from it, and its shivering turns to violent convulsions that actually tear it apart.

Vrell studies the images appearing on his screen with renewed interest. He knows at once what Orbus has used. He knows about sprine, but possesses none and knows nothing about its basic formula. Orbus fires again, and again, leaving disintegrating creatures clinging all about the pair of them.

Vrell abruptly opens up communication. 'Continue along your present course until you reach the bulkhead wall. Turn to your right and proceed along the wall until you reach the bulkhead door, which I will open for you.'

'That you, Prador?' asks Orbus.

'Who else did you expect?'

'Sarcasm from a Prador?' says Orbus, glancing at the drone.

'Seems so,' Sniper replies.

'Do not let any of those mutated third-children into the rest of the ship,' Vrell warns. 'And please desist from destroying them completely, as I am currently studying them.'

'Right,' says Orbus, switching over to standard explosive bullets.

They proceed as directed by Vrell, the Old Captain shooting one or two more of the attacking mutants, but Sniper keeping them at bay mainly with his tentacles. Vrell meanwhile orders two of his mobile corpse crew down to wait on the other side of the bulkhead door, then sends the instruction for it to open just as Sniper and Orbus reach it. Orbus goes through first while Sniper bats away persistent mutants, then Sniper goes through, slamming the door quickly shut.

That King Oberon is agitated seems plainly evident. The envoy from one of the powerful but normal adults in the Prador Kingdom was granted a personal audience with the King and, as is usually the case when the King gives a personal audience to those who must not know what he has become, the luckless envoy did not survive it.

Sadurian gazes around at the resultant mess. The King has torn off all the envoy's limbs and strewn them around the nice white floor of the audience chamber, then opened the envoy's carapace horizontally to eviscerate it. Sadurian peers down at one palp eye lying detached on the floor a few inches from the toe of her right boot, then abruptly turns away. The ship-lice will deal with most of this carnage, then the King's staff will come and remove the indigestible shell. Thereafter, the absorbent material of the floor will suck up the stains and self-bleach, returning to white sterility. Why the King favours all this open, eye-aching whiteness around him when all other Prador prefer their stinking caves remains a puzzle to her.

Sadurian heads for a distant door – one only large enough to allow access for herself and the armoured third-children that serve her. Beyond this she mounts a spiral ramp, moulded with long step-like indentations, and keeps climbing till finally stepping off onto a long gallery that runs across a sheer chainglass screen as high and wide as a cliff. She glances out onto the busy vacuum lying between Oberon's ship and the accompanying dreadnoughts, then halfway along the gallery seats herself in a single padded chair. After a moment she opens her visor and takes a slow breath, before removing her helmet and gloves.

Though slightly lacking in oxygen, Prador air is as breathable for her as air on any high mountain on Earth, but Sadurian usually keeps her visor closed while moving about the ship, because her suit's enclosed air supply keeps the more unpleasant odours from her nostrils – a frequent occurrence, since the Prador tend to leave their dead and the remains of their meals to the ship-lice, only cleaning up remaining carapace, bones or whatever when they become an inconvenience. Her armoured suit she wears constantly because, around Prador, it is all too easy for a soft Human to receive the most severe injuries through simple accident. But up here she is relatively safe, for this place is visited only by herself, her two servants and the occasional adventurous ship-louse. Unhooking her palmtop from her belt, she begins updating her journal, pausing occasionally to gaze at some distant dreadnought, or one of the smaller ships busy shuttling between the assembled dreadnoughts and the King's ship.

The ripped-up envoy, a first-child, arrived from the Kingdom on one of the dreadnoughts and was then ferried over by its captain. Apparently there is trouble back home: a feud between two adults, whom the King has managed to keep from attacking each other for many years, exploding back into life now the King is out here at the border. One of the adults has been slain and now the remaining one is squabbling with the King's Guard about the ownership of certain territories on the homeworld and also certain vessels in orbit about it. The King's irritation is understandable, for normal Prador simply behave like vicious children once he isn't nearby to keep watch over them, but that was hardly the first-child envoy's fault. Sadurian feels a degree of pity for the victim, but this is tempered by her years in the Kingdom and the non-stop vicious brutality she has witnessed here. Perhaps, Sadurian thinks, the time has come for her to return to the Polity and reacquaint herself with her own humanity . . .

Almost as if this last thought had initiated it, Sadurian's comunit speaks into her right ear. 'I need to see you,' says the King, speaking perfect Anglic with vocal apparatus grown inside his body nearly fifty years ago and supported by surgical alterations to certain structures of his brain.

Oberon is the only Prador Sadurian knows who can speak Human languages and understand the precise meaning of the words he uses. Most Prador struggle with translator machines that simply delete vague Human terms like altruism, philanthropy, friendship and love, or substitute them with some concoction like 'beneficial alliance'. The King certainly understands these concepts, though he doesn't give them much credence. He feels Humans are too often blinded by such words created in their primitive past, and which fail to accurately describe evolutionary reality.

'Where are you?' she enquires.

'Above you, on the main gallery,' Oberon replies.

Putting her palmtop away and pulling on her gloves, Sadurian heads over to the spiral ramp and climbs further. As always she feels a slight frisson of fear when heading for an audience with the King for, even though he has never attacked or even threatened her throughout many such encounters over the last century, that does not guarantee he will not do so this time. This seems especially true just lately, what with the King's behaviour becoming more and more erratic.

Departing the spiral onto the wide, heavily reinforced and, of course, white main-gallery road, Sadurian gazes at her patron. Perhaps the King likes to surround himself with all this wide-open whiteness because he feels it serves to de-emphasize his sheer size? Perhaps so, but nothing can de-emphasize the primal horror he inevitably inspires in any individual, whether Prador or Human. With the light so bright and the surroundings so white, his dark chitinous angles, the dark red, green and black of his carapace, stand out in utter contrast.

The King turns, his great complex feet crumping down on the gallery road, causing slight indentations, so that Sadurian can feel the reverberations under her own feet, then he abruptly surges forwards to loom over her. Sadurian gazes up into the massive angular outer mandibles and sees how green Prador blood still stains them, and she listens to the sound of his inner mandibles sharpening themselves against each other like glass sickles.

She quickly closes up her visor. 'What's the problem?' she asks.

'Prador are the problem,' declares Oberon, his voice issuing breathy and wet-sounding from a slit just below his main mouth. 'How can they ever advance?'

'*You* have,' Sadurian observes.

'I wish that were true,' the King replies. 'I now struggle to attain the next stage without losing myself.'

Never ever has the King been clear about what he is intending.

Whereas all the Guard take viral inhibitors, stick to a rigorous diet of foods that also inhibit viral growth, and strive, at the King's instruction, to retain some integral Pradorishness, the King does not. He eats viral meat – homeworld food animals long infected with the virus – and regularly experiments on himself with chemical and nanomechanical control of the virus, using robotic surgical equipment taken from a cache of the Golgoloth's long before Sadurian even entered the Kingdom, so as to install in himself machinery and organic grafts of his own design, and somehow he now possesses a species of conscious control over the virus growing inside his body. But to what purpose?

'What is this next stage?' Sadurian asks, utterly sure she will receive no reply.

'The stage when I become what the virus has intended to make me.'

Sadurian takes a pace back, dumbfounded. Is the King at last going to reveal his aims, and will Sadurian herself be allowed to survive that revelation?

'And what will that be?'

The King's inner mandibles grow suddenly still. 'Do my latest children grow satisfactorily?'

Sadurian feels a deep disappointment. 'Yes, Oberon – one third of them have survived to implantation and, going on past experience, we should lose less than ten per cent of them afterwards.'

'And my third-children can continue this process?'

'They can.'

'Take this.'

Oberon twists his massive body suddenly, and something lands with a wet crack on the floor below him. Sadurian gazes at a segmented object the size of her own forearm – some part of the King's hugely mutated underhands. She has seen this sort of thing before because, over the years, as the King's form has perpetually changed, he has shed numerous chunks of himself, as if running through all the various mutations the virus can cause, then abandoning them. Swallowing drily, Sadurian steps over underneath the monster, glances up at the regular pattern of carapace on his underside, then stoops to pick up the deposited object before quickly moving back out of the shadow.

'What am I to do with it?'

'Study the viral form and then bring me your conclusions.' Oberon turns away to gaze back out into space with eyes the colour of obsidian.

The two armoured Prador both bear particle cannons. Glaring at them, and conscious of that horrible churning in his stomach, Orbus finds it difficult to accept that what stand here are merely two corpses wrapped up in mobile suits of Prador armour. Perhaps his earlier feelings upon seeing that dead Prador inside the moon should be re-examined: a good Prador is indeed a dead Prador, but only if it exhibits the generally accepted signs of death – like not moving around.

'I guess I should be used to seeing the walking dead,' he observes, trying to keep his voice level.

The two of them part, and one gestures with its weapon along the wide corridor. For a moment Orbus expects to be disarmed, but the two undead make no other move.

'These ain't reifications,' says Sniper. 'No minds of their own and, if you think about it, they're not really dead.'

'Not dead?' Orbus repeats. 'Yes, quite.'

The Guard are virally infected so, despite having their nervous sytems burnt out like strands of fusepaper, whatever now resides inside those suits certainly isn't really dead. The virus will be perpetually trying to mutate them into something more able to successfully feed it, just like those mutants inhabiting that part of the ship behind them, yet contained like this it will perpetually fail. Then, without nutrients will it finally die, devolve to some basic form, or become dormant? He feels this last option to be the most likely, for he knows that virally infected life can hibernate for centuries. He just hopes that whatever writhes inside that metal cage doesn't figure out how to get out, because if it does it will be very very hungry.

Checking the exterior atmosphere display on his arm console, Orbus notes that it is at the Prador norm, and so he thumbs the control to open his visor. It is a mistake, for the smells inevitable aboard a Prador ship of this size hit him hard, driving dire memories to the surface. Suddenly predominant in his mind is the clear sharp image of Humans, crammed into a corridor like this one, being herded forward by second-children, those at the rear regularly being jabbed by claw tips. On that first occasion, as they were driven from Imbretus Station onto the dreadnought, those same claws were often used for their usual purpose, which resulted in torsos split open and bulging out their contents, arms and legs shattered, and the occasional crushed skull. Dying and dead were then dragged off by the second-children, and Orbus remembers two of them fighting over the corpse of a man and tearing it in half.

The Captain quickly closes his visor. However, it seems that those smells, having once entered his nostrils, will not go away. It is as if, like some organic key, they have unlocked some unwanted part of his consciousness. Wasn't it at a junction like the one just ahead that the first-child appeared to watch the screaming crowd being hustled past, and picked out those showing any obvious signs of injury for immediate extermination? Hadn't Orbus shuffled past and seen the mound of corpses behind the Prador, and seen how it stood in blood an inch deep on the floor?

While negotiating the numerous corridors, every surface, angle or item of Prador technology continues to impel horrific memories back to the surface of Orbus's mind. They finally enter a wide-open area, where all around can be seen the bones of the ship. Orbus feels some relief now, for he never witnessed a place like this in that *other* ship, just similar corridors and finally that low-roofed chamber into which they were all crammed for the duration of the journey to Spatterjay . . . surviving on Human flesh.

'The drone will remain there,' says Vrell, speaking from one of his undead servants, and even as he speaks, further armoured Prador enter from side tunnels or from other gaps in the structure all around them.

'Not sure I like that idea,' says Sniper.

'Nor am I sure,' Vrell replies, 'that I like the idea of you getting any closer to me. I have now scanned deep enough to detect that you possess the armament sufficient to penetrate armour, and have much else besides concealed under internal chameleonware.'

Sniper spreads his tentacles helplessly. 'Sorry, I can no more disarm than a Prador can lose his claws.'

'Captain Orbus alone will accompany my Guard,' Vrell states.

'Not a problem,' says Orbus, walking after the pair as they head for a nearby tunnel. But it *is* a problem, for they are once again entering parts of this ship that seem all too familiar. How long did it take that other ship to get to Spatterjay? The likely figure is two or three months, though it then seemed like a lifetime. Of course, upon arriving on that world the nightmare did not end.

The two Guard lead him to a long wide corridor, large enough to be used by adult Prador. He notes a burnt-out war drone lying against one wall, disfigured by weapons damage and scorch marks, while nearby lies a burnt-out suit of armour obviously in the process of being cannibalized. Then within a moment they stand before a wide set of doors that he guesses must be the entrance to the Captain's Sanctum. Very shortly, it seems, he will be face to face with Vrell.

The doors grind open, rolling back into the walls from their diagonal split, the two Guards moving over to either side of them, and Orbus enters. Further signs of battle damage in here, and some huge piece of hydraulic equipment parked off to one side. Nearby stands a single highly modified suit of armour, closed but motionless. Then there is Vrell himself, turning away from an array of screens and pit consoles to face him. And Vrell wears no armour.

Orbus gazes at this monster, and is conscious of heat rising up through his own spine and sweat breaking out on his skin. Abruptly he distinctly remembers Vrell coming for him and his crew and then, one after the other, dragging them off to be enslaved. He remembers when his own turn came, a claw crushing his torso as Vrell dragged him away, then the surgical equipment slicing into his neck, and the spider thrall burrowing into his flesh like a huge iron tick. He feels a surge of livid anger, yet behind it a weird kind of tired acceptance and, almost without thinking, finds himself raising and pointing his multigun.

Vrell bubbles and clatters his mandibles, while the disembodied voice of a translator says, 'Captain Orbus.'

Orbus's finger tightens on the trigger. Yes, they could negotiate, offer an amnesty, whatever, but wouldn't it be better if Vrell just went away? Here he is standing directly before Orbus, a virally infected Prador out of his armour; and here stands Orbus holding a multigun that fires sprine bullets. Orbus just cannot find any holes in his reasoning and, further, this might be the only opportunity he will be presented with. He pulls the trigger, though for a brief second it is not entirely clear to him that he meant to.

A stream of explosive bullets hammers across the sanctum, taking Vrell straight in the mouth, but then passes through him to detonate on the far wall. Unable to accept what he is seeing, Orbus switches to the sprine particle-beam and fires again, but the red blade of that passes straight through Vrell too, turning into a hazy cloud beyond. Finally accepting he is merely shooting at a hologram, Orbus turns round, knocking the gun to another setting, drops to one knee and fires at the closed suit of armour now already turning towards him. Conventional explosive bullets detonate all over the suit, but to little effect. The real Vrell lunges forwards, tears the weapon from Orbus's hands and its power feeds from his suit, then hits him in the chest with his other claw, to send him sprawling.

'Now I understand the basis of our negotiation,' says Vrell.

'I fucked up, Sniper,' Orbus sends via com.

'Yes you did,' Sniper replies. 'I am watching.'

Orbus sits up, taps his wrist display on, and calls up the menu for his suit's Lamion assister motors.

'What did you expect?' he asks Vrell. 'That I've forgiven you for what you did to me? What you did to my crew?' But somehow his vehemence has gone, and he feels merely foolish. As Vrell slowly advances on him, Orbus glances at the menu, spots a certain power setting, and with a flick of his finger pushes it all the way to the top. He springs to his feet, feeling as if he wears no armour at all and his body has lost half its mass, then hurls himself towards Vrell, only to be smashed to one side by a swinging claw and sent crashing into a wall. Before he can even slide down it, the side of Vrell's claw slams against him again, pinning him to the wall.

'What are you doing, Sniper?' he sends.

'Oh, I'll be there when I'm ready,' Sniper replies. 'I'll just give you girls time to sort out your differences while I figure out what to do about the fifty armoured ghouls now surrounding me.'

Orbus gets his hands behind the claw and manages to push it

away, dropping to the floor just as the other claw swings towards his head. He rolls down beside the Prador, Vrell's leg is nearby. Orbus reaches out, grabs it and twists, feeling something give with a gristly crunch.

With a shriek Vrell pulls away and swings round, bringing one claw down like a hammer. Orbus catches it above his head, feeling the sheer impact drive his knees partway into the deck.

'Have you presented our negotiating package yet?' Sniper enquires. 'That might be a good idea.'

Orbus heaves the claw to one side, dives and rolls, snagging up a big metal beam lying beside the hydraulic machine.

'So I tried to kill you!' he shouts at Vrell. 'That doesn't mean Earth Central's offer doesn't stand. It just means I don't fucking like you.' Orbus brings the beam down hard on the top of the visual turret of Vrell's armour. The beam shatters, but leaves a dent, and Vrell staggers drunkenly. Orbus flings the stub of the beam hard at him, but it bounces off an abruptly raised claw.

'What negotiating package?' Vrell demands.

Orbus now realizes Sniper has been using open com so Vrell can listen in.

'I can send it to you,' Sniper suggests. 'Once you stop trying to kill the good Captain.'

'Why should I?' Vrell wonders, again advancing. 'Under your own laws of self-defence, I have the right.'

'Okay – I'll send it anyway.'

Orbus eyes the open doors leading out into the corridor, calculating if now might be the time to run. But Vrell pauses, frozen in place, claws held up high. Is that as a result of the package? The Prador abruptly turns and hurtles over to his pit consoles, armour hingeing away from his claws, as they enter two pits before him, underhands meanwhile reaching down to insert themselves into pits below him. Orbus realizes that if he attacks now he might stand a better chance, but then the entire vessel suddenly slams sideways, hard enough to send him staggering.

'That you, Sniper?'

'No, it seems we have a visitor.'

The Golgoloth feels some satisfaction at having its patience justified. Vrell's dreadnought being that close to the sun certainly presented some problems, since the EMR there would tend to interfere with the Golgoloth's network of ganglia, and there was always the possibility that Vrell might take advantage of that. However, the arrival of what is obviously a covert ECS vessel of some kind has finally lured Vrell out. *Perfect.* The other vessel, after Vrell's attack on it, jumped out beyond the gas giant and is of no further concern to the Golgoloth. If it interferes again its remaining existence will be numbered in seconds. The Golgoloth focuses solely on the dreadnought.

Vrell's ship is of an old design and undergoing substantial repairs, but either there is more damage than seems evident or something beyond recent events has been distracting Vrell, for, throughout the long two seconds it takes the Golgoloth's massive ship to surface from U-space and open fire, there is no reaction. The stealth missile, which is really just a refined version of a Prador kamikaze with the frozen mind of one of the Golgoloth's children controlling it, initiates its U-drive to take it across the intervening four million miles in no time at all, then opens up its fusion drive and slams into the dreadnought's side, detonating to excavate a half-mile-wide crater and hurl out a cloud of debris. This gets Vrell's attention.

The dreadnought abruptly accelerates and beam weapons cut across intervening space, shortly followed by a swarm of conventional missiles rising on the white stars of their drives. The Golgoloth's ship, its hull a fifty-metre-thick layer of exotic metals and superconducting grids, simply soaks up this energy, even utilizing some for the ship's own systems.

The Golgoloth meanwhile studies its surroundings. This system has a meagre supply of worlds: one molten ball close to the green sun, and a dead giant orbited by a couple of planetoids, but one of them will do. The Golgoloth focuses on the chosen planetoid and studies data. Its atmosphere is mostly nitrogen and sulphides, but there does not seem to be too much volcanic activity or heavy weather, at least not in its present location; and, protected by the magnetic field of the dead giant, it isn't subject to too much of the solar wind either. In fact, surface conditions are such that any Prador, with an air supply only, could survive there for an appreciable length of time.

Using standard Prador codes, the Golgoloth sends the coordinates of the planetoid directly to Vrell's ship, then launches two more U-drive missiles, which leap across the intervening gap, fusion reactors winding up to speed within them. The Golgoloth watches his detectors and notes the familiar signature of a U-space drive being brought online within the dreadnought. *So predictable.* The moment one of the missiles starts up its fusion drive, a particle beam stabs out from the dreadnought and the missile detonates with a massive EMR flash. The other missile, briefly undetectable by the dreadnought's overloaded sensors, needs only to position itself with steering thrusters, then its systems fire up to create a massive magnetic bottle effect around it, almost simultaneous with it turning most of its substance into plasma. The briefly lived particle weapon spits its energy down into the dreadnought, punching through to a specific target. A detonation within glares through its superstructure, and the U-drive signature goes out. Vrell will not be leaving this system now.

Next the dreadnought flips round, its fusion drive and steering thrusters at full power to hurl it, once it completes its turn, straight at the Golgoloth's vessel. The Golgoloth prepares his own ship for evasive manoeuvres, wondering if Vrell intends some ploy like he initially used against Vrost's vessel – crashing his own ship directly into it then boarding. Even though confident of thwarting any plans Vrell might have once he has boarded, the Golgoloth does not want that to happen – best to be cautious with such a potentially dangerous intelligence. However, it seems Vrell intends nothing of the kind, for he makes another abrupt course alteration. Ah, he is trying to run for the sun, hoping to hide in the chaotic EMR output there. Another U-drive missile appears in the dreadnought's path and detonates. A warning only. The Golgoloth again sends the coordinates of the planetoid.

The two Guards enter the Sanctum shortly after the first impact, and since they are both carrying particle cannons, Orbus guesses that Vrell has finished playing around.

'Leave,' Vrell orders him, which seems a good sign, since Orbus hasn't yet been fried on the spot. He walks out between the Guards, who return him to join Sniper, where the drone waits surrounded by fifty of their fellows either standing in a ring immediately around him or ensconced in the surrounding exposed internal superstructure of the ship, though as events progress, even they begin to move away.

Massive accelerations set the ship's structure groaning all about them, and explosions can be heard deep within it. Orbus's visor closes automatically and he simultaneously notes a stratum of smoke in the air – which has to be poisonous or his suit would not have reacted so. Then come steady rhythmic sounds, machine sounds, and abruptly two more of the Guard put away their weapons and head off. Later, two Guards return carrying great loads of equipment and begin welding beams and heavy armour across one tunnel entrance.

'What is that noise?' Orbus asks.

'Onboard manufactories,' Sniper replies.

Orbus nods. 'We need to find out what the hell is going on here.'

'Vrell ain't very chatty at the moment,' Sniper observes. 'But maybe he'll let me ride some of his sensors.'

Sniper turns and cautiously begins to head towards one wall. The remaining ten Guards simply follow his course with their weapons, but otherwise show no reaction. Snaking out a couple of tentacles Sniper drags a great clump of fibre optics into view. Obviously that is a step too far, for five of the Guard immediately leap down from the surrounding superstructure and close in on him.

'That got his attention,' says Sniper, then, after a pause, 'Ah, seems he doesn't mind us taking a look now, since he's no idea what he's dealing with.' Sniper picks out several optics, wrapping some of his minor tentacles around them. His eyes glare and a wall nearby dissolves into a view looking directly onto vacuum. Distantly, a steely orb can be seen, then after a moment magnification brings it right up close.

'I don't recognize that,' says Sniper.

'Can you give me some scale?' Orbus asks.

A rule appears along the bottom of the image. The thing out there, which looks like a melon with one segment excised, bears a similarity to some ECS dreadnoughts, but its surface texture is composed of conjoined hexagons, like the honeycomb screens the Prador use, and it is all of ten miles across.

'I am receiving further data,' says Sniper. 'That first missile U-jumped, so either whatever is aboard yonder ship possesses some very advanced technology or it isn't bothered about sacrificing minds.'

'Prador kamikaze?'

'Very similar but much more refined and accurate,' Sniper replies. 'The second missile is a plasma converter – that's what took out Vrell's U-space engines.'

'This is in the Graveyard,' Orbus notes.

'Yeah, so either that ship got in using some pretty superior chameleonware or it got in even before all the border stations were built. There's no record that I know of regarding anything like this.'

Further acceleration then, for which Orbus's suit helps him compensate. He sees one of the Guard lose its footing and go crashing to one side, which is unusual, since they possess considerably more legs than he does. Suddenly he doesn't feel quite so calm about all this. If Vrell intends getting into a stand-up fight with that thing out there, it is probably all over for every one of them.

Vrell is trying to communicate, but the Golgoloth ignores that attempt and waits. The dreadnought turns again, decelerating and laying in a new course to the planetoid, but certainly Vrell hasn't given up. Scanning deep into the dreadnought, the Golgoloth notes a great deal of activity, analyses it in an instant, and realizes that the young Prador is preparing to be boarded. Vrell is also pumping energy and materials into the onboard manufactories. Doubtless the result of that activity will become evident in due course. The Golgoloth follows, but keeps the distance between them at a steady four million miles.

Seventeen hours later, objects begins to spill from the dreadnought and apparently disappear. Interestingly, the young Prador has managed to put together some stealth mines. With a thought, the Golgoloth jumps his ship straight ahead, arriving twenty million miles ahead of Vrell's ship, and waits again. Stealth missiles next, a great pack of them spearing out ahead of Vrell's ship. The

Golgoloth shifts his great vessel aside, then checks all relevant vectors before sending three of his U-drive missiles in return.

The missiles flash into being about the dreadnought, discharging all their substance in plasma beams at various targets on its hull. Two major steering thrusters simply explode and the ship's course diverts just so, before the main fusion engine blows out a red cloud of radioactive gas, then sputters and dies.

Grav simply winks out and Orbus awakes, floating up from the floor to grab hold of a beam. Even though constantly under threat for twenty hours, sleep finally took hold of him. Fire gouts from a nearby tunnel, and then out through open superstructure into their surroundings. With no gravity to give it shape, it burns in Mandelbrot patterns through the air, perpetually going out and reigniting as it loses and finds whatever it is feeding on.

'Don't worry,' says Sniper. 'This isn't hot enough to singe your ass.'

'Right,' says Orbus wearily. 'What just happened?'

'The attacker knocked out Vrell's fusion drive too, and some steering thrusters,' Sniper replies. 'This ship is now effectively rudderless.'

Orbus has watched Vrell's failed attempts with the stealth mines and missiles, and realizes the Prador is now in a cleft stick. He gazes at the image of the distant ship that Sniper is still projecting on the wall. It does not seem to be moving in for the kill, but that does not mean it won't. He almost wishes it would.

'I think we need to go and find Vrell,' says Sniper, revolving slightly to observe the remaining five of the Guard. Orbus notes something odd then: one of them is tilted over on its side and struggling in zero gravity to regain its place in the superstructure, and all five keep making odd inadvertent adjustments to their balance.

'Has Vrell got anything yet to say for himself?' he asks.

'No communication at all.'

Orbus releases the beam he was clinging to and turns towards the tunnel leading up towards the Captain's Sanctum. The gecko function of his boots engaged, he begins to head in that direction. After a moment, Sniper disconnects from the fibre optics and his screen projection blinks off, then, with his tentacles lightly touching the floor, he propels himself after Orbus. As the two enter the tunnel and step out of view, the Guard show no reaction at all.

Everything is going quickly and badly wrong. Vrell knows of no vessel, either in the Polity or the Kingdom, that could so quickly disable a Prador dreadnought like this. Checking his sensors he sees he is now on a course that, even if he does use the remaining thrusters, will finally crash his dreadnought down on the surface of the planetoid. Best, then, to save power in order to make that landing just a bit less hard. But what happens then?

The big vessel is still keeping its distance, when in reality it could now come staight in and carve up the dreadnought at its leisure. Why does it want the ship down on that planetoid, why does it want Vrell down there? What the hell is it?

But these aren't the only problems. The sealed-off section of the ship containing the mutated third-children has been breached, and already they are spreading throughout the ship, and now there is something definitely wrong with the Guard. He noted it first with the sluggish response of some of them to his direct orders, and the diagnostic probe he sent has revealed a steady corruption to their programs, those complex sub-AI programs. He has tried wiping and reloading copies of the original program to those worst affected, which worked for a little while before they started corrupting again. It seems it isn't the program itself that is at fault, but some sort of hardware failure. This can only mean one thing:

what is living inside those suits is beginning to penetrate their internal systems. He curses himself for neglecting one simple fact about Prador armour: it might be virtually invulnerable from the outside, but the same does not apply from the inside. How long, he wonders, before the fast-eject routine is tripped on some of them?

'Vrell,' says a Human voice.

Vrell swings his attention to one side, and sees that both the Human and the drone are entering his Sanctum.

Should have closed the door.

Through his control units, he links to those members of the Guard that were watching over these two and finds their programs so corrupted and so much processing space wiped out that all that remains of computer power is being employed just to keep them on their feet.

'What's happening, Prador?' asks Orbus.

Vrell just gazes at the man for a long moment. ECS has offered him sanctuary, and this man and accompanying drone came to negotiate the terms. It is all irrelevant now.

'We are going to crash,' says Vrell simply.

10

It is possible to store the mind of a Human in a piece of crystal no larger than the tip of one's little finger, and world-controlling artificial intelligences can fit into something the size of a tennis ball (larger crystal is more stable but tennis-ball AIs still exist). Both of these can be copied easily, ad infinitum. We know of three extinct, but once extremely powerful, star-spanning civilizations and, unless they were all like the Prador, they must have possessed their own artificial intelligences and ways of storing their own minds. It is therefore, a complete fucking certainty that, somewhere out there, something extremely dangerous is just waiting for someone to press the wrong button. Hey, you might be wandering the surface of an alien world when you spot an extremely pretty-looking stone at your feet. You could pick it up, and the warmth of your hand might call back into existence something that once moved suns about just for its own convenience.

– From HOW IT IS by Gordon

The dreadnought hits the thin atmosphere of the planetoid, its hull glowing red-hot and scoring an orange trail of burning metal, which spreads into a black smoke as the metal reacts with atmospheric gases to form strange nitrides and nitrates. The young Prador uses the ship's remaining steering thrusters to keep it skating far above the icy plains and jagged mountain ranges, hoping perhaps to bounce it back out into space. However, the ship does not now have sufficient speed to escape the pull of even so small a planetoid. Its course arcs round, orbital, gravity and thin air dragging it down.

The Golgoloth wonders for a moment why Vrell even attempted to bounce the craft back out, but then, making some rapid calculations, realizes there was a 10 per cent chance of success wholly dependent on atmospheric conditions difficult to measure. Now drawing his own ship in closer, he watches the tumultuous descent of the big ship. Vrell is obviously making calculations all the way down and trying to select the most suitable landing site. He manages to institute a bit of grav-planing, but the ship is too damaged to achieve more than 40 per cent negation of its weight.

Managing one entire orbit of the planetoid, Vrell must have mapped everything below, and then included that in his calculations. Jetting the steering thrusters, he ramps up acceleration for a moment, seemingly intent on taking the ship to a particular equatorial plain. The Golgoloth realizes something more will be required, because a line of obsidian peaks, like black canines, now stands in the way of the optimum approach vector.

Vortices all around the angular ship create a long vapour trail, with the curious effect of CO^2 snow falling below it. The ship speeds over one mountain chain, just the shock of its passage causing thousand-ton rockfalls behind it, and then the obsidian peaks lie ahead. Vrell fires the remainder of what must be a diminishing stock of missiles. They stab out ahead of the hurtling ship, the bright white of their fusion drives leaving a green trail in this atmosphere, and slam into the lower slopes. The ensuing massive explosions throw tons of brittle rock into the air, and two of the peaks begin to sag and collapse. Now particle cannons fire up, lancing here and there at specific targets within this falling mass just to speed its descent. Snagging outcrops are turned laval, great masses of hard water-ice melt in areas that lubricate their descent. The Golgoloth wonders if Vrell has miscalculated the speed of all this, perhaps not sufficiently accounting for the low gravity here.

The dreadnought hits falling debris, collision lasers firing non-stop but not sufficient to prevent great chunks of ice and rock exploding into fragments against the armoured hull. Some penetrate through unrepaired gaps to then tear through superstructure, and in some cases set fires burning within. The ship strikes one peak that has yet to fall all the way, tearing off a great shield of brassy armour, which tumbles along behind it to slam down into the plain beyond, throwing ahead of it an avalanche of shattered ice. Perhaps, after all, Vrell calculated it exactly right, for the impact has slowed the vessel considerably.

Now follow further stabs of fire from both the ship's particle cannons and its lasers, aimed at somewhere far ahead, on the plain. The Golgoloth studies this target, and notes Vrell is cutting a trench at his impact point. Very clever, but will this work?

The trench tracks the angle of descent into the ice, then slowly ascends in steps. Within a minute the ship hits the start of it and begins skidding, peeling up ice like a braking ski. A great cloud of vapour explodes from the hull as this ice hits something hotter than anything that has been down there for millennia. The ship hits the first step, shuddering and tearing up more ice, this time in thick broken slabs, before rising up over this. It hits a second step, and the same thing happens, though the ship is moving much slower now. Four steps later its speed is down to that of high-speed monorail, but still thousands of tons of momentum need to be accounted for. Exiting the end of the trench it continues skidding, piling up a glacier ahead of it. Finally it hammers this into the lower slopes of the next chain of mountains, causing disruptions that bring some of them crashing down. The scar of Vrell's crash landing extends for eighty miles, but is no longer visible from space, what with a boiling line of clouds now forming above it.

The Golgoloth emits a bubbling sigh. *Perfect.* Vrell has demonstrated just how quickly and accurately he can make calculations under appalling circumstances. Obviously he has done this sort of thing before, to evade being killed on Spatterjay and to then take over Vrost's dreadnought, but the Golgoloth had not witnessed that. Understanding perfectly the situation it has manufactured here, the Golgoloth can more accurately assess the mind of the Prador below. Vrell is dangerous, perhaps as dangerous as the King himself, and the Golgoloth has made the right choice in deciding to immobilize and isolate him first. Now, however, it is time for study, experimentation and investigation.

The ancient hermaphrodite Prador places its massive vessel in close orbit about the planetoid and initiates an external ganglion. Immediately reacquainted with certain ship systems, it runs a diagnostic, the results of which are within safety parameters, then sets in motion those same systems. Great blocks of internal structure shift on ancient hydraulics, seals detach and reattach elsewhere, explosive bolts blow, and thruster motors fire up.

Over the surface of the vessel, lines of division jag around the intersection points of hexagons within the honeycomb structure covering its surface, thus outlining a misshapen area some ten miles across. This whole area then begins to extrude, the whole lot easing out like a segment of geode. Meanwhile, interfaces begin to separate, dividing off scattered ganglion control systems, but then a radio connection establishes between them. Along with itself, the Golgoloth is now separating out part of its distributed mind along with the excised chunk of ship. Contact by radio will continue with that part of its mind still residing within the main vessel, but that isn't as good as direct optic or electrochemical connection. Anyway, the Golgoloth does not feel it will require the full power of its own mind for the chores ahead. Vrell is dangerous, but not *that* dangerous.

★

'The dreadnought is down intact,' Gurnard observes.

In the forward screen the image of the dreadnought, resting at the end of a long scar running across a planetary plain, now fades away, and that other enormous vessel once again comes into focus. Drooble gazes in awe as it extrudes a great chunk of itself, which then begins to descend towards the planetoid. First the dreadnought attacking, the captain and Sniper heading over, and now this? It is all just too much for him, lying as it does outside the simple routine of annoying his Captain, being punished, recovering, then doing the whole thing again.

'A lot of it appears to be of Prador manufacture,' remarks Gurnard, 'but I daren't scan to find out for sure.'

'Daren't?' Drooble echoes. He still feels slightly unwell. The damage done to his body by the Prador rail-gun in Montmartre has healed, but his body mass is down by 20 per cent, whilst the viral mass is up at its previous levels. There is a definite imbalance between the two, which effects the way his mind works. Those around him seem slightly crazy . . . though on some level he recognizes that he is the slightly crazy one, while those around him have changed not at all.

'I am just collecting sensor informaton, passively – not using any form of active scan,' Gurnard replies. 'But just that reveals layers of sensor and scanner complexity on the unknown ship's surface – almost certainly whatever is inside will know at once if I start scanning. It probably knows we're out here anyway. It seems improbable to me that, just by chance, it chose to attack shortly after we were driven away.'

'Just scan it anyway,' Drooble says abruptly. 'Let's see what we're up against.'

Poised just to one side of him, with its tail resting down on his horseshoe console, the drone Thirteen revolves to inspect him.

'Maybe we shouldn't too readily antagonize a ship that's ten miles across and can deploy U-space missiles,' Thirteen suggests. 'It's got enough firepower and accuracy of firepower to disable a Prador dreadnought. If it wants rid of us, it can be rid of us in less time than it would take you to say "Oh shit", Drooble.'

'The Captain gave *me* the bridge,' Drooble complains.

'That holds no weight here,' Gurnard says. 'Orbus was appointed by Cymbeline, but he cannot appoint his own replacement. I am in charge.'

Drooble feels a degree of resentment about that – but also relief. 'What do we do, then?'

'I am in communication with Earth Central,' Gurnard replies. 'It appears that no ship like this has been seen entering the Graveyard over the last seven hundred years. It seems to be of Prador manufacture, and in attacking Vrell is likely to be doing the King's bidding. Perhaps it is sufficiently advanced to have avoided detection while entering the Graveyard, in which case the entire population of the Polity certainly has something to worry about. We have been told therefore to watch and gather information, without putting ourselves at too much risk.'

'What about my Captain?'

'Your Captain is perfectly able to look after himself, and there is nothing we can do to make him any safer.'

'Yeah, right.'

'However, we can move much closer, for though, as Thirteen says, it will not do to antagonize whoever controls that vessel, we are in fact no safer out here than up close, since a U-space missile can remove us from existence just as quickly in either case.'

Thirteen merely snorts at that.

Gurnard adds, 'Moving closer will also give us a better view of events, and greater option to react to them. I calculate that this will be a risk worth taking.'

The *Gurnard* begins accelerating, then abruptly all the screens grey. Drooble feels the odd twisted pull of U-space and it kicks something crooked in his mind onto a new path. He suddenly feels optimistic about being closer to his Captain, and thus closer to the action, and though Gurnard is not actually obeying him, it certainly seems to be doing what he wants.

The screens once again show the outside view. Far to their right rests the dead giant, a silvered orb without cloud to soften the intricate wrinkles extending over its surface. Ahead lies the planetoid, that same big vessel clearly visible in orbit about it. Drooble realizes that the *Gurnard*'s fusion drive is still firing and that they are steadily drawing closer to this diorama. Magnification brings the vessel right up close, and Drooble sees at once that a great splinter of the ship is pulling out of the cavity already left by the departure of that other chunk now heading down to the planetoid's surface.

'I take it that this all started happening the moment we arrived here,' says Thirteen.

'It did,' Gurnard replies, 'but at least it's not a U-space missile.'

Once its point is clear of the main ship, the splinter swings round like a compass needle, perspective contracting it down into a metallic jewel – it is now pointing directly towards them. Then it flashes briefly out of existence, reappears much closer, and begins to swing round again.

'So far and no further?' Thirteen suggests.

Gurnard begins to decelerate. 'So it would seem,' the AI replies. 'But now at least we can see the surface.'

The forward screen image changes to show a clear view of the downed dreadnought, and the first chunk that detached from that other vessel lying ahead of them now settling on the plain nearby.

'And so the stage is set,' says Gurnard.

'What's playing tonight?' asks Drooble.

'A drama of life and death, as always.'

Drooble nods thoughtfully, then stands up and departs the bridge, a determined set to his expression.

By slow degrees the soldier attains consciousness, knowing itself as Ebror, yet even throughout the process also knowing that Ebror the Prador is just an organic recording, a sub-component of itself, the point of the needle it uses to puncture the membrane separating itself from existence. Instinctively it retains that conscious component so it can review Ebror's memories and understand the world it now finds itself in. It does all this for limited and clearly defined purposes: for the survival of itself and its squad and also for the destruction of the enemy.

Studying genetic tissue contained within its viral body, the soldier thoroughly understands Prador and all they are about. Reviewing substantial samples of DNA from Human beings, it gains some understanding of them too. All are the enemy. Its own species are the enemy outside its squad. Anything living – other than itself and its squad – is the enemy. This rules out confusion.

When the squad's spaceship was attacked all those eons ago, and forced to crash-land on the planet, their time had been limited. They knew their present physical bodies would not be able to survive the ensuing attack, and so they took a very unusual route. Upon discovering the surrounding ecology of the planet to be dominated by a complex viral mycelium, they spliced this with the nano-mycelium that maintained both their vessel and their own bodies, incorporating into it their own genome and direct recordings of their long memories. It remained part of the vessel and part of themselves until the expected attack arrived, destroying both them and their ship, whereupon their bastard child spread in the oceans. They became somnolent then, sleeping, and incorporated as part of an ecology.

With an internal awareness that was a major evolutionary advantage of its kind from the beginning, the soldier explores its body and gradually understands the processes that have brought it to consciousness. The plan was for resurrection to ensue some brief years after their destruction, but the programming was too hurried, mistakes were made. Having incorporated them, the mycelial virus should have, after the running down of an internal biological clock, recoded some of the creatures it went on to infest, and turned them into exact copies of the original squad. Instead, the clock stopped and the virus just kept incorporating, at first at random, genetic samples taken from the creatures of its own world – burying the squad deep. Evolution then played its part too, so that this incorporation of genetic tissue became a tool for viral survival. Had there been no outside interference with that world, the soldier would have remained sleeping for ever.

However, the virally infected Prador, of which Ebror is one, were killed by a specific nanite that completely wiped out their nervous systems, leaving only a blank slate. They were thereafter left confined in armoured shells, completely cut off from any food supply. The result was a sequence of mutations within the shell, as the virus tried every single one of its strategies for survival, but failed. With nutrient diminishing, it worked its way through its whole eclectic genome collection until finally hitting upon what lay at the bottom: the alien genome of the squad itself. And, given the chance, that squad certainly knew how to survive. The evolutionary program of the virus had been to mutate only its given body and not to venture outside that. Once he was in control, even though unconscious, the soldier immediately turned the virus outwards; survival did not lie within, but by penetrating the simple electromechanical systems that surrounded it. And, whilst that penetration proceeded, the soldier woke.

'The technology is primitive,' comes a simple communication through the electronics of the armour.

'But useful.'

'It can be adapted, even in this environment.'

'This ship has crash-landed. I see exterior conditions. Sharing now.'

And so it goes, as the squad calls in. As the soldier absorbs a squirt of battle code detailing the location of the vessel, exterior conditions and interior conditions, it surmises that their number is greater than it had been before the attack upon their own ship, and yet also that some of the squad is missing, but this is inevitable. Some soldiers have been multiply duplicated, whilst some have not achieved consciousness at all. It is as it should be: the strongest predominate.

The soldier now draws back his internal focus and studies the larger-scale organic make-up of his being. Most of the original Prador body is gone, while muscle, vascular systems and the organs required for running a body this size have grown, including the entwined ganglia that contain his consciousness. He has not grown bones or a shell, the armour still sufficing. However, everything is greatly stunted since he lacks nutrients, sugars and sufficient oxygen. Exploring Prador memories, he quickly locates needed information and, extending one of his internal leech mouths, manages to turn on the internal oxygen supply of the armour, thus enabling what will be a short-lived boost of energy as he further burns up the substance of his own body just to keep mobile. A quick squirt of battle code alerts his fellows to this option too.

'Weapons cache found,' notes one of the others.

'Primitive again, but adaptable.'

Now turning his attention fully outwards, he gazes at his surroundings through wholly Prador eyes that the virus did not see fit to discard. He crouches in a corridor, a welding device clutched in one claw and a maglev tool chest toppled over on its side beside him. He heaves himself to his feet, discarding the welder, and, again sampling Prador memories, turns and heads up the corridor towards the nearest larder. Thankfully, the door is lying open, but the next bit is problematic: how to get some of the abundant food stored here inside him.

Again the Ebror memories do not let him down. The soldier shifts another leech mouth to some internal controls and manipulates them, and with a clunk the section of armour that once covered Ebror's mandibles hinges open in two parts. There is pain as it rips away from internal musculature, and much bleeding, but at last the soldier manages to extrude a collection of leech mouths that start boring into a selection of Prador homeworld fish steaks and large misshapen lumps of flesh that are likely to be some kind of mollusc.

Nutrients flood through him, directly sucked into the virus itself without the intercession of a stomach. The soldier immediately begins using these to improve his internal structure, selecting from his own genome since it remains utterly superior to those of Prador, or Humans or any life-form deriving from Spatterjay. But of course it is, it being the product of some tens of thousands of years of genetic engineering.

He begins building bones against which to brace his muscles, rather than using the armour for support. He grows a stomach and digestive system, expands his circulatory system and all other support organs. He quickly replaces the rest of his electrochemical nervous system with one wholly electrical, operating so much much faster.

'Energy supplies located,' another notes. 'Moving to secure.'

'Main weapons located. Moving to secure.'

'Force-fields located and secure. Adaptation in progress.'

The soldier contemplates this input then adds, 'If crew still survive, they must be found and killed.'

'Searching,' another replies.

As the ship shudders into stillness, Vrell struggles to break through the paralysis of an unaccustomed terror. He does not recognize the code running on the screen of his armour's CPU. It is fast, incredibly complex even for him, and seems to be shifting huge chunks of information that are changing even as they retransmit. It seems he is acting as a relay in some network, but a network formed between different suits of armour that are no longer under his control.

His first guess would have been that the sub-AI programs in each of them have made the leap to sentience, but the data format is too alien and cannot possibly arise out of the original programs. But, more important than that, the same code is running in the control units bonded to his carapace, and so invading his nervous system. Through that connection he can *feel* a cold nihilistic logic and terrifying intelligence.

Fighting the growing fear, Vrell tries to apply some logic. Actually using either his CPU or control unit to obtain information would be a foolish move, for whatever is operating inside his ship would immediately become aware of him and, as far as he can see, it can take control of his armour. Just by monitoring the data flow, its sheer capacity and utterly alien format, he confirms that he is not seeing AI sentience arising from his original programs. Could it be that somehow the Old Captain and the drone have penetrated his security? No, something odd was happening with the Guard even before the pair boarded. There seems only one logical conclusion: the Guard are being controlled by some alien within the unfamiliar vessel that forced him down onto this planetoid. But he cannot just lie here pondering the purpose of this invasion while that other vessel has him at its mercy; he suspects that if he waits too long he will soon be dead.

The big hydraulic clawjack, having slid across the Sanctum to knock him from his pit controls, has trapped him against one wall. If he tries to push it away, the assister motors in his armour will cut in, immediately alerting those other *things* aboard to his presence in the network. He just has to hope that the hydraulics of the manual fast-eject routine will be up to the task. Probing with his mandibles into the pit controls within his armoured turret, he initiates the routine. The top half of his armour pushes out, against the wall, whilst lubricant flows around his limbs. This sets the hydraulic jack sliding away from him, then, as the lid of his armour hinges up, the jack topples over with a resounding crash. Compressed gas throws Vrell out as his armour thumps down flat. The edge of his carapace hits the wall and he turns, but by chopping a claw against the same wall, he rights himself and comes down on his feet. At once he reaches down, grabs hold of the control units bonded to his shell and yanks them free, sending them skittering away from him.

'Drone,' he instructs, in the Prador language now because his translator is part of the armour. 'Destroy my armour.'

The drone has secured himself in the doorway to the Sanctum, wrapping some of his tentacles around the Old Captain whilst using the rest to prevent both of them being thrown about. Sniper's tentacles now unwrap from the Human and send him sprawling.

'Why?' Sniper asks, in the same clattering, bubbling speech.

'Controlled by dangerous intelligence,' Vrell clatters back.

Just then the suit begins moving, tentatively stretching its limbs and snapping closed one claw. The lid begins to close.

Before Vrell can say anything more, Sniper shoots into the air and, with a loud crackling, spits a stream of missiles straight down inside the armour. A series of detonations blows free the hatch, so it slams against the ceiling. With a bright fire burning inside it, the armour tries to right itself and turn, just as Sniper crashes into it, tentacles entwined around its limbs, his face directly into the flames. His particle beam stabs out next, and gobbets of molten metal spit out around him as the interior of the armour turns blast-furnace hot. Vrell sees the drone has focused the beam directly on the internal location of the CPU. The armour struggles to right itself, then for a moment the colour of internal flame flashes bright red, and it slumps. Sniper releases his hold and rises again, hovering in the air, tentacles twitching.

Vrell has no time to feel gratitude, for now he is running out of breath. With his body mutated and interlaced with the Spatter-jay virus, anoxia will not kill him. However, it might cause further mutations and, knowing what he knows now, that is not a prospect he relishes. He scans all about to see the deck lying tilted, and chunks of superstructure protruding through it like shattered ribs, but what catches his attention is a frost on some surfaces, indication of an atmosphere breach.

'What is controlling that armour?' Sniper asks in Prador speech.

Vrell ignores the question and points at one of the storage alcoves. 'Blow that door.'

Sniper drops down beside the storage alcove indicated, grabs protrusions in the wall surrounding it, inserts tentacles and simply tears the door off. Vrell watches this with a degree of chagrin. He has seriously underestimated this Sniper, in fact he should have ejected the drone from this ship at the first opportunity. However, circumstances have changed and now the drone's presence might even prove welcome. Sniper reaches inside the alcove and drags out a Prador harness incorporating integral breather unit, com hardware and numerous little niches for numerous weapons.

'This what you want?'

'Yes,' Vrell replies, moving forwards.

'Then I am going to need a bit more detail.'

By now the Old Captain is on his feet and saying something. Vrell listens to it for a moment, simply not realizing he is understanding, then something clicks in his major ganglion. His earlier encounters with Humans, on many levels, and his recent use of a translator have provided all the data his enhanced intelligence needs. He now understands the Captain perfectly.

Orbus has just said, 'What the fuck is going on?'

Vrell is not equipped with the vocal apparatus to provide him with an answer.

'That's what I'm trying to figure out,' says Sniper, giving the harness a shake.

'Something hostile has taken control of the Guard,' Vrell states.

'What did he say?' asks Orbus.

Sniper ignores the man. 'Something from that attacking ship, then. How did it penetrate your security?'

'I do not know, but logic dictates that this is the case,' says Vrell. But, even as he says it, Vrell does not want to admit to himself that, though all the evidence seems to confirm his supposition, he does not *feel* it to be true. He cannot shake off the feeling that the source of the alien code lies *inside* each suit of armour.

'What's that?' Orbus demands.

'Somehow,' Sniper tells him, 'the attacking craft has managed to take control of those suits of armour.'

'How?' asks Orbus.

'Who cares?' Sniper tosses the harness to Vrell. 'We're in big trouble, however you cut it.'

Vrell initiates the harness CPU, but with the com function shut down, then checks readouts in the mask to be sure nothing has invaded it, before quickly donning the equipment.

'So what's the plan now?' Orbus asks Sniper.

'Beats me,' the big drone replies. 'You got any ideas, Vrell?'

Vrell eyes the two of them and can think of no reply. The dreadnought came down hard and will not be going anywhere for a long while, especially now his previous workforce lies beyond his control. Perhaps they can stay aboard and fight, but he needs time to formulate some method of attack – time he suspects he will not be allowed by the alien-controlled Guard.

'Did you recognize that attacking ship?' Vrell asks, now using a translator.

'Nope,' says Orbus, glancing at Sniper. 'We thought you might be able to tell us about it, because obviously whatever is aboard it has an overwhelming interest in you. Could it be King Oberon sent it?'

'If it was the King, then why did it not destroy me when given the chance?'

The Human shrugs and his expression changes in ways Vrell cannot read. The drone remains as inscrutable as ever. The only way Vrell could know whether they are telling the truth would be to take them both apart and read the information directly from their minds, which is not an option at this moment. He shakes himself, and abruptly moves back over to his pit controls and array of screens. Many of the controls have been damaged by the sliding clawjack, and a lot of the screens are out but, inserting his claws and underhands, he finds some controls he can still use.

As yet there seems no corruption in the instruments and data available to him here, and what he now finds is both awesome and frightening.

'The Guard are on the move,' he says at last. 'They first broke into food caches located throughout the ship, and are now securing critical areas. All the remaining fusion reactors are out of my control, as are the main weapons and force-field defences.' He studies a screen which shows two members of the Guard taking apart a hardfield projector. They are moving with the kind of speed he has only ever seen achieved by sophisticated robots. Vrell takes a moment or two to mull this over. How can he fight something like this? As he is witnessing, the Guard can now move horribly fast and are rapidly removing the ship from his control. Even as he studies the screens, internal security systems go down and blocks of computing space are hijacked.

Abruptly coming to a decision, he calls up one of the remaining security programs – one created by Vrost and held in reserve – and initiates it. Screens begins to blink out one after another as a destructive power surge sweeps through all the internal ship eyes and scanners, burning them out. He then inspects a screen which briefly gives him a view outside the ship before it too winks out. It shows a great segment of the attacking ship now landing ten miles away across the icy plain.

'The area of this ship you first entered after boarding is presently unoccupied,' Vrell observes, whilst removing his claws and underhands from the pit controls, as some more screens blink out and others begins running weird writhing patterns. He backs away and turns, heading over to the alcove storage. In there he quickly begins selecting items and affixing them to his harness: a particle cannon, a rail-gun, further power supplies, oxygen, grenades and a selection of mines.

'We gonna hide?' Sniper wonders.

'I intend to hide and then to watch,' Vrell replies, turning and rapidly moving up beside the drone, to peer out into the corridor beyond. 'Since part of the attacking ship is now landing outside, it seems likely its occupants might be heading here. That might present some . . . opportunities.'

'There might be another option,' suggests Orbus. 'It might be possible to call in the *Gurnard*?' He goes over and picks up the weapon Vrell took from him earlier, plugging its leads back into his suit.

'Yes . . . possible,' Vrell acknowledges, as he steps out into the corridor.

Almost mirroring him, one of the Guard steps into view at the far end of the corridor, its shape now oddly distorted and its armour taking on a blue hue, and with blinding speed swings a rail-gun round to bear. Everything seems to shudder into nightmare slow-motion for Vrell. As he swings up his own weapon, he just knows he is not moving fast enough. He can normally get the drop on any Prador, or Human, or on any living thing he has previously encountered, but this thing moves as fast as a machine. His senses heightened to pinpoint and painful clarity, he sees the rail-gun aimed precisely at his unprotected mouth, and the Guard's claw simultaneously closing to fire it, whilst his own weapon is only halfway up towards firing position. Then a missile streaks past, its passage noted only by the subliminal flicker of a black line sketched across the air. Perfectly targeted, it enters the barrel of the Guard's rail-gun and detonates. Even as the explosion disintegrates the weapon, and part of the claw holding it, throwing the Guard backwards, Sniper slides in front of Vrell and continues firing. The war drone is thrown into abrupt silhouette by sun-bright explosions, as it turns the far end of the corridor into a furnace.

'Run,' Sniper advises.

Vrell spins round and, with Orbus falling in behind him, heads at high speed for the opposite end of the corridor. Then, obeying instinct, he abruptly flings himself sideways and clambers up the wall, both his weapons pointing towards his destination. One of the Guard shoots into view, and its rail-gun swings up already targeting Orbus before the Old Captain has a chance to react. A stream of projectiles slams into the Human, but amazingly he stands his ground, with shattered metal ricocheting from the front of his suit. Vrell aims carefully and fires both his weapons, target-ing power supplies, and the Guard is lifted up on an explosion that finally flings Orbus to the floor. Yet, even as this particular Guard's rail-gun sputters out, and it rises amidst the blast, another of its kind is appearing behind it.

'The wall,' Sniper sends over com.

Vrell flings himself from one wall to the other, then down on to the floor. The drone turns, twin-particle cannon beams stabbing out and cutting a hole through the corridor wall, even while his launcher turns like a chameleon eye and spits missiles straight down the corridor, past Vrell. Vrell feels a series of impacts in his back and sees one of his own legs go skittering past him. Rail-gun missiles racket off the wall beside him, then firing ceases upon the two detonations behind. Ignoring the pain, he surges forward as a great chunk of the wall falls through. He grabs up Orbus as he goes, not quite sure why, and, as he flings himself through, slaps two proximity mines on the floor. Sniper follows, his thinking much the same as he too sticks some device beside the hole.

Vrell falls twenty feet into a long cylindrical room through which run numerous power ducts and pipes. Scattered along its length are the huge pumps that keep all areas of the ship supplied with water and various necessary gases. He quickly inspects these, then pain surges up from his claw as it is wrenched open. Vrell has almost forgotten he is still carrying Orbus, and drops him like an unpleasant insect.

11

Unlike the independent drones produced throughout the war, or those AI subminds that sometimes either buy or are given their own independence, the security drone for ever remains part of an integrated security system. This is because its mind, on its own, is not actually an artificial intelligence. In any exchange, conversational or informational, with one of these machines, it would seem to be an independent entity, but it is not. The security system itself is the AI (usually the submind of a larger AI), but of a format similar to that of an intelligent hive of social insects. Such machines are just not complex enough to either deliberately or inadvertently build sufficient ego within themselves to wish for independence. Of course, the observant reader will immediately point out cases in which such drones have achieved independence, but those are usually parts of very old security systems that are breaking down – suffering a hivemind version of schizophrenia.

– From THE WEAPONS DIRECTORY

Sadurian gazes into the clean-tank, at the chunk recently shed from the King's body. The first cursory scan of genetic material from this makes it utterly plain to her that the spermatozoa used to fertilize the latest batch of eggs are not the product of the King's present body. Sperm produced by something with a genetic make-up like *that* simply would not produce Prador. If it could fertilize even the modified Prador eggs the King's females are producing, which is doubtful, the product would resemble the King himself.

How Oberon managed that, Sadurian has no idea, but manage it he had. Quickly running comparisons on her screens, she sees that the sperm recently used closely matches that of a previous mating, some twelve years ago. Somehow the King retained sperm inside him untouched by the devastating viral changes he has undergone since. Or else, since these matings are never witnessed, he has used some other means to preserve and then inject it.

'Okay, quit the scan, Delf, and let's start from the basics.'

The chrome-armoured third-child inserts himself into the space made for his kind within the nanofactor apparatus, where he can operate with multi-limbed precision the nanoscope and the array of nanoscopic tools. This is one great advantage the Prador have over Humans for this kind of work, for they simply possess more hands to employ more tools. It is a shame they perpetually need to overcome so many prejudices and mental blocks to conduct such work – then, again, perhaps not. If they had been as adroit as Humans at manipulating genetic code, the outcome of the old war might have been very different.

Screens now display an image comprising both nanoscopic maps and computer-generated images of the King's present genome, which consists of that which is active, the enclosing viral framework, and the virus's own eclectic collection of inactive genetic tissue – the stuff it uses to transform its host when survival becomes an issue.

'Weigh it,' says Sadurian, 'before we start with molecular deconstruction.'

Prador glyphs appear along the bottom of Sadurian's screen, first detailing the overall weight then the separate weights of the three main components. She studies these for a long moment so as to be utterly sure she understands what she is seeing.

'Yaggs.' Sadurian glances over her shoulder to where the other chrome-armoured third-child is currently working the laboratory pit controls. 'Give me data on the unit weight for the mating batch, and then correct for meiosis.'

On a second screen appear recorded images of genome collected from the King's sperm. Prador meiosis, that process of cell-division that produces the half chromosome weight for spermatozoa, closely resembles that of Human beings, but with the Spatterjay virus introduced into the equation things become a little complex. The spermatozoa carry this parasite which, even at a microscopic level, views anything other than its immediate host as food. This is precisely the problem Sadurian was brought into the Kingdom to solve, and has solved. She therefore knows that her instruction to 'correct for meiosis' is no simple matter of doubling up chromosome weight. She sits back and watches the third-child's calculations as they appear on her screen, mentally checking each one. Finally, Yaggs solves the problem. Sadurian nods to herself and smiles. Her two protégés have, over the last decade, reached the point where they can now take over from her, which is good, because at last Sadurian has begun to conclude that it is time to draw to a close her time here amidst the Prador.

Now running a comparison between Yaggs's result, which basically gives the weight of the King's genome from twelve years back, and the result from the tissue currently in the clean-tank, Sadurian sees that the present sample is three-quarters the molecular weight of the old one. She nods to herself, considering the timing of all this: the King began instituting major changes in himself from about the time Ebulan, Vrell's father, made his illegal excursion to Spatterjay. Oberon must have expected Ebulan to make certain discoveries about the virus or, because of Ebulan's excursion, have come to the conclusion that those discoveries were inevitable somewhere, and so then began pushing whatever he is doing to himself to the limit. Either that or this is coincidental. Sadurian doesn't believe in coincidence.

'Yaggs,' says Sadurian. 'Take control of the other nanofactor – that should help us get through this a lot quicker.' Yaggs turns from his pit controls and heads over to the second factor positioned on the other side of Delf from Sadurian. 'Now, let's begin deconstruction and mapping.' She pauses for a moment, considering. 'I want you to give me a full factual report on this, but no speculation and no prognosis – just stick to the facts of the now.' Prador are as good at that sort of report as they are bad at anything involving imagination.

Even as, molecule by molecule, Delf and Yaggs begin pulling apart the viral genome, Sadurian can see that only a small portion of the original Prador stuff that made Oberon is still there, and that a lot of the virus's eclectic collection of Spatterjay genetic material is also missing. Why, then, if Oberon is seeking to *become* something, is he stripping away all these options? Then Sadurian remembers the alien material, that stuff down deep, and realizes Oberon must be steadily stripping away genetic options to reach it. But why?

'One moment . . . Delf.' As the Prador pauses, Sadurian stares at her screen. Throughout all her long years here, the alien genome and its effects have been irrelevant to her. Somehow it is locked, some activating principle missing and, though it is quite evidently there, it has no bearing on the reproductive studies, experiments and work she has been conducting. It just sits there: chunks of complicated intertwined molecules which reproduce themselves during cell division but otherwise effect nothing. But Oberon obviously knows different.

'Delf, I want you strip the King's viral genome of all Spatterjay, Prador or other known genetic material, leaving only that alien junk. Then map it and run the data over to my station.' Sadurian stands up and heads for the door. 'Call me when you're ready.'

Orbus rolls clear and leaps to his feet, backing away from the Prador. On some level he knows that, armoured as he is, Vrell could not have crushed him, but the Prador grabbed him and picked him up just like it had picked up all his crew, and just like when it grabbed him and dragged him off to install a spider thrall in the back of his neck. All he can think of is that time, as if reliving it. But things are different now, because he is armed with something more effective than a skinning knife. He begins trying to shove his multigun power plug, which has pulled free, back into this suit, but the suit motors amplify the shaking of his hands.

Vrell studies him for a moment, unreadable and hideously alien, then turns and fires one short blast from his particle cannon straight into a particular pipe, and gas begins to gush out, rapidly fogging the entire area.

'This way,' Vrell instructs, setting off. Passing two of the big pumps, he stoops over a wide hatch, rapidly undogs it and flings it back on its single hinge. 'Down here.'

Orbus moves over by the hatch, his multigun clutched close to his chest, but he still hasn't managed to plug its power supply back in. He stares at the hatch until a tentacle prods him in the back.

'No time to take in the scenery,' warns Sniper.

Orbus jumps down and Sniper follows, turning as he enters the narrow space below. Vrell follows but his carapace jams and he hangs there struggling for a moment, then the proximity mines above detonate and the shockwave shoves him down, breaking off chunks of his shell. He hits a floor hard, lies there apparently stunned for a moment, then abruptly heaves himself to his feet and reaches up with one claw to pull down the hatch and dog it back in place.

'Where now, Prador?' asks Orbus.

They need Vrell to guide them through the maze of his ship, but at some point Sniper should be able to take over and the Prador will become superfluous. Then Orbus pauses that line of thought, a sudden doubt inflicting him. He has already tried to kill Vrell once, and afterwards regretted it. Is the situation any different now? Why such anger at simply being snatched up in the Prador's claw? Yes, yes he knows why; it is because Vrell does not save lives out of any altruism, but because they might be useful to him. No doubt a spider thrall awaits Orbus eventually, wherever Vrell is taking him . . .

Vrell just beckons them after him as he is forced to crouch his way along. Judging by the size of this passageway, it was made for third- and second-children only, doubtless the ones given the shittiest jobs aboard a ship like this. The passage curves down, becoming increasingly steep, and Orbus realizes that, with ship's gravity out, up and down is now governed solely by the planetoid it rests upon. Ahead this steepness makes the transition into a straight drop, and Vrell struggles to find footholds to prevent himself slipping down. Orbus feels one of Sniper's tentacles wrap round him like a climbing rope, and glances back to see the drone is managing to extend other tentacles to every possible nook and cranny surrounding them. Abruptly Vrell slips, his legs scrabbling and clattering against the walls, then he begins sliding downwards.

'Seems like the quickest way,' observes Sniper.

The war drone draws Orbus in close, then releases his holds and begins sliding too. The slope soon turns into a vertical drop, which then starts curving inwards, and Orbus now reasons this passageway must run in a ring around the inside of the ship. There is no impact, fortunately, and Sniper is sliding again, whilst ahead of them Vrell folds his legs and claws in close, his weapons and other equipment clutched tight to his belly. For a short time they skid down a gradually decreasing slope, making a sound like a sack of tools dropped down an air-conditioning duct. Vrell eventually slides to a halt, lying on his back, while Sniper, his external coating obviously smoother, continues sliding and rams straight into him.

Like this they skid another twenty feet before once more grinding to a halt.

'Handy getaway,' Sniper observes.

As Sniper spills Orbus free, the Captain stands up and, in one movement, finally plugs in the power supply to his multigun, and the cross-hairs reappear on his visor. He swings the gun towards Vrell, bringing those cross-hairs right over the Prador's belly. Vrell just lies there on his back, utterly vulnerable, for there is simply no room here for him to right himself. Gripping the ceiling of the passageway, he can push himself along for a little way, but even that will take some time.

'I am . . . inconvenienced,' says the Prador.

'Yeah, looks that way,' Sniper concurs.

Orbus walks over to Vrell, his aim not deviating. 'You know, Sniper, we could solve one of our major problems right now.'

Vrell is still in the process of folding his legs back out again, but now he freezes. Is he wondering to himself how quickly he can bring one of his weapons to bear before Orbus pulls the trigger? Surely he must realize Orbus can fill him full of sprine bullets before he can hope to respond. And, then, respond with what? Orbus now knows for certain that Prador close-combat rail-guns cannot penetrate his armour. Will Vrell's particle cannon prove equally ineffective? Whatever he uses, Vrell will still die. Orbus knows well what sprine does to anyone infected with the Spatterjay virus, for he once used it to execute a member of his own sailing-ship crew.

'I guess we could,' Sniper replies. 'We could go ahead and wipe out the guy who just saved your life.'

Orbus hears the words but can't quite make sense of them. After puzzling over this for a moment, he realizes his aim has wandered a little, and quickly snaps it back.

Sniper continues, 'Just one sprine bullet and Vrell ceases to be a problem, and afterwards you, Orbus, will be all better and hardly fucked up at all.'

'This isn't about me,' says Orbus, knowing he is lying. And even as he speaks he finds his anger beginning to recede.

'You mean it ain't about you starting to lose grip on your widely scattered marbles the moment you first got a sniff of this place?' Sniper enquires. 'Let's put this in perspective: Prador or not, infected by the virus or not, Vrell doesn't deserve to die. On Spatterjay he expected to be blamed for the crimes he commited while under the control of his father's pheromones. He tried to escape, and one of your crewmen died. Do you even remember the man's name?'

Orbus reaches up to scratch his head, only remembering he can't when his fingers clonk against the side of his helmet. 'That's not important . . .' he begins.

'Do you recall the names of any of those you killed just to stay alive when you were a captive of the Prador?'

'Ah fuckit,' says the Old Captain, closing his eyes and abruptly swinging his weapon away from Vrell. As the surge of anger continues to recede he knows, instantly, what this is all about. Yes, the smells of this ship evoke nightmares and, yes, the sight of any Prador is enough to scare him. But the anger? It is just a conditioned response, something acquired over his years as the sadistic Captain of a crew of masochists. He wonders just what other natural emotional responses are left within his skull. Any at all? Yes, there have to be. He laughed quite naturally whilst still aboard the *Gurnard*, and therefore knows he still possesses the capacity for pity, for empathy. Maybe it is simply the case that stress pushes him back into old habits. He opens his eyes to to find himself looking straight down the mirrored barrel of Vrell's particle cannon.

'This Human hates me,' says the Prador.

'Don't flatter yourself,' says Sniper. 'He hates all your kind, but hates himself even more.'

'That is not a logical survival trait,' remarks Vrell.

Just those words alone seem to cut right down to Orbus's core. He is not quite so screwed up as he was aboard the *Vignette*, but he still has a long way to go. Behaving as he has been recently, he does not reckon much on his chances getting out of all this alive, but the most critical question he needs to answer is: *Do I want to live?* He needs to answer that question now, to himself, deep inside. He runs his tongue over his teeth and remembers stringy flesh caught between them, and knows the answer at once. *He wants to live.* He owes it to all those who didn't. He owes them more than his wasted centuries; so much more.

'Are you going to pull the trigger on that thing,' Orbus snarls. 'Or are we going to get moving?'

Vrell slowly swings the weapon away from him and returns it to the clips in his harness. 'Fifty yards further along here, we can break through into the section I secured for the mutated third-children. Some minutes ago the Guard were not present there, but that may have changed.'

'So we just need to get there,' says Sniper. The drone reaches out with his major tentacles and slaps them down on the rim of Vrell's shell. 'You move ahead, Orbus.'

Only a small gap runs down alongside Vrell, and Orbus eases himself into it, edging past the big mutated Prador, which is fine until Vrell suddenly moves, whereupon Orbus slams himself back against the wall. He realizes his breathing is uneven and recognizes the phobic horror he is feeling but, with rigid determination, pushes himself on. Once safely beyond Vrell, he moves quickly down the passageway and turns to look back. Sniper, his smaller tentacles unfurled all about him, begins pushing, Vrell grinds along slowly at first, then with increasing speed as Sniper edges himself along too. This goes on for some minutes until Vrell calls out, 'Here – this is the spot.'

'Where do I cut through?' Sniper asks.

'Right below me.'

One spatulate tentacle tip stabs down beside the Prador, going through the floor with a high whine and spurt of metallic dust. Sniper continues cutting in a wide circle and halfway round the floor begins to sag. Further slicing drops the floor lower till, with a whistling sound, Vrell slides from sight and crashes down somewhere below.

'C'mon!' Sniper yells, following the Prador down.

Just for a second Orbus considers finding his own way, but realizes that will be suicidal, since he won't last more than a few minutes if he encounters one of the Guard. Reluctantly he moves to the yawning gap, ups the light amplification of his visor, and sees Vrell and Sniper making their way down a sloping floor, pushing wreckage aside as they go. The floor itself lies twenty feet below him, which even at one-gravity would not hurt him. He steps over the edge and drops, landing with a thump and not even bending his legs to absorb the shock, and then strides after them as fast as the low gravity will allow.

Even as he catches up, he sees Sniper batting away one of the mutated third-children.

Then a beam of a particle cannon cuts through wreckage, strikes Sniper and splashes, then catches Vrell on one side, blowing away part of his shell and three of his legs.

'They're here,' Sniper announces.

So Gurnard isn't going to venture any closer to the planetoid and intends to sit out here as a spectator only, but Drooble is damned if that is all he himself is going to do. He applies the multidriver to the fixings all around the wall panel, quickly winding them out and sending them clattering to the floor, and meanwhile wonders how long it will take the AI to catch on to what he's doing. Maybe it'll stay distracted by that thing sitting out there keeping an eye on them.

Eventually the panel swings down on one remaining lower corner fixing, to expose bunches of fibre-optics and a couple of superconductor feeds sheathed in plasticized ceramic. Drooble unholsters his solid-state laser pistol and studies them for a moment. If his earlier reading of the ship's schematics is correct, then all the optics and the lower feed are the ones he needs to deal with. He therefore points at the feed and pulls the trigger.

The laser beam crackles as it hits the ceramic coating but, since the purpose of this coating is to prevent the possibility of a short of thousands of amps, it takes a little while to burn through. The moment it does, however, a massive arc flash cuts a crater into the metal behind, the blast throwing Drooble back against the opposite wall of the corridor. The arc burns for a while longer as vaporizing metal erodes the superconductor away, then some safety device kicks in and shuts it down. The corridor lights dim for a second, then come on again.

'What are you doing, Drooble?' Gurnard enquires.

Drooble staggers to his feet, emitting an odd giggle, wipes his face then wishes he hadn't, as a layer of skin peels off to dangle free. He pulls it off and discards it, then glances up towards the ceiling, half expecting a security drone to drop into view, before approaching the panel again.

Metal is still glowing inside there and most of the optics are burnt through but, being methodical, Drooble takes careful aim and severs the rest of them, before turning away and heading over to a nearby bulkhead door.

'You are not going to answer me?' Gurnard enquires.

As expected, the control panel beside the door is dead, and

Drooble has to use its manual mechanism to open it. He strides on into the suiting room beyond, tears open a locker that is also without power, pulls out the spacesuit inside and dons it.

'Ah, I think I see,' says Gurnard.

'You do?' Drooble wonders. 'Bit slow for an AI, ain't you?'

'What makes you think that object out there will let you past when it won't allow me past?'

'There's one way to find out,' Drooble replies.

'You are not thinking clearly, Iannus Drooble.'

'No? Really?' Drooble opens the next bulkhead door into the shuttle bay and carefully closes it behind him. Then he walks over and operates the door control to the shuttle, which is powered by the shuttle itself, and enters. He takes the pilot's chair and pulls back the ivory-handled lever to close up the shuttle's door, then after a pause pulls back the lever next to it to open the space doors. If he has this right, a safety system will have kicked in. This is so that, should the *Gurnard* come under attack and lose its internal power, the shuttle's own internal power supply can still be used to open the bay doors

A ship's bell begins ringing and he jerks in surprise, before gripping the shuttle's helm and shuffling into a more comfortable position in the chair, with his feet down on the foot pedals. The space door cracks open with a bang, and a wind begins whistling as the air inside the bay squirts out into vacuum, the noise growing fast to a steady shriek. Obviously the power supplied by the shuttle is enough to open the doors, but not enough to operate the bay-evacuation pumps. Eventually all the air goes, and then Drooble pushes the helm forwards to slide the shuttle out into night.

'Do you think Orbus will approve of this?' Gurnard enquires from the console.

'I don't care either way,' Drooble replies.

'Yes, of course . . . you get to risk your life and, if you survive and the Captain does not approve of what you have done, just maybe he'll punish you for it . . .'

'That's not what this is about.' But Drooble wonders to himself just what this is about. He wants to be there, not just spectating from the bridge of the *Gurnard*. He wants to help out as best he can. Doesn't he?

The shuttle falls away from the big cargo ship towards the icy marble of the planetoid, and towards that other object which, from this perspective, lies just off to one side of it. He opens up the fusion drive, the seat punching him in the back, and grins. Whilst the planetoid seems to grow only marginally, the object that has placed itself between *Gurnard* and it is rapidly increasing in size. Within minutes it is large enough for him to study some of its detail. It does look like just a big chunk, a big splinter of metal hanging in the void, though now he can see shapes like a cross between fossils of ancient life-forms and old circuitry seemingly etched into its surface. He waits for some reaction from the thing, but there is nothing, not even as he draws parallel to it, then speeds past.

'So you survived that,' Gurnard observes.

'I thought maybe this shuttle would be too small for it to even bother with,' Drooble replies, uncomfortable with the fact that he is feeling a species of disappointment.

'There's the main vessel to contend with yet,' warns Gurnard. 'Then the one down on the planet, and maybe Vrell and his dreadnought too.'

'Not a problem.' Drooble increases acceleration towards the distant orb.

Since boarding the dreadnought, Sniper had been perpetually scanning the areas immediately surrounding him. Some of the Guard were active at the beginning, but only conducting Vrell's ongoing repairs of his ship, and others were simply grinding to a halt. However, from half an hour prior to Vrell saying, '*Something hostile has taken control of the Guard,*' the activity of those armoured corpses aboard the dreadnought has ramped up. The motionless ones have started moving again and those still working have downed tools and moved off. At first all this new activity seemed utterly chaotic, but then a pattern began to emerge as the Guard started isolating reactors, weapons systems, and the ship's various drives. Next, even worse, some of them faded from view as they brought online some form of chameleonware. And now they are here.

In irritation, Sniper slaps a mutated third-child out of the way and spits two missiles towards the hazy source of that particle beam, then fires off both his own particle cannons at points within the wreckage where he predicts the near-invisible attacker might have gone. The two missiles impact, a double blast casting aside twisted beams and buckled wall panels. Briefly, something that definitely does not look like one of the Guard is flung back out of sight by the blast, whilst another of the same variety is picked out by one of the particle beams.

'There's things in here that don't look like your Guard,' he observes.

'They must be from the other ship,' Vrell replies.

'Then they got in here bloody quick.'

Something odd about all this, something very odd . . .

Absorbing data from these brief appearances, Sniper reconfigures his scanning routine and gets a snapshot of the attackers' positions throughout this particular area of the ship. Five of them are here within this sealed-off area, and others are converging from outside it. Then, abruptly, the scanning routine ceases to pick up anything, as the creatures he now sees reconfigure their own chameleonware, quick to work out what data Sniper just acquired. They are fast – horribly so.

Sniper doesn't know what plans Vrell has been formulating. It certainly seems the Prador wants to find somewhere to hide, so as to formulate them further and begin some furtive attack upon the invaders of his ship. But these new creatures will not give Vrell the time, and now the Prador is crippled too.

'We have to get out of here,' announces Sniper. 'Things are gonna get too hot to handle in here very quickly.'

Vrell is struggling along, managing to keep up for a short distance, then collapsing as the two legs he has left on one side fail to support his weight, probably because of damage to connecting muscles, and maybe because of the pain. However, where the chunk was burned from his shell the wound is already skinning over and bulging, and it seems likely the Prador will not be without legs for too much longer.

'Help him,' Sniper says to Orbus.

'Help him?'

Another cripple, thinks Sniper. Orbus was not the right choice for this little venture. Maybe a few decades cruising round as the Captain of a cargo ship would have resulted in him obtaining some stability, maybe not. But certainly getting thrown straight into conflict with those who damaged him in the first place seems to be undermining the already shaky bulwarks of his mind. Sniper wonders how long it will be before Orbus again decides Vrell is surplus to requirements, for his anger seems to be surfacing in a regular pattern. However, he did manage to control it this last time.

'Yes, *help* him.'

Orbus reluctantly moves up beside Vrell and, none too gently, jams his shoulder underneath the place where the Prador has lost its legs. Vrell hisses, but says nothing.

Still scanning about, Sniper realizes their only option now lies far down to his left, where a break in the hull opens to the outside.

But what then? In here they will be subject to constant and increasingly lethal attacks, but that does not mean such attacks will cease once they depart the ship.

'Keep moving.'

Sniper plots out the area down below, then tears away a tangle of beams to give them access to the start of an exit route. Knowing that the enemy may second-guess him, be begins to reprogram some of his missiles, choose alternative routes, prepare mines and other incendiaries, and formulate solutions to various forms of attack. Certainly, he isn't going up against simple Prador – or their drones – here.

Prador drones . . .

'What about your drones?' he abruptly asks Vrell.

'I am ahead of you,' Vrell replies. 'I have recorded orders for them, and I possess the codes to access the drone cache, but I cannot open communication without being detected and leaving myself open to viral attack.'

Sniper picks up a signal from Vrell's CPU, opens a channel and downloads the data the Prador sends him. Sniper next begins running programming routines to punch him through to the drone cache, but with the static out there, and the alien code running in so many of the ship's systems, this is like negotiating a briar patch growing on the surface of a swamp.

'Down here.' Sniper leads the way down through a gap.

Orbus and Vrell dutifully follow, though Sniper has to help the Prador down through. Even as he lowers Vrell to the floor below, he turns and fires two programmed missiles along their intended route, whereupon, a hundred feet ahead, they swerve into surrounding wreckage. The first explodes, flaring out an EM pulse, whilst the second simply settles, then winds up to speed its chemical reactor in order to power its esoteric hardware. Its nose falls off and it begins projecting. A hundred feet ahead, holographic copies of the three escapees proceed through the wreckage, and abruptly find themselves at the confluence of two particle beams and a stream of rail-gun missiles.

Sniper returns fire from his present location, his two particle beams stabbing out, and has the satisfaction of briefly seeing one of the invaders lose a claw as its own particle cannon explodes. The holograms leap forward, simultaneously opening fire, and the EM pulse has sufficiently scrambled instrumentation for the unknown attackers not to know which of the figures they see are the real ones.

Leading the way along a different course through the wreckage, Sniper again picks up enough data to penetrate his opponents' chameleonware, and again gets a snapshot of their locations before they reformat. In response to this, he drops a series of mines from his store, and begins flinging them all about with deadly accuracy. Where they hit, their gecko function kicks in and they stick. Simultaneously he sends specially designed programs to each. Some will detonate if touched, some upon picking up regular patterns of air movement, others will blow if a weapon is fired within their blast radius. All of this Sniper very carefully designed. He knows he stands no hope of taking out more than one or two of these creatures. He just needs to delay them enough so that he, Vrell and Orbus can get out of here.

Vrell seems to be getting along a bit better, showing a speed of recovery that would be remarkable in any normal Prador, but Sniper has long been associating with those infected with the Spatterjay virus; he knows what it can do for them. It also occurs to him, knowing the other effects of the virus, that Vrell will soon be needing something to eat, or else he might risk undergoing some nasty changes.

Through . . .

Abruptly Sniper finds himself accessing the drone cache.

Through internal ship eyes, he observes rank upon rank of the spherical drones all locked into their storage alcoves along the walls of one massive chamber – in fact hundreds of them. On sending the first code Vrell provided, he observes clamps slowly disengaging from the drones like claws opening up. Meanwhile he sends to each of them Vrell's instructions: *The Guard are hostile, and in collusion with invaders attempting to take over this ship. Hunt and destroy them all without regard to ship structure.* As soon as the command arrives, the drones begin departing their alcoves, but just then, some massive explosion rocks the entire chamber, flinging many of them about like loose ball-bearings, and yet more of those creatures he has already seen start to enter, with weapons blazing. Sniper feels both chagrin and not a little fear, on seeing how incredibly fast they react. He intercepts data from the cache, again breaking the enemy's chameleonware format, and sees that some of them are already withdrawing from around him to counter this new danger. But not enough.

Particle beams lash down all around them. Orbus takes a hit, spins out from his position of supporting Vrell, then opens fire with his multigun.

Time to go.

Sniper fires a series of missiles which shoot ahead of him and then curve down. He advances to grab a floor panel, tear it up and cast it aside. From below comes the first detonation. He snakes out a tentacle, wraps it around Orbus, whose armour is smoking, and drags him in close. Vrell, however, having worked out what the drone is doing, hurls himself to one side, a particle beam splashing on and incinerating wreckage directly above him, then lurches forward and down through the hole. Sniper flings himself after him, powering up his fusion drive as he drops, swinging the flame chambers around a full one hundred and eighty degrees, so he is essentially propelled shell-first downwards. Passing Vrell, he reaches out to snag the Prador and draw him in below the two drive flames. He hits burning and molten wreckage from the first missile explosion, and punches straight through it. Further detonations ensue as Sniper punches his way through three more weakened conglomerations of wreckage. Particle beams and streams of missiles from rail-guns create a storm of fire and metal fragments all about them. Above, mines begin going off, igniting a rapidly receding inferno.

Finally Sniper cannons hard into an unweakened wall of crash-foam directly under a lattice of beams. He drags himself out of the crater he has made, swinging his drives round again, and uses both them and his free tentacles to propel himself, and the other two, across the wall. He fires another missile, which curves down through a hole in the wall and detonates, filling all nearby spaces with burning crash-foam, then hurtles down into this gap and out into icy twilight, bounces on hard ice before releasing his two companions, then skids for two hundred feet before driving his tentacles into it to bring himself to a stop. Orbus and Vrell go skating on past him, finally drawing to a halt some fifty feet further on.

'Run for that.' Sniper stabs a tentacle towards an outcrop of ice and stone situated between them and the distant vessel which, now down on the icy plain, looks like the giant fortress of some VR fantasy called *Lord of Winter*. The two obey him, moving swiftly away. However Vrell is again signalling with his CPU and clearly wants to send Sniper something more.

'This may be of use,' Vrell reports. 'I tried to use it just a moment ago, but I cannot get through. It is the detonation code for the fusion tacticals inside the Guards' armour.'

'Not much use against these other buggers,' Sniper observes.

He squirrels the code away for future use, puts online his internal antigrav and rises twenty feet into the air, turning to face their exit point from the ship. With spurts from his steering jets, he steadily moves away, keeping himself between the exit and his two companions. Whilst doing this, he checks his supplies of munitions and power. Both are severely depleted and, for what is to come, he doubts even the full load would be enough. At intervals he begins cutting holes down into the ice and then shooting off the occasional preprogrammed missile. He needs to stack the odds in his favour.

The Golgoloth realizes that something very untoward is occurring aboard the dreadnought and, on examining the fragments of com it is picking up, knows at once that the source of these events is neither Human nor Prador. The ancient hermaphrodite Prador has never seen code like this before, to the best of his knowledge, anyway. It begins running a search through its extended mind, putting online ganglion after ganglion and, as a precaution, leaving them running, the processing power of his mind and his sheer intelligence growing moment by moment. As a further precaution the Golgoloth begins applying some of those ganglia to the weapons systems of this vessel fragment and the main vessel above – systems it did not previously consider necessary for dealing with a downed dreadnought and its single mutated Prador occupant.

Up above, it readies U-space missiles, reformatting their U-fields so they can actually penetrate down into a gravity well to reach the surface of a planet, their target the dreadnought itself. The Golgoloth begins running hardfield generators up to power, and provides numerous back-up systems for them. It lines up reception dishes on the ship fragment to receive high-powered microwave beams from the fathership – an excess of power the Golgoloth may shortly require. It onlines generators that can produce force-fields of rather esoteric design – the product of a century-long thread of research it finished fifty years back. It now runs diagnostics on equally esoteric beam weapons whose output combines the radiative spectrums and particle emissions in strange and useful ways, and readies its most powerful full-spectrum white lasers. Then it turns its attention to information now becoming available.

For a brief moment the Golgoloth is surprised at the source of this new information, which is a ganglion it brought online only recently: in fact the one that stores all its knowledge about the Spatterjay virus. The Golgoloth knew the virus harboured something entirely alien – a trihelical genome – and the special search reveals that the alien code presently being employed aboard the dreadnought closely matches feedback from those trihelical structures caused by induction scanning. This is an odd fact, but still doesn't explain what is happening in that ship out there.

Its intelligence now thoroughly heightened, the Golgoloth again reviews what it knows. Oberon wants Vrell destroyed and, even though the Golgoloth is not completely allied with the King, the old hermaphrodite is currently the King's most powerful resource within the Graveyard. Because of the possible Polity response, sending in ships is not a safe option, yet the King seems ready to now do even that. Vrell, though a dangerous virally mutated Prador, does not seem to represent a sufficient danger to merit being countered by such drastic measures, yet now it appears that the Golgoloth has somehow underestimated him. Whatever is happening aboard that dreadnought is perhaps exactly what Oberon feared.

The Golgoloth returns its attention to its telescopes and scanners, realizing that some sort of battle is occurring within the dreadnought itself. Focusing on two Prador war drones as they pursue something escaping through an upper hatch, it sees an object hazy with chameleonware effect even though repeatedly being struck by weapons fire. Then one of the big rail-guns mounted in the ship's hull opens fire, slamming quarter-ton missiles into the drones and blowing them apart. The hazy thing returns to the ship, its chameleonware shutting off, and Golgoloth glimpses briefly an insectile armoured shape. Next, figures come careening out through one of the holes in the bottom of the ship, and begin heading towards an outcrop of stone and ice lying midway between the Golgoloth's vessel and the dreadnought. The old hermaphrodite cautiously focuses all its weapons on them, before studying them intently.

One mutated Prador who is very likely Vrell, one armoured Human and one Polity war drone. This is all very odd. The Golgoloth watches them with interest.

12

Like the Human race the Prador developed electronics by beginning with simple switches and going on to thermionic valves, transistors and then, as they first ventured beyond their world and physical weight became an issue, the integrated circuit. Again like Humans, from this they developed computers to handle the increasing complexities of their civilization. However, because of the ruggedness of the Prador physiology and their lack of regard even for their offspring, and because their biotechnology of that time was so advanced, their thinking machines soon incorporated parts of the surgically excised brains and nervous systems of their children. Later, as Prador understood the possibilities inherent in creating artficial intelligence – something that might eventually prove superior to them – they chose to use the whole brains of their children rather than go that route. AIs were therefore never developed in the Prador Kingdom, and the penalties for either importing or researching them are severe.
– From QUINCE GUIDE *compiled by Humans*

Sadurian puts the stack of crystal memtabs down on her console and returns to her seat. The tabs contain programs she has not used in many years, first because they are something the Prador very much do not like, and second because long ago she singled out the main reasons for the King's inability to breed. Mainly it is about the virus being carried as a parasite in the King's spermatozoa. The issue, however, was not one of Prador genetics, but instead about turning off the chemical switch that sends the virus into survival mode by stunning it prior to fertilization. These programs were constructed to explore what all different kinds of genetic tissue can produce: a computer womb but also something else.

'It is done?' she enquires.

'Done,' replies Delf, typically laconic.

Sadurian studies the tangled molecular maps on her screen, displaying millions of fragments of alien code that are wound up in the mycelial tangle of the Spatterjay virus. Her problem is that, before she starts predicting what the genome produces, she needs to first put it all together. It will be like rethreading a million beads back on a new string, but exactly in the right order. Sadurian begins loading her programs which, requiring no further input from her, now slot themselves together. She glances across at Delf and Yaggs, checks a couple of subscreens, and sees that Delf has now returned to the deconstruction and mapping of the King's genome. However, it does not matter that these two Prador are here, because they have known about these programs for years, doubtless reported them to Oberon, and so far nothing untoward has happened.

The last crystal memtab goes into the tab-reader slot, then, after a moment, pokes out like a tongue and she extracts it, returning it to the stack.

'I am ready,' says a voice from the console, speaking Human Anglic.

'Okay, Sphinx, check kernel four. You'll find some interesting data there.'

'I see,' replies Sphinx, who is an artificial intelligence.

Because the Prador do not like AIs, those caught experimenting with them tend to end up on the hot end of an electrified spike somewhere in the central caverns of the Prador homeworld's capital city. That way, it usually takes Prador offenders a week to die. Humans caught smuggling such technology into the Kingdom die more quickly, but that is only a matter of physiology, since the same sort of spike is generally employed in both cases. However, none of this applies to Sadurian, for she is under the King's protection and knows that if she ever displeases Oberon sufficiently, her end will be quick, messy and dispensed by the King himself.

The AI continues, 'We seem to have here the cellular component of the Spatterjay virus, comprising numerous pieces of a genome I do not recognize and other components relating to some form of quantum storage.'

Sadurian nods briefly to herself, absorbing the words she already expected to hear, before abruptly realizing that Sphinx is telling her more than she expected. A cold talon drags itself down her spine.

'Quantum storage? What do you mean "quantum storage"?'

'Molecular components constructed in the format of quantum-storage units, and nested amidst the alien genome.'

'What do they store?' Sadurian asks, still not quite grasping what she is hearing.

'Since I am at present only studying a computer model, I cannot tell you that. A much deeper analysis of the actual physical units will be required – the superpositions and entanglements of the atoms concerned – and then only a general idea might be obtained,' Sphinx replies. 'And even to do that will require the work of a specialized AI somewhat more powerful than me.'

'Right,' says Sadurian, sitting back. 'Right . . . I want you to start finding a way to put that genome back together. I want to find out what it *makes*.'

'Easy enough. It is trihelical, so there are fewer base combinations, fewer ways the pieces can link up, than with a double helix.'

Even as the AI speaks, the images on the screen change. Lengths of alien genome, represented as simple rods of varying lengths and colours, stand up like skittles in endless rows, flickering and swapping places. On a second screen, rods being selected out are joined, separated, and rejoined with other lengths. As Sadurian knows perfectly well, the whole graphic is a huge simplification intended for her benefit, but it is satisfying to see at least some of the process.

'Interesting,' comments Sphinx.

'An eye,' says Sadurian, peering at the recognizable anatomical image of an eye plus optic nerve and some other related structures.

'Yes, in one incarnation it is little different from a Human or squid eye, however, it is becoming increasing clear how a large series of related alleles cover a whole range of options.'

The image changes, the eye slowly transforming into a brush-like organ, then a jointed antenna, which then collapses back into an opaque receptor of something other than visible light. Sadurian feels a further prickling down her spine when she recognizes something resembling the King's present midnight eyes.

'These are only a few of the options,' Sphinx adds. 'And it seems that there are also many further options for other physical structures.'

'Any conclusions?'

'My conclusions are, at present, that much of this is too well ordered to all be a simple product of evolution. Instead, I would guess evolution plus a great deal of genetic modification over a long period of time. It is also interesting to note that this creature has the facility to grow nerve tissue with a pure electrical basis, also to grow very hard bone or shell – often with molecular honing to sharp edges – as well as very dense muscles, and numerous ways of delivering potent venoms.'

'Products of a hostile environment?'

'Creatures capable of genetic modification at this level only have hostile environments that they themselves create.'

Sadurian doesn't need any more hints. Before entering the Kingdom, she was at the top of her profession for a good reason.

'This is a soldier,' she decides.

'So it would seem.'

Sadurian wonders just how much further she wants to go with this. She has learnt what needed to be learnt, and now it is time to see Oberon. 'So the quantum storage is its mind, I guess.'

'Seems likely,' says Sphinx.

Sadurian stands up and heads for the door. Somehow, Oberon knows all this, she is sure, but what does the King want to do with such knowledge? Does he want to learn everything known about and *by* this soldier . . . or soldiers? Or, thinking about his recent actions and his paranoia regarding the Prador Vrell, does he want to utterly stamp such knowledge out of existence?

'Ah, bollocks,' says Sniper, as three armoured figures simply shed their chameleonware, thus demonstrating that they don't feel the need to hide from him. He studies them carefully, using all his scanning routines, and is utterly baffled.

They seem to bear some similarity to Prador, being also crustaceans and clad in armour of the same exotic metal as the Guard's. However, their armour is a deep blue in colour, and extends into lobster tails at the back. They each possess four thick legs and their claws are mismatched, one of them possessing three jaws and the other just one jaw extending into a long scythe-like spike. Their heads are separate and protrude from their bodies on short necks, just like Vrell's, and are loaded with sensory apparatus and with two gleaming blue forward-facing eyes. Their weapons reveal a similar format to Prador weapons he knows, but are much altered and blended into their bodies. Each possesses the mouth of a particle cannon at the base of that scythelike spike, and other suspicious-looking openings ranged about their bodies. Scan data reveals how they also *blend* with their armour. It appears he is facing insectile cyborgs.

'I don't suppose you want to talk about this?' Sniper enquires.

A particle beam, spectrally shifted from blue to green, stabs from the middle one of the three, to splash on the hardfield Sniper projects. The force of the blast sends Sniper skidding backwards, for that beam possesses a kinetic component he has never encountered before. Almost immediately the hardfield generator Sniper uses begins to behave oddly, and strange resonances feed back through its power supply. The blast is feeding a computer virus to him straight through his own projector. Flinging himself high, he shuts down the field and, onlining another generator, he intercepts a second beam strike from another of the three, while he tries to damp the resonance in the first generator.

Sniper shuts off grav and drops, not wanting them to pursue him into the sky, and as he hits ice again they advance. He watches them carefully pause to study the ice, then circumvent a churned area directly ahead of them. Sniper sends a detonation signal and a mine explodes below one of the three creatures, flinging it high. Of course he didn't bury the mines where he churned the ice. He opens fire on the remaining two, his particle beam splashing against a hardfield disc. Just a distraction. The one still hurtling upwards through the air manages to correct its tumble just in time for one of Sniper's preprogrammed missiles to slam into it from the other side of the ship. The explosion slaps it down hard on the ice, where it bounces, snapped partially in half like a cooked prawn. But, even as Sniper watches, it begins tugging itself together. Sniper is about to hit it again, when suddenly the ice all around it begins fragmenting, and he hears the recognizable smack of bullets hitting home.

Orbus.

The Old Captain is positioned three hundred yards away,

down on one knee and aiming carefully. Beyond him, Vrell is still struggling towards the distant vessel. As the two remaining creatures launch themselves into the air, intent on avoiding any further mines, missiles whicker out from them. Sniper manages to hit each projectile with his laser, but the blasts knock him weaving backwards. A second later the particle beams are back, grinding against his hardfields, their viral load trying to work its way inside him.

The wounded creature down on the ice begins to shiver, then rattle against the frozen ground. Suddenly it shoots straight up making a sound like a big angry hornet, hovers for a moment, then streaks off sideways to slam into the side of the dreadnought, where it shatters like brittle porcelain.

Lucky strike, thinks Sniper, *but at a cost*, as Orbus and Vrell also come under fire from the remaining two creatures. Then, seemingly out of nowhere, *Gurnard*'s lamprey shuttle roars in over the top of the dreadnought, a stream of rail-gun missiles playing across one of the opponents and knocking it tumbling through the air. The shuttle turns hard, briefly playing its fusion torch over the second creature, so that it falls a hundred feet with smoke pouring from its armour.

The shuttle belly-lands just beyond Orbus and Vrell, skidding round and sliding, while trying to bring itself to a stop with its steering jets and sun-bright bursts from its fusion torch. For a moment Sniper allows himself some optimism, but both creatures have simply corrected their flight once the shuttle is past, and they open fire again.

Vrell, the bigger unarmoured target, is now down on his belly, a spatter of green blood staining the ice beyond him, and a great smoking groove carved across his back. As the shuttle settles in a great cloud of steam on the ice behind, Orbus goes down on his knee again, sighting on one of the distant creatures as it tumbles through the air. With the gun's menu up inside his visor, he checks through the options, but again returns to the sprine bullets. The simple fact is that if Sniper is having trouble taking down those two monstrosities with his array of weapons, then Orbus stands no chance of succeeding with the conventional firepower of this weapon he holds. He just hopes instead for another lucky hit, another hole punctured by Sniper or by that rail-gun hit from the shuttle, to enable him to get some sprine inside creatures that must be infected by the Spatterjay virus.

He fires one burst, completely on target, but to little effect. As he turns to aim at the other creature, now steadying itself and beginning to rise again, a series of explosions track across the ice towards him. A blast lifts him from the ground and then something else slams into his chest and spins him round in midair. He hits the ground winded, still clutching his multigun, the front of his suit now a molten mess and error message after error message displaying on his visor. Heaving himself upright, he is glad the creatures seem to be saving their big stuff for Sniper, or else he would be nothing but a smoking crater now. Time to run, he decides.

'Cap'n!' A distant shout, immediately echoing in Orbus's com gear.

Orbus turns and gazes across at the shuttle. Its side door is open and Drooble standing out on the ice, beckoning to him. But how did Gurnard get the vessel here so quickly? Did the AI somehow work out that they would abandon the dreadnought like this?

He quickly moves over to Vrell. 'Can you stand?'

Vrell tentatively moves his legs, then abruptly heaves himself up on to them, tilting over as two remaining legs on one side begin to shake under the load. Orbus considers just making a run for the shuttle, then with a surge of anger quickly moves over and jams his shoulder underneath one edge of the Prador's carapace. He has made his choice: Vrell is an ally, and that's the end of it. Slowly they begin to make their way towards the vessel, while Drooble moves out to meet them.

'Come on, Cap'n!' he shouts. 'Why don't you just leave that fucker!'

Abruptly Vrell jams one claw down into the ice, bringing them to a sudden halt.

'Go to the shuttle,' he orders.

'I'm not going to leave you now,' says Orbus. 'It took me long enough to accept that you deserve to live.'

'The shuttle,' Vrell observes, 'is too small.'

Orbus gapes at it for a moment, then calls himself all kinds of fool. Of course, how the hell does he expect to get the big mutated Prador inside a vessel like that?

'I'll bring it back here and you can cling to the outside,' he says. 'We can get you clear.'

'Yes,' Vrell concedes, but that is all.

Orbus eases his shoulder out from underneath the Prador, and watches it start to sag, before breaking into a loping run. He notes that Drooble is not accompanied by Thirteen, a fact that makes him suspicious.

'Why did Gurnard send you?' Orbus asks over com.

'He didn't,' Drooble replies. 'This was my own idea.'

'Probably not a great one, then.'

'Probably.' Drooble raises his gaze to the ongoing battle between the drone and the two unknown creatures, and to the dreadnought lying beyond them. 'That don't look promising.'

Orbus glances back. Movement on the summit of the dread-nought, then something blurs momentarily, and a thunderous crackle cuts the sky. He swings back in time to see Drooble turning back towards the shuttle.

'Ah shit,' says Drooble, then he flies apart in an immense eruption of ice dust and random fragments. The shuttle bucks and lifts, deforming as if wriggling in pain under multiple impacts, chunks of its flying away in all directions, but also a great spray of splintered metal spraying out to carve scars across the ice beyond it. Then something detonates inside it, and it disappears in a hot globular explosion. Not for the first time, Orbus finds himself at the brunt of a shockwave. In a storm of ice chunks, shattered metal and and seemingly liquid fire, he hurtles backwards, hits the ice on his back and skids, his armour smoking and spatters of molten metal gleaming across his visor.

Fuck you, Drooble, thinks Orbus. *Fuck you.* Something at the surface of his consciousness wants to rage at the world, go charging back and attack whoever fired the big rail-gun from the dreadnought, and then to spend himself against any that remain. But the feeling seems a skin over a hollow emptiness. And when the storm abruptly ceases, truncating unnaturally, and out of it an invisible claw snatches him up and draws him in, he doesn't fight it – just lets it drag him away.

Orbus, Vrell and Drooble have disappeared amid the massive eruptions caused by the rail-gun, and Sniper does not suppose it will be long before the same weapon is turned on himself, though he will not make so easy a target. He absorbs and accepts the loss of those three, somewhat surprised at how much he regrets it, despite him knowing them for so little time and theirs not being the most likeable of characters. This isn't something he can ponder for long, however. He needs to finish this soon, finish it before more weapons or more opponents are put into play.

Brute firepower is not the answer here, for Sniper simply does not possess enough of it. The wily tricks he previously used to take out Prador and their drones had always worked to his advantage.

Maybe not again, though. No, even as Sniper retreats under the impact of those green virus-laden beams, his two opponents methodically start probing down below with lasers, to wipe out the missiles he also concealed in the ice. They then launch, all around them, a cloud of small ball-bearing-sized objects that go speeding away. Incendiaries of some kind, doubtless to intercept any other preprogrammed missiles. Sniper is rapidly running out of options.

One of his hardfield generators is resonating high, a virus forming – under induction from it – within his processing space and feeding back to interfere with the function of the generator itself. Only seconds remain before he needs to shut it down, or before it shuts itself down. He has one spare inside him which he brings online, but even that is already being interfered with. He searches desperately for options and finds only one. He regularly used a supercavitating drive to travel at high speed through the oceans of Spatterjay, and this produced a conefield ahead of him by bonding water molecules into a frictionless layer. Shutting down the most unstable hardfield generator, he tries the conefield. It intercepts and refracts the beam, which plays over his shell, but even so reduced, it blisters the nano-chain chromium and induces further viruses into his system. One of these propagates in the control hardware for his antigrav, and he drops like a stone. Maybe he should learn something from this?

Sniper loads some of his own attack viruses, and fires them by com laser even as he falls. One of the attackers abruptly shuts off its beam and drops. Working? No, the thing steadies and rises again as Sniper finally crashes down into the ice. A missile then slams into him, the blast sends him skidding a hundred yards. Two tentacles are now gone and a large chunk of his shell missing. But the force of the impact shakes something loose in his crystal mind.

Sprine bullets? Orbus was firing sprine bullets.

Knowing that this is all now coming to an end, Sniper launches missile after missile, depleting his supply. He fires his particle cannons, draining himself of energy and the particulate matter ionized for the beams. A com laser strikes him, engages his sensors, and he just cannot shut it out. Inside him the computer viruses begin linking up, and he feels himself downloading through the laser. They are stealing his mind, all his knowledge, everything he is, and the looting seems utterly methodical: enough for him to know what will be taken next. In the few seconds remaining to him, he loads the code Vrell had sent him into the next portion of his mind that he expects to be stolen, and it goes.

Above him two sun-bright lights flash into being, as the two alien creatures disappear in tactical fusion explosions. Ice boils into steam around Sniper as the shockwave picks him up yet again, just briefly, then slaps him down again, skidding up a hillock of fragmented ice behind him. The viruses, however, will not disperse so easily, and he continues to fight an internal battle: wiping portions of his own memory and closing down processing space like an army burning crops before an invader. Only after a few minutes does he regain enough control to once again re-engage his senses.

Carbon-dioxide snow falls all around him and fog banks, shot through with persimmon-yellow stains, roll away to his right and left. Like hornets disturbed from a hive, creatures just like the two he already killed depart the dreadnought and fly towards him. He is out of ammo, very low on power, and has lost nearly two-thirds of his mind. These things will not fall for any more tricks, and certainly they would soon analyse what just happened and respond to it. There will now be no access to the fusion tacticals inside them.

Sniper does not even have the power to destroy himself. He gropes out with ragged tentacles to snatch up chunks of hard ice, deciding he'll throw rocks at the fuckers if that's all that remains to him.

One creature, some way ahead of the main group, begins to descend out of the sky towards him. Abruptly a silver bubble appears around it, then just as suddenly collapses and winks out. From the space the creature occupied drops a compacted ball of smoking matter, which hits the ice and flies apart. All the others simply draw to a halt in mid-air, contemplate the situation for all of half a second, then turn and retreat.

The fact that sprine killed these creatures, and the detonation of the fusion tacticals inside his two attackers, is all the evidence Sniper needs. Issuing from the alien ship behind him, this field-tech attack on their fellows is further confirmation. The unknown creatures aren't invading the dreadnought from that other, alien, ship; they are the dreadnought's erstwhile crew.

Orbus gasps chill air and shudders, needles of cold piercing into his skin. He opens his eyes on eerie, green-tinted illumination, feels a cold floor beneath his back, and under his palm.

Iannus Drooble is dead.

He can't quite grasp that, for Drooble was his crewman for centuries and seemed almost an extension of his being. Orbus feels hollow now and oddly devoid of anger. Trying to analyse this feeling, a quite drily unemotional and horrible thought occurs to him. Drooble's death has severed yet another link to his own past; it has cut through the anchor chain linking him to the *Vignette* and somehow cast him adrift. The death of the crewman might well be the cure he needs and, though he resents that notion, it is a resentment without the power to turn itself into rage.

After a moment he sits upright, muscles creaking, then gazes down at himself, realizing his armoured spacesuit has been removed. Now glancing to one side, he observes Vrell lying down on his stomach, remaining legs sprawled. The clatter and bubble of Prador speech issues from somewhere, and Vrell, still wearing his harness though disarmed, replies to it, and now the harness translator, obviously just turned on by Vrell, supplies the words to Orbus.

'I will not,' says Vrell.

'Why not?' asks an unknown Prador, its voice now also relayed through Vrell's translator.

'Because I choose not to.'

'But you must be suffering from the injury hunger engendered by the Spatterjay virus, and there beside you is a source of nutrient.'

The penny finally drops and Orbus realizes that the 'source of nutrient' is himself. He stands up and, in a way he hopes isn't too obvious, moves away until his back rests against a curving black wall. At least now he will have time to react before Vrell makes a grab for him. Whatever camaraderie Vrell is feeling for Orbus will soon depart as the virus continues its work inside the Prador. After all, Humans suffering from injury hunger for long enough will eat just about anything. Orbus remembers some of the gruesome stories he has heard about Hooper crews stranded on the islands; and about how quite a few crew members mysteriously disappeared, and how the survivors don't much like discussing the matter. And Prador tend to be even less concerned by moral issues bearing on their food supply.

'I find that very interesting,' continues the voice. 'My understanding of the effect of this mutation is that it produces a beast much better able to survive. One would suppose, being Prador, that survivability equates to ruthlessness; while in Human society a degree of altruism, whether with an evolutionary or moral basis, works better than unrelenting viciousness.'

With shaky effort, Vrell manages to heave himself to his feet, still tilting to one side where the two legs remaining fail to adequately support his weight.

'Who are you?' Vrell asks.

A long pause ensues, then the same voice replies, 'I have now weighed up the pros and cons of telling you the truth. I am the Golgoloth.'

Orbus is surprised at Vrell's reaction. The Prador instinctively cringes like a dog expecting a blow, which puts him out of balance so that he staggers to one side to rest one edge of his carapace against the wall furthest away from Orbus. His legs are visibly shaking again, and Orbus suspects this has nothing to do with the physical strain they are under.

'Who is the Golgoloth?' Orbus asks.

'A myth,' Vrell replies. 'A story used to frighten offspring.'

Orbus contemplates that statement. Taking into account the fact that Prador fathers rather enjoy eating alive some of their own children, if this Golgoloth is something used to scare the young, it must be terrible indeed.

'Yet here we are almost certainly aboard one section of a massive vessel,' says Orbus, 'a vessel the Polity has no knowledge of and which it seems likely was either built in the Graveyard or hidden in here before the border defence stations went fully online. So tell me about this Golgoloth.'

'I don't know very much,' confesses Vrell. 'It is supposedly a monster that can travel through darkness to any location, where it cuts out and eats the organs of young Prador. It is claimed to be immortal, and to control the destinies of all Prador . . .'

Through the intercom, or by whatever other means this Golgoloth thing is using to talk to them, comes a clattering and bubbling. Orbus waits for a translation, but there is none forthcoming. He suspects he has just, for the first time ever, heard Pradorish laughter.

'In Prador culture, myth-making indeed struggles to produce anything coherent,' says the Golgoloth. 'But Vrell, like all myths, about which your companion doubtless has greater knowledge, being the product of a society where myths easily propagate, the ones concerning me do possess an element of truth.'

'So what's *true* about them?' Orbus asks.

'Vrell,' says the Golgoloth, 'you really should exercise more control over your food.'

'Why don't you answer the question Captain Orbus has asked?'

The eerie glow increases in intensity, then the walls slide into translucence, revealing vague lights lying beyond, then gradually into transparency. Studying his surroundings, Orbus realizes they are enclosed in a cylinder, within a larger chamber. Turbid water, about a foot deep, slops against the outside of the cylinder wall, and the place is packed with optic and power cables and pipes plugged into blocky monoliths of a technology that appears to be more about plumbing than electronics. Platforms mounted on single pillars support other conglomerations of technology, and numerous other cylindrical tanks – much narrower than the one they now occupy – contain organic components blended with hardware and wired in to the whole mass. Here and there, multi-jointed arms terminating in complex manipulators are in the process of either assembling or disassembling various components. Independent robots like segmented iron starfish move through it all, and in the water itself living organisms and odd machines constantly bumble or dart. However, taking all this in at a glance, Orbus's attention is inexorably drawn to the individual squatting on a platform that seems to be at the focus of all this hybrid technology.

'The Golgoloth?' he wonders aloud.

Vrell just jerks away from the transparent wall and moves over to Orbus's side of the cylinder. Orbus isn't afraid, realizing that

Vrell isn't moving over to take advantage of this 'source of nutrient', but just getting as far away as he can from the thing on the platform.

The creature bears some resemblance to normal Prador in that it possesses a similar number of limbs, a carapace and a visual turret. However, it is distinctly asymmetrical, its colouring ranging from a sick yellow to white, its carapace so covered with lines and mismatched depths of shell that it seems to have been decorated with a montage. Orbus recognizes these marks as surgery scars: the result of shell-welding. It is also linked by numerous optics and pipes to two monolithic machines positioned behind it. Things also crawl over its shell, things like mechanical ship-lice. Its turret eyes don't match: too small on one side and too large on the other. Its palp eyes are also mismatched: one of them blind white and trailing wires from its centre straight into an array of electronic eyes mounted on its back, the other big, and bright green, almost glowing.

'Is this what your myths describe?' Orbus asks.

'It is,' Vrell confirms.

'So, let me get this straight,' says Orbus. 'A young Prador survives the death of his father and manages to get safely to his father's ship underneath the Spatterjay ocean, where he is subsequently mutated by the Spatterjay virus. This young Prador manages to get his father's ship running again, go up against a fully-armed Prador dreadnought and survive yet again, subsequently exterminating the whole crew of that vessel and taking control of it. Yet now this same Prador is frightened by a fairy tale?'

Vrell abruptly jerks away from the wall and swings his nightmarish head towards Orbus, who suspects he himself has unwittingly just made the transition from ally to food. Certainly Vrell looks greatly in need of something to eat: his belly plates run in parallel with his upper carapace, and the distance between the two has decreased to less than a foot. Where he lost his legs the shape of new legs can now be seen neatly folded underneath a taut translucent skin.

'I am weakened,' says Vrell, his mandibles grinding, and a black saliva dripping from the lower part of his mouth.

Orbus takes a pace or two back, whereupon Vrell leans forward and takes one unsteady pace towards Orbus.

'I see,' says the Golgoloth, 'that despite your strength of mind, Vrell, that viral-injury hunger is at last winning out. However, having scanned both yourself and the Human enclosed in there with you, I see that the result of any contest between you is by no means assured.'

A large arm swings over, above the cylinder they occupy, and at its end is an object shaped like an inverted cup. This clamps down, causing the floor to shudder underneath them, then in the ceiling a hatch divides centrally, the two halves hingeing downwards to drop something inside. It hits the floor with a heavy wet thump, spattering purplish blood across it and up the walls. The animal source of this great chunk of raw flesh, with jagged black bones almost like ribs, is a mystery to Orbus, but the smell clicks some switch even inside himself and his mouth starts watering. It has, after all, been many hours since he has eaten, too.

Vrell totters towards the flesh and almost falls upon it, legs sprawling and head lunging down. He tears up a large flap of it in one claw, brings it to his mouth and saws at it with his mandibles, whereupon it quickly disappears into the grinding plates inside his mouth. He severs another chunk, then another, eating so fast he is scattering loose gobbets of it all about him. Orbus moves over and takes up one of these fragments, bites hard and worries off a mouthful. Whilst chewing, he tries not to think about how its texture so much resembles raw human flesh. He swallows, expecting nausea, but though part of his mind feels disgust at this meal, his digestion is not so picky. His stomach rumbles alarmingly, and he continues to eat.

Again the floor shudders underfoot, and Orbus glances up at the hatch again, expecting another load of food to drop through it, but the hatch remains firmly closed. Returning his attention to Vrell, Orbus notes how the membrane is tearing along his wounded side, and small soft legs are folding out.

'The speed of regeneration is indeed astounding,' the Golgoloth observes, 'yet there could be severe penalties to pay. For it seems the Spatterjay virus is what you Humans would describe as a Trojan horse.'

'Oh, you're speaking to me now?' Orbus remarks.

'I find you interesting, Human.'

Orbus guesses this is one of those situations where if you aren't of interest you are merely rubbish to be discarded, or more likely just food. However, even being an object of interest does not ultimately guarantee fair and equitable treatment. This Golgoloth creature strikes Orbus as no better than any other Prador, where any interest in an individual might result in vivisection just to satisfy that interest.

'However,' the Golgoloth continues, whilst turning on its platform as if to gaze, through all the surrounding equipment, at something lying far beyond this vessel, 'exigency overcomes my curiosity about you – and about Vrell. It seems that those rather strange alien entities of yours out there have decided I am a threat that must now be countered.'

At first Orbus feels some amusement at hearing this creature describe others as 'quite strange', but then wonders what is meant by 'of yours'.

'It is time for me to put some distance between us and them, so I can have more opportunity to decide what needs to be done next,' the Golgoloth adds.

13

Throughout those initial and immediately hostile encounters with the Prador, Humans only witnessed first- and second-children. Not until some three years into the war was an adult male actually encountered, and the first females were seen only some years after the war was over. However, just from the Prador genome, forensic AIs were quickly able to surmise much about their life cycle, all of it later confirmed. The males are aggressive, intelligent, and use pheromones to force perpetual servitude from their children until they themselves achieve adulthood . . . if they are allowed. They keep harems of the less intelligent females, also pheromonally controlled, which they mate with regularly. The females develop their eggs in oviducts, then inject them via ovipositor into the soft bodies of bivalve molluscs like giant mussels. The eggs hatch and, feeding on the host molluscs, the young Prador grow into the first stage of their lives – a stage very few of them progress beyond.
— *From* QUINCE GUIDE *compiled by Humans*

The dreadnought is changing even as Sniper watches. Creatures still scuttle around outside, working on the hull, but now numerous specialized robots are joining them. The work is being carried out at a pace he has only ever seen once before, and that during the war, inside one of the big AI-guided warship constructor stations. Some sort of chemical disintegrator has spread out in a wave, causing the piled-up ice debris around the vessel to smoke away into a fog bank that is only now dispersing. The entire structure of the ship has tightened so that it no longer looks like a rotten pomegranate sagging to the ground, and the numerous gaps in its hull are being knitted together. Also, every now and again, momentary geometric distortions appear in the surrounding haze, as if the creatures are testing force-fields just as esoteric as those projected by the vessel that is down on the ice behind him. Sniper understands, with utter certainty, that something nasty has been unleashed here, but what the fuck it is he has no idea.

Slowly, incrementally, Sniper's fusion reactor recharges the laminar power storage inside him. However the reactor is running out of hydrogen and certain other essential elements, so he uses one tentacle to bore down through the ice beside him, sampling as he goes. Upper layers consist mainly of CO^2 ice with occasional layers softened by liquid nitrogen, which outgasses the moment he reaches them. He needs water ice, which he finally hits ten feet down. Now boring through this, he begins drawing water-ice dust inside himself, heating it until it becomes liquid, then electrolysing it out, the hydrogen going to the reactor and the oxygen into a pressure vessel inside him.

It is a slow and meticulous process that could result in disaster if he does not monitor it constantly. His energy levels are so low that the amount of energy input to keep the fusion process running eats up nearly 90 per cent of the consequent output. Of the remaining 10 per cent he employs much to keep *himself* powered up, to heat the water, electrolyse it and run the oxygen compressor, and also to power the tentacle still boring down into the water ice. In total the available energy going into laminar storage is climbing from a piddling 1 per cent of reactor output – just about enough to power a food processor.

'C'mon,' Sniper mutters to himself, then in annoyance notes how much power is used up by just speaking out loud.

Bugger.

It will take him at least an hour to build up useful reserves, and now he needs to think about how to use them. Even fully powered up and fully armed, he still stands little chance against whatever it is the Guard has turned into, so what other options are available? Deciding to use up a little of the slowly accumulated power, he eases forward from his shell, turning his head to gaze towards the spot where the shuttle was destroyed.

Wreckage is strewn across the surface over there, though covering only a small percentage of the whole because most of it has melted its way down into the ice. A splash of red blood marks where Drooble died, and scattered around it lie gobbets of flesh and what looks like three-quarters of a skull emptied of its contents. There is no sign of Orbus, though Sniper realizes that rail-gun hits on his armour could have heated it enough for it to melt his remains downwards out of sight. No red blood where he was standing either, but then Old Captains don't really have much of the stuff running round in their veins. However, it is odd that there seems to be no sign at all of Vrell's remains. He would not have melted into the ice and, having been struck by a rail-gun, the Prador should have left a lot more than that little spatter of green gore on the surface. No sign of any chunks of black carapace, nor stray legs or chunks of Prador flesh either.

Trying to replay his memories of those events makes Sniper painfully aware of how much memory he has lost, but one thing is becoming plain: whilst there had been force-field activity before him, when some sort of spherical field crushed one of his attackers, there must also have been similar activity behind him. So perhaps Orbus and Vrell are still alive? It seems most likely to Sniper that, somehow, whatever is occupying that larger vessel has snatched them up. He needs to find out for sure, and to find out he needs to get aboard that vessel undetected, which is problematic since he doesn't even possess the energy to pull himself out of this hole.

Half an hour passes and his laminar storage has risen to 8 per cent. Having detected traces of the three naturally occurring isotopes of hydrogen – deuterium, protium and tritium – he takes the risk of refining these out, since not so much energy is required to fuse them. After that he choses his moment, then reconfigures his reactor injectors to utilize them. It pays off with a short-lived energy boost that knocks his laminar storage up to 14 per cent. He draws off some of this to power another of his tentacles, merely to clear the powdered ice from his shell. This ploy allows a larger proportion of the meagre light available here to reach the photovoltaic cells scattered about his surface. It takes another half-hour for their input to match the energy he has expended in cleaning himself, but by then his laminar storage surpasses 30 per cent.

Sniper now possesses sufficient power to get moving, though not enough to employ antigravity or any of his energy weapons. However, he remains precisely where he is. Despite one of the ex-Guard being destroyed by some type of field projected from the ship behind, there is no guarantee that such a field will not be deployed against Sniper, and there is also no reason to suppose it will again be used against those alien creatures if they decide to come after him again. Over the ensuing hour he bleeds a minimal amount of power to run diagnostics and to instigate those repairs he can afford to make. By the end of this time his fusion reactor is operating at optimum, and he can afford to store hydrogen isotopes as well as oxygen, and also bore down into the ice with more tentacles. Soon afterwards he is fully back up to power and it is time to move.

Sniper carefully eases himself up, extracting tentacles from the ice, then turns over until his head is pointing down into the hollow he previously occupied, whilst keeping one sensor-loaded tentacle aimed towards the dreadnought. He needs to get to that other ship fast, but in a way that has at least a partial chance of going unnoticed. From inside himself he extrudes the iron cylinder of a thermic lance now connected to his internal oxygen supply, begins blowing oxygen through it, and ignites that with a stab of laser. The tool, which in past times he used to bore through the armour of Prador war drones whilst in close combat with them, now burns as bright as a sun. Driving the tips of his tentacles again into the ice to brace himself, he thrusts the lance down, thus turning the ice below him into an explosion of CO_2 gas. As he bores down, he detects a response back at the dreadnought, and the ice above him explodes into fragments under rail-gun fire, even as he himself drops into the hole he has been making.

Good, thinks Sniper, as rail-gun missiles glance off his shell and punch into the ice all around him. This attack from the dreadnought will prevent whoever controls the ship ahead from seeing what he is doing. Twenty feet down he enters the water-ice layer, and starts turning it liquid whilst still vaporizing the CO_2 ice. The pressure from the gas forces the liquid back behind him along the hole he is making, where it refreezes, though with outgas holes worming through it. With any luck the outgassing at the surface will be attributed to hot rail-gun missiles like the one that just bounced off him.

Moving ahead at a slow crawl Sniper makes some calculations based on the steady ablation of the thermic lance, and realizes that its iron will run out before he reaches his destination. He begins employing his lasers, since they are the only energy weapon left to him, and occasionally heaves chunks of ice out of the way with his tentacles. Above, the rumbling attack from the dreadnought ceases and he wonders if the creatures are on their way out again. He keeps tunnelling hard for another ten minutes before some huge detonation above flashes light down through the ice and shakes his subterranean world, sending cracks shooting down all about him. An electromagnetic pulse temporarily disables systems inside him now inadequately protected by his damaged shell, and he realizes that either a CTD or some nuclear device has been deployed. It strikes him as very likely that it was not actually directed at him – more likely that the dreadnought's occupants were now turning on the other mystery visitor here.

The yards count down, and the thermic lance grows shorter and shorter, finally burning the last of the iron in its ceramic clamp and sputtering out just as Sniper begins to make his way back up to the surface again. Here, however, the ice is thoroughly cracked, possibly as a result of that recent blast, but more likely from the huge monolithic weight currently resting upon it. Sniper pauses to use the cutting function of his one remaining spatulate-tipped tentacle and also brute force to cut and tear out chunks of ice immediately above, before steadily working his way upwards again.

He passes some kind of anchor strut bedded deep down into the ice beside him, then finally breaks through into an open space. He studies a scorched wall of thermal glass all around him, then peers up into a ceramic tube lined with the business end of a force-field containment system, which even now is forcing dust particles away from the walls. Quickly he drags himself sideways, and working frenetically with both tentacles and laser, begins to cut under the thermal glass, having just realized he is sitting right inside the blast ring of a big fusion engine. However, the wall begins to lift – everything above him begins to lift – and gravitic eddies begin flinging about chunks of ice. The ship is lifting on antigravity, but at any moment those fusion engines could kick in. Sniper gropes his way outside the thermal ring, finding indenta-tions and ceramic bracing struts, and pulls himself up, sticking, like a snail going into hibernation, in the gaps available between blast chambers of the fusion-engine array.

Then his world abruptly turns very bright and very hot, as fusion torches ignite all around him.

★

Rail-gun fire hammers into a hardfield with unexpected force, the missiles turning to plasma and the feedback reaching all the way to the source generator. Through internal ship eyes, the Golgoloth observes the generator involved immediately glowing red, over-loading thermal converters until they blacken and shrivel. The energy now reverts to kinetic shock, slamming the generator out of its mountings, punching it back through a heavily armoured and insulated wall, and then through a hundred feet of structure beyond. Safeties cut in, sealing the area and evacuating it of air so as to put out the fires.

Locating the active rail-gun, the Golgoloth fires a probing shot with a standard particle cannon. The beam bounces off an angled hardfield projected up from the dreadnought, and plays over the icy plain, churning up a thick cloud of vapour. The Golgoloth next fires a white laser, aimed off-centre to account for hardfield diffraction. It strikes home perfectly on centre on the rail-gun, blows a crater in the top of the dreadnought, then causes further damage somewhere else inside, so that fire spews from several adjacent ports. This tells the ancient hermaphrodite just how substantially things have been altered inside the ship, since standard Prador rail-guns are buffered for feedback. He suspects this is not a mistake the creatures down inside there will make again.

As its vessel rises above the plain and accelerates into the sky, the Golgoloth contemplates, with increasing disquiet, the data relayed by its own ship's sensors. The creatures within the dread-nought have adapted its technology, actually altered its structure, use field technology as good as the Golgoloth's own, and against the drone they killed out there have deployed complex weapons combining both the destructive potential of particle cannons and the invasive properties of viral computer warfare. Nothing like this was going on prior to the ship landing; this means they have achieved all this within a matter of hours – which does not bode well for the future.

'So tell me about *these*?' the Golgoloth says, returning its attention to Vrell and Orbus whilst simultaneously initiating a bank of screens and turning them to face towards the two prisoners. All the screens display an image of one of the new creatures currently residing inside the dreadnought.

'How the fuck should we know?' asks Orbus. 'You sent 'em.'

Interesting.

The Human does not seem to know where the creatures come from. However, the dreadnought is big enough to hide anything inside, so Vrell must have somehow kept knowledge of these entities from Orbus. It strikes the Golgoloth as likely that Vrell has conducted experiments using the Spatterjay virus, probably on survivors of the original crew, to produce some variety of super-soldier, which has then turned against him. Is this what Oberon feared? Interesting to speculate, but other problems begin arising.

Green lasers now strike the hermaphrodite's ship, refracting through its fields just as the Golgoloth has refracted a laser through theirs. The power of the beams is not sufficient to damage armour, but straight away the Golgoloth begins to receive warnings of invasive viruses. This needs to be stopped, *now*. Operating the ship's internal robotics, the hermaphrodite's logistical, ballistic and martial ganglia assemble components into a chemical warhead based on magnesium and selected thermal catalysts, and spit it down towards the surface. It swerves as it hammers down on the dreadnought and the Golgoloth protects it as best it can with field-tech. It strikes the icy plain and detonates, spewing its burning load across an area of ice a mile across. The reaction is immediate: thick clouds of vapour boil up, and they will shroud the dreadnought totally within minutes. It is a murk even those green lasers should not be able to penetrate.

'You are notably quiet on this matter, Vrell,' the Golgoloth observes whilst, with a whole set of programming ganglia, it oversees the destruction of computer viruses generated by those same green lasers. Worrying, because without that growing vapour cloud, the Golgoloth might have lost that battle.

'You did not send them,' Vrell states, his body unnaturally still.

Even more interesting.

The Golgoloth has spent centuries dealing with conniving Prador, and immediately recognizes that Vrell is showing confusion, doubt and a degree of fear unrelated to its presence here.

'I did not send them,' it affirms.

Oh, what now!

'Oh, right,' says Orbus. 'The buggers just materialized out of thin air?'

The cloud is drawing across the dreadnought, but out of it punches a missile, a very odd-looking missile, shaped like a Prador's palp-eye. The Golgoloth quickly fires a particle beam at it, but to no effect. The thing is riding up under a domed hardfield umbrella, power being fed into it from underneath by a microwave beam. White laser now, at full intensity, but the power goes nowhere. Golgoloth abruptly shuts the beam weapons off, having realized what is happening. The *missile* itself is firing the microwave beam. It is feeding power back down to the dreadnought. This means insolent crustaceans down there are using the Golgoloth's weapons as an energy source. The hermaphrodite launches a single missile which shoots down, under massive acceleration, to detonate against the umbrella. An eye of nuclear fire opens below, which is just a bit more energy than the missile can handle.

As the fire burns and fades, the Golgoloth's vessel clears atmosphere and heads back towards the fathership. The hermaphrodite begins sending instructions to the vast resources stored within that main ship, making further preparations. It knows this isn't over, not at all.

'They are the Guard,' says Vrell abruptly.

Orbus turns to him. 'The Guard are all dead and, you know, those didn't look like armoured Prador to me.'

The Golgoloth considers this for a long moment. Unless Vrell is lying, and managing to do so very convincingly, which might be possible what with him going the same route as Oberon, something very odd is occurring here.

'How did you kill the Guard?' it asks.

'I used a nerve-tissue-eating nanite keyed to the King's genome,' Vrell replies. 'Though as individual Prador they all died, as organisms they did not.'

'So,' says the Golgoloth, 'the virus has resurrected something.'

'Those ain't leeches,' says Orbus.

'You don't know.' Vrell swings his head towards him. 'I discovered that, at its heart, the Spatterjay virus holds genetic tissue that is alien to us here, and to any life-form on Spatterjay.' Vrell gazes back towards the Golgoloth. 'It seems I am not the only one to have discovered this.'

'Genetic tissue ain't intelligent,' Orbus argues. 'It doesn't spontaneously generate a brain full of the knowledge to take over a dreadnought and turn itself into some insect cyborg.' He gestures towards the screens.

Quite.

Neither Vrell nor Orbus possesses a clear grasp of what is happening, nor does the Golgoloth either. It seems only one being knows the answer here. As the hermaphrodite turns its great splinter of a vessel to reinsert into the father ship, it decides the time has come for another conversation with Oberon.

★

Sadurian pauses in the wide white corridor, tilts her head to listen for a moment, then takes a few paces back and walks over to an alcove set in the wall. Having some knowledge of ancient Earth history, she describes these frequently provided spaces as 'overtaking lanes'. Their purpose is to offer refuge for junior Prador when their larger brethren come by. Indeed, without them, smaller Prador can end up with shells cracked and limbs missing if they happen to get in the way of their larger kin. Aboard the vessels of normal Prador these refuges are made for third-children to avoid second-children, or for both to avoid the usually belligerent first-children. However, things are rather different here aboard the King's ship.

Enabling Oberon to produce children was the first of many problems Sadurian overcame during her time here in the Kingdom. Making it possible for those children to grow up was the next and most lengthy task. On Spatterjay, relying on a diet of offworld food and viral inhibitors, the virus-infected children of Humans manage to reach adulthood without too many problems, though there can still be some when they hit adolescence.

However, Prador children, pheromonally controlled by their fathers and heading for permanently inhibited adolescence, grow in violent spurts punctuated by regular shedding of their shells. This process causes the virus's survival mechanism to switch on at every such occasion. Controlling this requires a cocktail of viral inhibitors, and sometimes even surgical intervention. A small percentage of the children do not survive the process, others need to have their growth halted early. The moment one of the King's children reaches either first-childhood or some earlier point when the growth spurts need to be halted, it goes into armour. Therefore the usual juvenile hierarchy is somewhat different here. These alcoves are provided for third- and second-children still growing, and therefore unarmoured. Corridor space is given as a priority to all stages of children, just so long as they wear armour. And these are what Sadurian is now avoiding.

The floor vibrates with the approach of an unusual number of Prador to be encountered in this portion of the ship. Sadurian peeks out and along the corridor, to observe a host of over twenty of the Guard thundering towards her. Some of them are small and wear chrome armour like Delf and Yaggs, most wear brassy armour matching that usually worn by the first-children of normal Prador, and a few wear the armour of normal young adults. However, it is debatable as to what stage of development all of these, being Oberon's children, have reached. Some of the large ones could be either first-children or old virally-developed second-children. The mid-size ones could be at any stage, either under- or over-developed. And even the small armoured ones might easily be stunted second-children.

They move at such a pace and in such a chaotic manner that some are clambering over others to proceed. The din they make is incredible, aggravated by the fact that many of them carry weapons and other equipment, and as this riot passes Sadurian's alcove, showering her with flecks of metal and ceramic, they leave an oily haze of lubricants in the air. She steps out to watch them go, then continues at a saunter towards a destination she is none too anxious to arrive at. But arrive she does.

Diagonally divided, as in most Prador entrances, the twin doors are high and arched but specially fashioned to accommodate something that looks nothing like the general run of Prador kind. Sadurian hesitates before them, laying one hand on the top of her palmtop, where it hooks onto her belt, as if resting it on the butt of a gun. Right then she is thoroughly aware of her vulnerability. Oberon may have set her on a course to discover the data now residing in her palmtop, but that doesn't mean the King is going to like it. After a moment she walks over to the pit control positioned over her head beside the door, reaches inside and toggles the inner control, feeling something stab into the back of her hand as the pit samples her genetic tissue. She then stands back.

The doors do not open at once, which is usual as the pit control requires approval from Oberon before they do. First comes a grinding clonk inside the walls on either side, then the doors themselves draw ponderously back, allowing a gap no wider than a few feet to give her admittance. She steps into a huge high-ceilinged atrium, pausing for a moment to glance around at the heavy weapons mounted in balcony-like excrescences ranged about the walls.

'Where are you?' she asks.

After a pause the King replies, his tone sounding distracted. 'I am in my control centre.'

Sadurian heads for the wide corridor directly ahead, grateful at least that she isn't to be greeted in the audience chamber, where too many of the *terminal* audiences are conducted. Along this same corridor she notes some large and dangerous-looking ship-lice feeding on the remains of the King's last meal – thankfully nothing sentient this time – and she steps warily round them. Periodically these lice need to be exterminated as, becoming infected with the Spatterjay virus, a few undergo transformations that make them even less savoury creatures. Finally she reaches the control centre.

The King is resting his great weight on a series of bars set just a few feet above the floor, his legs drawn up spiderlike above his main body. As Sadurian enters, Oberon keeps his attention focused on the array of hexagonal screens that honeycomb the wall ahead of him, his underarms at rest in a series of pit controls situated directly beneath the bars he rests upon. Sadurian focuses briefly on this monstrous entity before her, then swings her attention to a second monster now displayed on the screens.

The Golgoloth.

Though she knows about this creature, has seen images constructed from hearsay and heard descriptions, and has always been amused by the mythology, Sadurian has never actually seen the thing itself. Its grotesqueness has not been overly elaborated on by the taletellers, yet Sadurian merely gazes at it with analytical curiosity. She has seen worse monstrosities chewing their way out of the King's birth molluscs, while the one right beside her certainly takes some beating.

'You have a Human with you, I see, how coincidental,' says Golgoloth. 'Why exactly do you have a Human with you?'

'I needed someone to solve my reproductive problem,' Oberon replies. 'Prador possess neither the elasticity of mind required nor the ability to distance themselves from such research work.'

'But in solving your problem, the Human becomes a problem itself?'

'Not really,' replies the King, 'since the Polity AIs have been aware of my condition for some years.'

This is news to Sadurian and seems to confirm some of her own speculations about why the King might be lurking here, by the Graveyard. She folds her arms and waits. That the Polity AIs know about the King makes it more likely he will allow her to return to the Polity, yet being privy to conversations like this one might not be healthy.

'So in destroying Vrell your ostensible purpose of preventing Polity AIs or others finding out what he is, and thereby revealing what you are, is actually a lie.' The Golgoloth is right on the button of course, but why, Sadurian wonders, is the King even speaking to this creature?

'I think that you know that already, Golgoloth. I take it you have located Vrell, and that this coincidence you mention somehow concerns that fact?'

'Astute as ever, O King. Observe.'

A small collection of screens blank down in one corner of the main array, then flicker on again to show a big bulky Human with his back resting against a glassy wall.

'A Hooper,' says Sadurian, peering at the man curiously. She herself has taken great interest in the work of one Erlin Taser Three Indomial on the planet Spatterjay – the woman who revealed much about the virus's lifecycle. One day she intends to go there herself, simply to closely study Hooper Humans like this.

The King swivels his monstrous head round to gaze at her, and she wishes she'd kept her mouth shut. Though they converse with the clatter and bubble of Prador speech, the conversation between these two creatures seems easy and relaxed, and that puts her off her guard. Best to keep silent and remember her true position in Prador society. She lives simply at the King's will, when otherwise she would be considered little more than food. Very highly paid food, but lunch nonetheless. The King returns his attention to the screens.

'As my Human has noted: that is a Hooper. I also recognize this human as being involved in killing one of my agents in the Graveyard. He is an Old Captain by the name of Orbus. Perhaps you can elaborate on why he now appears to be a prisoner aboard your ship?'

'Because he was with my other captive, Vrell.'

'You have him?'

'I have him.'

The lower screen image changes to show a black mutated Prador. Sadurian studies Vrell intently, noting the differences between him and Oberon. The King is obviously a lot further along than Vrell, and has been deliberately forcing mutations on his own body for some years, yet Vrell's appearance does not match that of the King when the latter was the same age. Sadurian knows that for sure after being allowed to study the King's personal physiological files.

'Then why is he still alive?' asks the King.

'Whilst I was still considering your offer, certain complications arose,' says the Golgoloth.

'Explain,' the King clatters, and Sadurian takes one careful pace away from him. When the King uses single-word interrogatives like that, it usually means he is getting pissed off, which in turn usually results in blood spattered on the walls.

'I drove Vrell's ship down onto a planetoid so as to facilitate my extracting him from it, since I knew that, wanting him dead, you would want proper evidence of his demise. However, I did not even need to extract him for, along with this Orbus and a Polity drone that was subsequently destroyed, he fled his ship – pursued by some distinctly strange creatures.'

'Creatures?'

The King's mandibles snap open on the final clonk of the Prador word and he rises up slightly, his big ribbed body now tense as that of a scorpion about to strike. The lower screen image changes yet again, this time to display some sort of cyborg insect.

'Identify,' Oberon instructs.

'Vrell's ship has been taken over by these creatures,' the Golgoloth explains. 'And it is apparent that they were once members of the Guard, but somehow transformed by the Spatterjay virus into what you see. Presumably the virus is working with some ancient alien genetic tissue it holds, but that would not explain how these things are able to wield advanced technologies. Perhaps you, Oberon, should now "identify".'

Oberon settles back with a sigh that seems to have some elements of pain in it. 'It has happened,' he intones.

'What, precisely?'

Oberon raises his head. 'You clearly did not look deep enough into the viral store, if all you found was alien genetic material.'

Sadurian cannot help herself. 'Quantum mem-storage – the mind of a soldier, or perhaps the minds of many soldiers.'

'As the Human says,' declares the King.

The Golgoloth shudders as if those words possess a physical force, then speaks very slowly as it, no doubt, ransacks its 'ganglion' storage. 'And that being so . . . considering the likely age of the virus in its present form, these soldiers were created by one of the three extinct races: the Jain, the Csorians or the Atheter.'

'Discount the last two,' Sadurian interjects. 'You're not up-to-date on recent research.'

'Why?' asks the ancient hermaphrodite.

'Because the genetic sample I've been studying does not come anywhere close to matching that of those we now know to be the descendants of the Atheter – the gabbleducks of Masada. Nor does it match pieces of genetic material recovered by fossil genome techniques from what Polity AIs are sure is the body of a Csorian.'

'The Jain, then,' the Golgoloth continues. 'The ones who liked to rearrange solar systems and even destroyed a few suns. Something very dangerous has been unleashed.'

'Yes, it has,' replies the King, 'and now I must destroy it.'

Sadurian feels the world shift and the walls seem to distort all around her. Prador shielding is not as good as that on Polity ships, but in either case she knows instantly when any ship she is aboard has shifted into U-space. The Golgoloth fades from the main screens, but the picture of the Jain still hangs in place.

'I wonder what they looked like before they started changing themselves . . . before they advanced enough . . .' Sadurian wonders aloud.

Oberon just swings that great head of his towards her again.

Sadurian thinks it politic not to add: . . . *before they could change their physical form at will . . . just like you, King of the Prador.*

Gurnard regrets the death of Iannus Drooble, but it is not for AIs to limit the free will of Humans, even if they make stupid choices and get themselves killed. AIs only limit that free will when it might result in others dying.

'We cannot rescue Orbus,' says Thirteen, perching with his tail wrapped round one arm of the Captain's chair, 'or Vrell either.'

Gurnard could not agree more. With Sniper down, and quite possibly destroyed, there is no one now to send to the rescue, and going up against so large and obviously powerful a vessel would be suicidal. Such an effort would most likely only increase the chances of the two captives dying. All Gurnard can do therefore is watch, and again send out a request for advice.

The larger chunk from the big ship out there is heading back to the main ship with Orbus and Vrell now aboard. However the other splinter sent out to prevent the *Gurnard* getting any closer remains on station. Still no idea where that big ship comes from, and less idea what those creatures down on the planet are. Initially the AI assumed the big ship used some kind of U-jump – like it did with its missiles – to put alien assault troops aboard the dreadnought, but subsequent events have shot that theory down.

'Any word from Sniper?' Thirteen asks.

'Nothing,' Gurnard replies, contemplatively, whilst trying to analyse some particularly odd readings it is picking up on local com. 'Nor have I received any response from the Polity fleet stationed at the border.'

'That seems a bit strange.'

'Perhaps they are still analysing the data.'

The local com is laser-based, and Gurnard is only intercepting a small portion of it, but even that is enough to realize it is dangerously loaded with informational life. Gurnard now recognizes it for what it is: this is splash, overspill from a computer warfare laser. Triangulation along the length of its own ship's body gives Gurnard the source of the splash and thus the laser's true target: that splinter deriving from the big ship out there. Analysis of how the laser is being deflected reveals that the beam is playing along the length of the splinter from somewhere down on the planetoid. If the attacks made upon the larger shuttle portion of that ship were not enough, this confirms the hostility of those life-forms below. Gurnard wonders if the crew of that big ship knows what is going on.

But then, before the AI can speculate further, it receives an urgent exterior request to open a U-com channel. All the codes are correct and it seems, from data accompanying the request, that it is opening from a distant location, via the runcible network and the Polity fleet. Gurnard accepts the request and allows Thirteen to listen in.

'The data you dispatched is interesting,' says the entity at the far end of the channel, and Gurnard feels for a moment as if it has tried to open conversation with a couple of individuals on the side of a mountain, and the mountain itself has replied. The ship AI knows instantly that this is no normal AI speaking; this is Earth Central itself.

'Interesting in the sense of an old Chinese curse?' Gurnard suggests.

'Quite possibly,' concurs Earth Central. 'Due to the sensitive nature of relations between the Polity and the Prador Third

Kingdom, we have been disinclined to initiate any large-scale intervention in this matter and, despite your data, this disinclination remains unchanged.'

'We've got a massive unidentified vessel, possibly of Prador manufacture, here within the Graveyard,' Gurnard observes. 'And we've got alien assault troops that seemingly have appeared out of nowhere.'

'Let me clarify matters for you: that large alien vessel is the property of a creature called the Golgoloth, a being that fled the usurpation of the Second Kingdom.'

Gurnard receives a data package and absorbs its contents instantly, now knowing precisely what this Golgoloth is, and also learning that Earth Central and the sector AIs have known about the creature for centuries.

Earth Central continues, 'It seems likely that, despite the Golgoloth having previously been hunted down by King Oberon, it is now acting as his agent in this matter.'

'And those aliens down there?'

Another data package arrives, from which Gurnard learns in great detail about the Jain soldiers the Spatterjay virus holds at its core. The ship AI also studies with interest the results of data extraction from the Jain quantum storage: about how these soldiers can alter and adapt their bodies at will, how they are hostile to any but those in their own squad, how certain elements of the knowledge held in storage have yet to be properly interpreted even by autistic-savant forensic AIs. However, these scientific details are not all of the data Earth Central is providing. Gurnard also learns about the long and troubled deliberations, between Earth Central and the Sector AIs, about what exactly should be done. On numerous occasions the whole planet of Spatterjay has come close to annihilation at their hands, so what held the AIs back? The answer was a reluctance to destroy such a unique source of data about the Jain, rather than any question of morality regarding planetary destruction and genocide.

'You will not intervene here,' says Gurnard. 'Yet what is now happening here is precisely what you feared.'

'As of this time, intervention is not required.'

'But if no action is taken against them, they get a chance to grow stronger.'

'But action *is* being taken. King Oberon, in his capital ship, along with twenty of the most advanced Prador dreadnoughts, is already on his way.'

Gurnard isn't entirely sure this means the situation has got any better.

'So what should I do?'

'Though you were formerly employed by Earth Central Security, that employment is now considered at an end, and you are once again a free agent,' Earth Central replies. 'My advice, therefore, is that you get out of there just as fast as you can. Our border defence stations will let you through, if you do this right now. However I cannot guarantee that they will let anything pass through later on.'

The channel closes.

'Ever get the feeling you're just a pawn on a chessboard?' Thirteen asks.

'Often,' Gurnard replies.

'So what's the *real* agenda here?'

'My guess if that if King Oberon deals with this problem the Polity gets a bit of a negotiating advantage, what with him being the one to have broken their treaties. However, if things get out of control, Oberon might end up dead and quite a few of his major ships could be smashed up, then the Polity moves in to finish off the Jain – after which it has another kind of advantage.'

'For attack?' suggests Thirteen. 'Attacking the Kingdom?'

'No,' Gurnard replies. 'I've information about this Golgoloth now, and about how that creature is basically what held together the Second Kingdom, and further data on how Oberon alone is what holds together the Third Kingdom. Remove both of them from the equation, and Vrell too, since he might become as capable as either of the other two, and the Prador will start attacking each other again, and the Kingdom will fall apart.'

'Then, I suppose,' says Thirteen, 'after letting them tear each other apart, ECS goes in to clear up the mess.'

'Neat, don't you think?'

'Not very moral.'

'Whoever accused us AIs of morality?' Gurnard wonders.

'So we run now?'

'Of course not.'

Gurnard returns its attention to the splinter of ship still visible out there. The attempts at computer warfare have ceased, and it is now turning away to head back towards the father ship. Perhaps it has managed to fend off those attacks, but if otherwise Gurnard suspects it will be seeing the results of that failure quite soon.

14

The residents of Spatterjay, the so-called 'Hoopers', range from the toughness of a heavy-worlder to, in the case of the Old Captains, something stronger and more difficult to waste than the most advanced combat Golem. However, luckily for us, as with ancient fictional characters like Achilles or Superman, they've got one critical weakness, and in their case it is sprine. This poison, refined from the bile of the oceanic leeches of Spatterjay, kills the virus that grants them virtual immortality combined with the strength to rip arms out of sockets, and, since the viral fibres pierce every cell of their bodies, this leads to complete physical breakdown. So a man capable of tearing out a bulkhead door with his bare hands can be killed by the prick of a needle. Had there been no weakness like this I doubt that Hoopers would have been allowed to range so freely throughout the Polity. As it is, the security services of every Polity world store caches of sprine weapons – bullets, particle beamers and sprine gas – all kept ready to bring down one of these supermen should he go rogue.

– From HOW IT IS by Gordon

The splinter ship the Golgoloth shed in order to keep that Polity vessel at bay, is tardy in returning to the main ship, but the old hermaphrodite is not surprised, for many of the computer systems and the ganglia inside the splinter are very decrepit. Upon its return, it will be time to run a diagnostic and then perhaps discard old pieces of the Golgoloth's former children's minds, and load their data to new tissue. Many of its children still ensconced in their frames within the main ship are ready for harvesting to that end.

'King Oberon is coming here,' warns the Golgoloth, now eyeing its two captives.

'Great,' says Orbus. 'Should I wash and change, do y'think?'

'I think the King is only concerned about what creatures wear when it is armour,' the Golgoloth replies, meanwhile focusing on Vrell's reaction.

The mutated Prador shows little indication of fear, so perhaps he has simply given up. However, he is looking much healthier now, his soft new white legs having grown visibly during the last hour, so that they now nearly reach the ground. And, anyway, the Golgoloth suspects that 'giving up' is not in the young mutant's mental lexicon.

'Did the King send you here from the Kingdom?' Vrell abruptly asks.

The Golgoloth appreciates that: Vrell is still trying to gain an advantage.

'I have been in practical exile in the Graveyard since the fall of the Second Kingdom,' it replies.

'But, like other Prador here, you seek to gain favour.'

'It is not quite like that.'

Vrell clatters and bubbles with Prador laughter. With some amusement itself, the Golgoloth realizes that, not having the option of some physical form of escape, Vrell is now trying the psychological route. This might be interesting, but again other exigencies must be considered.

The Golgoloth's surroundings shudder as if in sympathy with that thought, as the shuttle segment, which it used to get down to the planet, slots neatly back into place in the father ship. The hermaphrodite now returns its attention to its screens and sensors to monitor the rest of the docking procedure, before switching over to the greater data-flows of its main vessel in order to scan the planetoid. There is some sort of disruption down there, a heavy chameleonware effect aggravated by the murk the Golgoloth created with the weapon used to block those green lasers, for its detectors cannot now locate the dreadnought. However, if the thing launches from down in a gravity well, the Golgoloth feels confident this will cause sufficient disruption to reveal it, no matter what concealing technology is being used. The Golgoloth loads the known coordinates of the dreadnought to one of its U-jump missiles, and lets the ganglion that the missile contains run the required calculations to fling itself down the gravity well. This should take just a few minutes.

'Not quite like that, in what way?' Vrell enquires.

'My relationship with Oberon is complex.'

'I would have thought it quite simple: you escaped and have remained an embarrassment to him for centuries. I imagine he has a heated spike prepared especially for you.'

'Only the King and a select few others know about me.'

'The King knows about you, and that's all that matters.'

'That is a rather crude attempt at manipulation.'

'The truth tends to be crude – not complex.'

Such a poor showing from the young mutant, and yet the King is indeed a complex being, who might have been able to fool even the Golgoloth over the years. What use exactly is the Golgoloth to the King? Even here, in the Graveyard, the old hermaphrodite has essentially failed. Yes, Vrell is now a captive, but the real danger that needed countering has since manifested, and now the King feels the need to break numerous treaties with the Polity so as to come into the Graveyard to deal with the matter. Slightly troubled by this line of thought, the Golgoloth returns its attention to the planetoid.

'I recollect an obscure reference to the Golgoloth as a "king-maker",' says Vrell suddenly. 'You were the true power in the Second Kingdom.'

Astounding: Vrell has just made a quite correct assessment based on very little data.

'You are correct,' the Golgoloth allows.

'You escaped with your life before Oberon even knew you existed.'

Another incredible, and correct, leap.

'Just so.'

'King Oberon,' Vrell continues, 'does not want any knowledge of what kind of creature he is to reach the Kingdom, for possessing that knowledge means power. Do you think for one moment he will allow someone who is not utterly loyal to him, that is, a member of his family, to gain that kind of power over him? Do you think Oberon will want, inside the Kingdom, that power to be in the hands of a creature who once controlled that same Kingdom?'

This observation goes like a needle straight through the Golgoloth's mind. *Foolish creature*, it chides itself. *You have not been paying attention.* Is it loneliness, it wonders, that has led it into such straits? The Golgoloth wants to live for ever but is not prepared to risk using the Spatterjay virus to extend its life, even though the virus demonstrably works, yet it is prepared to risk trusting a Prador King with its life? *Stupidity.* The moment it seized Vrell, it should have fled and not concerned itself with those strange creatures down below.

Focusing back on its screens, the Golgoloth sees that the missile is nearly ready to launch. This could all be over long before the King arrives, and the Golgoloth can then remove itself far from here. But why even launch the missile? Those creatures down there might be dangerous, but are not necessarily the Golgoloth's concern. The King will doubtless arrive here with massive forces at his command, in order to solve this problem – and, if it remains here, to simultaneously remove the Golgoloth from all further equations. That most certainly must not be allowed to happen.

The murk below continues to roll away, revealing a churned-up landscape and utterly no sign of the dreadnought, as is only to be expected if the ship is using chameleonware. However, the Golgoloth did not expect to see that a great tunnel, precisely the girth of the dreadnought, has been bored down into the ice and rock, and so realizes that chameleonware is not involved. The Jain obviously moved the dreadnought shortly after that murk concealed it, using some sort of disintegrator technology, perhaps.

'You are, of course, correct, Vrell,' says the Golgoloth. 'Remaining here might be unhealthy for me, so I shall remove myself at once.'

'What about us?' asks Orbus.

'You will come with me, of course. I still have much to learn from you.'

The ship splinter is now sliding back towards its docking cavity, but it is travelling too fast. The Golgoloth sends orders to slow it, but the ten-thousand-ton splinter slows not at all. Something very badly wrong here. The ganglia within the errant vessel fall out of contact, and the other systems the Golgoloth uses to access it abruptly close off. The Golgoloth quickly instructs the ganglia aboard the father ship to prepare, and numerous force-fields spring into being, clawing at the surface of the fast-approaching splinter, but their power simply is not enough to cancel out that level of momentum, and even as they grope for purchase, informational life begins feeding back through them. The Golgoloth understands at once that, whilst it was concerning itself with the Jain down on the planet, they themselves were thinking ahead, and formulating an attack up here. The splinter is now theirs.

Launching counter-programs throughout its systems, the

Golgoloth soon realizes that only one option now remains. It simply cannot allow this vessel to dock. Action follows upon thought, with massive steering jets exploding to life about the father ship. It begins turning immediately, thus swinging the splinter's docking cavity away from it. However, the Golgoloth at once discovers huge resistance to this ploy, and finds that many force-field generators have been hijacked and now aren't trying to push the splinter away but clinging to it. The thing swings along with the main vessel, explosions lighting giant flashbulbs in the father ship's structure and hurling chunks of ceramic out into space as force-field generators exceed their loading limits. Tracking down the hijacked generators, the Golgoloth isolates and shuts them down. But still this simply isn't enough.

The narrow nose of the splinter enters its docking hole, though off-centre, then the first thousand feet of the rogue craft penetrate the father ship before it hits the side of the cavity. The father ship shudders as the splinter peels up superstructure, and chunks of its own hull tear away. Debris fountains from the contact point, as from a knife shaving across ice. Internally, fire rolls through long-abandoned corridors, ancient safety systems cut in, swiftly evacuating air. Inner wall plates flex and break away from surrounding structure, pipes rupture spilling water and other fluids, oxygen and other gases. Further explosions ensue, along with violent chemical reactions, and corridors evacuated of breathable air now evacuate poisonous clouds. Then finally, with a crash that sends the Golgoloth staggering to the edge of its support platform, the splinter slams entirely home.

The real attack begins.

The frame keeps the first-child's muscles in prime condition, while the screens and punishment shocks keep its other muscle, its major ganglion, its brain, in prime condition too. Like all the father-mother's children confined here, it is highly intelligent and absorbs enough of the wide, eclectic mix of educational data presented by the screens for it to understand its position in the world. Just swinging one palp-eye to look at the slightly older first-child beside it, and remembering what happened to the one that occupied the empty frame beyond, provides it with enough information for it to foresee its future. The nearby child is now without legs, without a claw, and it is also missing parts of its internal organs. Such harvesting will continue until the damage becomes too much for it to sustain, then its major ganglion will be removed for installation in one of the father-mother's machines, the rest discarded. There is no escape, and the horror for each child here is that it perfectly understands this.

The movement of the ship and its recent occasional shaking signify that the father-mother might be involved in some sort of conflict, which has given it brief hope that it instantly suppresses. It knows where such hope leads: to the mind-breaking and the punishment shocks increasing, finally being pushed up to lethal levels by the father-mother as it makes its regular rounds. When the screens blank out the first-child briefly hopes for a respite; some time to apply its mind to trying to find some way – any way – for it to escape. However, the screens come back on again, running strange and alluring patterns, then filling with data it does not recognize. The child feels itself becoming angry and frustrated as those odd patterns implant themselves into its major ganglion, and there propagate, seemingly riffling through its mind. Then it experiences a sudden euphoria, as its mind explodes with light, with clarity, with coherence.

Next comes data it recognizes: the schematics of the father-mother's vessel, the onboard locations of weapons, power supplies, main conduits, generators – everything a neophyte saboteur might need – and finally the location of the father-mother itself. Then the clamps that have held it in place since its limbs grew big enough to be manacled suddenly open, and it drops to the floor. Throughout the nursery, it hears the sound of deformed young Prador hitting the floor similarly, and glances across at them as they shake themselves experimentally and test their limbs. The liberated first-child heads for the nearest door, determined to arm itself and go after its tormentor, the father-mother . . . determined never to be confined again.

In defiance of treaties with the Polity, King Oberon is now flinging his capital ship, along with a fleet of state-of-the-art dreadnoughts, straight into the Graveyard, aiming to attack creatures which are yet to show themselves to be a genuine enemy. This seems a typically Pradorish move to make, but Sadurian is puzzled. Yes, enough has been learnt about the Jain to know that they possessed a highly advanced and dangerous technology and, yes, it seems that these creatures resurrected in the Graveyard are Jain soldiers. But why does it seem such a personal issue to Oberon? Why is the King risking so much to move in on them so quickly? And what more does the King know?

'You could have left them alone,' she suggests. 'There's no certainty they will head in this direction. They might head for the Polity instead, and become a problem for the AIs.'

'If these creatures are allowed time to develop, they will become everyone's problem,' says the King, speaking Human words.

Now that the tiers of screens are out, the lighting in here is sinister and concealing, despite the surrounding whiteness. The King lets his mandibles rest on the floor and now seems soaked in shadow, immobile as some baroque sculpture fashioned out of wrought iron. Sadurian can feel implicit threat in the air. She is too close to discovering things that might cost her her life, but that is a risk she is now prepared to take.

'How can you be so certain?'

'Because I know them,' says the King, his voice hissing with an unhuman edge. 'Long ago a Polity captive described to me Human nightmares, and I never understood what he meant until I experienced them myself, mere decades after I was first infected with the Spatterjay virus. Perhaps because of those nightmares I chose to halt the virus's progress within me and simply rule – however, after four centuries of rule I saw stability around me, but also stagnation. With me eternally at its head, the Prador civilization will never advance, will never have the opportunity to become something that won't then fall apart without me. And also I was bored.'

The King shifts one of his heavy limbs, his hard carapace scoring a glittering scratch in the floor. Sadurian resists the urge to step away – to just leave quickly.

'But you let the virus start growing inside you again,' she surmises.

'I did, and the nightmares returned with redoubled force. I realized then that much of the data surfacing in my consciousness could not have my own brain or memories as its source. That's when I began studying the virus more deeply than I had on first acquiring it, and that's when I found the quantum storage within the Jain genome.'

'You've known about this for so long?'

The King brings his mandibles up off the floor, snaps them open and shut again with a sound like branches breaking, then focuses a dark-eyed regard on Sadurian. 'I saw visions of power, technological advantage that could flatten the Polity. I picked up scraps of knowledge even in my dreams: elements of science that we have since used. But I still wanted to get to the source of it. Every time the virus changed me, I felt myself getting closer to that source of knowledge, and my studies have shown me that, if I strip away all the stored animal genetic tissue the virus carries and finally begin using the Jain genetic schematics, this will give me access to the quantum storage – for activating the tissue activates the storage.'

'And you have access now?'

'It is knowledge that can kill.'

'All knowledge can do that.'

'Those scraps of knowledge I acquired derived not from simple computer storage but from the minds of powerful, aggressive and hostile entities.'

'That's interesting, coming from the King of the Prador.' The moment she says the words, Sadurian feels herself sweating in panic. Perhaps she has gone too far.

'To use Human vernacular,' says Oberon, 'compared to these Jain, we Prador are just pussies.'

Perhaps not.

'They are dangerous,' says Sadurian, making her words neither a question nor a confirmation.

'Truly accessing that quantum storage so as to obtain *real* knowledge might kill me, because I would be accessing their minds, and they would then seek to seize control of me. I might thus become one or all of them.'

'But still you try . . .'

'I still try, but slowly – and very very carefully.'

'I am surprised that they are stronger than you.'

'The introduction of technology slows the process of evolution, but it never actually ceases,' the King explains. 'And when technology advances sufficiently to be applied to the bodies and minds of those wielding it, it becomes a tool of evolution.'

'That is understood.'

'The Jain were all hard individualists, whose civilization rose and fell over tens of thousands of years, constantly specialized, and changed . . .' the King continues. 'They divided and fought, they learnt and they changed themselves and built up layer upon layer of technology, plumbing depths far beyond the universal secrets we have only just scraped. They fought battles that lasted longer than either of *our* civilizations have been in existence. Fighting amongst themselves, they evolved into something even the King of the Prador is justified in fearing.'

'All this from your nightmares?'

'All of this, yes. The Jain are what the Prador could become if we were to survive a million years.' The King pauses and, to Sadurian, seems suddenly weary. 'My research has led me to deduce that these Jain soldiers are inherently hostile to any form of competition, even from others of their own kind. And just the scraps of knowledge I have gathered about their technology have made it clear to me that if unleashed with such technology, they could exterminate all Prador. There would be nothing left.'

'Are the Polity AIs aware of this?'

The King jerks as if coming out of reverie and begins to shift his legs. Sadurian realizes the time is *fast* approaching for her to depart.

'They have been aware of this for longer than I have, and they are certainly well aware of what is happening in the Graveyard.'

'And will Earth Central Security ships be coming?'

'They will not.'

'Why?'

'Because your AIs realize that I and my children have the potential to become Jain ourselves, and as such we represent a huge danger to the Polity. Because they sent me an ultimatum: I must demonstrate that I am quite capable of keeping my house in order, in other words capable of dealing with virus-infected Prador who have been turned into Jain.'

'Ultimatum?'

'Whilst my Kingdom stagnates, your Polity advances. I have therefore no doubt about the result of a conflict between the two: we Prador would lose. Earth Central Security would do it quickly, using weapons based on your runcibles and upon what your AIs already know about Jain technology. They would move fast to nullify any chance of me trying to resurrect Jain soldiers to use as a weapon against them. Prador civilization would collapse; the Prador race itself would be lucky to survive.'

'That still doesn't explain about this ultimatum.'

'It has been a balancing act. The cost to the Polity of a war against my kind would be heavy even now, but all that has held off ECS so far has been the fact that I am judged sane; that I do not try to turn my children into Jain soldiers, do not try to turn them into a weapon to use against the Polity. But the greatest fear of your AIs is that at any time it could happen by accident, some-where out of their sight, within the Prador Kingdom.'

With frightening speed for something so massive, the King heaves himself to his feet.

'It is a fear, indeed, that first brought them close to attacking me, and a fear only calmed over a century ago by the knowledge that I have the power to detonate fusion explosives in the armour of each and every one of my children. However, in recent years that fear has grown again, especially now a Human genius has enabled me to breed and the population of my children constantly grows.' Sadurian begins backing away as Oberon takes one step, his complex foot crunching down like a sawn log landing end-on.

'I must demonstrate to the Polity that if such a situation develops within my Kingdom, I can control it. Demonstrate this I must, or my family dies and my erstwhile species ends up back down in the ancestral mud.'

'The AIs will do this?'

'They are not so kind as you Humans would like to believe,' the King hisses.

Sadurian turns and walks away, determined not to break into a run.

Something is knocking this ship about, that is evident, but Orbus guesses it isn't some malfunction that causes the imprisoning cylinder around them to rise like a belljar being lifted. Water washes in about his feet and, being an Old Captain from the seas of Spatterjay where only the unsound of mind will ever get their feet wet, he peers nervously at the odd mechanisms and organisms swimming within it.

'We have a problem,' the Golgoloth informs them.

Control systems, honeycombs of screens and other unidentifiable devices sprout on stalks around the Prador's platform, and bend in close like attendant priests. The Golgoloth stabs with its claws, while all its underhands are inserted into a bank of pit controls, and optic connections plug themselves into ports in its body like pins driving into a big bug. The creature is moving fast, turning from system to system, inputting data, sending certain devices away and summoning others in. Technology swarms about it like starving metal animals falling eagerly on the only source of food.

'*We* have a problem?' Orbus enquires.

'Yes,' the asymmetric creature continues, and Orbus realizes its voice cannot now be issuing from it personally, for it is also using its mandibles to operate all these swarming machines. 'You perhaps understand that if I had intended to kill you both, you would already be dead by now. However, if what is now attempting to take over this ship succeeds, your deaths, and mine, will become a certainty.'

'The Jain,' says Vrell.

Even as he delivers the words, his whole body jerks as his new legs extend, splashing down through the water to the floor, green blood suffusing them and their outer layer rapidly blackening and hardening. He swings round towards the Golgoloth, splashing up water while squatting as if about to spring, but then, between them and the Golgoloth, the air shimmers and Orbus notes a line of division cutting through the water below it, as if a sheet of glass has just dropped into place. It seems the Golgoloth has thrown up a force-field between itself and them, almost as an afterthought.

'Your weapons are in the container sitting to your right,' it declares.

Vrell eases himself back up into a fully standing position, then swings his head towards the direction indicated. The top half of an upright cylinder splits diagonally, hinging its upper section down into the water. Within the cavity now exposed rest Vrell's weapons, Orbus's multigun, and also the weird sculpture of his folded suit. He wades over to inspect these items more closely. The suit is battered, partially melted in places, cracked, too, and has been cleanly sliced through with something used to open it. He picks up his multigun, unplugging its armoured lead from the belt port and putting it aside, then turns the suit over to access the two flat power packs inset at waist level on the back. Toggling a manual control inside the suit releases them, whereupon the universal plug of the multigun's cable plugs neatly into one power pack's port, and he inserts this pack into one pocket – the other going into his other pocket – then hefts his weapon. He won't have the targeting and finesse of control provided by operating it through the suit, but he can still inflict plenty of damage.

'You expect us to fight these Jain for you?' Vrell enquires, snatching up his rail-gun and particle cannon just as Orbus moves aside.

And abruptly that fact comes home to Orbus: those creatures severely fucked over a war drone Orbus would not himself like to go up against even with an attack ship.

'I am fighting the subversion software now, but the Jain remain somewhere inside the planetoid – for the moment at least,' says the Golgoloth. 'However, their attack has caused some other problems inside this vessel that I am not currently able to deal with, and twenty-eight of them are heading here directly. They are my children and they are adequately armed.'

'Order them to desist,' says Vrell.

'I do not have the pheromonal control of normal Prador, and have never really needed it until now.'

'Why should we fight your children?' asks Orbus. 'And why are your children such a danger to you?'

Vrell clatters a Prador laugh and Orbus realizes his second question was a stupid one. Prador children usually only obey their father because he controls them pheromonally, and because the alternative to obedience is death. However, Orbus still needs an answer to his first question.

'You have little choice in the matter.' The Golgoloth takes time out from its frenzied activity to gesture towards a door opening into an adjacent corridor. 'You are between them and me, and they will be arriving here soon. Do you think they will go round you to get to me instead of through you?'

Vrell finishes plugging in the power leads to his weapons and he now clutches one in each claw. Turning his head carefully, he inspects their surroundings, and Orbus guesses he is wondering how he can get to the Golgoloth.

'This is a big ship,' Orbus observes. 'If that thing's children can get here, then the internal defences must be offline. Let's just get as far away from our friend here as we can, and let him settle his own family disputes.'

'There will be a good reason why we shouldn't,' observes Vrell.

'Of course you are correct, Vrell,' says the Golgoloth. 'As I told you, I am fighting subversion software. If I die, that software wins, and then either the Jain arrive here shortly afterwards or this ship will be destroyed. In the unlikely event that neither of these scenarios applies, it will take you, Vrell, a long while to get control of this ship and fly it out of here – time enough for King Oberon to arrive.'

'And if we defeat these children for you, what do we gain?' asks Orbus.

'You stay alive.'

And that seems to be the end of the discussion.

Vrell rapidly scoots towards the door, and Orbus wades laboriously after him, making a selection on his weapon's display. Vrell moves ahead of him out into the corridor, swinging his head from side to side to check out each end of it. Orbus then moves out, too, feeling the tug of a current against his calves. Water is rushing down drain gratings positioned along the base of the walls, and heaping detritus there which is crawling with ship-lice, tangled with lengths of optics and various organic-looking pipes, and scattered with insectile machines. Orbus is interested to note these last, for they are the kind of robot you find aboard Polity ships, but which Prador tend not to use. Somehow, because it uses robots, he now feels better about the Golgoloth than any other Prador, except perhaps Vrell.

'Here they come,' says Vrell, now retreating towards the doorway.

By its size, the creature splashing into view at the end of the corridor is a third-child version of the Golgoloth: a pathetic limping creature which doesn't seem to know what it is doing. It freezes upon seeing them, makes a chittering sound, then turns and flees. Orbus sights on the point where it disappears, and moves over into an alcove on the opposite side of the corridor.

'Maybe they won't attack,' he suggests. That creature hadn't looked particularly aggressive – in fact, Orbus feels an ambivalent pity for it. Who would want a parent like its own?

Vrell laughs again – he seems to be doing a lot of that lately – then launches himself up onto the uneven surface of the wall and climbs to the top, stopping just below some air vents.

The second-child that appears next seems wrapped in silvery tubes and holds some kind of wide flat weapon. It fires it once down the corridor, then flings itself out of sight. Multiple impacts cut a broad line of splashes through the flood, then a series of explosions ensue, filling the air with flames, whickering fragments of metal and great sprays of water. Orbus turns his head, only to feel something thump into his back. Reaching round he levers out a chunk of shrapnel, then squats to sight again along the corridor. Another second-child appears and he hits it twice, then has to duck back as it fires its weapon before advancing. It calmly takes aim again, seemingly unaffected by his shots though they have punched through its carapace. Orbus ducks further out of sight as the stretch of wall adjacent to his alcove explodes into flinders.

Damn, fuck-up.

He has made the stupid and automatic assumption that these creatures are infected with the Spatterjay virus, yet sprine bullets do not affect them. Nothing from Vrell yet, as the Prador carefully edges along just below the ceiling. Orbus hurriedly alters the setting on his weapon for rail-accelerated P-shells packed with a high-pressure explosive fluid, but the creature will not let up sufficiently for him to lean out far enough to fire. He will just have to take some hits, then. Using the uneven wall surface, he climbs higher inside the alcove, then lunges out. Something smacks into his thigh, partially spinning him round. He shoulders into six inches of water, then rolls and comes up seating his multigun against his shoulder. A short burst of four shots slam into the Prador's mouth, sending it staggering back, then they detonate inside the creature, bursting it into fragments like a shattered coconut. Orbus glances down as chunks of the second-child bounce off the walls or spatter them. His own thigh is sliced open to the bone. Reaching down he clamps the wound closed with one hand, waits for a moment, then takes his hand away. The wound remains closed but he can still feel its weakening effects. Orbus limps forward and fires just as four third-children scuttle across the junction ahead. One slams against the wall with half its side gone, then slides down into the water and is washed against one of the drains.

Where the hell is Vrell?

Glancing up, Orbus can now see no sign of him, but he doesn't want to search too long as that might give away Vrell's position to these attackers. More second-children appear, carrying something between them. A detonation over to the right, and part of the wall collapses like shattering stone, to expose a grid underneath and pipes leaking a fluid like bile. Orbus fires, shakes off his limp, and charges towards them. Numerous rapid detonations send one of them up into the air, spinning and shedding limbs, and split another evenly in two. Orbus reaches the survivor before it can bring its weapon to bear. He kicks it hard, lifting it up off the floor and feeling carapace breaking under the impact of his boot, then catches hold of its bigger claw and cannons it into the nearby wall.

Ahead a whole second-child host swarms into view. He drags his latest opponent before him as a shield, and aims over it, firing short bursts to horrible effect. It is odd that though these crippled oddities are trying to kill him, he still feels sorry for them – but only until his second-child shield disintegrates under returned fire, while the walls all around explode with flinders and spray fills the air. Then suddenly a powerful rail-gun opens up, and he recognizes the sound. As he hits water on his back and skids, he sees the crowd of second-children disappearing as if being fed from the front end into an invisible shredder. From this lower position he can also see that a grating in the ceiling has been torn open. So that's where the bugger went.

Ears ringing, Orbus lies half submerged in cool water and wonders just how badly injured he is. Are his guts hanging out? Will he soon be growing a leech tongue as the virus starts making drastic changes to his body? He doesn't feel any damage, however, other than the stiffness in his leg. No time for idle speculation, so he jerks himself upright and again raises his weapon, checking its display before inspecting himself. He is covered in green gore and gobbets of flesh, while chunks of Prador carapace, sharp as shattered porcelain, are embedded in his chest. He pulls them out and discards them and, seeing no damage more serious than that, he stands up.

The corridor is now a charnel house. Vrell must have killed twenty or more of the creatures with that prolonged blast. Bits of them heap about the drains, spatter the walls, or float in water turned peppermint-green by their blood. Some are still whole, some still moving. As Orbus advances, one of them pulls itself to its feet, eyes him for a moment, then, with a clattering, gobbling sound, turns and flees. With his multigun up against his shoulder he tracks its progress to a turning at the end where it ducks out of sight, then he lowers his weapon and switches it over to laser, for only few of the explosive bullets remain.

'What are you doing, Vrell?' he wonders out loud.

Advancing, he reaches the turning and abruptly steps round it. Ahead stands another crowd of both second- and third-children, some armed with cobbled-together projectile weapons, the rest carrying only items of metal to use as clubs. The whole crowd, which was advancing cautiously, comes to an abrupt halt. Orbus considers his chances. He is covered with blood and bits of their kind, and has just come through their better-armed advance force, of which nothing much now remains. He roars and charges towards them, and the whole crowd just turns and flees, disappearing into side corridors, through gratings or scuttling up walls to get out of his way. Orbus grins to himself, then turns to head back to the Golgoloth's Sanctum. But by no means is this all over. For there were no first-children amidst those attackers, and certainly Vrell is up to something.

15

When Humans went into space it did not take long for their vessels to be occupied by unwelcome stowaways. Modern ships possess subminds whose sum purpose is pest control. Microbots patrol ducts to laser down fleas, mosquitoes, sandflies and houseflies. Slightly larger robots are deployed to catch and digest a mutated cockroach that is capable of existing on a diet of plastics, whilst mice and rats can usually be exterminated by general ship-security systems. Other unwelcome visitors include more alien forms: the blade beetle – a creature with razor-sharp edges and a penchant for laying its eggs inside anything large, warm and soft; sugar worms which seem to have acquired a taste for the organic dust of skin cells which Humans perpetually shed; and sheeter colonies that spread like coral whilst busy metabolizing aluminium. The list is endless and also includes numberless microscopic forms, blooms of nanomachines and even 'wild' robots, so it is therefore unsurprising to discover that Prador ships are similarly colonized. However, those crablike aliens approach the problem in an entirely different way. Whereas Humans perpetually try to clean house, the Prador let their small passengers clean house for them. Their ships swarm with decapod crustaceans, ship-lice, who clear up the remains of their meals, and such remnants as are left by their frequent violent encounters with each other.
– From QUINCE GUIDE compiled by Humans

The ceiling space extends into darkness on either side, but is only just deep enough to accommodate Vrell, who is now inching forward on his belly, occasionally having to pause to carefully and quietly tear out a supporting strut that is blocking his way. He assumes the first-children moving ahead of him stand no real chance of creeping up undetected on the Golgoloth, for surely the old monster would never have allowed such a hole in its defences. However, the three first-children are trying this route anyway, dragging with them thermic lances and plasma cutting torches, and maybe they will provide Vrell with an opportunity to exploit.

Vrell pauses by a ship's eye that is dangling before him on a single wire, then turns his head as an orange flicker cuts through the darkness, leaving after-images in his harness mask. The lead first-child is carrying a scanning device and a powerful gas laser, to detect and then destroy all the sensors in the vicinity. It seems these three know they cannot hide their present position from their parent, but are trying nevertheless to conceal precisely what they are doing. Perhaps, given time, they could cut their way through to the Golgoloth, but Vrell suspects that either they will not be allowed enough time, or a reception is already being prepared for them.

The three finally reach a curving wall and begin setting up their equipment. Vrell carefully eases back to put himself out of range of the light they will shortly be generating. He settles down and adjusts his mask to a reactive setting so the glare will not blind him, even temporarily. As expected, a plasma torch flares into life and one of the three begins cutting through the lower part of the ceiling space, beside the wall. The one with the scanner and gas laser stands guard, as lopsided and pathetic-looking as its fellows.

Vrell sets his harness to quiet running, just in case the scanner is sensitive enough to pick up its electrical activity, but when the laser suddenly flares and leaves a macula in his mask, he assumes for a moment that this precaution was not enough. However, something then flares behind him and, slowly turning his head, he observes the remains of a small robot burning and folding its legs up like a dying spider. The Golgoloth obviously decided to send some mobile eyes up here to watch the proceedings.

With a clang, a circular section of ceiling drops out of sight and the plasma torch gutters out. First down through the hole is the one with the scanner and laser, and numerous flashes ensue as it knocks out any ship eyes found immediately below. As the other two first-children follow it, Vrell eases himself into motion again and heads over to the hole they have cut. He then pauses. The gap itself is too small for him, and following them directly will only lead him straight into whatever reception the Golgoloth has prepared for them. Better that they work as a distraction. He eyes the curving wall ahead, remembering precisely how he gained access to Vrost aboard the dreadnought, then edges his way round it to put some distance between himself and the hole the first-children have made, but not so far as to come within the compass of any still-functioning ship eyes. Then, abruptly, he stabs out with one claw.

Its sharp tips punch through a layer of light aluminium alloy, before he closes the claw, tearing through the metal, and pulls away a chunk of it. As he expected, this layer was put in place merely for containment, so that the space between it and another wall further in could be injected with insulating foamed porcelain. Vrell opens his claws wide, stabs in just one jaw, then works it round like a can opener, finally tearing out a section of metal sheet that is wider than himself. Next he begins working on the porcelain, which being old and brittle quickly breaks into chunks. After a few minutes of frenzied activity, he makes a hole large enough to insert himself, right through to an inner wall of ceramal armour. He pushes himself inside, then, like a crustacean forcing its way through sand, uses all his limbs simultaneously to tear chunks of the surrrounding material free and push it behind him, steadily working his way upwards.

It is slow and methodical work, and meanwhile Vrell begins mulling over everything that has happened so far. It seems that the peak of his achievement since leaving Spatterjay has been to seize control of Vrost's dreadnought, but thereafter everything started going downhill, yet it isn't the major events – like the Golgoloth forcing him to crash-land or the resurrection of Jain super-soldiers – that cause him the most mortification. His response to those was simply inadequate because he lacked sufficient resources, and even retrospective analysis of his actions causes him no shame. No, it is some of his un-Pradorish behaviour that bothers him, and its unintended consequences.

It would have been eminently sensible to have ejected both Sniper and Orbus from the dreadnought at once, either that or to have used the Guard to eliminate them immediately. Certainly the drone would have taken some killing, but with the forces then at Vrell's disposal he could have managed it. However, even though his decision at the time *should* have been wrong, Sniper later saved his life. Then Orbus: the Human tried to kill him once, then contemplated it again, so surely Vrell should have eliminated him? But Vrell just did not want to kill him. *Am I becoming a soft-shell?* he wonders. It seems so, for what Prador other than a puling coward would feel such fear upon encountering these Jain, and then feel such terror when encountering a mythical creature used to scare him as a third-child? Vrell decides the time for fear is at an end; it is time for positive, violent action.

At about twenty feet up, the armoured wall begins to curve down to form a ceiling, and at his back the thin aluminium alloy is supplanted by another layer of ceramal armour. Soon he exposes a pipe running along above the ceiling, and follows it to another armoured wall ahead, which curves sharply away to his right and left. The pipe enters this wall through a flange that is secured in place with ceramal rivets. Vrell pulls his particle cannon from his harness, then unplugs it from its main power supply so as to leave it reliant only on its internal battery. Dialling down its power to the minimum, and then setting it for one microsecond burst, he centres it over one rivet and triggers it.

The beam is barely functional, but still produces a loud crack and flash of greenish light. Moving the weapon aside, he observes that part of the flange is now missing, along with the rivet head. He moves on to the next one and the next, to burn away all the rivet heads in turn, then, levering with his claw, he pulls the flange free from the rivets and slides it back along the pipe before jutting his head forward and tilting it so that he can insert one palp-eye through the gap.

Amazingly, the Golgoloth's defences aren't as rigorous as Vrell supposed. This ceramal wall, which is only a few inches thick, forms a cylindrical chamber via which numerous pipes and optic ducts enter the sanctum below. Turning his eye, Vrell obtains a very good view of the Golgoloth, still frenetically working its machines as it fights the Jain computer-life attempting to seize control of this entire vessel. It will take, Vrell estimates, just seconds with the particle cannon at full power, to cut through, though that will drain its remaining charge of particulate matter. Still, he has enough projectiles available for his rail-gun to turn that creature below him to slurry. Not yet, however; first let the Golgoloth rid the ship of its Jain worms and viruses, and only then will Vrell change the current situation, radically.

A micro-drone rises into position before the Golgoloth's natural eye, presenting on its flat viewing face a green-and-white schematic of a far sector of the ship, the various locations of hijacked components highlighted in pulsating yellow. Also monitoring this activity in two internal ganglia and one external one, the Golgoloth issues countermeasures and the yellow begins to recede in some areas; however, it begins to blossom elsewhere.

Not good enough.

The Golgoloth issues further instructions resulting in power surges aimed to bypass its own safety protocols, and the old creature observes the effect in that same sector through its optically linked eye. A long row of fuses blow along the interior of a mirrored square canister, as it rapidly fills with inert gas. Where the fuses disintegrate, white arcs flare as an excess of power surges into a circuit that should have shut down. A short distance away, a large laminar power supply suddenly explodes underneath a superconducting cable, severing it. Other cables throughout the ship are severed in a similar manner, and lasers, particle cannons, field generators, rail-guns and missile arrays instantly power down. The Jain computer-life might manage to access those other weapons, but simply will not have the current to operate them; though neither will the Golgoloth itself. However, one item of the hull weaponry remains usable: the U-jump missile the Golgoloth intended to fire at the dreadnought, and which it now controls through a secure channel it sacrificed several other systems just to preserve.

The old hermaphrodite now focuses on one of the stalked arrays of screens. Vrell and Orbus have driven off the remaining third- and second-children, a few of which can be seen still cowering in wet crannies here and there within the ship, and those brave first-children working their way down the outside of the Sanctum, to where a false ship's schematic details a weakness in the walls, will eventually be dealt with. However, killing this Jain computer-life is like trying to stamp out a fog. The Golgoloth returns its attention to the micro-drone, and banishes it with the touch of a claw, whereupon another drone leaps into place. More schematics reveal that same sick yellow almost entirely shrouding a node in the ship's systems which is surrounded by control icons: a ganglion. A simple instruction delivered here sends a coded pulse along an isolated wire to it, to operate a plunger that injects a lethal poison, and the ganglion dies, its entire nexus shutting down and killing the Jain worm growing within. Already it has been necessary to sacrifice sixty-two ganglia like this, also to isolate entire ship's systems and to physically sabotage power lines to the main U-space engines, as just achieved with the hull weapons.

The Golgoloth feels a growing anger as it comes to understand that, no matter what worms and viruses it kills inside the main ship, they are still being propagated from the splinter. But it knows it will eventually win this battle, though the sacrifice that victory entails will be a big one. The real problem, however, is time. Even now something major is occurring within the planetoid, indicated by massive outgassings. The Jain are up to something there requiring vast amounts of energy in order to have such a wide-spread effect. Then there is the other problem: King Oberon will be arriving sometime soon, long before the Golgoloth gets a chance to repair those power lines and put the engines back online.

Out of necessity the Golgoloth kills off another two ganglia and, as a result, feels itself becoming just a little more stupid. It then observes the Old Captain returning to the Sanctum, covered in Prador gore, to plump himself down on the cowling of a filter pump beside the entrance. But where meanwhile is Vrell? That, it seems, might be another problem for, despite his size, Vrell managed to worm himself up into the ceiling vents, and from there to ambush the second-children to such devastating effect, but now he has completely disappeared. The Golgoloth is all too aware how those same vents give access to the ceiling space the first-children were using to reach the Sanctum's inner wall, whilst knocking out a great many sensors, and that Vrell might currently be using that blind spot to do . . . *something*.

The Golgoloth was intending to send more robots into that same area to find out just what he might be up to, but unfortunately a Jain worm is now chewing its way through the control software of the robots in this same sector of the ship. Perhaps it should have acceded to Oberon's request right from the beginning. Taking out the dreadnought upon first coming within range of it would have been easy – then no Jain, no Vrell and no utterly imminent Oberon.

No time for regrets.

The Golgoloth sends instructions to the only engines it still controls: the steering thrusters. Many of them instantly fire up about the equator of the ship, sending blue blades of flame spearing out into vacuum. The ship begins to spin ponderously at first, then faster and faster. The Golgoloth monitors the current situation through ship eyes and sensors it still controls within the vicinity of the splinter. Stress readings come through first, as damaged structure there begins to shift. A micro-drone rises into position to receive instruction, and a tap from one claw sends its isolated program on its way. The spinter did not hard-dock properly, merely crashed into its berth in the main ship. The program slips past the sick yellow of Jain infestation and trips numerous switches to a network of superconductors that in turn are connected to cylindrical charges of chemical explosive. They now detonate about the splinter in an even pattern, for the explosives were initially positioned there to drive out docking bolts for rapid escape, should the Golgoloth ever need to use the splinter for that purpose. Given an initial shove by these blasts, and assisted on its way by the main vessel's spin, the splinter begins to ease itself out. The Golgoloth shuts off the steering jets, not now wanting another impact between the main vessel and the departing splinter, and grunts with satisfaction as it watches optic cables begin to tear loose, cutting off much of the flow of Jain computer-life from the splinter.

Immediately the portions of ship's schematics currently presented by the micro-drones begin to look better as the Golgoloth's hunter-killer programs make headway. Some ganglia and the systems they control begin to reconnect. However, the process is still a laborious one because, though physical connections with the splinter have been broken, the electromagnetic ones have not. Viruses and worms are still being transmitted to the main vessel's sensors. The Golgoloth sends another instruction to the steering jets, the moment the tip of the splinter clears the ship's hull, first turning its docking hole away from it, next moving the main ship away. The old monster then summons to itself a micro-drone that is standing ready.

The splinter reaches a distance of two miles before its own engine abruptly flares into life. Doubtless the plan now is to crash it into the main vessel, but it is too late. The Golgoloth taps the micro-drone, which transmits its signal to the U-jump missile. The rail-gun launcher in which the missile sits now powers up and spits the missile out into vacuum. A mile out from the main vessel, a particle beam probes out from the splinter to lick on the missile for a fraction of a second, but the missile drops into U-space, disappearing from reality for the remaining mile.

The splinter seems to briefly turn transparent as the missile detonates inside it like a flashbulb inside a glass bottle. It bucks and bends at the point of detonation, starts to separate into two halves, but they disintegrate and are then vaporized in the spreading spherical blastwave. The Golgoloth reaches over to grab the stalk of one of its screen units for support, as the main vessel shudders under the blast. Through exterior sensors, where they survive for long enough, it observes the outer hull distort then heat up briefly, before internal layers of superconductor redistribute the heat. Numerous damage warnings call for its attention, but it ignores them, focusing on just one alert nearby, as it sends a single instruction.

Over to one side, a section of wall spins on a central axis, bringing three very surprised first-children right into the sanctum, while they are still cutting into the side of a wall that until then was an exterior one. After a pause they raise their paltry weapons, but a flat hardfield slams them back against the wall and pins them into place. Having rapidly defeated two attacks, the Golgoloth feels a surge of joy, until a concentrated blast above rains down chunks of broken ceramal, molten metal and a single mutated Prador wielding a rail-gun.

The shockwave and ship's spin try to scour Sniper from his niche between the throats of the fusion engines, and his temperature rises in concert with his surroundings. He clings on grimly as molten metal rains down on him. Sensory input from his surroundings arrives both blurred and fragmentary, and internal diagnostic routines clamour for his attention with their lists of faults. Aware of what many items on these lists indicate, the drone simply deletes them. He can resist massive point temperatures from weapons strikes by distributing the heat about his body through an internal s-con grid. He can vent heat by emitting evaporants and convert it, sometimes, to other usable forms of energy. But sitting for over an hour in close proximity to a fusion torch has been like surfing on the chromosphere of a sun, and now this blast on top of all that is taking many of his internal components beyond the point of recovery.

The forces trying to fling him into vacuum slowly ebb, and the molten metal spattering his exterior begins to harden. He reaches out with tentacles that now bend like jointed limbs because so many of their motors, each previously operating like a separate vertebrae, have now melted and fused to adjoining motors. Laboriously he drags himself clear of the engines and scans his surroundings.

There.

An array of infrared radiator fins protrude a hundred yards away, almost certainly connected to internal superconductors – a typical construct to be found on any ship this size which is likely to end up in combat, their purpose being to shed internal heat caused by beam and missile strikes or imploding field generators, or to redistribute heat like that produced by this most recent blast. Sniper drags himself across to it, careful all the way to insert his tentacles in whatever nooks and crannies he can find, eventually pulling himself right up beside the array and wrapping red hot tentacles around it . . . and then sighing.

His temperature begins dropping rapidly, the cherry glow fading from his body and hardened metal flaking away, unable to bond to his outer layer of nano-chain chromium. He begins to inspect those diagnostic lists more closely. The coils of his particle cannons and the wiring to his rail-guns have fused, his lasers are scrap, his ability to communicate further than a few hundred yards is non-existent and his gravmotors just aren't responding. He gives a little shrug. At least he's fired off all his missiles down there on the planetoid – some of the chemical warheads would have been detonated by his recent roasting and left nothing but an empty shell. However, as his temperature drops, the routines finally begin reporting some good news. Parts of his internal toolkit remain functional; being mostly fashioned of high-spec ceramal, his steering jets and fusion drive still work; and his crystal mind has not cracked. He is seriously injured but not totally crippled.

What now?

Orbus and Vrell are still somewhere inside this ship, and he feels his first duty is to find them. He needs to sneak inside – and sneaking is something he has always been adept at – but this won't be so easy in his current condition. First, then, he needs to find the resources hereabouts to repair himself. Again closely scanning his surroundings, he focuses on a nearby construct on the hull, which looks like a ring of iron standing stones. Doubtless they encircle some sort of weapons port and, if the design of this ship in anyway matches that of both Prador and Polity ships, the weapon will reside inside some blast-proof, partially self-contained blister – the kind of place he should be able to quickly isolate and which likely contains resources he can use.

Sniper lets go of the heat sink and begins towing himself across to the ring of extrusions. It is fortunate, he guesses, that this area of the hull has taken such a pounding, as that probably will have wiped out any sensors able to detect him. Finally reaching one of the monoliths, he clings to it and peers down into a dish formed within the hull, an octagonal opening at its bottom. His eyes are better now, since internal programming has been busy ironing out optical distortion caused by lens damage. The opening is some sort of rail-gun port – obviously not for launching inert missiles because it is just too big, yet conveniently big enough for Sniper to haul himself inside.

Easing himself down the slope, while still clinging to the monolith, he reaches out for the edge of the hole, grips it as best he can, then releasing his other hold, pulls himself over the edge and, scanning downwards, discovers that this particular weapon does not seem to be live.

Positioned in each angle of an octagonal tube leading down inside the ship is a rail: crescent-section, inner face micro-ridged all the way down, with doped superconductors. Coolant pipes, s-con cables and various control systems run through the jacket enclosing all these, and the only way out of this barrel and into the surrounding chamber will be either by cutting a hole through the barrel's side or trying to open the loading mechanism far at the back. Sniper holds up his one spatula-tipped tentacle and inspects it. The microscopic chainglass teeth around its edge only extrude while actually in use, and are resistant to temperatures exceeding those he has recently experienced, but there is a short in the power supply somewhere.

Sniper sends a minibot telefactor scuttling like an ant down inside the tentacle. Halfway down, it finds the problem: a lump of something incredibly hard and glassy has penetrated, and split the coating over an s-con wire, shorting it against one adjacent motor. A simple enough problem to solve, if it wasn't the case that thousands of other such failings must be dealt with inside him. Directly controlled by Sniper, the minibot cuts the wire free from its short point, reinserting it into its broken clamp, and welds that, then sprays over the break in the coating with a speed-set insulator. Next he reinstates an internal fuse and has the satisfaction of watching his cutter blur up to speed, before he inserts it into the wall of the rail-gun barrel and begins slicing.

At that moment one of his internal sensors, made to register disturbances in underspace and which he has assumed was burnt out, alerts him. Quickly analysing the signal he realizes that the sensor is running at less than 20 per cent efficiency, and only reacting now because something huge has arrived nearby.

Sniper pauses, then heaves himself to the mouth of the rail-gun and looks around, not even having to raise magnification to spot the massive upright ship hovering out there, just above this vessel's horizon. Numerous smaller, silvery objects gather about it and, slowly increasing magnification, at each stage having to correct errors, he brings those objects into focus even as the vessel he clings to rolls slightly, throwing them higher above the ship's horizon and also bringing the planetoid into view. He sees Prador dreadnoughts surrounding a ship that reaches fifty miles from top to bottom. Perhaps this isn't such a great time to be crawling about in the throat of a rail-gun, but Sniper ducks down again and sets to work.

To Gurnard's perception, the U-space signature is like a bomb going off, and when, moments later, a giant Prador dreadnought roars past, the ship AI realizes it might just be time to move. But to where, and then to do what? Gurnard focuses now on the Golgoloth's vessel. Certainly the Jain were attacking it informationally, hence the destruction of the splinter vessel, but perhaps it is still under attack and, it having sustained some damage, an opportunity to somehow get to Orbus and Vrell has opened up there? Gurnard fires up its fusion engine and speeds in that direction, not yet sure what to do, but certain that leaving the scene right now will be of no help at all.

'So good King Oberon just arrived,' observes Thirteen. 'I wonder what comedian AI decided to give him that particular name?'

'It is a name he chose himself, apparently,' Gurnard replies.

'A Prador with a sense of humour? Sounds like a dangerous precedent to me.'

'This entire planetary system is full of dangerous precedents,' Gurnard observes.

Thirteen gives an electronic snort and rises from his position on the console. 'Other than your telefactors, which are basically blunt tools, I am your only means of getting to Orbus and Vrell, and I am now ready.'

'And eager, it would seem.'

'We have lost Drooble and we have lost Sniper . . .'

'A drone you have known for many years.'

'Yes, Sniper and I have been through a lot together. He gave me my independence and much else besides.'

'It is not certain that he is dead,' suggests Gurnard. 'He could merely be damaged and unable to communicate. If he is damaged he has probably gone to ground to repair himself, or might even have ejected his mind canister from his body for later retrieval. That last option is not one available to Orbus and Vrell, who in my opinion are in greater danger. If we survive whatever happens next, we will search the planetoid for him.'

'All predicated on the notion that any of them are alive at all.'

'I don't see this Golgoloth creature seizing both Vrell and Orbus simply to kill them. It could have left them to the Jain or shot them down from its own vessel.' Gurnard pauses as the scene on one of the forward electronic screens changes from a view of the Golgoloth's vessel to one of King Oberon's ship and its attendant dreadnoughts, the planetoid lying just beyond them. 'As for Sniper, if he has survived at all, then it seems likely he will continue surviving – he is, after all, a very old and wily war drone.'

Thirteen turns in midair and starts drifting towards the rear of the bridge. 'I don't possess the propulsion to throw myself across large distances.'

'What would be your preference: rail-gun or telefactor?'

'A rail-gun will get me there quicker, but I might have a problem upon arrival. Very humorous, Gurnard.'

'AIs can have a sense of humour too.'

Tracking the little drone with internal cams, Gurnard watches it making its way down towards the docking ring. Meanwhile the AI inspects, by other means, two suitable telefactors which, unlike the handler robots, possess chemical rocket drives. These two objects, looking like sculptures of water beetles nearly ten feet long, hang suspended in a framework within their own little bay. Gurnard powers both of them up, whilst allowing a diagnostic program to check them over, itself focusing on their ability to hide. These things do not possess modern chameleonware capable of subverting *active* scanning; however, they do possess sufficient 'ware in their wing cases to make them invisible to a *passive* search.

Diagnostics reveal nothing wrong with either telefactor, though one has been used recently and therefore contains less oxygen and hydrogen fuel. Gurnard chooses that one, because quantity of fuel probably won't be an issue, and it is always best to employ a machine that has recently been run up to speed, despite what the diagnostics say. One portion of his consciousness now inhabiting the little machine, Gurnard lifts one wing case and opens the concertinaed hatch in its back.

'Any padding?' Thirteen enquires, now entering the bay and rising above the hatch.

'Once you are inside I can inject crash-foam,' Gurnard replies. 'I can also eject you at high speed should the telefactor itself come under attack.'

Thirteen settles into the cavity, but just as the cover begins to slide across, pokes his head back out. 'When will you launch me?'

'Within fifty minutes I will be as close as I dare get to the Golgoloth's ship,' Gurnard replies, only part of its attention focused on the drone, and a great deal focused instead on King Oberon's fleet.

Something is happening there, something that might not bode well for Sniper if he is still down there somewhere on the planetoid. Perhaps best not to mention that to Thirteen.

Standing on the wide highway of the King's viewing gallery, Sadurian keeps her eyes closed until the nausea passes, for the effects of U-space transition seem worst here, this close to vacuum, then opens them to observe the white wall of opaque glass in front of her. After a moment its blank whiteness turns to a cloudiness which, in turn, drains away as if some pump is sucking smoke from between two sheets of glass. Her first distinguishable view is of one of the new Prador dreadnoughts drifting across and turning, but its passing soon reveals the planetoid lying beyond. Obviously, the war vessel was ordered to this prime position so that King Oberon, presently standing twenty feet away from her, can watch the show.

Sadurian studies the planetoid beyond. From its cloudy atmosphere a gaseous ring fans out, which is not how this object looked in the library pictures.

'The latent temperature of the planetoid has risen by three degrees,' Oberon observes.

'That's a lot of heat,' Sadurian replies, feeling that she needs to say something – anything.

The King dips his head as if focusing on some particular aspect of the planetoid. 'The Polity's automated warship factories did not produce as much even during the height of the war.'

'It could signify inefficiencies,' Sadurian notes.

'It could, but probably only those that can be ignored for the sake of speed.'

'They know they need to establish a foothold fast, in order to survive.'

'Precisely,' the King agrees. 'I would be very interested to know what is going on inside there, but we cannot afford the time to find out.' He swings his head sideways to observe the dreadnought. 'And very shortly the temperature there is going to rise considerably.'

Gazing also at the dreadnought, Sadurian can see no change, but guesses it has just opened fire. She again focuses on the planetoid as straight lines flash into existence throughout its cloud layers, then the hot bloom of impact points becomes visible from below. This indicates near-c rail-gun missiles – carrying no explosive load themselves other than the hard material of their bodies – turning partially to plasma as they hit gas, and then releasing huge amounts of energy as they penetrate the planetoid's crust. Each impact yields megatonnes. They are the most immediate weapon to use, perhaps killing the Jain themselves, or at least slowing them down. However, the next wave of firings from the dreadnought is intended to make certain.

Silvery missiles speed from the dreadnought's launchers, though not at near-c, since such a level of acceleration would breach the antimatter flasks inside them. Some miles out, each of them ignites a bright white fusion torch, and accelerates. Meanwhile, blastwaves from the surface disrupt the cloud and blow it, in gouts thousands of miles across, out into space. In one area a plume of magma, just like the uncoiling stalk of some red vine, gropes into vacuum and then begins to come apart, rolling out lumps of molten rock that will soon enough solidify into asteroids.

'They do not seem to be responding,' remarks Oberon.

'Perhaps they're dead, now.'

'It would be nice to think so.'

Decidedly pessimistic, thinks Sadurian. But then perhaps the King is contemplating what he might need to do if the first strikes made here should fail. Sadurian knows what that augurs and doesn't like it at all. If the Jain can survive what is still to come, that means they are beyond Prador state-of-the-art weaponry, so then it isn't just a case of more force needing to be applied, but greater knowledge . . . knowledge the King does not, at this moment, possess. Knowledge the King *could* possess, but only at a very great risk.

The distant white dots of the missile fusion drives enter gas clouds dispersing from the planetoid, which is now becoming visible, its surface blotched with volcanic activity and other darker smokes. As one, they slam into the crust, disappearing from sight. A long pause ensues, and for a moment Sadurian wonders if the Jain have somehow disarmed these weapons. Then it seems as if some angry god takes hold of the very substance of space and begins squeezing it out of shape. The planetoid distorts like a soft egg about to hatch, and begins to expand. For a moment it is thrown into dark silhouette as an unbearably bright light glares behind it, then a crescent cuts across its surface and the same light glares from that too, photo-actively blotted by the glass directly in front of Sadurian. Flame and seas of molten rock explode outwards at thousands of miles per hour – an appalling act of planetary demolition – but, on this leviathan scale, the blast proceeds in seeming slow motion.

Sadurian feels like a cloistered intellectual suddenly faced with harsh realities. Ensconced within the white halls of the King's ship, concerning herself with biological matters generally below the microscopic, she has lost sight of just what kind of power the King of the Prador can wield.

The great cloud of hot gas and molten rock continues to expand, lightning storms flashing in its interior. *How can anything survive that?*

'Any sign of them?' she asks.

The King bows his head, mandibles clonking briefly against the glass. 'We are scanning,' he intones, 'but the disruption is great.'

Abruptly a ten-foot square etches itself into existence in the glass before the King, and reluctantly Sadurian walks closer to take a look. Within this square the view is magnified once, then twice, till it seems the cloud of destruction boils just on the other side of the glass. The scene then changes five times, showing different aspects of the chaos, then flicks away into open space, where it centres over a ship.

'Is that them?' Sadurian asks, gazing at the odd, fish-shaped vessel.

'A Polity ship,' Oberon replies. 'The Human we saw with the Golgoloth came from it. It should not be here.'

The view changes once more, this time bringing into focus a larger vessel, shaped like a melon with various parts of it excised. Sadurian recognizes it at once.

'If the Jain have survived and should they reveal themselves, we will respond,' says Oberon. 'Meanwhile I have other business to conduct here.'

In the larger view Sadurian observes four of the King's dreadnoughts accelerating away on a course taking them to a point far out from the expanding cloud. She concludes that the Golgoloth is also about to learn about the power the King can wield.

16

The massive amounts of EMR produced during space battles, making it increasingly difficult for our AIs to control telefactored weapons, resulted in the increasingly independent subminds which became our war drones. It then became necessary to increase their independence when they were used for assassinations and other covert missions, and to this end they were constructed with the ability to change just about any component of their bodies, and even to find replacements amidst stolen Prador technology. Sometimes these drones would come back almost unrecognizable, and some were even mistakenly destroyed because they so closely resembled Prador weapons. Over the intervening years since the war, such drones are still being found, like those Japanese soldiers hidden in the jungle after the Second World War on Earth, faithfully maintaining themselves in the remains of the Prador bases they destroyed, and unaware that the war they had been fighting ended centuries ago.
– MODERN WARFARE lecture notes from E.B.S. Heinlein

Vrell lands with a crash, his bulk demolishing one of the stalked arrays of screens, and nearly falling from the platform. He snaps out one claw and closes it on two of the Golgoloth's diseased-looking legs either to drag the creature closer or to drag himself fully onto the platform. With a gristly crunch the two legs are torn free, whereupon the Golgoloth emits a gobbling shriek and swings one of its claws at Vrell's head. Still scrabbling for balance, Vrell raises his rail-gun to block the intended blow, then finally manages to propel himself off the shattered screen array and onto the platform, to ram the barrel of his weapon just below the Golgo-loth's lower eyes. Then he hesitates.

'You kill me, you die,' says the hermaphrodite, its whole body quivering. 'My external ganglia are killing off the last of the Jain computer-life, but earlier I had to cut the power supplies to both the weapons and the engines.'

'That still does not explain your threat,' says Vrell.

'Perhaps, given time, you will be able to supplant me aboard my own vessel.' The creature flexes itself a little, getting its quivering partially under control. 'But to do so you will have to kill all my ganglia that are distributed throughout it.'

Vrell grinds the barrel of his weapon against the Golgoloth's scarred shell, wondering if he is only doing so to somehow reassure himself. He eyes one of the lice-things on the Golgoloth's body and notices that it appears to be half machine and half animal.

'But you do not have time,' the Golgoloth adds.

One of the arrays of screens still within Vrell's view, which until then had been showing a scrolling schematic of some kind, abruptly displays a view of the distant planetoid, with impact sites now glowing on its surface. A moment later the whole planetoid erupts.

'This was recorded while you were still lurking in the ceiling spaces above me.'

The creature seems more confident now, its quivering com-pletely controlled. Now the view pulls back to show King Oberon's ship and its surrounding dreadnoughts, before switching again to what Vrell presumes is a realtime view showing a spreading sphere of furnace-hot gas and chunks of magma.

'I am propelling us away from the blastfront by using steering thrusters, which will double the time before it strikes.'

'How long?'

'Four minutes,' the Golgoloth replies. 'This ship can survive most impacts, but if one of these hits us' – the screen view now focuses on a slowly distorting magma asteroid the size of Gibraltar, which is spewing out hot streams of lava from inside itself, like an ameoba groping for prey – 'we'll end up inside it, whereupon one of two things will happen: the heat will eventually overcome us, or we'll end up trapped inside a cooling asteroid.'

'What do you suggest?' Vrell asks.

'I suggest you let me just get on with what I am doing, which is repairing the power supplies to three fusion engines – enough for me to manoeuvre us out of the way of anything big that approaches. After that my intention is to repair the power supply to the U-space engines, though of course we will not be leaving here any time soon.'

'Why?' Vrell asks.

'The U-engines cannot be deployed whilst this ship is still surrounded by such a density of gas and rock. Using the fusion engines, it will take four hours to get clear before we can employ the U-engines and, it seems, having demolished the planetoid and presumably the Jain too, Oberon is now taking an interest in me.' Another change of screen display, now showing four of the big silver dreadnoughts heading straight towards them. 'They will arrive here just a few minutes after the blastfront itself arrives.'

Vrell just stares at the image before him. He'd successfully wormed his way into the chamber and now holds a gun at the Golgoloth's head, but that seems to be all the victory he can achieve.

'Can you fight them off?' Vrell asks.

'Bearing in mind my current circumstances, why should I bother?'

'Because Oberon will kill you.'

'The pair of us certainly seem to have a problem which needs to be solved within the next minute, if I am to get those fusion engines functioning in time.'

Vrell suddenly very much wants to spread this creature's brains all over the interior of the Sanctum. He needs to think, and think hard.

'The moment I step away from you, I end up pinned against a wall behind a force-field.'

'What do *you* suggest?' the Golgoloth enquires.

It will take too long for Vrell to usurp control of this ship, but perhaps there is a simpler solution to his present dilemma. He turns his head slightly to glance over at Orbus, who is now standing right by the force-field currently separating him from this diorama. 'Drop that hardfield wall.'

The Golgoloth doesn't seem to like this idea much. 'You mean let the Human in here?'

'Yes, let the Human in here.'

'What can he possibly achieve for you?'

'It is always better to have allies,' Vrell replies, groping with one of his underhands for various items attached to his harness. 'And it is always better to have insurance.' The sticky mine detaches and Vrell reaches out to press it in place underneath the Golgoloth's mandibles.

'Drop the field,' says Vrell, feeling a slight bubbling amusement as the other creature tries, with its one good palp-eye, to peer down past its mandibles. 'The mine I've just attached to you I now control through my harness.' Vrell's underhand is back at the point where he detached the mine, one hard little finger poised ready inside a small pit control. 'You may be able to crush me to slurry with one of your force-fields, but will you be able to do it quickly enough?'

The hardfield shuts down and water sloshes as it finds its new level. Vrell watches Orbus wade across to finally halt beside the platform, which stands head-high to him. The Old Captain rests his multigun across his shoulder and peers carefully at the Golgoloth.

'You got the bugger then,' Orbus observes. 'Maybe we should get in touch with Gurnard now?' Obviously he has not heard the previous exchange nor seen the images on the screens.

Vrell abruptly withdraws the barrel of his rail-gun from the captive's head. 'Make your repairs, Golgoloth.' Vrell moves to the edge of the platform, turns and abruptly drops off it to land beside Orbus. 'Prador dreadnoughts will be arriving here within minutes,' he explains to the Old Captain, 'just shortly after the blastfront from the planetoid they destroyed.'

'Get him to use his weapons against 'em,' Orbus nods up at the old creature, which is again calling in its micro-drones and issuing silent instructions. 'He's got some really fancy gear aboard this ship.'

'How long will it take you to reinstate your weapons?' Vrell asks.

'About forty minutes too long,' the Golgoloth replies, knocking one drone away, then backing up to insert several underhands into pit controls. There comes an immediate surge that sends Orbus staggering, and causes a wave to splash up against the hardfield behind which the first-children still struggle helplessly.

'So how are you going to survive this, then?' Vrell asks.

'I am going to throw myself on the King's mercy,' the old creature replies. 'Which is to say, I do not think I am going to survive this.'

Vrell does not think he will either, though is determined not to give up easily.

The rail-gun is dead, its power supply cut, and it is a simple matter to find and sever the fibre-optic control system and then, in very short order, to dismantle a great deal of the hardware housed in here. Sniper finds motors which, with just a little alteration, can replace some of his own. He feeds lengths of optic fibre inside himself to be snatched up by his internal toolbox, which uses it to replace damaged optic looms inside him. He is repairing his com gear when the sleet of electromagnetic radiation hits, and he scuttles back out to the mouth of the gun.

'Right,' says Sniper, much appreciating the scale of the destruction he is witnessing. He watches the show for a little while, steering thrusters hurling up blades of flame all about him as the vessel he currently occupies tries to gain some distance from the blastfront, then he spots the approaching dreadnoughts. 'Ah fuckit.' Sniper ducks back inside and begins working again just as hard and fast as he can.

Two of his minor tentacles he sacrifices, so as to use their working motors to replace irretrievably scrapped ones in his other tentacles. He replaces some of his sensors with ship eyes and other such devices, pillaged from all about him. The moment he puts these online, he feels a surge of nostalgia, for during the war he had often looted available equipment and self-repaired like this. In fact, trying always to be prepared for any eventuality, Sniper had this new drone shell of his deliberately fashioned so that it could adapt to just about any fitting or wiring system. Accurately sliced lengths from the rails of the big gun here now replace the ones in his own, then a section of bar sliced into short lengths supplies at least a little ammunition. Rewinding the coils for his particle cannon will take too long – better to find something inside the ship for that, just as a gravplate from inside can be worked into a suitable replacement for his trashed gravmotors. He is quickly reassembling one of his tentacles when the whole ship shudders and a low thunder echoes from its inner reaches – the blastfront has arrived.

Hot gas gusts in from outside the rail-gun chamber, and a momentary hail of lava spatters through the hole Sniper has cut through the barrel, instantly cooling to stone as it strikes against metallic walls. Using some of his tentacles as shock absorbers, Sniper braces himself and continues working; rapidly rejoining vertebrae motors and replacing nano-chain chromium rings, then finally locking on the pointed sensor tip. Next he fires up the cutting spatula of one of his main tentacles and uses it to slice round a section of the blister's inner wall, with a couple of lugs at its centre, and employing this as a shield, holds it before him as he re-enters the rail-gun barrel and eases his way up to the hull.

The shield takes a buffeting from hot gas, and rattles like a tin roof under hail. Far to his right, he can see the glare of a fusion-drive torch throwing out a long red contrail as it also burns surrounding spaceborne matter. Across the hull of the ship pass waves of molten-lava sleet, and every now and again something bigger hits, to spatter and release odd sparkling thermal reactions. However, even as he watches all this, the sleet begins to disperse as a massive shadow falls across him, and Sniper looks up to see the silvered hull of a modern Prador dreadnought blotting out the burning sky, its own drive flame slicing like a white scalpel drawn across blushed skin to release a trail of blood. He watches this vessel for a moment, then attempts to locate the other three – one over there, on the ship horizon, but no others in sight. They are positioned evenly about this ship, but what now, and why so close? Perhaps the environment prevents them using their usual weapons from a distance? No, silly idea.

Within the hull of the dreadnought, a row of ports opens and the nubs of what might be missiles poke out. Sniper retreats a little way, ready to take cover inside. But, upon seeing that those nubs possess wide flat faces, Sniper realizes he is in little danger from them. After a moment, the first of the row shoots out trailing a black cable. Some yards out, it ignites a series of small thrusters behind its head, to propel itself, and the huge weight of cable behind it, across the gap. The thing thumps down a hundred feet from Sniper, where it flares arc-light as it welds itself to the hull. Only as it hits can its truly enormous scale be assessed. The anchor head lies ten feet across and the cable – some form of braided metal – is two feet thick. A second of these comes hurtling across, then a third. Sniper ducks down again. No response from the vessel he is aboard probably means that not just this rail-gun but all its weapons are offline. Soon, those inside will become Oberon's captives – unless Sniper can do something about that.

Carefully controlling his internal toolbox, he makes some final adjustments to his newly repaired com gear, and sends a coded radio broadcast. There is a good chance that all the surrounding crap will block it, but he has to make the effort.

'Hey, Gurnard, can you hear me?'

After a lengthy delay during which Sniper picks up nothing but static, a surprisingly clear reply comes through. 'Now, why is it that I'm not surprised to hear from *you*?'

''Cus in your heart of steel you knew,' Thirteen interjected, 'that old drones don't die. That just happens to everyone else.'

'What is your status?' Gurnard asks.

'Seriously fucked over, squatting in a rail-gun blister trying to make some repairs.'

'Your timing, is as ever, exquisite, Sniper,' Gurnard observes. 'Thirteen, currently residing inside one of my telefactors, has just landed on the surface of the Golgoloth's ship.'

'The Golgoloth's ship?'

A package of information arrives and Sniper opens it in his mind. *Right, the Golgoloth.* Sniper feels sure he had picked up on something about this during his past, and has the sneaking suspicion the information is part of his missing memories.

'Getting ideas above your station again, Thirteen?' he asks.

'Hey, I was the last chance for Orbus and Vrell.'

'Right,' says Sniper.

'Where are you exactly?' Gurnard enquires. 'I cannot triangulate in this mess.'

'The rail-gun blister sits directly below one of the dreadnoughts—' Yet another of the tow lines slams down only a short distance behind Sniper, the hull shuddering, and a wave of magma spatters and arc-fire passing over his position. 'In fact the blister sits right on a line of towing anchors, one of which missed me by about twenty feet just a second ago.'

'From my point of view, all the lines are attached, so you must be below the one ship that is hidden from me.' Gurnard pauses, perhaps trying to fit Sniper into whatever crazy plan it is now developing. 'What are your requirements, Sniper? Perhaps I can get away with sending the other telefactor . . .'

'I take it the Prador just ignored you?'

'Yes.'

'Well, let's keep it that way.' Sniper considers for a moment. 'I take it your telefactor has gravmotors, com lasers and the usual arrays of stepper motors? Does it have limbs as well?'

'Yes, yes, yes – and yes,' Gurnard adds. 'I think I see your location now, though not you. Take the starting line of anchors as twelve o'clock, and look to about two.'

Sniper gazes over in that direction and picks out something making its way across the hull towards him. Only when it turns to circumvent one of the anchors does he take in its shape. The thing is struggling under a load of hardening stone, he sees.

'If your telefactor is a big metal bug,' says Sniper, 'then I already see it.'

'It is indeed a big metal bug,' Gurnard replies.

Sniper settles down to wait until the thing finally drags itself to the edge of the rail-gun port, now moving like some sea creature loaded down with a heavy layer of coral. It pauses for a moment at the edge, then drags itself down, and Sniper feels like a trapdoor spider waiting for its prey.

'Did your plans include getting Thirteen out of this thing?' he enquires.

'I can use an explosive ejection routine,' Gurnard replies.

'Well, don't.'

Sniper scours away some of the larger chunks of rock before propelling the telefactor through the hole into the rail-gun blister, and then towing it inside. Here he removes even more of the mess, slinging chunks of glutinous magma out into the barrel. A wing case rises, and a concertinaed hatch slides back to reveal a mass of crash foam which, in the next instant, is sliced through from the inside by a laser. Shaking off pieces of foam, Thirteen propels himself out.

'Let's get to work!' the little drone says cheerfully, splitting his tail into a two-fingered manipulator.

Sniper grunts agreement, already spinning the telefactor over and beginning to pull off its legs.

'I want you to release your first-children,' says Vrell.

Orbus looks across at Vrell and wonders if the Prador has lost his mind. Pinned up against the wall there is as good a place as any for those buggers, and the only improvement to their situation he can see is if the Golgoloth should move the hardfield tight up to the wall, turning them into organic paintwork.

'That will have the same effect upon me as you detonating that mine,' the Golgoloth replies. 'They will turn their weapons on me instantly.'

'Yeah, now why is that?' Orbus mutters.

Vrell persists, 'You will withdraw the force-field far enough to allow them some freedom of movement, but retain it in place between us and them.'

Very odd, thinks Orbus, perhaps Vrell is remembering his own traumatic upbringing and feels some sympathy for them – a particularly un-Pradorish reaction.

The force-field abruptly withdraws, dropping the first-children to the floor. Whilst two of the children just cringe back against the wall, the other one shakily moves to the hardfield, presses a claw against it, then raises a gas laser and fires it, but with no target in mind. The beam, just visible in the moisture-laden air, strikes the hardfield and loses coherence. Orbus feels the warmth from it wash across him, but that's all. The child shuts the beam down.

'Do you want to live?' Vrell addresses the three of them.

They make no reply.

'They're just aggressive fucks, like all Prador,' remarks Orbus, then glancing at Vrell, 'present company excepted.'

'Prador are aggressive because to behave otherwise means death,' says Vrell. 'Those sufficiently aggressive and motivated get to survive into first-childhood, and in that state can live for some time and even extract some pleasure from life. A very few even get to become adults.'

Orbus snorts derisively. That seems an overly indulgent explanation of Prador aggression, and pleasure for a Prador first-child usually means stomping on its smaller kin, pain for all enemies of the species, usually followed by them being turned into dinner.

Vrell continues, 'But no such options have ever been available to these, have they, Golgoloth?'

The Golgoloth doesn't reply.

'We are born, we grow and we are dismantled,' comes the translation through Vrell's com gear. It is the first-child with the laser that is speaking, even now backing away from the hardfield to rejoin its fellows. 'We remain inside our confinement frames, our minds and our bodies constantly exercised to achieve prime growth and health for eventual transplantation.'

It takes a moment for Orbus to absorb all that, but still he can't quite make any sense out of it. 'What's he on about?'

Vrell points one claw down at the yellow limbs he tore from the Golgoloth's body. They float in the water, jerking here and there as ship-lice feed on them. 'Those legs are not the Golgoloth's own. This is how it stays alive.'

Orbus gets it. All those second-children out in the corridor, the ones he has killed and the ones Vrell massacred. Up till then, he had seen only the kind of creatures that tormented him in the past: horrible beasts to be annihilated as quickly as possible. No wonder they came here to kill their parent. He feels suddenly sick at having been there to stop them.

'Confinement frames?' he asks.

'It has taken me a moment to see past the myths to register what is evident before me,' says Vrell. 'I now understand. The Golgoloth is a hermaphrodite and both father and mother to its children. Being such a close genetic match to it, they provide a ready source of transplant replacements to keep it alive. Obviously the Golgoloth will not want any creatures running free which likely possess its own innate intelligence, and who it uses for such an essential purpose.'

'So they spend their lives locked up in frames, being regularly harvested for their parts?'

'Yes.'

Orbus considers putting a few explosive bullets straight into the creature up there on the platform, but since Vrell himself hasn't yet chosen that option, there has to be a reason. Most of his life he thought there could be nothing worse than Prador, yet here is the Golgoloth, which is something else again. He swears to himself that, once this creature ceases to be essential to his own and Vrell's survival, he will not hesitate on the trigger.

'Do you want to live?' Vrell asks again.

'We want to live,' the first-child agrees.

'This is the situation . . .' Vrell explains it in short staccato sentences finishing with, 'The Jain will kill you, Oberon and any other Prador will automatically kill you, your parent here will put you back in your frames and harvest you. Only with me do you have a chance to live.'

The first-child abruptly turns away, to go into a huddle with its two fellows.

'Do they really understand?' Orbus asks.

'The Golgoloth kept their minds functioning, and those minds are like its own. They understand.'

The first-child turns back. 'What do you want of us?'

'I want you to gather all your fellows,' says Vrell. 'Your parent will then provide you with better weapons, which it almost certainly has aboard. Then I expect you to be prepared to fight, and probably die.'

'Agreed,' says the first-child.

'What is you name?' asks Vrell.

'I have none.'

'I will call you Geth,' says Vrell, then turns away. 'Golgoloth, drop the hardfield.'

The telefactor lies in pieces all about them, and Sniper feels so so much better, as if he is surrounded by the remains of a hearty meal. He and Thirteen have installed a gravmotor within his shell, his laser and hardfield generators are up and running, one of his particle cannons too, and even provided with the necessary particulate matter made by grinding up the telefactor's wing cases, while all his tentacles bend and twist in their usual satisfyingly squirmy manner. All he needs now, to really get up to spec, is a nice supply of programmable missiles and mines, but that is perhaps too much to ask from the hardware currently available.

'Okay,' he says, 'let's see what these fuckers are doing.'

Thirteen follows him into the rail-gun barrel, and on out to the ship's hull.

Space beyond is no longer filled with flame and magma sleet, but has by no means returned to black vacuum. The Golgoloth's vessel sits in a cloud that is the colour of pink grapefruit juice, threaded with veins of deep red. As Sniper surveys his surroundings, he observes one of the big anchors detaching and slowly winding back into the dreadnought hovering above. Others have already detached, their cables black scribbles in the pink sky, clouds of rock-shards spreading from where they are being wound into their ports and some mechanism strips away magma hardened on them. Another detaches and then another. Soon all the cables nearby retract, and the dreadnought spits out a long white fusion flame that scores bloody smoke from the surrounding firmament as it begins to move off, finally revealing the King's ship a thousand kilometres beyond it, but rapidly expanding in dimensions as they draw closer to it.

A further force wrenches at the Golgoloth's ship, nearly unseating Sniper from the throat of the rail-gun, and sending Thirteen tumbling away. Sniper spears out a tentacle that snags the little drone, dragging him back.

'What the fuck?' Thirteen wonders.

'The other achors are still attached,' Sniper replies. 'The other dreadnoughts are slowing us – I reckon we're on the docking side.'

'That a good place to be?'

'I dunno.' Sniper focuses on the King's ship, upping magnification. He can now see three massive docking tunnels extruding from a point midway down its fifty-mile height. They are tubular, with blocky structures distributed some half a mile back from their outermost tips, and definitely aren't the universal kind that finds the correct airlocks and adapts to them. The tips are sharp and barbed, so the docking procedure is going to be a violent one. Also, a swarm of familiar objects clusters in the area, like flies over shit: King's Guard, thousands of them.

'C'mon.' Sniper withdraws down the rail-gun barrel and back inside the blister, turning his attention to where he has already cut away part of the inner wall. Spearing out his main tentacles, both cutters now running, he shears through a layer of foamed porcelain, quickly shoving blocks of it behind him, exposing an s-con cooling grid and numerous pipes and fibre optics lining the main outer armour of the blister, then exposing a cap beside the loading mechanism at the back of the barrel itself, through which all of these connections are admitted.

'I could go through the door,' Thirteen observes, 'and take out the eyes.'

Sniper glances round at the little drone, who is pointing one division of his tail at a maintenance hatch underneath the rear of the particle-cannon barrel. The thing is quite small, so obviously isn't for Prador use but for little robots – like Thirteen.

'Then why are you still here?' he growls.

Thirteen descends on the hatch to quickly tear off the covers over its various locks and then manually click them back. The little drone starts to labour at the hatch itself, but Sniper snakes out a tentacle, levers it up off its seals and slides it aside. Whilst Thirteen pulls himself through, Sniper turns back to the cap and exposes the rest of it. The outer armour of blisters like these is usually cast in one piece, so actually cutting through the armour to get out is not an option. He could do it but the whole process would be far too noisy, and would deplete his power. Here beside the loading

351

mechanism, however, where all the power cables and optics enter, lies a capped hole just large enough for him to get through. He cuts away one skein of optics and drags it aside, exposing the weaker metal of the cap, stabs a hole through with his spatula-tipped tentacle and, as low-pressure air jets in, inserts another tentacle with its sensory tip active, and takes a look around.

Here, behind the blister, is a much larger chamber in which lie the mechanisms that rotate the whole blister like one giant eyeball. Over to one side lie the loading pincers, now empty, but one gleaming missile is partially visible in clamps situated behind it. Sniper recognizes it as one of the U-jump missiles this ship used against Vrell's vessel earlier. Swinging the tip of his tentacle round, he watches as the outer maintenance hatch eases aside a little. Ruby light flashes and ship eyes positioned in the surrounding wall flare and smoke, scattering shards of a material like mica, then the hatch swings completely aside, and Thirteen shoots out.

'Clear,' he calls, 'though I don't think they were working anyway.'

Sniper rapidly tears away further cables, slices around the end cap and, shoving it before him, slides out into the same chamber. After a quick scan of the interior, he tows himself over to a rack positioned along one wall, which holds maintenance robots folded up like long-legged brass woodlice.

'Seems this Golgoloth don't mind using robots,' he observes as he tugs one of the devices from its rack and begins slicing round it as if peeling an orange.

'What are you doing?' Thirteen asks.

'If there's maintenance robots here, they'll have an ID,' Sniper explains. 'Can't have the ship's security systems reacting every time one of 'em gets down to work.'

The robot's controls are simple and, plugging into it via the sensory tip of his tentacle, Sniper quickly riffles through what passes for its mind. He soon finds what he wants: a coded signal the thing broadcasts as it goes about its work. This message tells the ship's security systems to simply ignore it, so he records the signal, sends a copy to Thirteen, and they both begin broadcasting.

'Think this will work?' the little drone asks.

'So long as nothing with a mind is watching,' Sniper replies. 'Anyway, this Golgoloth thing is soon going to have a lot more to worry about than us.'

To the rear of the chamber stands a door large enough to admit Prador, but opening up this chamber, which via the blister now lies open to vacuum, will kick in emergency systems. Maybe that will attract the attention of the Golgoloth, but maybe not, since this area of the ship seems to have already sustained a lot of damage. It is a risk Sniper will have to take. He tears out the door's pit control and works the optics behind it. The diagonally divided door begins to grind open, and air and a moist fog blast through. Immediately, streams of yellowish-green fluid jet from holes in the walls. Where this substance lands it foams and expands rapidly. The door shudders to a halt, the emergency systems shutting down all power to it. Sniper reaches into the gap as, behind him and Thirteen, the chamber begins filling with a great amoebic mass of expanding crash foam. He then tears the doors open and the two push through into the familiar interior of a Prador ship. Behind them, the crash foam oozes through the door, hardening in the atmosphere of the corridor, and the atmosphere breach seals.

Sniper samples the distinctly organic-smelling air. With a laser ping or two down the length of the corridor, he checks the aim of his rail-gun and particle cannon, then reaches out with one of his main tentacles to negligently crush a ship-louse to slurry. He feels like he has come home.

★

As the hardfield drops, the three first-children all immediately swing their weapons towards the Golgoloth. Vrell expected this and sends a signal to his own rail-gun, noisily spinning up the barrels, and three sets of mismatched palp-eyes swing towards him.

'You do not kill the Golgoloth,' he says.

'Seems like a good idea to me,' says Orbus.

Vrell glances at the Old Captain, noting that he too is training his weapon on the hideous creature. A beat passes when it could go either way, then the first-children lower their weapons. Vrell has judged the situation correctly. He now watches Orbus for a moment, and the Old Captain finally, reluctantly, lowers his weapon too.

'What is the current situation out there?' Vrell asks the Golgoloth.

The old hermaphrodite just cringes lower on its platform and does not reply.

Vrell points his rail-gun towards the creature and asks again, 'What is the situation out there.'

'We are about to dock,' the Golgoloth replies. Behind it an array of screens abruptly displays the scene beyond the ship. When he sees the massive spears of the invasive docking tunnels approaching, and the surrounding horde of King's Guard, Vrell feels utter dismay, but refuses to show it.

He turns to Geth. 'Summon the rest of the children.'

'I already have,' the first-child replies, turning one palp-eye towards the door.

A second-child and an even smaller and more obviously distorted third-child move into view.

'Golgoloth,' Vrell continues, 'we need weapons.'

'Once I have provided you with them,' replies the old creature, 'there is no logical reason why you should keep me alive.'

Vrell has to admit the old monster has a point. How then to persuade it to provide what he wants? Vrell fires, rail-gun missiles punching holes into one of the floating pillars behind the Golgoloth. Shattered metal explodes out of the back of the pillar, power arcs inside it, and miniature lightnings skitter over its surface. It drops abruptly, crashes against the edge of the platform and topples, tearing numerous pipes, optics and cables from the Golgoloth's body as it lands with a hissing splash in the water below. The Golgoloth shrieks and bubbles, backing towards the other pillar, green blood and other fluids dribbling from the holes torn in its body.

'Provide us with weapons,' Vrell repeats, 'or I shoot out the other one, then I send the signal to detonate that mine you're wearing.' Sometimes the simplest solutions are the best.

Immediately afterwards, a pillar – like the one that contained Vrell's and Orbus's weapons – rises out of the floor; however this one splits vertically in numerous places around its circumference, and then opens like a flower to expose its contents. These are disappointing to say the least: merely three particle cannons, two rail-guns, and a couple of short solid-state lasers.

'These are not enough,' Vrell observes.

'They are all I have!' the creature clatters.

Of course, it makes sense that the hermaphrodite would only have weapons for itself, seeing it is the only one aboard it would want to possess them. This, then, must be the Golgoloth's personal arsenal.

'Geth, go collect them and hand them out to those best able to use them.'

Geth and his two fellows splash forwards, and begin tugging the weapons from the pillar. Other children now enter the Sanctum: second- and third-children who all gaze up at the Golgoloth on its platform as if some terrifying god squats there. But of course, to them that is precisely what the Golgoloth has always been. This is exactly why Vrell expected the first-children to hesitate when given the opportunity to fire upon their parent.

The three first-children take up the cannons, whilst a selection of second-children take the rest. Other makeshift weapons are redistributed.

'Now can we kill the father-mother?' Geth asks.

At that moment a thunderous sound echoes throughout the ship, and the floor tilts, causing all the water to flow to one side of the Sanctum. Vrell staggers, sees Orbus slip over and numerous children caught in the flood.

'Move out into the corridor!' Vrell instructs.

Many of the children begin retreating hurriedly as Vrell regains his balance and aims his weapon at the second pillar. Abruptly some mechanism thumps below and the Golgoloth's platform slowly sinks to just above floor level.

'We have docked with the King's ship,' the creature intones.

'Send to my harness a schematic of this ship's interior, with all those docking points detailed,' says Vrell. 'And, believe me, I will know if the information is right.'

'And then you will kill me,' says the Golgoloth.

'Send me the schematic.'

'I will not.'

Vrell fires again, hitting the second pillar. The thing drops end-on, then goes over like a falling tree, again tearing its connections out of the Golgoloth's body. The creature shrieks once and goes over on its side, then rolls from its platform, leaving a trail of blood, and splashes down into the water, with its limbs thrashing.

'We know this ship,' says Geth, from behind Vrell. 'We can find what you want. Now kill the father-mother.'

They want him to do it, for they still hold this creature in too much awe. Vrell keeps his rail-gun focused on the Golgoloth, strangely reluctant to end the life of this ancient monster who, aware that its end is close, is now backing away.

Dragging himself to his feet, cursing and shaking off water, Orbus moves up beside Vrell. 'I'll finish the bugger, if you want.'

'There is no need,' Vrell replies, now identifying the reason for his own reluctance. He is about to kill a legend, to extinguish a large chunk of Prador history and remove from the universe something utterly unique, no matter how horrible. He studies the creature for a moment longer, then glances over at Geth . . . perhaps the Golgoloth is not so unique? Time to end its life now. But odd the way it is moving, turning and raising itself . . .

Vrell realizes something is wrong just a second too late, even as he fires his weapon. Rail-gun missiles slam into a sharply curved hardfield wall, some of them just flattening and dropping, but others ricocheting away. Half a second later, Vrell sends the signal to detonate the mine. No matter that a hardfield lies directly before him, that signal will bounce around inside the ship and quickly reach its destination. Only then does Vrell realize he has sent the signal too late as well. The Golgoloth is not standing entirely on the other side of the hardfield. One mandible, part of its mouth and an expanse of carapace below it now drop, and green blood belches against the hardfield that sheered them away. Then the attached mine detonates, blowing these severed parts to fog. The Golgoloth staggers drunkenly over to the nearby Sanctum wall, and the hardfield fades out as a section of that same wall revolves the creature out of sight.

Vrell hisses with annoyance, aware he has been played. Only by detaching the creature from its pillars did Vrell allow it to get itself into a position to escape. 'We get out of here, now,' he says, turning and heading for the door, only pausing to snag Geth – who has frozen to the spot – and send him reeling towards the door too.

17

Prador language being a series of clicks, clatters and bubblings, we must be very careful of the words in our own language that we apply to them. We are told that our translation machines choose the word 'king' to describe the leader of the Prador, rather than autocrat or dictator, because Prador society is almost feudal in nature. The reality is that 'king' was settled on during the war because there was no need to demonize creatures our AIs had already seen fit to go to war with. The King, we are told, apparently chose the name Oberon for himself, but I do not believe that for a moment. I believe such appellations are all an attempt to mythologize the Prador, so that it becomes easier for us to accept the slurs against their nature and some of the frankly unbelievable stories of their cruelty. We must always remember that they are merely products of evolution like ourselves. They are not demons, nor are they devils sent from the Pit. They are not monsters and in fact are no better or worse than ourselves. There are no genuine monsters.

– Anonymous

The docking tunnels spear into the Golgoloth's ship, causing great chunks of armour to tip like huge scales as the arrow points find their way between, punching through walls and superstructure, ripping out beams and shoving aside massive internal components. Only when the midway chambers impact with the outer hull does their progress halt. The tips of the docking tunnels open inside like the jaws of conger eels, ripping up further internal structure. King's Guard, all geared up for a major assault, pour from the tunnels and begin to spread throughout the ship like some infection. Many of them, the Golgoloth notes, are moving directly towards its own Sanctum. It has considered fending them off but, though some of its internal weapons can penetrate that armour, the resulting mayhem will destroy most of the vessel, and then the King need only send more of his troops.

Crash foam, both from the ship itself and from the stores around the midway chambers, continues to well out, much of it getting blasted like snow into vacuum by the escaping atmosphere, but nevertheless the wounds are gradually sealing.

The melon-shaped vessel now rests right up against the King's ship as if rolled against a cliff face. Squads of the Guard, out in vacuum, jet down to its hull and land with a racket that can be heard deep inside here in this emergency Sanctum. They quickly begin to open airlocks or otherwise tear their way in, efficiently searching, isolating and sealing off areas as they move through.

The Golgoloth whimpers both at the sight of these invaders and from pain as optics and pipes extend on telescopic arms from a new control pillar to mate into the dripping sockets in its body. Meanwhile a surgical robot, mounted on the end of a hinged arm, poises over the creature's forward wound like a brass tree and, having already sprayed the area with coagulating and analgesic foam and carved out the remains of the Golgoloth's mouth, is now knitting in missing muscle structure with a set of its spidery limbs. The Golgoloth glances at its emergency supply in the transparent cylindrical canisters arrayed along one wall, each containing various chunks of its children floating in preserving fluid, nerve tissue spread about them like water weed. Another robot attaches its flat cobra head to the top of one of these, and reaches inside with long insectile limbs to divide up a set of mandibles and the outer rim of a mouth so as to provide the Golgoloth with a replacement. Further down the row of canisters, a similar robot is carefully extracting some legs. All around, the small Sanctum is filled with the busy movement of complex surgical robots poised on the ends of big mantis arms, amid slithering ribbed tubes, and the scuttle of smaller robots resembling steel spiders.

Returning its attention to the screens, the Golgoloth realizes that Vrell and the Human – and its own remaining children, now numbering twenty – are making their way along a zero-gravity shaft towards the area where the upper one of those docking tunnels debouches. As they move, they methodically knock out ship eyes and security systems, with the result that internal countermeasure lasers keep going offline. The Golgoloth considers what to do next. Though no weapons are available to it in that part of the ship, it can easily power up a gravplated section near the end of the shaft, and thus turn that escape party's progress into a one-mile high-gravity drop. The Golgoloth very much wants Vrell and his pet Human dead, but accompanying them is its main stock of body parts. Most likely such a drastic fall would smash all its children beyond usefulness, yet ironically Vrell and the Human, infected by the Spatterjay virus, might survive it.

Communication comes through.

'You have been injured,' Oberon observes.

The Golgoloth watches the surgical robot as its fellow swings over with one mandible and a set of outer mouthparts – muscle groups, tendons and stringy nerves hanging wetly from the back of them. The robot takes this replacement and threads nerves into the tips of long needles, stretching them tight to inject into raw flesh, there reconnecting them with microscopic carbon sheaths. Tendons next, pulled out with larger manipulators and cinched into place with organic clamps.

'So what do you want?' the Golgoloth asks, speaking through its control pillar.

'I want you, alive,' replies the King of the Prador.

'Yet you take my ship by armed assault.'

'You have Vrell aboard, and for all I know there are Jain there too,' says Oberon. 'How do I know I am even talking to the Golgoloth and not some simulacrum using our communication channel?'

The robot now moves the mandible and mouthparts into position out from the wound, after withdrawing the tools that reattached tendons and nerves. The Golgoloth can just about feel these new parts, feel them aching, whereupon a subliminal instruction bring another spray of analgesic foam. Reaching behind the new transplant the robot then begins connecting up muscles.

'Stop playing with me,' the Golgoloth says to Oberon.

The King dips his flat head in acknowledgement. 'Very well, I want you under my power, totally under my power, then I will decide what to do with you. I want Vrell too, grovelling on his belly here before me.'

'Now that sounds much more like a Prador King.'

Another robot is fetching over a piece of carapace, perfectly shaped to fit around the new mandible and mouth, its edges glistening with shell glue. And yet another robot waits in the queue, replacement legs ready.

'I have to say I admire your surgery there,' says Oberon.

'Developed over a thousand years,' Golgoloth replies grumpily. 'I possess knowledge and expert technologies in advance of much found in the Kingdom.' Always a good idea to press his case and thus try to dispel that image, planted in his mind by Vrell, of a heated spike with the name 'Golgoloth' engraved on its base.

'Prador and Polity technology integrated, I note,' says the King.

'I do not share the Prador antipathy to intelligent machines.'

'Yet I trust you have nothing operating there like the Polity artificial intelligences?'

'No,' says the Golgoloth. 'I have my children.'

Everything surrounding it, like everything in the ship, is controlled by ganglia that are in turn linked through the control pillar to the Golgoloth's mind. With a little effort it can *become* those machines surrounding it, like it can *become* its own ship. The repairs currently being conducted on its body are almost like the action of an autonomous nervous system.

'When you are well again,' Oberon says, 'I want you to give me a location conveniently near to you where my Guard can collect you. Meanwhile I want to know where Vrell is.'

The Golgoloth checks throughout its ship. The Guard now control at least a third of it and are currently locking down fusion reactors and external weapons systems. But they have as yet to find the shaft Vrell is traversing.

'They are here,' says the Golgoloth, sending the location of the same shaft.

'Thank you,' says Oberon, his image winking out.

The shaped piece of carapace goes into place, steam rising from the glue as it instantly sets. The robot then squeezes glue around the holes ready to take the base of the mandible and the exterior shell of the mouth. These items, still poised slightly out from the Golgoloth's body, muscles, tendons and nerves stretched like elastic, it allows to pull back into place. More steam as glue sets. The robot now attaches numerous pipes to holes that had been drilled through the new carapace, and fills any intervening gaps with collagen foam. For a moment the Golgoloth watches its new legs and new claw being carried over, then turns its attention to the ship eyes positioned in the vicinity of the shaft that Vrell is evidently reaching the end of. The Guard begin to close in, rapidly.

Orbus propels himself to the next safety-hold, a recess specially designed for a Prador foot, catches hold of it and halts his progress for a moment.

'We are taking the attack to the King,' Vrell said earlier.

The Old Captain thinks that a bad idea, but can't think of a better one – not for Vrell at least. For Vrell to throw himself on the mercy of this Oberon creature makes about as much sense as Orbus throwing himself on the mercy of the leeches in his home sea of Spatterjay. Generally, Prador do not do mercy; they do torture and killing and eating. Orbus shudders as he gazes at the horde of the Golgoloth's children propelling themselves past him.

The only other option would be to try and get themselves to the *Gurnard*, if it is still out there. Maybe find a shuttle . . . but that is hopeless too. They are securely docked with the King's ship, totally surrounded by dreadnoughts and King's Guard. Really, if there is to be an escape route, it will only be one the King himself allows. And here is Orbus's main problem. The King wants Vrell, he wants the Golgoloth, but Orbus is probably an irrelevance. King Oberon might even let him leave unharmed, even assist his departure, just to make political capital with the Polity. But for that to be an option, Orbus must abandon Vrell and go his own way, and certainly he should not be now involving himself in some insane and utterly doomed attack on the King's ship.

Orbus shoves himself back into motion, catching Prador footholds to throw himself up to speed again and quickly catch up with Vrell. Whatever Vrell does now, the end will be the same: no more Vrell. Orbus damns him, and damns the situation, but finds himself unable to abandon this mutated Prador.

'So you've got it all planned out?' Orbus asks.

Vrell is moving more slowly, he realizes, probably reluctant to reach his destination.

'I infiltrated Vrost's dreadnought,' Vrell reminds him. 'I managed to get to the Golgoloth . . .'

'But what's your plan right now?'

Vrell takes a long time replying. 'The plan must be easily revised . . . the King's ship is immense and there will be places in it where we can hide ourselves. If we can acquire some armour, we can proceed unnoticed and then find a way to the King himself.'

No plan, in other words.

Vrell abruptly draws to a halt and Orbus catches hold of the edge of the Prador's shell to halt himself too.

'Your weapon is loaded with sprine bullets,' says Vrell.

'Certainly, but they don't penetrate armour.'

'I am not thinking of armour.'

Orbus feels a sudden tiredness wash over him. 'Spell it out for me.'

'If I am to be captured . . .' Vrell begins, then abruptly swings his head round to watch one of the first-children.

It has missed its hold on the wall and just tumbles past them, its limbs moving spastically. Glancing back, Orbus sees that others seem to be losing control of themselves too, and with his next breath he feels a tightness in his lungs and smells an odd perfume in the air.

'Gas!'

Vrell shuts his mask at once, reaches out to close a claw about Orbus's arm, and propels them both forward. From behind, a detonation lights the shaft, a shower of debris flying ahead of a cloud of fire unshaped by gravity. The blast travels along the shaft, tumbling the Golgoloth's children ahead of it, chunks of shattered metal cutting into many of them like shrapnel. By the time the fire reaches them, and then Orbus and Vrell, it has turned to hot smoke. Beyond it, Orbus can see King's Guard swarming into the shaft, all of them carrying short trumpet-shaped weapons which they at once begin to deploy. The first shot sends a black egg projectile screeing along the shaft. It hits amidst a group of the children, and small lightnings arc from it to surrounding bodies, then outwards to the shaft walls. But the children don't react, the gas obviously having knocked them out. So why aren't he and Vrell unconscious? The Spatterjay virus, as always.

'Stunners,' explains Vrell.

Polity stun-guns are nothing like this, yet Orbus supposes it unsurprising that this weapon is new to him, as certainly they are not in common use by these creatures. Most Prador weapons tend to have one setting only: lethal and messy.

'Let me go,' says Orbus and, as Vrell's claw releases him, he throws himself forward. Both of them go rapidly hurtling ahead of the children, the end of the shaft now in sight. Behind, the Guard now reach the children, simply batting them aside and coming on. They aren't interested in them; it's Vrell they want. Then, at the end of the shaft, a glint of brassy colour, and the inevitable appearance of King's Guard there too.

Vrell drives his legs against the edge of the shaft, skidding up glitters of metal. Orbus catches hold, the force wrenching his arm and spinning him round to cannon into the shaft wall. Vrell opens fire on the pursuing guards, but what use is a rail-gun against so much armour? Orbus realizes exactly what use when a cloud of the stun eggs disintegrates barely fifty yards away from them. Orbus clicks his multigun over from normal explosive bullets to those containing sprine.

'Do it now,' urges Vrell.

Orbus takes aim, utterly reluctant to pull the trigger, as yet another egg gets through, impacting the wall behind Vrell and scouring him away from it in a harsh bright discharge.

Vrell manages to clatter out something further, his translator obviously shorted by the stunner. Probably it is another demand for Orbus to end his life. Orbus sees black eggs hurtling towards him from two directions. He pulls the trigger just before the shocks turn his body into a stiff arc of flesh, and bright fire extinguishes his world.

The Guard drag out the crippled-looking Prador children in big cable nets. Two of the armoured creatures tow out Vrell between them, his legs enclosed in manacles and heavy clamps about his claws. Orbus they do not seem so concerned about, because he is in one of the nets too. All have been disarmed and are now either unconscious or dead. Sniper turns the tip of his sensory tentacle, where it protrudes from the nearby air vent, and watches Thirteen.

The little drone has coiled himself into something snail-like and attached himself to a twisted girder amidst the wreckage caused by the opening end of the docking tube. He looks just like another piece of hardware and the numerous Guard scattered throughout the area do not notice him.

'Well, I could try and grab them,' Sniper suggests.

'You will not succeed,' Gurnard replies.

The AI is right. Sniper has already played through a few scenarios in his mind. Certainly he can move quickly enough to secure Orbus and Vrell, but then, once burdened with them, he needs to get out of this ship, and as he does so, hundreds of the Guard will come down on him like a hammer. He might survive that, but it is highly likely that Orbus and Vrell would not.

The two Guard towing Vrell enter the docking tube first, and next come those towing the four nets loaded with Prador children. The moment the net containing Orbus draws near to his girder, Thirteen uncoils himself to shoot across like a jellyfish sting, quickly disappearing amid a jumble of limbs and distorted carapaces.

'I'm in,' he observes. 'I detect traces of a short-acting derivative of Hazon nerve gas, though it appears Orbus has sustained a massive electric shock that even stunned his virus.'

'He's alive?' Sniper asks.

'Yes.'

Now the nets disappear into the tunnel, and Sniper wonders if that is the last he will see of any of them.

'Where are you now?' Sniper asks Gurnard.

'Ten thousand miles out,' the AI replies. 'One of the King's dreadnoughts just shifted over to my position and turned to face me. It seems they are paying attention to me now the main threats have been countered.'

'So no chance of you zipping in here if I was to try grabbing them?'

'No chance. They'd turn me into Swiss cheese.'

Sniper growls to himself, then ponders what the hell to do next. He is outgunned here and no matter at what angle he views the situation, and no matter how much of his centuries-long experience he calls upon, there is no way he can rescue Orbus and Vrell.

'Perhaps it is time to talk to King Oberon,' Gurnard suggests.

'Whaddabout?' Sniper does not like that idea at all.

'Our mission here in the Graveyard was to neutralize Prador agents, and when Vrell arrived it was either to neutralize him or bring him over to our side. Events have now moved on and Vrell *is* now effectively neutralized. Perhaps we can now concentrate on using a little diplomacy to try and get Orbus back?'

'Fuck our mission,' says Sniper.

He turns within the cramped space he occupies, first scanning the wall he cut through in order to enter, then welded back in place once inside. Beyond it three of the Guard busily plug cables from their armour into nearby computer systems and, because of the signal that Sniper constantly broadcasts, detect nothing more threatening than a nearby maintenance robot. He turns to another wall, beyond which lies a tunnel the Guard have already checked and secured. He starts to cut.

'I agree,' says Gurnard.

Sniper is surprised.

The AI continues, 'I was instructed to withdraw and leave this whole situation to Oberon, but I cannot just leave behind those I transported here. Vrell is beyond our help, I think, but we must get Orbus back and safely withdraw. I will now attempt to open communications with the King of the Prador. You, Sniper, should return to me here.'

Fuck that, thinks Sniper, but doesn't communicate that sentiment. 'Best of luck,' he says instead, as he peels out a section of wall.

Numerous bracing structures lie underneath it. Sniper cuts through them also, slices through foamed porcelain, then through the farther skin of the wall, finally spearing his tentacles through to draw himself into the tunnel beyond. He jets his fusion engine once, its flame rusty yellow and sputtering, and hurtles down towards the end of the tunnel, scanning always ahead. There lies a T-junction, its righthand tunnel curving towards the hull. One of the Guard is waiting just around the corner and, as he speeds towards the junction, Sniper detects it moving to investigate the sudden burst of radiation from the fusion blast. He onlines his rail-gun, sets his particle cannon to a wide focus precisely measured to the size of the Guard's visual turret, fires a steering thruster to slow himself a little and to divert his course just so. Shame he doesn't have any missiles – he'll just have to work with what he's got.

The armoured Prador moves into view, the top of its carapace facing towards Sniper. It tilts upwards just in time to receive the blast of the particle beam straight into its eyes, before Sniper careers into it at full speed. The Guard smashes into the opposite wall, making a large carapace-shaped dent. The wall itself ripples with the shock, sending several panel fixings gyrating through the air. Sniper wraps his tentacles about the creature as it tries to bring its own particle cannon to bear. He rips the weapon from its claw and sends it tumbling away. No point trying to kill this damned thing as its armour is too thick, and anyway there is the possibility of it detonating the fusion tactical inside.

Sniper tries another approach. Now narrow-focusing his cannon, he burns out his opponent's temporarily blinded eyes and with his tentacles probes into sensory pits for the other detectors it uses. A claw closes on another part of Sniper's own damaged shell and begins to bend it upwards, but Sniper manages to turn the creature sideways, find a couple of its steering jets, and fire his rail-gun into them. The soft metal of the missiles he uses impacts inside, and Sniper thrusts himself away, snapping the creature's claw free, and firing up his fusion engine again. The blast, centred on the Prador, sends it tumbling away, whilst Sniper hurtles on up the new tunnel. That particular creature will not be able to pursue, but now the others will have become aware of Sniper's presence.

Slamming into the wall beside a Prador door at the far end of the tunnel, Sniper tears out its pit control and concentrates on subverting its optics. The door divides and starts to open. Glancing back, he sees the tunnel is still empty, but knows he has very little time. Scanning beyond the door, he observes another tunnel leading towards the internal spaces immediately around one of the big fusion engines. *Good.* Sniper turns away from it and heads off to his right, accelerating fast to where the next tunnel hits a large junction from which seven others branch off. Again he uses a wall for braking, then chooses the particular tunnel he wants, and heads up that one. Any pursuing Guard will hopefully assume he has gone through the door and then waste time searching for him in the complex around the engine.

Via further tunnels and by sometimes cutting through walls that aren't armoured, Sniper finally reaches a portion of the ship that has sustained a great deal of damage. A corridor, so crushed that he has to turn himself on his side to negotiate it, terminates against a wall of crash foam far ahead. He fires up his engine again and shoots along the corridor like a bullet up a barrel, hammering into the foam which fractures enough for the air pressure in the tunnel behind him to blow chunks of it, and himself, out into vacuum. In passing Sniper snags a long twisted beam and swings round it to again halt his progress abruptly, this time thumping down into a distorted tangle of metal that was once a docking tube. He glances back at the hole he just made as new crash foam boils into it, then up towards the pinkish firmament far above him. He is sitting at the bottom of that deep crevice in the Golgoloth's ship formerly occupied by that splinter craft the creature was forced to destroy. This is Sniper's quickest way out.

Again the war drone fires up his engine, accelerating up towards freedom, finally hurtling away from the ship and out into space the colour of pink grapefruit, in the lee of the King's ship. Unfortunately he is not alone, since over five hundred of the King's Guard are hovering there expectantly in what is not quite vacuum.

'Fuck,' says Sniper.

'You, drone, have caused me enough problems already,' says a voice speaking through the com channel Sniper has open with Gurnard, 'You will now surrender yourself to my Guard.'

'Surrender, Your Majesty?' Sniper enquires, scanning about and detecting precisely four hundred and eighty-eight particle cannons all aimed at him, plus a large bastard rail-gun swivelling on the nearby King's ship so as to aim at him too.

'I know the word is probably not one you are accustomed to, but if you want your Human and that curiously shaped little drone back in one piece, it is a concept to which you must rapidly become accustomed. I can perhaps overlook the fact that you terminated my agent at Montmartre, but I will not countenance any further attacks upon my children.'

Sniper points all his tentacles in one direction. It is a gesture any Human might recognize, were there any up and down in space and if the direction he is pointing them is upwards.

'Alright, no need to get tetchy.'

Orbus feels like someone has taken a hammer to every bone in his body individually. He opens his eyes, but everything is too white and bright, so he closes them again. He is slumped down on a cold floor, gravity operating, and around him he can hear the familiar sliding and clattering movement of Prador.

Did I get him? He wonders. Did he manage to put a sprine bullet into Vrell and thus close another chapter of his own life? He hopes for Vrell's sake that he did, but still regrets the killing. Odd, after all this time, to actually feel some sympathy for such a creature. He opens his eyes again. Still too bright, and he realizes that the floor he lies prone upon is pure white.

'How you feeling?' asks a voice.

Orbus tracks his gaze along the floor and focuses blurrily on the ribbed tail resting against it. He tracks on upwards to see Thirteen hovering there, gazing down at him with seemingly demonic topaz eyes.

'Been . . . better,' he manages, his mouth feeling like it has been sandpapered.

'That degree of shock would have killed any normal Human, and was clearly enough even to kill some Prador – not all of the Golgoloth's children survived – but then King Oberon was intent only on capturing Vrell.'

'Yeah, I figured that.'

'The Golgoloth's surviving children, and you and me I think, are just here now to satisfy his curiosity.'

'How did you get here?'

'I snuck into the Golgoloth's ship with Sniper—'

'So the bugger survived. Should have expected that.'

'—then I concealed myself amongst the prisoners. Not well enough, though. The Guard must have spotted me 'cus they grabbed me the moment we entered the docking tunnel. They captured Sniper too – just outside the Golgoloth's ship.'

'The King?' Orbus rolls onto his side and gazes, beyond Thirteen, at a group of the Golgoloth's children all clustered together protectively. One of them is the one Vrell named Geth. He is glad to see the crippled creature has survived and realizes that, over recent events, something has utterly changed inside him. How is it that he can now *like* a Prador? Beyond the children lies a distant white wall, and high above is a white ceiling inset with elliptical vents. This seems a very odd place indeed.

'The King,' Thirteen repeats.

The little drone's tail divides, one fork of it rising to point behind Orbus. The Old Captain heaves himself up on to one elbow, then slowly up until he is in a sitting position and, not yet trusting his legs to support him, he spins round on his bottom. When he sees what lies beyond the shimmering upright posts that surround him and the others, he very much wants to be up on his legs and running. Those posts, he realizes, must comprise some sort of electric fence imprisoning them. But he is glad they lie between him and the *thing* looming only a short distance away.

Here then is the King of the Prador. Supported on its eight thorny armoured legs, the creature stands ten feet high at its back, and when it now shifts one complex spiky foot, the entire floor vibrates. It is all chitinous angles of dark red, green and black, and its body is thirty feet long and louse-like, with unidentifiable items of technology surgically grafted into it, even down the length of its long saurian tail. The armoured segments of the body end in a spiked skirt radiating above the sockets the legs extend from, while clamped to its underbelly, Prador arms terminate in manipulatory hands of varying design. Because its forelegs stand higher and heavier than the three pairs behind, its body curves upwards to where it ends in wide armoured shoulders, from which extend its clawed arms, and from between these shoulders rises a long neck supporting a wide flat head. This resembles the head of a giant ant, though without antennae and possessing a complicated array of mandibles. The outer set are sawtoothed and jointed, and presently hang downwards like mantis arms, as if ready to snap out and grasp. An inner set, positioned directly over the mouth, look like sets of lubricated scythes.

'Mother of fuck,' says Orbus.

The King hears him and swings his head in his direction, revealing two midnight-black eyes, and Orbus involuntarily cringes back.

'That is the usual reaction from Humans on first seeing him,' says a voice.

Orbus glances over to see a woman standing outside the fence, eyeing him curiously. She is clad in some sort of armoured suit, and has cropped grey hair and mild brown eyes. She reminds him of someone, but that being the normal reaction of those of his extreme age upon encountering almost anyone, he is about to dismiss it until he realizes who: her face resembles that of a lover from long long ago.

'How long did these Humans survive afterwards?' he asks, shaking himself briskly, then clambering to his feet.

'Well,' she says, 'the Humans usually brought before him are either criminals or ECS spies he wants to question, so they don't last very long after the talking has stopped.'

'And what about you, then?'

'I work for him.'

'And you are?'

'Sadurian.'

Orbus recognizes the name, though is not sure where from, but it isn't that of the lover he once knew. He swings his regard back to the King just as Oberon returns his attention to the figure immediately before him. Down there, on the floor, squats Vrell, securely manacled, and with his head tilted up like a dog awaiting punishment from its master. Orbus missed, then. He focuses on a couple of fresh grooves across Vrell's shell just beside his neck, realizing that's where the sprine bullets ricocheted off.

Now Orbus begins to study some of the other contents of this unusual room. To the left of Vrell are positioned arrays of hexagonal screens of typical Prador design. Immediately before these lies some sort of framework with pit controls below it. Beyond the King, part of the wall is taken up by a huge window displaying a vista of pink space in which a silvery dreadnought glitters. Other mechanisms rise here and there like chalk monoliths, or lie prone like white tombstones, with pit controls in their surfaces and much space between so the King can gain easy access to each. Returning his attention to Vrell and the King, he realizes the two are talking.

'What are they saying?' he asks.

Sadurian waves a gloved hand at Thirteen. 'Your drone can translate.'

Orbus glances sideways at the iron seahorse.

'They've just got through the initial introductions – and threats – but now it's getting complicated,' says Thirteen. 'I'd better translate direct.'

'. . . I used a counternanite based on the Polity Samarkand model,' the King says, Human words seeming to issue directly from him, for Thirteen is using some form of voice-casting. 'My Guard introduced it into the Golgoloth's ship before entering, and it is also part of the Hazon nerve-gas derivative I used against them.' The King swings a claw round and snaps it shut with a gunshot sound, towards the Golgoloth's children. It strikes Orbus that something so big and evidently heavy should not be able to move its limbs so fast. 'You are now clear of it, as is most of the Golgoloth's ship. Vrost's ship appears to be gone, along with the planetoid, so perhaps, apart from a few surviving examples the counternanite has yet to reach, it is no longer a threat to me or my children.'

Vrell dips his head in acknowledgement. 'I am unfamiliar with this "Samarkand model" you mention. Did the counternanite attack the calcite structures or sodium bonds?'

The King abruptly surges forward, past Vrell, then settles himself down on the framework of bars arrayed over the pit controls before the screens. 'Observe.'

The screens come on, displaying complex molecular maps and scrolling Prador glyphs. Vrell tries to turn his head, but cannot get it right round. The King glances back, and, with a crackling sound, the manacles drop from Vrell's legs. He spins around and for a moment Orbus thinks he is going to run, but instead he moves up beside the King and peers up at the screen.

'Interesting approach, but I would have targeted those sodium bonds. They were the weakest point.'

'What the fuck are they on about?' Orbus asks.

'The nanite Vrell used to destroy all those aboard the dreadnought he took control of,' Thirteen explains.

Orbus returns his attention to the two Prador.

'Show me how you constructed those bonds,' the King has just said.

Vrell looks over to one of the tombstone devices. Another set of manacles, like a solid frozen chain, unseen until then, clatters to the floor, thus freeing his underhands. Then, with two loud cracks, the clamps drop from his claws.

'Your King is a damned sight more trusting than I would be in the circumstances – Vrell is no walkover,' remarks Orbus.

Sadurian glances over at him. '*My* King is even more danger-ous than he looks.' She glances down as a ship-louse scuttles over, and steps carefully out of its way. Orbus notes that the louse is bigger than any he has seen before, and has trilobite divisions to its body. It tries to run past one of the posts to get to the prisoners. A jag of lighting crackles out, constant and glaring as an arc welder, and, with the smell of burning stew, fries the thing on the spot. This is a salutary reminder, because things seemed to be getting just too *convivial* here.

Vrell heads over to the tombstone, inserts three of his under-hands into three small pit controls, and one claw into a larger one. A hatch slides aside to the fore of the tombstone and a mask-like device rises up before Vrell. He inserts his head into that, manip-ulates the pit controls for a moment, and then the images on the screens change.

'As I suspected,' says the King. 'Perhaps you can now explain to me . . .'

The lights abruptly dim, for a moment, and Orbus wonders if Vrell has managed to do something clever operating through those pit controls. Perhaps the King thinks the same, for he shoots from the framework and comes down with a crash directly over the smaller Prador, his legs on either side, and a claw instantly in position about Vrell's neck. He then slowly withdraws the claw, head coming up and black eyes focusing on the screens as columns of Prador glyphs begin to scroll down. He turns his head, and the entire far wall of the huge room, the one incorporating the window, becomes one massive screen.

Oberon steps away from Vrell. 'It wasn't enough,' the King intones. 'I must *become*.'

'God help us,' whispers Sadurian.

Orbus glances over at her, realizing she must be a very old Human indeed to instinctively use such a curiously archaic expression. Her face is pale now and she looks very scared. Groping down, she takes a palm console from her belt, and with shaking hands keys into it. He realizes in an instant that her fear is not of what is occurring outside, but because of the King's words. Orbus returns his attention to the massive screen.

The image that lies before him resembles a nebula, straight contrails of orange vapour spreading out behind chunks of cooling magma set on courses unlikely to deviate for millions of years. Yet, within this, a dark spot appears and grows gradually into a spherical shadow. Along the bottom of the screen, bright light blooms, and a sudden acceleration sends everyone staggering. Ahead, a dreadnought slides into close view, then begins to recede as the King's vessel draws away fast, and to either side the other dreadnoughts now fall into view. The King steps away from Vrell and quickly returns to his framework of bars, which have been bent by his recent rapid departure.

Vrell begins to rise from his own position, but the King glances over at him.

'Stay where you are – I may need you,' orders the King, then turns aside. 'Sadurian, I must do it now.'

The enormous dreadnoughts move rapidly into a quadrate formation positioned between that growing darkness and the King's ship.

'What is that?' Orbus asks, but when he looks to Sadurian for an answer, he sees her heading over to the King. To one side of the room a door opens and in scuttle two small chrome-armoured Prador, towing behind them a levitating upright cylinder bearing some resemblance to the kind of devices the Golgoloth uses. They hurry after Sadurian, and soon all three are standing ready beside the King.

'Any ideas?' Orbus asks Thirteen, puzzled.

'Sniper is watching,' replies the little drone, 'and even he's not sure about what's going on.'

A square, ten feet across, etches itself into existence inside the big screen, magnifies once to bring one dreadnought up close enough seemingly to reach out and touch, then once again to take in the view beyond, then once more to spread that mysterious darkness all the way across it. At the centre of this shadow rests a weird bastardized vessel: a triangular dish resting in a structure bearing a vague resemblance to a collection of giant bones formed of brass. Attached to one edge of this, Vrell's original ship is only just recognizable.

'It is sucking up energy from the surrounding cloud,' observes King Oberon. 'I cannot even guess how.'

A star ignites at the centre of the triangular dish, and from that point a beam of . . . *something* spears out. It glares like the output from a particle cannon, yet along its length it is plaited like a rope. Just as King Oberon cannot guess how that strange vessel is now sucking up surrounding energy, Orbus cannot guess how this ship of bones produces such a thing.

Abruptly the view leaps out again, this time to show a dreadnought silhouetted against a vast electric-blue surface. Orbus has only enough time to realize he is witnessing the impact of that beam against a massive hardfield, just as white fire erupts from numerous ports in the dreadnought's surface, and the field flickers out. The beam strikes hull, turning like a drill, and chunks of the big ship begin to break away like swarf, then briefly the same beam punches out the other side of the vessel in a shower of debris, before finally shutting down. Burning with numerous fires caused more by damage to its own internal systems than by heat from the weapon that struck it, the dreadnought rolls in a debris cloud, cored out like an olive – a mere husk.

'Fuck,' says Sadurian.

'I am inclined to agree,' replies the King.

Thirteen rises from the floor and moves over to hover in the air at Orbus's shoulder. 'It seems the Jain weren't destroyed after all.'

'Ah, *those* buggers . . . then I agree with her too,' says Orbus.

18

Even as the first primitive computers were being bolted together, so were their diseases and parasites. Computer worms and viruses, so named because of their similarity to the real thing, were designed to penetrate computers in order to tell you about the latest tooth-rotting drink, to spy or simply to trash everything out of sheer malice. These things both evolved and were deliberately improved, in some cases even by those selling the cure for them, and in later centuries they became ever more complex. We still use the same names for them, though a better description would be 'computer life', for they include destructive programs that might be better described as sharks, scorpions, poisonous spiders and snakes, and – ranging into mythology – why not demons, imps and evil gnomes? It is rumoured that programs even exist that can penetrate living minds merely through the senses. As with all life, however, some parasites became symbionts and mutualists, or utterly independent entities. Some programs developed to fight the parasites even became malignant themselves. It was all a very fast evolutionary process that still continues and, though we may bemoan the latest picture worm wrecking our personal files, we should also remember that another product of this same process is artificial intelligence – for good or evil I leave you to judge.
– From HOW IT IS by Gordon

The powerful disruption of a USER shudders underspace, and in an instant Sniper realizes its source is that weird ship out there. The Jain, now manifesting in the debris cloud, have just ensured that no one will be taking off outsystem for some time. Win or lose, this is to be the battleground. They have also ensured that neither the King nor the Golgoloth will be firing off any U-space missiles. Now checking back towards the retreating King's ship and its escort of dreadnoughts, Sniper observes that dropping from it are numerous dodecahedral objects, and one other item: for the Golgoloth's ship is now loose out there, jetting steering thrusters to get its spin under control, and occasionally snapping out a fusion flame as it begins to manoeuvre.

'Whoot,' Sniper exclaims. 'The shit just hit the fan.'

'This is not a matter for any amusement,' replies Gurnard.

'Um, I guess you were quite close to that last one?'

'Close enough to bend my spine – and that weapon used some form of U-tech I know nothing about.' Gurnard pauses. 'This does not bode well for any of us, Sniper.'

'No shit.'

Sniper surveys the Guard surrounding him. None of them is pointing a weapon at him, and some are now heading towards those dodecahedral objects, which he consequently assumes are not mines. Now might be a good time to make his escape. However, far in the distance, the ship of bones, judging by the blackness spreading around it, is recharging for another blast; while heading directly towards him and the surrounding Guard, with nothing in between but chunks of cooling magma and dispersed gas, comes a swarm of about two hundred Jain soldiers. Obviously the Jain intend to use their big weapon to take out the King's dreadnoughts, but have dispatched a portion of their number to mop up everything else. Looks like it is going to be a stand-up, knock-down, brawly mess out here, and Sniper would not have missed it for anything.

'Hey, who's in charge here?' Sniper asks, broadcasting on the same frequencies the Guard are using.

Unintelligible code bounces back at him, then abruptly transforms into Prador language, which Sniper has no trouble either understanding or speaking.

'I am Frordor,' comes the reply.

Sniper triangulates the signal by using the tips of two of his raised tentacles, and thus locates the armoured Prador in question. The only way this Frordor is distinct from all the rest is that he seems to be hauling around a big missile-launcher that isn't integral to his armour.

'I fought these same fuckers down on that planetoid,' Sniper explains, 'and there's some stuff you need to know about their techniques.'

'Do you know battle language Aleph?'

'I do.'

'Tell me, then.'

Sniper searches his own memory and finds, thankfully, that the old battle language of the Prador is not something the Jain have stolen from him. He likes the lingo, because it is utterly pragmatic. Using it, he now broadcasts his earlier experiences down there on the planetoid, detailing the viral attacks and the other methods the Jain soldiers employ.

Frordor begins to issue orders: 'Move back to weapons caches, triclaw formation and rotate hardfield defence.'

'If they get under your armour they'll go straight for your suicide bombs,' Sniper warns.

After a brief pause, Frordor says, 'Disable approved by King. Tacticals manual detonation only.'

The armoured Prador begin falling back into a three-pronged formation, with the dodecahedral objects ranged behind them. These are now being opened up by others of the Guard and their contents distributed. Sniper spots big lasers, portable hardfield generators, some more of those large missile-launchers and numerous belts and packages of missiles and mines.

'Um, any chance I can get me some of that stuff?' he enquires.

'Help yourself,' Frordor replies.

Sniper draws in his tentacles from the gesture of surrender, assuming he is now no longer a prisoner. It strikes him as unusual for Prador, even the Guard, to adapt to a new situation so quickly, but then these, being with the King, must constitute the elite. He fires up his fusion engine and speeds over, scanning more deeply the armaments currently being distributed. The missiles are of about the right size, so he begins adapting his rail-gun to take them. As he approaches, the Guard unloading this particular dodecahedron, and flinging packages on courses to other Guards, suddenly sends three of the rolled-up missile belts in his direction. Sniper decelerates, fielding them with his tentacles, and then abruptly unravelling one of them. Closer scan reveals that the missiles contain balls of high-pressure metalized hydrogen wrapped about a layer of very dense explosive with a plutonium core. To the rear of each lies a chemical drive, and steering-jet holes ring the equator. Even as he tries to fiddle with the computer hardware inside them, Frordor sends him the access code. Sniper opens a hatch just above his rail-gun and begins feeding the missiles inside himself, as if eating sweets, reprogramming them as he slots them internally into his missile carousel.

Now Sniper jets over to another weapons cache, from which spherical crates of mines are being distributed. Again some packages get diverted his way. The mines are simple enough: they possess no propulsion but can be programmed to detonate in varying circumstances. He feeds a good number of these inside himself for later use, the remainder he sticks to his shell for easy access. Then he pauses to survey the overall situation.

The Guard seem as ready as they can be, Frordor having successfully deployed the claw formation, with its rotational use of hardfields to prevent too many of his comrades taking too much of the load at once. The Golgoloth's ship has stabilized, and distanced itself behind and to one side of this formation, and now some of the Guard abandon it to join those already here. Perhaps the Golgoloth is hoping it will not need to get directly involved.

Sniper now considers his own position. He could easily take up a place within this formation and fight with the rest of the grunts, but that isn't how he likes to operate. He prefers to bring in something from outfield, something others have not thought of. In fact he likes to win, not just slug it out. He therefore sends a probing signal to the Golgoloth's ship, to try and open up some communication.

After a moment the creature replies. 'Yes, I did note that you've survived, Polity drone,' it says. 'And it appears you managed to gain access to my ship without me noticing. How did you do that?'

'I got in through one of your rail-gun ports then I used your maintenance robot ID code – you might like to take a look at that, because if I can do it, then so can the Jain.'

After a pause, 'I now see where you came in. I have therefore randomized the code, and now all maintenance robots possess a personal code, to be altered on a randomized schedule.'

Fast.

'Are you in this fight or not?' Sniper asks, deliberately including Frordor in the communication.

'Since the Jain have seen fit to strand us all here, it seems that I am in,' the Golgoloth replies. 'I do not think these creatures recognize neutrality.'

'So what have you got?'

'You expect me to detail the firepower I possess to a temporary ally and potential enemy?'

Sniper shrugs as he again focuses on the approaching Jain. Five of them are clustered about an object shaped like a doughnut, which has various receptor and transmission dishes dotted over its surface. The rest don't carry anything more than those Sniper originally faced and, despite them being very very dangerous, there is only so much energy that creatures of this scale can individually deploy. He considers what he would do if he were one of them, intent on destroying a defence just like this.

'You're gonna be the main target,' Sniper informs the Golgoloth. 'They won't fully engage the Guard here, but they'll go for you. They like to hijack and subvert, and your ship is perfect for that purpose. If they get to it, they'll enter and force the Guard to fire on you.'

'I agree,' Frordor interjects.

Steering thrusters suddenly fire up on the Golgoloth's big melon-shaped vessel, and it begins to draw nearer to the formation, whilst Frordor issues orders in battle code, moving that formation over towards the approaching ship. Even now missiles are zipping towards them from the converging Jain, and little time now remains to get the defence properly organized.

Sniper now watches the approaching doughnut-shaped object, noting how it is being kept to the centre and rear of the Jain formation.

'What is that damned thing?' he broadcasts.

Immediately the Golgoloth sends to him a recording of the problems it earlier encountered while leaving the planetoid: how the Jain contrived to use the same energy the hermaphrodite deployed against them. It seems likely that this object serves a similar function, or is a relay from the vessel back there within the cloud, or both, so it needs to be taken out, quickly.

Clearly visible because of the surrounding dust and gas, green lasers spear up from the Jain. They blur and fray as they strike hardfields, but still enough gets through to form a viral attack.

'Colour-shift all sensors,' Frordor instructs.

Now why didn't I think of that? Sniper grumps to himself. He does the same as all the Prador do, excluding the green of those lasers from the spectrum he can receive. Almost immediately these lasers shift to blue.

'Keep shifting,' Frordor instructs.

'Watch for feedback through hardfields,' Sniper sends.

'Rotating.'

The Prador positioned to the fore of the formation break off and circle round to the rear. Now particle beams spear up, splashing on hardfields. The lasers start rapidly shifting their spectrum, and the Jain begin manoeuvring in a swirling pattern. Now they are so much closer, Sniper begins firing his own laser, loading it with the code Vrell passed to him when they were on the planetoid – the one designed to detonate the tacticals within the Guard these assailants once were. No response; they've obviously disabled that option, even as Frordor just did. He accelerates, curving out between Frordor's formation into the gap between it and the Golgoloth's ship. Distantly he observes another object approaching from off to one side, fusion engines at full blast: the *Gurnard*.

'Come to join the fun?' Sniper enquires.

Gurnard's reply is less than polite.

Now the Guard launch missiles, and in moments the space between the two opposing forces begins blossoming with explosions. The projectiles impact on hardfield walls, flaring scales of energy into existence. Particle cannons probe from either side as the Jain come in closer, then, from a point on the exterior of the ship of bones deep in the cloud, a beam spears out, only visible because it heats the dispersed gas and dust along its course. Microwave beam, Sniper realizes, as it strikes precisely at the centre of the doughnut, and from there divides into a hundred narrower beams, licking out to be intercepted by a select few of the Jain. From these issue particle beams of incredible intensity, all focused on Frordor's formation. The first three Prador forming the tip of each claw simply rupture as first their hardfield genera-tors blow and then the beams hit them. Explosions of claws, legs and chunks of armour carapace spread, and others of the Guard cannot rotate into position fast enough to replace the casualties.

'Break for individual combat,' Frordor instructs needlessly.

From the moment he regained consciousness and found himself a captive of King Oberon, Vrell decided he would not beg, he would not grovel, and he would grab any opportunity that comes his way to fight for survival. However, on finally coming before the King, he has realized that he does not face a creature who will want those satisfactions from him. He has found himself before an entity even more frightening and even more potent than the Golgoloth, and which functions on a level far above himself. Upon having his restraints removed, he perhaps should have made some futile gesture, hopefully thus speeding his own end. But he did not, because he knew when he was utterly outclassed.

Probing the controls made available to him, Vrell discovers he has been allowed a great deal of leeway. He can call up onboard information within the mask, which provides him with a three-dimensional virtuality. Some of this data is classified even to members of the Guard. He can also open private com channels and run the kinds of complex calculations and programs he is accustomed to. He can access sensors aboard this same ship, and the dreadnoughts, and even those carried by individual Prador out there, so through the mask he can see every detail of the desperate fight taking place out in space. However, the ship's weapons, defences and command channels lie outside his remit. Instead he opens another channel to send a probing signal, and then waits.

'Gotcha,' Thirteen replies, his voice relayed through small speakers in Vrell's mask and the words also displayed as Prador glyphs should he need them. 'Orbus is in the circuit too.'

Vrell turns his head to glance over at the prisoners, the mask moving with him and responding to his wish by providing an outside view, then turns his attention back to the King, his attendant Human and the two chrome-armoured third-children. The two small Prador are currently attaching optics, power feeds and various fluid pipes to the numerous devices woven throughout the King's body, thus connecting him to the mechanisms of the pillar. As yet Vrell has been unable to access any information about what is occurring there.

'Any idea what's going on?' he asks.

'I am scanning,' Thirteen replies, 'but the technology is awfully complex.'

'Whatever it is,' says Orbus, 'the thought of it is scaring that Sadurian character even more than those nasty buggers out there are.'

'How do you know this?' Vrell asks.

'Trust me,' the Old Captain replies. 'She started shitting herself the moment the King told her he "*must become*" – whatever that means.'

Vrell studies the King further, trying to put aside his initial reaction of awe and terror. The King is obviously a creature already well advanced in mutation by the Spatterjay virus. But now he has decided he '*must become*' after being faced with the evidently superior firepower of the Jain. He has obviously decided on an option he was reluctant to choose before and, if Orbus is correct about the reaction of the Human woman, whom Vrell has ascertained to be a first-class Polity mind specializing in reproduction and genetics, it seems likely this choice is a dangerous one. Vrell already has some idea of what that might be even as he seeks confirmation from the masses of data made available to him, but numerous searches render him nothing more than an arrow pointing directly towards the King's private files. Vrell takes a long hard look at the codes needed to give him access, and proceeds to formulate programs that might enable him to crack them.

'I can't see how he can become anything worse than he is,' Orbus adds.

Vrell cannot find the spare processing power within his own mind to respond, as he inserts every available limb into pit-controls and frantically works his programs. He calls up data from ship's systems, programs or fragments of the same that are stored there. He combines them, alters them, tests them, puts them through high-speed computerized evolutionary processes. Trying to cover every bet, for he feels sure he will have only one chance at this, his mind goes into overdrive. Then, almost on a level that is not quite consciousness, he launches his programs against the King's files and finds himself in an informational battle that seems to mirror the chaos unfolding in vacuum outside.

He punches through firewalls, and then has to either disinfect or sacrifice the programs he uses for that purpose when they become loaded with killer viruses from the walls themselves. He has to weave together his own programs to fight killer programs deployed against him, has to even reformat his own thinking and sensory input so as to prevent some of the things sent by those same killers from loading into his own mind – but the King's earlier attack on him aboard Vrost's ship has prepared him for this. At many points he finds himself making no headway at all, being diverted into blind tunnels or lured towards data precipices, and every time he finds he has to exert more effort in pushing the functionality of his mind to its limits, and beyond its limits, yet finding something there even so. Reaching a certain depth in he knows there is no turning back, as this determined penetration becomes a fight for survival. His breathing accelerates to its limit and hunger grows inside him as his mind constantly sucks up and burns nutrients. His brain becomes hot and his heart pumps at its maximum, to feed it food and oxygen and to draw away heat. Some of his limbs and some internal organs shut down, superfluous to this process. Then, when it seems he is about to be crushed under those powerful defences, he is through, all of them collapsing simultaneously around him. He feels he has been deliberately tested to the utter limit, which in itself seems far too neat to be coincidental.

'So you are in,' says something, and Vrell cringes, exhausted, immediately expecting to come under either an informational attack or a physical one. For the thing here is something the Prador so much dread: an artificial intelligence.

'What are you?' Vrell asks, unable to think of a more coherent question.

'I am Sphinx.'

'Are you Polity?'

'I am,' replies Sphinx. 'I am the property of Sadurian, though of course I also belong to myself. She fed me into the ship's system about two hours ago, when she realized just how badly fucked-up things might get here.'

'How do you intend to react to me?' Vrell asks.

'I do not intend to react to you as you fear,' the AI replies. 'My own presence here is as unrequested as your own.'

As his breathing and heart rate slow, Vrell mulls that over. This AI could be either an enemy or an ally. Certainly it can find information more quickly than he can . . .

'What is the King doing?'

'He is in the process of opening up quantum Jain memstorage inside himself, so as to provide himself with the knowledge to defeat them,' Sphinx replies, simultaneously opening and presenting files in a quickly growing virtual space. These show Vrell the details of the operation, which Vrell briefly inspects.

'It is, as you might imagine,' says the AI, 'a risky venture which will probably result in the mind of some Jain soldier taking complete control of him. He believes, however, that he can control things for long enough to obtain the necessary knowledge.'

Vrell peers across at the King. All the pipes, optics and cables are finally attached, and the pillar now quietly humming to itself. The effect upon Oberon is noticeable already. Clear fluid drips from gaps between sections of his carapace, and he is swinging his head from side to side as if in agony. Perhaps he is.

Vrell inspects the information contained in the files, but is still not up to speed. 'How is he doing this?'

'He is using nanites to kill off the last of the Spatterjay genome stored inside every one of his cells, thus leaving only Jain DNA, the virus itself and those quantum stores. The disruption to his cellular machinery is very great, and many of the cybernetic mechanisms spread throughout his body are there just to keep him alive.'

'So in the end it will be just his mind pitted against whatever comes out of quantum storage,' Vrell notes.

He is starting to feel better now, almost euphoric. With the kind of access previously denied him, he initiates searches into the files. It surprises him to find that the only weapons in the near area are the wall-mounted defensive weapons in the atrium and a cache of the weapons taken from himself, Orbus and the Golgoloth's children. There is nothing he can gain control of from here to turn against the King. However he does find out how to open the small cache, and how to turn off the force-fence around his comrades, but this does not seem enough, for these same files also provide him with a great deal of data about the King's physical structure and the power of his mind. There is even stuff here Vrell simply cannot comprehend, and he doubts, if it comes to a fight, that he and the others can win. It would be like a crowd of Human children armed with bows and arrows attacking a fully-armed Prador. The result would likely be messy.

'And if you attack the King now,' says Sphinx, 'you'll probably destroy the only hope for survival any of us has right now.'

That is certainly a valid point, but another valid point is that if the King does manage to repel the Jain using their own knowledge, it will not be long before he becomes one of them too. This newly made Jain soldier controlling the King's body will then be right in the middle of its enemy, and with access to many conveniently placed weapons and primary controls. In such a position it could, given time, reactivate the Guard's tacticals and destroy them all at once, seize control of the dreadnoughts and force them to fire on each other, or send the codes to reactivate their self-destructs. Vrell needs to be ready.

Then he spots it: the one small chance they have.

'Our weapons,' Vrell tells Orbus, 'are in a store set into the wall over to your right, and I can deactivate the fence surrounding you. As soon as I shut down the fence and open the store, here is what we must do.'

The Prador formation shatters, its separate armoured troops now making less easy targets for the persistent particle beams. Along with the relay device they draw their energy from, the Jain shooters now hold back, whilst the rest come on. But still those beams are methodically incinerating members of the Guard. As if this was not bad enough, that plaited beam lances out again from the Jain ship's main dish, passing through the periphery of this skirmish.

Sniper tracks its course and watches it flash against a hardfield off to one side. There, two of the King's dreadnoughts are attempting to cover each other. As the first hardfield goes out, the dreadnought it issued from drops back shedding fire from numerous ports, and another hardfield intercepts the beam. The damaged dreadnought stabilizes for a moment, even whilst the detonations of hardfield generators star the hull of its replacement. It manages to emit an intermittent field, but this isn't enough. Something big then blows inside the replacement ship, hurling out a chunk of hull armour from a glowing wound, and its field winks out. At once the beam stabs through. It hits the vessel like a slow-turning metal drill, and just tears into it, spewing debris into space, before punching its way out the other side. However, this time it does not shut down but rips out the side of its target then bores into its fellow. The beam's first target is now just an unrecognizable mass of wreckage, while it cores its second and leaves it tumbling inert through vacuum. Meanwhile, the darkness surrounding the Jain ship begins to grow again as it draws in energy for yet another strike.

As the advancing Jain and the Guard defenders swirl into each other, Sniper finds himself passing within just a few miles of a formation of five Jain. He first focuses his rail-gun entirely upon one of them, and fires a fusillade of inert missiles. Then he launches ten of the Prador missiles, each in a different direction, all following the slightly adapted program he has just devised. Copying the Jain, he rapidly begins changing the spectrum of his laser, continuously loading it with a varied selection of viruses and worms. He is damned if he intends to lose out against these fuckers this time.

As he has calculated, they change their formation slightly, one of them accepting the impact of the rail-gun missiles whilst two others cover it, the remaining two focusing their attention on the missiles as they loop round. He ramps up his drive to full power, turns on his supercavitating conefield, and spears down towards their hardfields. The impact is massive, juddering Sniper almost to a halt, but it breaks up their formation and knocks out their hardfields. His own conefield gives out, blowing numerous internal fuses and slagging two of its five emission coils. Drive still firing at full power, he comes down on one of them and propels it away from the rest.

A claw closes on one of his tentacles as the creature tries to turn him round to face its particle cannon. Setting his spatulate cutter running, he spears it inside the mirrored barrel of the cannon and slices down inside, sheering power lines and components. The creature begins to extrude something tubular which ignites at its tip – a thermic lance – while the others now swing round to follow. Sniper fires his steering thrusters, spinning himself and the creature with precisely enough timing for his opponent to receive the brunt of a particle-cannon blast from one of its fellows, which cuts a smoking crater in its back.

Finally, tearing through its internal components, Sniper hits something vital and the creature's movements become sluggish. Using another tentacle Sniper selects mines from his armoury, withdraws his main tentacle and begins to insert the things inside his prey. The other four Jain are now otherwise engaged, as the ten missiles finally head back towards them and begin to prowl around them like piranhas. Sniper decelerates, allowing the four to fall in his direction, then propels their fellow towards them. His opponent crashes amidst them, some twenty yards ahead of Sniper, and meanwhile begins to move much faster and to correct its tumble. It has self-repaired astonishingly fast – just in time for the numerous mines inside it to detonate. Chunks of the Jain slam into its fellows, sending them into instant disarray.

Programmed to respond to this detonation, the prowling missiles now speed in. Sniper folds in his tentacles and puts his hardfield out to its maximum power and extent, set to roll back towards him at the precise time of the expected detonations, thus obviating some of the blast. Space turns incandescent, and Sniper finds himself hurtling away, his hardfield still functional though its generator is torn from its mountings and pressing against the back interior of his shell.

Flame clears to reveal that two more Jain are now toast, but the remaining two begin accelerating towards him. On either side, he sees Prador already copying his technique and engaging claw to claw. How will they insert mines, though? Numerous blasts rapidly lighting the firmament indicate to him that they are not, but instead are engaging then detonating their own internal fusion tacticals. He admires their dedication, but decides it is not a technique he himself wants to employ. It might be a winning formula, too, if not for that energy feed emanating from the Jain ship to that relay and thence to individual Jain soldiers. These particular troops continue to fire a sequence of immensely powerful particle-beams that pick off the Guard with devastating precision. How can the Guard win against that? And as he launches further missiles and accelerates towards his own two opponents, he wonders how just *he* is going to win as well.

Then, seemingly out of nowhere, erupts a dazzling white blast. One of the two Jain simply blackens and ablates away, and the second is sent tumbling helplessly. A bubble appears around it, closes then winks out, and a trail of shattered and molten debris mark its onward course.

'Very good, drone,' the Golgoloth sends. 'Now let's see what you can do about that relay.'

Checking out towards the relay, Sniper sees complicated duelling going on all around it, with the hardfields projected from the Golgoloth's vessel and from the Jain themselves taking on strange twisted shapes he has never witnessed before. Next scanning down towards the ancient hermaphrodite's ship, Sniper sees that about half the Jain force is currently heading towards it, under a hardfield umbrella, power being fed to them by that relay. White lasers probe up, and every now and again one of the Jain simply detonates like a fuse blowing in some circuit. The Golgoloth has also launched missiles, which circle round questingly. However, judging by their present casualty rate, at least twenty of the Jain will reach the Golgoloth's ship before this is all over, and just one or two of them might be enough.

'What cover can you give me?' he enquires, setting himself on a course that will take him round that hardfield action.

'Enough to keep them from close engagement,' the Golgoloth replies, then adds, 'Trust me.'

Sniper likes the creature's sense of humour.

He now concentrates on repairing some of the damage inside himself, dispatching minibots to weld his hardfield generator securely in the position it now occupies. Reinstalling fuses, he sets his three remaining conefield coils running again. This will give him three-fifths of a cone, which might mean the difference between life and death. He checks power, finds he is a quarter down, then loads more mines and missiles inside himself. The Jain spread about the relay obviously know he is coming, for many of them turn in his direction. A particle beam lances towards him, but splashes on an angled hardfield and deflects, losing coherence, and blasts past Sniper like the output from a flamethrower. Other Jain try to manoeuvre for a clear shot, but shifting themselves outside of their main formation puts them in the way of the Golgoloth's bubble fields. They, too, instantly become clouds of spreading debris. Others retreat to defend the relay itself, and he considers the odds.

'Unless you can take out the ten of them around that relay,' he tells the Golgoloth. 'I haven't got a fucking chance of knocking it out.'

'It only has to be out for less than a second,' the Golgoloth replies. 'Can't you think of something clever and *martial?*'

Sniper now knows what needs doing. He launches his whole

stock of missiles towards the relay, tweaking the programming of each as he fires them. *That should keep 'em busy.* Now for the mines, which he begins internally loading to his rail-gun and firing, their programs sets equally as varied. Because they do not precisely fit the rail-gun barrel, their accuracy isn't that great, but he wants nothing explosive left inside him for what is about to come.

'Get yourself ready,' he sends, whilst firing up his fusion engines to take him on a course behind the relay.

'I see,' says the Golgoloth. 'Our brief acquaintance has been an interesting one.'

About the relay itself, missiles detonate one after the other. Sniper is satisfied to see the tail end of a Jain tumbling away and a claw, glowing white hot, go spearing past him. One of the Golgoloth's fields then manages to punch through, and a brief sheer-plane slices two more of the Jain creatures in half horizontally. Then Sniper is bearing down on a seemingly solid bar of microwave energy. He fires up both his hardfield and conefield and falls into the bar. The remaining conefield coils last only a tenth of a second, while the hardfield generator persists for a further two-tenths of a second, the excess heat draining into his s-con grid but, once that becomes overloaded by microwave radiation, the grid simply turns molten inside him. Sniper's internal temperature ratchets up dangerously, even as he uses emergency measures to protect his most vital component: the crystal of his mind. Three of his minor tentacles simply fall apart, and one of his major ones explodes as the metal of a motor turns to gas. An age seems to pass in only tenths of a second, as he finally tumbles out of the beam's path. But has he cut off the microwave flow to the relay for long enough?

He has.

Through blurred visual input, Sniper watches numerous bubbles flash in and out of existence in surrounding space, strewing debris after them. A white laser blinks into hazy existence, deploys in a rapid circle that incorporates the doughnut of the relay, until the thing becomes a ring of burning gas. Sniper tries to fire up his fusion engine, but it merely belches a dirty red flame before sputtering out. He tries his particle cannon on a nearby Jain, but nothing happens. His mind seems to be filled with nothing but error codes, but at least he still *has* a mind. The nearby Jain swings towards him, other more distant Jain swing towards him too, but then that same white laser licks out to touch them, one after another, turning them instantly into puffs of glowing gas. Distantly, Sniper can see the remaining Guard now close to the Golgoloth's ship, and can see how the attacking Jain are swiftly being dispatched.

'Nice one,' he sends, then notes the error code informing him that a glowing slagged item inside him is all that remains of his ability to communicate.

'Bollocks,' he notes, as he falls away from the action.

It isn't over, not by any means. That swarm of objects now rising from the Jain ship is probably the rest of the buggers, and a brief brightness flooding surrounding space sees yet another dreadnought turned to scrap metal. Around that distant Jain vessel, the darkness is intensifying again, as it recharges to take out the remaining dreadnoughts, or the Golgoloth's ship, or even the King's ship. However, it is over for Sniper, and he thinks it doubly over for him when a hardfield bubble materializes around him and drags him to an abrupt halt. He waits for it to close down to a point, but instead it throws him in a different direction. Enough of his sensors remain for him to observe a set of crenellated hold doors opening, before he crashes down onto a ceramal deck, bounces and thunders into a rear wall.

Seems he is home, then, and he waits for Gurnard to find some means of talking to him.

★

The Golgoloth feels as raw and beaten up as it often used to feel after one of its siblings had attacked it – before it first learnt how to avoid them, then turn them against each other, then find other means to defeat them before it slaughtered them all. But at least this is a feeling to which it has been long accustomed. The reality, it suspects, is that little of its own original physical body remains for, over the long years, it has replaced all of its underhands, legs, both claws, numerous internal organs and something like 80 per cent of its major ganglion. Its mind remains its own, however, always its own. This, it seems, is precisely the King's condition, having lost or changed most of his physical body over the years. But now it seems the King is losing his mind.

'It *can* be done,' intones Oberon.

The Golgoloth checks its displays and once again begins integrating its exterior ganglia distributed throughout the ship. Certainly it has five U-jump missiles now ready for firing, but USER disruption within this system has turned underspace into a chaotic and ever-changing geometry.

'If I fire them, they'll be bounced out, probably turned inside-out too,' says the Golgoloth. 'There's no stability out there. Anyway, you've got your own kamikazes.'

'Not accurate . . . enough,' the King struggles to say.

The old hermaphrodite peers at the image of the King and gets a horrible inkling of what the mechanisms interlaced throughout his body, and the pillar they connect to, are for, and also what the Human female and the two chrome-armoured third-children are currently doing. At that moment, on other sensors, the Golgoloth watches another of the King's dreadnoughts die, and knows that its own ship would not last long if thus targeted. Perhaps it is time now to make a run for it, just using conventional fusion drive. The King and his remaining forces should keep the Jain occupied for a little while and, due to the U-space disruption, the Jain would only be able to pursue the Golgoloth by using conventional drive too. Perhaps the Golgoloth could stay ahead of them, using the techniques it long ago employed to first avoid Oberon's hunters; perhaps it could even lead the Jain into the Polity itself and let them become a problem for Earth Central and all its subordinate AIs.

'Stability is integral in space weave. Obedience is integral to success,' remarks Oberon.

Right, he is definitely losing it – for that isn't how the King talks at all. Meanwhile, other displays show that the nearest dreadnought is launching three bulky missiles the Golgoloth recognizes as the current Prador version of its own U-space missiles: large flying bombs piloted by first-child minds, suicide weapons.

Oberon continues, 'If you run, my five remaining dreadnoughts and my own ship have you in their sights. If you survive that, which I doubt, the kamikazes will follow you and, once you reach stable U-space, they will kill you.'

Ah, the King is back. The Golgoloth estimates its chances. The firepower remaining to the King does make fleeing an unlikely option. It doesn't matter how many hardfields the Golgoloth can deploy if it becomes the target of a few hundred rail-guns and as many energy weapons.

'Space weave?' the hermaphrodite enquires.

'Weapon a product of revolving singularity positioned across interface of U-space gate – effect focused through spiral gravity field,' says the King. 'You will all be erased, as is necessary for our survival.'

Oberon is swinging his head from side to side, his voice now produced by machinery rather than his own twitching and clashing mandibles. The Golgoloth also notes that the King's words confirm he has accessed Jain quantum storage, because he has just described technology that certainly does not exist within the Kingdom, and might not yet even exist in the Polity.

'You mean that weapon which just destroyed two of your dreadnoughts,' says the Golgoloth, pretending to be thick.

'That weapon . . . yes,' manages the King.

'What about positioning?' asks the Golgoloth, very much not liking what seems to be implied here.

'Yes . . . you must put yourself right in front of that beam, my old friend.'

My old friend.

Suddenly, those words seem to be enough, and the Golgoloth feels a great sadness surge through him. Oberon is also saying goodbye, it realizes. But the question remains about how to deal with what will certainly replace the King – a Jain soldier.

'It is indeed sad to lose a long-time friend,' says the Golgoloth. 'True replacements are difficult to find.'

'You know all . . . about replacements,' says Oberon. 'The first replacement . . . for me . . . will be dealt with. Arrangements have been made.'

The Golgoloth just has to trust that this is true, as it fires up its engines, turns its vessel so its least damaged side faces the ship of bones, and then accelerates towards it.

19

An esteemed colleague once pointed out to me that though it is convenient for major events in fiction to tip on some pivotal moment, for instance for Gollum to bite the finger off Frodo and thus send the ring of power into the fire, reality is rarely like that. He claimed that the march of history carries too much momentum for those small key events to knock it aside. I patted him on the shoulder and agreed, considering the assassination that led to the First World War, the bullet through Kennedy's skull, the positioning of an iceberg back in 1912 . . . Our stories do not pivot on one point but on thousands of them, moment to moment, every one of them a step in that same long march.

– Anonymous

As Vrell finishes his explanation, Orbus feels his legs grow slightly weak. Shit, his shooting isn't that great – he managed to miss Vrell – but now so much depends on it. He glances to one side at the Golgoloth's children, and notices they show the usual Prador signs of stark-staring terror. That is understandable, since both their task and Vrell's task are likely to get them killed.

'But with weapons we will be better,' observes the one named Geth.

'There will be no time,' Vrell replies, through Thirteen. 'Once the Jain soldier has taken him, it will try to destroy us all as quickly as possible. Though it cannot immediately detonate the fusion devices inside the Guard, because the King has switched them over to manual, or the self-destructs of the ships or access to their weapons, since they have been isolated too, it will go for control over the weapons of this ship, and those are formidable. With the help I have, I can freeze his pit controls, but it will not take him long to get to my own, or to others in here. He must be held back for long enough, or we all die.'

It is the longest speech Orbus has ever heard Vrell make, and he ponders its content. How coincidental that their weapons are cached here in this very room, and that Vrell has found Sadurian's AI hiding within the ship's system. And how fortunate that the dangers of informational attack from the Jain made it necessary for Oberon to offline those self-destruct mechanisms.

'How will you know when?' he asks.

'I am monitoring,' Vrell replies, through Thirteen. 'Oberon has just communicated with the Golgoloth, and I am now analysing their plan of attack for error.'

'They have one then?'

'They do but, since Oberon is currently being hijacked by a Jain soldier, there is no guarantee that the information underlying this plan is valid.'

'Not a lot we can do really, if it isn't.'

Oberon focuses his attention on the King, who now looks in a bad way, like some giant bug suffering a dose of Raid. The big mutant is shivering, his dripping fluids now turned pale jade as if tinged with Prador blood. He jerks sharply, snapping a hose from the pillar, jerks again and, with a shower of sparks, tears out a power cable. Sadurian gestures the two third-children towards the pillar, and they edge forward to busily set about reattaching both hose and cable.

'Oberon, tell me what to do now,' she asks him.

The King's massive head swings towards her and stops still, mandibles slowly opening and closing idiotically. Rods of drool dangle from them, and his inner mandibles clatter against each other briefly, spilling drool to the floor.

'Essential to eliminate competition,' announces the King, the translation still reaching Orbus through Thirteen. 'Racial survival imperative . . . subordinate to survival of squad. Viable alien superfluous.'

The King tilts his head slightly, then lowers his front end while raising his rear, his pose now resembling that of a scorpion or a devil's coach-horse beetle. Suddenly, his tail smacks into the side of the cylinder, hard enough to nearly fold it in half, before sending it end over end, scattering the two third-children as it hurtles across the room to crash into the wall. The two chrome-armoured children struggle back to their feet just as he emits a horrible whistling shriek, his main mandibles opening up to a span of ten feet. Then his head snaps down on one of them, and mandibles clash about its carapace as he wrenches it from the floor, pulls his main claws from the pit controls and, despite the third-child's armour, tears away its legs all down one side and then tosses it away. Weighing half a ton or more, the injured creature arcs for twenty feet before slamming hard into another wall, actually penetrating its surface and becoming jammed there.

'Right,' says Vrell, again through Thirteen, 'my friend in here just offlined his pit controls. We go now.'

The second third-child manages to get ten feet before the King comes down on it like a hammer, flattening it to the floor. His claws must be tipped with something incredibly hard and strong, for they drive down straight through the armour and body of the smaller Prador, the sheer impact denting the creature into the floor. Green ichor wells, then fountains up as the King extracts his claw. Sadurian is already running, but Orbus does not give much for her chances until the King's attention suddenly swings towards Vrell.

'I require access,' says the King – only Orbus knows that the thing standing there is no longer Oberon, has in fact ceased to be him for some minutes now. As the haze about them fades, he gazes at the imprisoning posts around himself and the Golgoloth's children, then immediately breaks into a run, heading to his right, towards where a diagonally divided panel is opening. The Golgoloth's children scramble away too, scattering throughout the room, heading for various control stations where they immediately begin digging in with their claws and distorted underhands to tear out components. The King leaps towards Vrell, blindingly fast, but Vrell leaps too. He shoots up from his controls and, with one claw crashing down, propels himself sideways. The King's claw just misses impaling him to the floor. One side of Vrell's carapace cannons into a wall, leaving a grooved dent, and he throws himself along the base of it, but the King ignores him as he sinks down over Vrell's pit controls.

Orbus is at the weapons cache, where he can see Prador weapons piled up, but not his own multigun. It must be somewhere underneath. Grabbing tangled equipment, he throws it hard behind him, towards where the Golgoloth's children are doing their ruinous work. Fire and smoke suddenly flare. Orbus glances round to witness the King shrieking and peeling himself up painfully, the controls under him sabotaged and burning. Multigun, there! Orbus grabs the barrel just as a rail-gun thrums. The King is moving fast, feet actually tearing up floor metal, and missiles ricocheting off shell that must be as hard as ceramal. *We're going to die*, thinks Orbus, *no way I can punch through that carapace*. Powering up the multigun, he sees disappointing figures on its display – ten shots only – ten sprine bullets for the purpose of regicide.

One of the Golgoloth's first-children is wrenched aloft, its rail-gun firing into the ceiling, but only as long as its bubbling shriek as the King's mandibles scissor the creature in half. Two of the smaller third-children are now scooped up in his claws, then thumped together to spatter like overripe fruit.

Just fucking concentrate.

Orbus goes down on one knee, takes a long slow breath, steadies the butt of the multigun against his shoulder as he aims. He lets out the breath just as a dark shape slams down on the King's back. Vrell is being foolishly brave. No, he's tearing away some of the machinery interlaced through that adamantine carapace, trying to make a gap. The King's head turns a full hundred and eighty degrees. One scissoring snip and Vrell's claw goes tumbling through the air, though lacking the green ichor already spattered about the floor by the Golgoloth's dying children.

Again Orbus steadies his weapon. Seemingly driven by hydraulic motors, a long claw closes on the edge of Vrell's carapace, cutting and crushing into it as if into pie crust. Vrell gives a shriek, but is victorious as, in his remaining claw, he waves some long silvery mechanism trailing dripping optics and tubes. Vrell is now slammed down on the floor, onto his back, that same long claw wrenching itself along his underside, gutting him. There, in the King's back, a hole from which trails vinelike electronics, leaking pale green. Orbus fires, just three shots, but then the King turns to scythe a second-child in half while snatching up another, bursting it. The detonations along the King's back are not even close. Powdery red in the air. And now the hole is facing away from Orbus.

'Just turn a little, you fucker,' Orbus whispers.

Vrell knows. Even open like a half-eaten trifle, he manages to right himself, drag himself across, snare one of the King's feet with his remaining claw. The King whirls, flipping Vrell upright, impales him on a claw and then discards him. Vrell bounces away trailing a confetti of internal organs. Geth fires a rail-gun at the King to draw attention to himself, just enough to turn the King around further. Three more shots towards that same hole. Two exterior detonations, but very close. Did the third actually go in? Orbus wonders if he will ever find out as the King, ignoring Geth and perhaps fully recognizing the danger the Old Captain represents, now hurtles towards him. Orbus knocks the setting of his weapon down to two shots, fires at midnight eyes just as the King slams into him like a monorail. Orbus adds his own impetus to the impact by throwing himself back into the weapons cache. Mandibles close on one half of the door, tear it out and skim it away, then they crash inside to close about the Sea Captain's body, dragging him out like a whelk from its shell, and raising him up before those inner glassy scythes over the glistening ridged tunnel of the King's mouth.

I don't think I can survive this, Orbus thinks, swinging his multigun round and firing his two remaining shots straight down the King's gullet.

The gathering darkness about the thing ahead is again reaching its optimum, and within minutes either one of those ships behind, including the King's ship, is going to die, or else the blast will be coming the Golgoloth's way. The ancient hermaphrodite opens new channels that key in more closely to its scattered ganglia, thus becoming them, becoming the ship itself. Through the U-space eyes of that ganglion from a first-child dismantled a hundred years in the past, it peers into the chaos of underspace: a five-dimensional ocean under storm, brain-twisting angles of non-matter revolving into existence then vanishing, waves mounting and rolling into each other, a maelstrom centred over that distant Jain vessel, where cords of the actual underlying structure of the universe suck down energy.

How can they win against this? How can they destroy something that manages to so ably bend the laws of physics?

The Golgoloth does not allow these questions to remain within its distributed mind for long. It simultaneously observes, through sensors both internal and external and across most of the emitted spectrum, the horde of Jain soldiers it rapidly approaches, and which is rapidly approaching it. Time to focus their attention. Almost as if they are its own limbs, the Golgoloth reaches out with hardfields and closes them like claws. It crushes Jain down to incredibly dense spheres a mere ten inches across, and then releases them, the spheres coming apart, materials recombined, incredibly hot, nothing of what they once formed remaining.

Next the ancient Prador stabs out with its white lasers, like the youngest type of Prador spearing small fish with the tips of its sharp legs. Hardfields scale space ahead, deflecting some of the beams, sometimes burning out, the Jain bodies projecting them raised to sun-surface temperatures and just evaporating into surrounding vacuum.

The intense beam of a particle cannon stabs back, powered via one of three new relays out there. The beam ploughs across the hull of the Golgoloth's vessel, its impact site one long explosion that cuts a trench fifty feet deep. White lasers reply, only again the Jain throw up hardfield defences that turn space refractive, the beams curving away on new courses, sometimes even turning at sharp angles.

The Golgoloth now tries its own particle cannons, probing here and there, again trying to predict each new hardfield configuration, whilst simultaneously opening five ports in its vessel's hull and bringing the noses of its U-jump missiles to the surface. Within the five missile-ganglia it rests the touch of its mind, feather-light.

Behind come the King's dreadnoughts and, following their attack in, the spaceborne Guard are struggling to keep up. The viruses and the Jain worms now arrive, a panoply of computer organisms invading through sensors, through the exposed gas-locked throats and crystal eyes of lasers, through transmission and reception dishes. Soon the Golgoloth is fighting internal battles, isolating what it can again, but otherwise shutting down and burning out its own software and hardware, and killing parts of its mind. One of the five missiles is invaded, and the Golgoloth instantly fires it, through normal sensors watching it depart the ship and vanish from realspace. In U-space the missile is rolled up in some multi-dimensional whirlpool, then splashes back out into the real, turning inside-out from front to back, a fraction of a second before its exposed antimatter touches the obverse and turns all into a massive detonation.

The ship passes through intense EM, and that is a relief almost, for briefly all the viral attacks cease. The Jain now lie directly ahead, and from behind the Golgoloth's ship the dreadnoughts fire into the host a seemingly liquid stream of rail-gun fire, shoals of missiles, and both visible and invisible beams. The Golgoloth, taking a lesson from Sniper, now concentrates hardfields ahead, interweaving them in a single configuration, cone-like, just like the field the war drone used – one the Golgoloth suspects was designed to allow it to travel quickly under water. Jain soldiers rattle off this defence like hail off a greenhouse, but they are nothing compared to what is coming. Ahead, in U-space, the cords draw in, and then, in the real, that ship-killer plaited beam screws out, heading straight towards the Golgoloth.

The thing hits the hardfields, rips them sideways as if flicking scales off a fish. Within the ship generators explode, twist out of their mountings, some even crashing through internal structure with the force of rail-gun missiles. The Golgoloth rails out its own U-jump missiles, directly towards the impact site on its hardfields. In underspace vision the beam appears clearly, a stretched-out spiral burrowing up out of chaos, and wherever it tears into fields, its end resembles a leech's mouth sliding back and forth against glass. The Golgoloth drops the four missiles out of the real, and with its mind hard-linked into them all, so that they are now parts of itself speeding away, it alters and touches and twists the function of each U-space drive, making nanosecond calculations upon the current position of the beam's end-point.

Two missiles bounce back up into the real, their subsequent detonations wiping out the rest of the Golgoloth's defence. As the plaited beam punches forwards, it scoops up the last remaining two like an eel snapping up grubs, and through their eyes the Golgoloth finds itself speeding down a curving well towards something utterly terrifying. In the real, the beam strikes the Golgoloth's ship and begins tearing up its hull, boring downwards. The missiles reach their destination, contact blurring away as they then choose – as they always choose so readily – to end it all. A hundred feet down into the Golgoloth's ship the beam tears, then just ceases. A microsecond later, a bright blue star flashes into existence at the centre of the ship of bones, growing in intensity and eventually occluding it. Next a blastfront spreads, tearing the strange vessel to shreds, converting material to fire and rolling out a doughnut-shaped cloud of luminous gas. In U-space the effect is visible too, as the source point of the USER maelstrom becomes a massive sphere rapidly collapsing in on itself.

The Golgoloth has killed the Jain ship. But now, as chaotic battle continues all about it, the old creature wonders if this will be a victory it can survive.

Shuddering to an abrupt halt, the King locks his mandibles tight enough around the Old Captain – perhaps tight enough to shear any normal Human in half. But with the Spatterjay virus so long occupying Orbus's body, Vrell knows the man will be as difficult to sever as something constructed of iron and seasoned wood.

Perhaps one day Vrell himself will be so tough, but only if he can survive this.

Three shots – one through the side of the King's body, and now two more straight down his throat. How long before the sprine will take effect?

The King abruptly jerks his head sideways, sending Orbus flying in a flat trajectory across the room, where he hits one wall hard, making a sound like a mollusc shell giving out. Orbus drops soggily from a deep dent in the wall, about which his rarely seen blood is spattered. Prone on the floor, little jerky movements in his body – where there should be no movement at all – betray his tenacious hold on life. Just like Vrell's hold.

Now the King begins shuddering, then suddenly he raises his head to emit an ululating shriek. He squats low, then hurls himself up with the force of a shuttle launching, his back slamming into the ceiling, then he drops hard, coming down with a crash, legs splayed momentarily in disarray. Then he is running, careering at high speed in a straight line, feet tearing up metal, though sometimes his gait slips out of control. Some of the Golgoloth's children scatter from his path, but he pays them no heed, just cannoning head-first into the far wall. There he just stands, mandibles buried deep in its surface, tail thrashing like an angry cat's.

And next he comes apart.

The King drips fluids now turned black from every joint, and then one of his back legs detaches from its carapace socket and topples like a felled tree. As it hits the floor, it breaks up into its individual segments, and what were once internal tissues like muscle, veins and tendons flow out in a black syrupy mess. His tail, at first flicking smoothly, now begins to lock up, this paralysing effect spreading from base to tip, and when that appendage finally grows still, the whole of it falls to pieces. Another leg goes next, followed by a primary claw, then his whole body just comes apart and collapses like an immense stone arch with its keystone removed. The head holds up for a little while longer, then it too drops like a boulder, leaving the sawtooth tips of his mandibles embedded in the wall.

I cannot begin to know how hard you fought, thinks Vrell.

Certainly the King fought against the Jain soldier he had resurrected inside himself, but he knew he might not win and so made careful preparations: severing his connection to the fusion devices inside the Guards' armour; severing his connection to the destructs of his own ships; placing the Old Captain's multigun here, ready to hand, loaded with sprine bullets; allowing Vrell access to this ship's computer systems; and very likely allowing Sadurian's AI free rein within them in the first place. Of course, the King did not make it easy for himself to be killed. Vrell can now see that Oberon had expected to either defeat the Jain soldier quickly or fight a long losing battle against it – a losing battle that would give the rest of them time to get to the multigun.

The King has knowingly made the ultimate sacrifice for the Prador race, and Vrell wonders if he could do the same.

I should be dead, he reflects. It does not seem right to be so severely damaged and still functional, or even regaining function. Already, with painful wrenching sensations, his sliced-open torso is closing. Not knowing what else to do, he reaches underneath and pushes torn and ruptured organs back inside himself, whereupon the speed at which his body is closing up increases. Unsteadily, he heaves himself to his feet.

'We succeeded,' says Geth, now standing with his remaining kin gathered behind him. They all gaze at the scattered fragments of the King, which begin to emit an oily steam – the result of mechanisms woven through his body shorting their power supplies.

'We succeeded only because he allowed us to succeed,' says Vrell, walking with great care over to Orbus, who is still lying flat on his back.

The woman, Sadurian, kneels beside him, some sort of medical box ready to hand. The drone, Thirteen, hovers above this.

'What can I do?' she asks.

Orbus makes only some mumbling liquid sound in reply.

'The direct translation of his reply,' explains Thirteen, 'is *The fucker broke every bone in my body.*'

'A reply that is not particularly helpful,' Sadurian observes.

'There is nothing you can do for him now,' interjects Vrell, 'except to make sure he is provided with a great deal of nutrient totally uninfected by the virus.'

Vrell is thinking much the same about himself, and hungrily eyeing the scattered remnants of those of the Golgoloth's children the King dismembered earlier. However, though this is not a usual Prador reaction, he feels it would seem ungrateful to start eating his one-time allies. He swings away to inspect the room, searching for still-usable pit controls. The children certainly did a thorough job of destruction, but over there in the far corner lies one access point that seems only partially trashed. Vrell heads over, inserts one claw and whichever of his underhands do not hang limp and dead underneath him. The unit's mask rises into position and he inserts his head, immediately accessing the ship's three-dimensional virtuality.

'You took your time,' says Sphinx, represented here as a glittering fog filled with cubic structures.

'I need to gain control of this ship,' says Vrell.

'You certainly do,' the AI replies. 'The remaining Jain are still fighting, and it is by no means certain that the Golgoloth and the King's dreadnoughts can defeat them.'

'There will be many traps throughout this system, and many

413

codes I will need to break,' says Vrell. 'King Oberon nearly killed me even just reaching out from the Kingdom to Vrost's ship, and breaking through to his personal files here tested me to the limit.'

'There will be no traps,' says the AI.

'You have eliminated them?'

'No, even I would have encountered severe problems had the King seen fit to put any hindrance in my way. He did not, however. He let me in here.'

Vrell is not entirely sure he trusts this artificial intelligence – it is Polity after all. How easy for it to let him now become entangled in lethal computer intricacies? How easy to thus eliminate another possible threat to the Polity?

'But I see you have doubts,' says Sphinx. 'I'll let someone else reassure you.'

In the virtuality, he slowly slides into existence: first a glassy outline like a vessel waiting to be filled, then colour and substance gradually fill him up, starting first from those great heavy feet pressing down on a non-existent floor.

'So I am dead,' says King Oberon.

Vrell almost leaps away from the the mask and pit controls, but manages to restrain himself.

'You are dead,' he confirms.

The King's image nods its head in a peculiarly Human manner, then begins to speak:

'When your father, Ebulan, travelled to Spatterjay, I sent Vrost there to destroy whatever then arose from that world, whether or not he or any of his children were actually infected by the Spatterjay virus. I could not tolerate competition. I would not tolerate any Prador family other than my own becoming infected and so becoming a danger. To this end I have been as ruthless as any Prador. I have exterminated entire families merely on the suspicion that they know about or have used the virus. Within the Kingdom I have denuded one entire world of life, because my Guard discovered Prador there who were infected. And to the Humans I returned as many of their infected blanks as possible, for purposes of disposal. I have made it illegal for any Prador to own such blanks, ostensibly because of our treaty with the Humans but mainly to free the Kingdom of the virus.'

Vrell just gazes silently at this representation of the King. Is this all just a recording or is it interactive? Is some portion, or even the whole of the King's mind here? Certainly, if there is the capacity here to contain a Polity AI, then there is also the capacity to hold a copy of the King's mind.

'I understand this,' says Vrell finally. 'On the merely Prador level, it is simple politics to eliminate any competition, but there was also the danger of the Jain—'

'Of course you understand, Vrell, which is why I chose to give you this opportunity.'

Opportunity?

'Under my rule, the Prador Kingdom has been stable, has grown wealthy, and managed to avoid extermination by the Polity AIs. It has also grown stale, stagnant, and the race as a whole has ceased to advance.' The King dips his head, mandibles opening and closing. Vrell needs to force himself to remember that those same mandibles are currently embedded in a wall outside this virtuality, and that the King's real body lies in steaming pieces. 'I do not know precisely when, during my long reign, I started to consider the question of the succession. Being Prador, one would have thought I would ever continue to cling to power, ruthlessly continuing to quash any opposition, even killing those within my own family who might rise up to usurp me.'

'If you have considered the succession, surely you should have prepared one of your own Guard for that position?' says Vrell.

'So you might think, but no, for one of my own would bring

nothing new to the position. One of my own would only continue the stagnation. So I chose you, Vrell.'

'You tried mightily hard to have me killed, or even kill me yourself,' Vrell notes.

'But you survived, which is all that matters,' the King replies. 'Had you not survived, you would not have been worthy, even in your encounter with the Jain soldier that destroyed me. When I sent the Golgoloth to kill you I knew its curiosity would prevent it from doing so, and I expected you to remove that creature from existence.'

Vrell considers that a very dubious claim, but asked, '*When* did you choose me?'

'The moment when, in almost impossible circumstances, you managed to board Vrost's ship,' came the reply. 'Now it is time for me to hand over power.'

System-access icons begin to flash into operation all around Vrell: a treasury of opportunity, of power. *But are they real?* Vrell decides the time for doubt is over, as the battle for survival still rages. Using those same icons, he begins to take control. First he calls up a view of the battle, along with tactical analysis, then he accesses the child minds that control the engines and through them fires up the fusion drive. He gazes at outside views down along the massive cliff face of the ship's hull and sees great fusion-drive flames indeed stabbing out. Then he pauses.

Weapons?

The icon for them is plainly evident and, if the King and Sphinx are lying to him, operating this will probably kill him. He uses it nevertheless, opens up schematics and control keys, then studies the weapons manifest and proceeds to online massive rail-guns, particle cannons, numerous designs of missiles sitting in silos as big as the entire *Gurnard*. He next reaches out to touch each of the dreadnoughts as they fight – and receives an unexpected response, an acknowledgement and proof that none beyond this room, excepting the Golgoloth, knows what has happened here.

'As my King commands,' responds each of the dreadnought captains in turn.

'Treat them well,' says the King, his colour now fading, some program scrubbing him from existence.

More underhands now becoming usable, Vrell inserts them into further pit controls, and then takes up the reins of power.

Orbus sits upright, his entire body creaking. He is starving hungry and knows that his brain isn't operating properly. He peers at the King's remains, looks over to Vrell, who is currently ensconced in one of those control thingies. Every now and again the mutated Prador removes his head from the mask, and with one claw snatches up gobbets of meat from a pile deposited beside him. At that moment a slight surge sways Orbus, and he puts a hand down to steady himself. The big ship is on the move and, the King being in no further condition to give orders, that seems likely to be at Vrell's behest. The Old Captain now turns to focus on Sadurian.

'Vrell has informed me that you require food, and lots of it,' she says. 'He need not have told me, though, for I know all about the viral-injury hunger.'

She gestures to one side, where stands one of the chrome-armoured third-children, the same one Orbus saw the King impale earlier. Green blood is clotted all about the hole through its armour, but the creature is mobile and now places a large plastic box on the floor beside Orbus, flipping it open with the tip of one claw. It then moves off to resume the task of levering its fellow from the wall.

Inside the box lie various packages that Orbus recognizes.

'My food supply,' says Sadurian. 'I get some regularly shipped in from the Polity and prepare some of my own here. There are plenty of foods I can eat in the Kingdom, but there are still some things I really miss.'

Orbus reaches in and picks up a large crusty loaf. His stomach instantly grumbles. He now picks up a large block of plastic-wrapped meat of some kind, unwraps it, splits the loaf with his thumb and inserts the meat, then crushes the loaf flat and consumes it all in a rapid series of bites, hardly bothering to chew before swallowing. Next a big carton of orange juice, followed by a box of currant buns, some meaty stew that turns out to be a hot curry, followed by rice that is still dry and uncooked.

Sadurian turns to gaze over at where one side of the room is again transformed into a big screen, but now this is divided into hexagonal segments displaying different views. Only partially sated, Orbus follows her gaze. In one segment a dreadnought burns and Jain soldiers settle down on its surface. Even as he watches, the vessel detonates, removing both itself and its attackers from existence. A separate segment shows another dreadnought duelling with the encroaching Jain, using beam weapons and telefactored missiles. Every so often it takes one of them out, but they draw ever closer. However, the most violent action concentrates about the Golgoloth's vessel, which is constantly disappearing behind weird hardfield distortions and intense detonations.

Orbus swallows more of the dry rice, washed down with orange juice. 'How's it going, then?'

'By no means decided, but the King has yet to deploy the weapons of his own ship,' Sadurian replies.

'The King?'

She nods towards Vrell. 'The succession has been decided, and the Prador don't bother with coronations.'

'Ah,' says Orbus, but can think of nothing further to add.

★

The Golgoloth at first was keeping a wary eye on the King's U-jump missiles, but so intense is the attack upon its own vessel that it has recently neglected to watch them, so some moments pass before it realizes one has winked out of existence, and that a subsequent detonation amidst the Jain is where it then rematerialized. Checking through U-space eyes, the hermaphrodite watches as another missile jumps and is amazed by the convoluted path it weaves, avoiding immediate destruction in the maelstrom, and taking itself just far enough so it can materialize again, fully amidst the Jain. Such guidance, the Golgoloth knows, requires massively complex and immediate calculations, so a first-class mind must be assisting the minds installed within the missiles themselves. The King has to be still alive and guiding those missiles. And now the Golgoloth sees the King's ship itself entering the fray.

But the Golgoloth has other concerns. The Jain are fast thinkers too, and are now managing to circumvent some of its hardfield defences. How they lock on to those fields and twist themselves round them, the Golgoloth has yet to understand. Certainly it is a tactic that requires a great deal of energy, and the hermaphrodite needs to understand the process quickly if it is to survive. Probing out with a white laser, it manages to pick off one of them, but realizes that, the moment the beam strikes, a burst of microwave radiation pulses from the target. Now it knows.

The Jain it is destroying are themselves transforming their death energy into a pulse of microwaves to supply yet other Jain with enough energy to bypass the Golgoloth's defences. For every one it kills, another manages to leap a stage closer. At this rate it might manage to kill two-thirds of its attackers, but the rest will eventually reach the ship's hull. The Golgoloth realizes it is just fighting a delaying action.

Communication.

It is the King's channel, so the Golgoloth opens it at once.

Oberon's image appears on some nearby screens, but hazy due to the surrounding disruption. Perhaps because he is so busy, the King merely sends a large tactical information package. The Golgoloth opens it and soon realises it contains a huge amount of redundancy – options to be applied should the first action fail. Since there seems little other hope, it absorbs and applies the first option at once. It begins to move its ship to a slightly different location, increasing the strength of its defence in one area whilst weakening it in another. The Jain react accordingly, like hardened soldiers suspecting any weakened defence is a trap, abruptly concentrating their attack on an area midway between weakness and strength, so as to be ready to take full advantage of either. With a degree of reluctance, because it has already lost so many, the Golgoloth deliberately overloads one of its hardfield generators, which is the one holding the shield to one side of the strong defence, and furthest from the weak area. The generator glows in its mountings and slumps, and a hole opens out there, which the Golgoloth apparently tries to cover using white lasers and particle beams.

Hardened soldiers or otherwise, the Jain take the bait. They make the perfectly credible assumption that, knowing a generator is about to blow, the Golgoloth has tried to lure the Jain away from the area it covers by creating weaknesses elsewhere. By also strengthening defences in yet another area, the Golgoloth has obviously tried to make it all look like an attempt at making a trap, so as to cover up its desperation. But now there is a hole, and the Golgoloth will have to either close it or reposition fields. Here lies the Jain's opportunity to end this confrontation quickly.

Twenty-seven of them burn out in vacuum, microwave flashing their combined death energy to their surviving fellows. The Golgoloth now realizes that those receiving the energy actually use it to take very short U-jumps themselves, which is how they bypass the hardfields. The rest of the Jain, over fifty of them, use the energy to hop through U-space. It is all perfectly calculated, and the Golgoloth is awed at how the King has managed to predict the shape of local U-space disruption as well as the reactions of these creatures. They all now materialize in one area which, stretching normal terms of geometry to breaking point, lies adjacent to one of least disruption in U-space. Three U-jump missiles, having negotiated a much greater portion of the maelstrom, materialize amidst them and detonate: three small suns igniting.

In a fraction of a second the Golgoloth shuts down several hardfields, then reinitiates them closer to the hull of its own ship. Even so, the shockwave from the triple blast sears five generators out of existence, rocks the ship violently, and punches lethal radiations deep inside it, though thankfully not deep enough to penetrate through to the hermaphrodite itself. The blast also destroys many of the weapons on the side receiving the impact. Steering thrusters firing, the Golgoloth spins its vessel round, bringing to bear lasers and cannons still workable, and begins hitting anything out there larger than football.

Now the King's ship is right in the middle of the action, rail-guns slamming five-ton inert missiles into Jain hardfields, particle-cannon beams a yard across lancing out and burning up the creatures like flies in an acetylene flame. The remaining dreadnoughts, the pressure now off them, begin to put more effort into attack than defence. Energy crackles through vacuum, ecosystems of missiles and other projectiles swarm, hardfields glitter like giant fragments of broken glass strewn throughout space. Then, within moments, it is all dying, the firing growing intermittent as the dreadnoughts, the King's ship and the Golgoloth itself pick off stray Jain weapons or fry any questionable objects drifting about out there.

But the Jain are all gone.

The Golgoloth looks at once to its further survival and begins considering some things it has had no time to consider until now. The King has shown himself quite capable of meticulous guidance of U-jump missiles, yet, like rulers everywhere, put someone else in line with a bullet to get the job done, only throwing himself into the fray when there seemed no other option. However, there are no more of his missiles in evidence out there. Quite probably he used them all against the Jain, but even if not, it might take him some time to get more ready to launch, and he might hesitate . . .

'About now you will be thinking of running,' says the image of Oberon on his screen. 'However, you are going nowhere.'

What?

The Golgoloth thinks fast, and quickly realizes its mistake.

The tactical package.

It is already open and fast spreading its concealed attack programs throughout the ship. The Golgoloth tries at first to close it down, then to limit its spread. The creature's external ganglia begin to go offline, and attacks to its systems begin to issue from other internal locations – other packages presumably planted by the Guard who came aboard. Next, the Golgoloth begins to detect movement inside the ship and, managing to reinstate some internal ship eyes, observes armoured Guard coming out of concealment and closing in on its own position.

Not all of them departed.

'Oberon prepared for this,' says that image of the King on the screens. 'You were never going anywhere but back to the Kingdom.'

The Golgoloth stares at the image as it fades, mandibles clicking together in frustration.

20

With runcibles established on just about every major Polity world or space station, and able to quickly transport both Humans and huge cargo loads from world to world, and with advanced manufacturing facilities on most worlds capable of producing just about anything conceivable, one would have thought there was no longer any need for the traditional cargo spaceship. However, when the Prador attacked, it was our over-reliance on runcibles that nearly brought about our downfall, so the artficial intelligences have since encouraged a return to the use of spaceships. Cargo ships are most active at the Polity border, where the runcible network peters out, and haul about cargoes within solar systems to make deliveries to outposts too small to warrant a runcible, like small space-based mining operations. They also make deliveries to Polity worlds of items that sell on their novelty value alone, and shift cargoes that certain individuals would rather the ruling AIs know nothing about.

– From HOW IT IS by Gordon

The sound of docking clamps engaging resounds through the *Gurnard* as Sniper runs yet another diagnostic test. He now possesses three operative minor tentacles and one workable major tentacle, as well as steering thrusters and a gravmotor cut from the *Gurnard*'s remaining telefactor. He has also replaced the damaged mind crystal by transferring its contents to new crystal whilst stitching the dislocated information back together as best he can. Of course, if and when he returns to Spatterjay, he will find out exactly how good a job he has done for, like all drones of his profession, he always keeps a few back-up copies of himself stored away safely.

'Seems like an odd request,' he observes.

'Who are we to question the King?' Gurnard replies.

Externally, Sniper knows he looks only a little different from before, the only evidence of his recent travails being tentacles still missing, and damage to his shell still evident in its distortion despite him having sprayed it with a chrome analogue, but internally he has changed drastically. Next to him lies a pile of technological junk: fried optics, cracked crystal, the melted components of a rail-gun, several lasers, a particle cannon and com hardware, cracked ceramic remnants of his fusion engines, unrecognizable slag that was once hardfield generators, and the remains of his underwater drive, along with numerous cyber-motors and sections of tentacle. Also here lie two dismembered earwig autohandlers, and various open plasmel component boxes. He has removed all the damaged components from inside himself, but found few suitable replacements for most of them from the cannibalized machines. Numerous raw voids gape inside a body once packed solid with state-of-the-art hardware, mostly of the lethal kind.

He feels naked.

'Why me?' Sniper asks, engaging his gravmotor to lift himself from the floor and using his tentacles to tow himself over to the door that opens into the *Gurnard* proper. 'You could send them over using an autohandler, or else he could send one of what have now become his Guard.'

'I asked just that, but he wasn't very forthcoming,' says Gurnard. 'Perhaps a royal arrogance has settled upon him along with the crown.'

'Prador don't go in for jewellery,' Sniper grumps, as he waits for the bay to pressurize. Once the pressures equalize, the door whumphs up off its seals and slides aside, and Sniper propels himself inside the ship, taking the familiar route down from the docking ring towards the cargo section. Shortly after, he passes through atmosphere doors, entering a zero-gravity hold space filled with inert gas and, with a flip of his main tentacle, sends himself drifting down an aisle leading through the quadrate frameworks. Over to his right, he sees the two halves of the crate in which he and Thirteen were stowed away, now carefully secured in place as if ready to receive them again. All along one wall of the hold, earwig-shaped autohandlers stir as if uncomfortable with rumours of what happened to two of their fellows in the ship above.

Finally Sniper draws to a halt beside three horizontal cylinders resting side-by-side, enviro-control consoles attached to their upper surfaces. His scanning abilities being severely limited now, he reluctantly prods at the controls on each console to check the condition of each cylinder's living contents. Those contents all seem fine and squirmy.

'Which one should I take?' Sniper asks.

'It doesn't matter,' Gurnard replies. 'Having just transferred over a huge sum in diamond slate to Charles Cymbeline, with the proviso that the profits will be shared with us, Vrell now owns the entire cargo of this ship.'

Vrell is thus paying back Cymbeline for the small part that the reification played in getting him on to the metaphorical Prador throne, but mostly he is rewarding Sniper, Thirteen and Orbus, and Gurnard for their crucial role. This makes the drone feel a lot better about boarding a Prador ship without his usual complement of weapons. He detaches one of the cylinders from its webbing straps and propels it back along the aisle. Once reaching the grav-sections of the ship, he engages a maglev unit on its underside, whose controls he programs so that the cylinder will follow him like a faithful dog. Then he finally passes through an airlock and into a wide docking tunnel – into Prador territory.

Three very battered members of the Guard await him in the docking tunnel, armoured as usual but carrying no visible weapons, and he feels something like a sympathetic severed-limb ache from his own missing weapons.

'You are to accompany me,' announces one of them.

Sniper recognizes the voice. 'That you, Frordor?'

'It is I,' says the Prador.

'Glad you made it,' Sniper replies, realizing he actually *is* glad. The severed-limb ache recedes a little as – accompanied by just Frordor, while the other two remain behind obviously to watch the tunnel – he enters a large Prador airlock, then the King's ship itself.

Things seem very busy inside, as Sniper notes a party of again rather battered-looking Guard escorting another of their kind, whose armour is clean and polished.

'Who's that?' Sniper asks.

'Ship Captain,' Frordor replies.

He must be the Captain of one of the five surviving dreadnoughts that are also docked to the King's ship, alongside the *Gurnard* and the Golgoloth's vessel. Sniper wonders if captains like this one, and soldiers like Frordor, yet know that their father, King Oberon, is dead. He also wonders if Vrell will even tell them, for it seems, according to Gurnard, that few of the Guard actually have any idea what their father looked like, and in his present position, Vrell should have no trouble disposing of any of those possessing inconvenient knowledge. It is the usual Prador way, politics and murder being nearly indistinguishable concepts in their multiple eyes.

Some way ahead of Sniper and Frordor, the Captain and his

escort reach a set of enormous doors. Sniper notices the Captain crouching slightly and picks up on the creature's apprehension. Perhaps this is the first time he has ever been summoned to an audience with the King himself, which as Sniper understands it, was often a terminal affair. The doors grind slowly open on dazzling whiteness within, and the first party enters. They then remain open until Frordor and Sniper reach them and enter too, then close resolutely behind them.

Sniper glances up at the weapons positioned in pits high in the walls, but notes with some surprise that these aren't tracking anyone's progress. As he and Frordor follow the other party, he glances through another set of open doors into a large room that seems to have recently seen quite a bit of action. He sees wrecked equipment, torn-up floor and dents in the walls. Prador blood-stains are everywhere, and through them some suspiciously large ship-lice scuttle delightedly. A section of wall also appears to have been chopped out. No actual body parts visible though, so some-one has at least done a bit of clearing up.

Next they enter a short tunnel that debouches into an area recently opened out, for Sniper can see where walls have been removed. An extent of white floor terminates at a wide viewing gallery equipped with enormous windows, which the drone assumes are comprised of some sort of chainglass rather than being massive electronic screens. Before these Vrell patrols restlessly below a raised platform, occasionally closing his harness mask across, probably to keep a sharp eye on everything around him – for miles around him. Much of the rest of the room is occupied by the Guard – like Frordor – who judging by the state of their armour are those that fought the Jain out in vacuum. All are grouped in ranks leaving a wide aisle to the viewing gallery. Near the front the dreadnought Captain joins his four fellows – a singularly shiny group. Then, Sniper notes something else to one side of the raised platform. It is the section of wall that has been removed from the room he passed earlier, with a pair of huge mandibles embedded in it, and resting below it lie pieces of the carapace of some immense creature.

'We go here,' indicates Frordor, leading Sniper over to a small group that stands utterly distinct from the rest assembled in this room. Here are the Golgoloth's surviving children, but amidst them the drone spies Orbus, with Thirteen hovering at his shoulder, and some Human woman flanked by two small chrome-armoured Prador.

'So you survived again,' says Orbus cheerfully.

'Most of me,' Sniper replies. 'So what's going on here? We about to see Vrell settling some old scores?'

Orbus nods. 'That'd be my guess.'

As Sniper settles to the floor, and instructs the cargo cylinder to park itself beside him, Vrell abruptly flips his harness mask aside and folds it down to his harness, before leaping up on to the platform in one fast fluid movement. It seems he will now make his inaugural address.

'All but a few of the Prador here,' begins Vrell, his voice amplified to carry clearly to everyone, whilst Thirteen runs a constant translation for Orbus, and maybe the other Human, 'will never grow to be adults. Not because your father kept your maturity chemically suppressed, but because the Spatterjay virus will never allow you to mature. However, every one of you here has been subject to Oberon's pheromonal and psychological control.'

There comes a great deal of shifting and clattering within the crowd, and Sniper finds out the reason for disturbance when Frordor swings towards him.

'This is not Oberon?' the Prador asks.

'I dunno.' Sniper decides to be economical with the truth. 'I was out there in vacuum with you.'

Frordor swings back to gaze at Vrell, and Sniper notices just about every member of the assembled Guard reflexively groping for weapons they do not now carry. Still, they are all armoured and Vrell is not. Unless he has some hidden defence, they could tear him apart in an instant.

'Your father, in our Prador terms, treated you well. Despite your enforced loyalty, you all have power and property, and want for only that thing you cannot have: adulthood. Now that your father, King Oberon, is dead, after having sacrificed his own life to defeat the Jain' – Vrell waves his single claw down towards the grotesque exhibit, and from the chunks of carapace resting below the embedded mandibles there arises a hologram of the fearsome creature they once composed – 'I, your new ruler, King Vrell, merely *demand* loyalty, and though it was within my power to enforce it directly through systems within your suits, I have shut down that option. Instead I demand loyalty in return for the benefits your positions grant you, in return for committing resources towards research that might finally lead to a way to raise you all to adulthood. And I demand that same loyalty to me for the good of the entire Prador race.'

The shifting and clattering amidst the Guard rises to a tumult, and Sniper wonders if some of them are about to rush the platform. Sniper suspects that, to ensure loyalty, Oberon used some kind of hormonal generator within each suit of armour, and perhaps some sort of continuous subliminal enforcement through each suit's electronics. So if Vrell has now shut these down, surely there are those here even now contemplating snatching power away from him? Then, again, the ultimate enforcement of loyalty is the fusion device inside each suit, of which Vrell has doubtless assumed control. Still, Vrell seems to be making a very dangerous gamble, and Sniper just hopes he understands Prador psychology – or rather the psychology of these Prador mutants – a lot better than Sniper does. 'Loyalty' as such is something that he reckons has to be *enforced* amidst this vicious species.

'You know how to signify your acceptance,' says Vrell. 'And I will prove to you my trust.'

Huh?

'Not sure I get that,' says Orbus.

'Me neither,' says Sniper.

Orbus turns to the woman. 'Sadurian?'

The Human woman's face twists into a strange smile and she shakes her head in amazement. 'You have to remember that many of those here are very old, aware that they are not true Prador, and are therefore not so hard-wired by their biology. Many of them have even acquired some wisdom.'

A Prador Captain, one of those in polished armour, abruptly steps out from the ranks and into the aisle, to directly approach Vrell's dais. The Captain draws to a halt and stands rigid and, after a moment, there comes a clonk and a hiss as the upper carapace of his armour separates from the lower, rising on silvered rods to then hinge back and reveal the monster within. This is no fast-eject routine, so the mutated Prador spends some time in withdrawing his legs, claws and underhands from their enclosing metal. Sniper studies the creature with interest. It looks soft, the head rising on a short, curving neck looks like that of a blind bird, while its legs bow under the weight of a bunched-up body that only gradually straightens out its kinks.

Vrell abruptly drops from his platform, flipping his mask back across in the meantime. He must have sent some instruction to the open armour, for sounds issue from within it as he approaches. He rears over it, reaches inside with his single claw, and pulls out some heavy coin-shaped component, which he takes over and places directly below the slowly fading hologram of King Oberon.

Vrell turns to address the naked mutant. 'Your armour's software has now been reformatted, though your personal data retained. You can check for yourself the status of the internal conditioning system – that system you have been aware of for over a century, Captain Vertos, and have been trying to overcome for as long.'

The blind birdlike head dips and turns to inspect the suit it has so recently departed. After lengthily studying some items within, the head dips in acquiescence again, and Captain Vertos climbs back into his armour. By the time the armour closes again, a queue is forming behind him, third in line being Frordor himself. Over the ensuing hours, Sniper observes a grotesque range of mutated Prador, and watches that stack of coin-shaped fusion bombs continue to grow and grow. Then, after the last two – the two small ones wearing chrome armour, one of whom needs assistance from the other for, despite its armour possessing all its legs, it does not – all gathered within this large room have become free for the first time in their entire existence. Sniper realizes that those assembled here are by no means all of the Guard, but just a representative few. Countless others are yet to be freed.

He wonders, too, what the major Polity AIs will make of all this: of mutated Prador, any of whom might turn into Jain supersoldiers, being thus freed of the devices that can destroy them at once. Then, again, this same possibility applies to every Human Hooper on Spatterjay, and they don't walk round with bombs permanently strapped to them.

'I offer choice,' says Vrell, once again back up on his platform. 'Now you can choose to either obey me or disobey me. You can choose to serve me or betray me. But, now that you have choice, you must be thoroughly aware that all choices have their consequences. I can no longer kill any of you in an instant, but choose to go against me and you may long for so speedy a death.'

'Ah, that's a bit more like it,' mutters Orbus.

'Carrot, then stick,' agrees Sniper. 'The former is for the older and wiser ones, the latter for those – like most Prador – who only understand the stick.'

'And now I shall offer another individual a choice,' says Vrell, raising his head to gaze towards the distant tunnel mouth, as even now a figure comes into view.

So that's the Golgoloth, Sniper guesses.

The crippled Prador hermaphrodite is limping along, trailing various tubes and wires, still surrounded by the members of the Guard that apprehended it. These Guards are all heavily armed and Sniper doubts that Vrell has released his control of them at all. They escort the Golgoloth before Vrell, and then all but two of them move back into the crowd. The two that remain close in on the creature and grab hold of its claws and misshapen carapace.

'And what choice might you offer me?' asks the Golgoloth, turning one palp-eye towards its children, who instinctively bunch together and back off a little.

'You possess knowledge and wisdom I will find useful,' says Vrell. 'You either choose to serve me or choose to die.'

'I never choose to die,' replies the ancient creature.

Again the Golgoloth peers at its children, no doubt coveting various parts of them, since some of those on its own body now possess an unhealthy hue and doubtless will soon be in need of replacement. Whilst the hermaphrodite is thus distracted, Vrell again drops from his platform. He shoots forwards and brutally stabs his claw right in beside the Golgoloth's mouth, where some of the recent repair remains weak. Shell crumbles and the creature shrieks, struggling between its two captors. Vrell grabs a rim of broken shell and wrenches it aside, exposing wet flesh underneath, now leaking green ichor.

'You said I could live!' the Golgoloth clatters.

'Yes, I did,' Vrell replies. 'I did not say how.'

And, now understanding, Sniper extends one tentacle to punch code into the console of the cargo cylinder and, after a moment, a hatch slides back. Inside lies a slimy bunched tangle of Spatterjay leeches, each measuring about a metre long. Now exposed to air and the possibility of prey, they begin to writhe more vigorously. One tubular, thread-cutting mouth probes up out of the mass, searching for flesh to bore into, for chunks of it to swallow down. All these horrible things are saturated with the Spatterjay virus. In fact they share a mutualism with the virus, for they spread it to turn their prey into a forever reusable food resource. It is the bite from one of these things that gave Orbus his endless life, gave the same to Vrell and King Oberon, and by proxy to all of the Guard.

Sniper wraps a tentacle around the more adventurous of the leeches and tugs it free, its body stretching to twice its previous resting length. Its tubular mouth grinds against the metal of his tentacle, producing a noise like eggs being crushed. With another tentacle, Sniper snaps the cylinder shut. He then engages his gravmotor to rise off the floor, and propels himself over to the Golgoloth.

'It might kill me!' The Golgoloth is in panic and, even armoured as they are, the two Guard have a problem holding the ancient creature steady.

'This is the only life you will now have,' says Vrell. 'You will no longer extend your own existence by dismantling your children.'

Sniper lowers the leech towards the raw flesh exposed beside the Golgoloth's mouth. The leech itself, sensing something more digestible, abruptly snaps its tube mouth away from Sniper's tentacle and stretches it towards that tempting flesh. A horrible keening issues from the Golgoloth as the leech mouth bores its way in, and green blood gouts around it. Sniper considers just letting the leech go. It would then bore right inside the Golgoloth, chewing through flesh and organs until sated, which is no more than the hermaphrodite deserves. However, in doing so, it might kill the Golgoloth before the virus has a good chance of taking hold. The end result would still be a living creature, but one without the mind that Vrell wants to use. Sniper pulls the leech free and observes a lump of Prador flesh sliding down the length of its attenuated body.

Enough. Sniper backs off and returns the leech to the cargo cylinder.

'The Prador Fourth Kingdom will be new and dynamic,' Vrell declaims. 'A new age has dawned, and now it is time for my kind to put their ignorance behind them, and rise from their long sleep.'

'Hey, did things just get any better?' Orbus mutters to Sniper.

'Buggered if I know,' the drone replies.

Orbus gazes through the big side-eye screen of the *Gurnard* as he drops into the Captain's throne. The King's ship hovers out there like some giant steel monolith transported into vacuum, and even now, as the *Gurnard* draws slowly away, the dreadnoughts are busy undocking. The Golgoloth's vessel, however, remains firmly docked, and Prador are all about it in vacuum, building structures that will permanently lock it to the King's ship. After a moment he turns his attention to the horseshoe console to one side of him, and its one empty chair, and a sadness rises up within him.

Orbus is now remembering things forgotten about Iannus Drooble during those centuries of madness aboard his sailing ship the *Vignette*. And now the crewman is dead. The lack of that man's often irritating presence leaves a raw hole inside him, but he knows the pain will fade. He knows, in fact, that Drooble's presence at his side served only to delay the healing process that began in his own mind underneath the seas of Spatterjay, whilst he was enslaved by Vrell. He must accept all this and move on.

'Take a seat,' he says, waving a hand towards the empty chair.

'Thank you,' says the woman, Sadurian. She has held back at the door for a little while, which confirms that she is much older than she looks and has therefore acquired some wisdom along the way. Orbus is glad to have her aboard for this visit, and looks forward to getting to know her better during the time ahead . . . that is, if she chooses to stay rather than return to the Polity, as seems to be her intent.

Sniper now looms in behind them, and Orbus feels comfortable with the drone's presence. However, he isn't entirely sure about the other two presently being taken on a tour of the ship, guided by Thirteen. But the two chrome-armoured third-children have been allowed, as free Prador, to accompany Sadurian over here, and he promises himself he will try to treat them with civility.

'So,' says Orbus, 'I asked Sniper earlier if what happened here is a good thing or a bad thing. Gurnard, tell me, what is the reaction of the Polity AIs?'

'Reserved,' replies the ship AI. 'They were happy enough with King Oberon, and since Vrell is his chosen successor, they'll not interfere. It also helps that Vrell is now pulling Oberon's remaining spies out of the Graveyard, and already talking about decommissioning the Prador defence stations – so long as the stations on the Polity side are decommissioned too.'

'But *reserved*, you said?'

'Vrell is a complex and dangerous creature,' Gurnard observes, 'and nobody really knows what his intentions are now. In a very short time he went from being a first-child trapped on Spatterjay to becoming King of the Prador. Some major AIs are also quite concerned about the way he managed to accurately fire U-jump missiles through disrupted underspace. The Polity will be watching him very closely.'

'You gotta admire the fucker,' says Sniper.

Ignoring the drone, Orbus turns to Sadurian. 'What do *you* think?'

'I am not sure my judgement is relevant,' she replies. 'I would suggest, however, that for building and maintaining a complex civilization, Prador natural aggression needs to be somewhat curbed. If Vrell is as intelligent as he would seem, he will know this fact too.' She gazes at him for a long moment. 'Personally I would like to hear what *you* feel, since that is surely more relevant. The Prador caused you great suffering in the past, yet you allied yourself with Vrell.'

Orbus sits back. He thinks Vrell is indeed a vicious and dangerous creature, but one sufficiently intelligent – and distanced from the rest of his kind – to be able to put racial issues to one side. But what does Orbus actually *feel?*

'Vrell knows that open war with the Polity, as well as quite possibly leading to the genocide of his own kind, would be merely a stupid waste. He'll open up the borders, and then take from the Polity what he can. He'll do very well.'

Sadurian tilts her head in acknowledgement. 'That would be my assessment, too.'

'So it looks like we've put the universe to rights,' interjects Sniper. 'What now?'

Orbus smiles to himself; the drone sounds bored already.

'The holds are empty,' says Gurnard. 'And Cymbeline has accepted your suggestion.'

'Huh?' says Sniper brilliantly.

Orbus turns his head in time to observe the King's ship firing up its fusion drives and beginning to draw away. The five dread-noughts then fire up their drives, too, and follow it.

'We've got no spies to hunt down in the Graveyard and meanwhile we need to acquire a profitable cargo,' says Orbus. 'I think a good place to look for one now will be beyond the Graveyard, inside the Prador Kingdom itself.' He turns to Sadurian. 'I'm afraid you'll have to find another way back to the Polity – if you're going right away.'

She gazes at him coolly. 'I think I'll stick around – this might be interesting.'

'Huh?' says Sniper again.

'Of course,' Orbus adds, 'with the new King establishing his position at the heart of things, there's going to be a great deal of contention.'

'Contention?' Sniper perks up.

'There's sure to be other Prador who'll dispute his claim to the title.'

'Yup,' concurs Sniper, his head nodding eagerly in his grounded shell.

Space distorts about the King's ship, generating a weird spiral light effect, then it is gone. One after another, the five dread-noughts flash out of existence too.

'It'll be dangerous in there,' Orbus warns.

Sniper impatiently rattles a tentacle against the floor. 'Are we going then, or what?'

Orbus grins. 'Gurnard, let's follow them in.'

The Fourth Kingdom: The events that led to King Vrell's rise to power are obscure at best, but everything he did afterwards has been well documented. By allowing more Prador children to reach adulthood, he caused massive population growth and this forced great societal changes. Allowing artificial intelligence to gain a firm foothold in the Kingdom, he enabled it to become a much more stable entity. And the new laws he introduced eliminated a great deal of the destructive competition between Prador adults. However, many cultural historians and xenologists are baffled about what has come to be known as the 'Prador Renaissance'. Everything Vrell has done, and is still doing, just does not fit the accepted biological and cultural profile of the Prador. It all seems just too humane. Many of the Prador themselves are baffled too, and very much resent King Vrell. They claim that the Prador of the new generations are soft shells, not having been subject to the traditional rigours of previous generations. However, those that object too strongly and loudly often fall prey to the most grotesque and fatal misfortunes, so my guess is that King Vrell, while not quite as vicious as his predecessors, ain't exactly about to turn vegetarian either.

– From HOW IT IS by Gordon